I0661727

SPACE CADETS

AND THE
LEGEND OF THE GOLIATHON

Brent Winzek

Space Cadets Studios

Cover Design, Artwork, & Maps by Monica Kay
with other designs by Jordan Stine

Based on the *Space Cadets Radio* podcast
(story by Brent Winzek & Jordan Stine)
& *The Space Cadets* video series (2005 – 2009)

The 20th Anniversary 3rd Edition

©2005 – 2025 Space Cadets Studios LLC

All rights reserved. No part of this book may be reproduced in any form or by any means, electronic or mechanical, including photocopying or recording, or by any information storage and retrieval system, without permission in writing from the publisher.

For more, visit spacecadetsstudios.com

The views and opinions expressed in this publication are those of the author and do not necessarily reflect the official policy or position of the publisher or its affiliates and partners. This is a work of fiction. Any names or characters, businesses or places, events or incidents, are fictitious. Any resemblance to actual persons, living or dead, or actual events is purely coincidental.

ISBN: 979-8-9885955-5-7

DEDICATION

To Monica for her unflappable belief in these stories.
To Jordan for carrying the light.
& to all my beloved Space Cadets: past, present & future.

ACKNOWLEDGEMENTS

This book would not be possible without the keen eyes of original Cliptorgian & supervising editor Dale McCarthy, nor the brilliant, probing mind of chief copyeditor Caedon Venné. It would not be enclosed in such a beautiful cover without the artistic talents of Monica Kay, nor would it have quite the continuity if not for her continued readership. Test readers Matthew L. & Laurel B. also deserve recognition for their eager contributions to this new edition.

This new edition would not be meticulous without the work done to previous iterations. Transonuscribe[1] Jesi Mullins deserves praise for her IPA notations and editorial input on early variants of the story. Additionally, the efforts of test readers Jordan S., Linda S., Zack G., & Matt A. deserve much praise for suffering through my early drafts.

Finally, the *Space Cadets* universe would not exist without the unwavering love and support of the original Space Cadets of Norwin Theater Club, the contributions of collaborator and dear friend Jordan Stine, the cast & crew of *Space Cadets Radio,* and the friends, family & communities who have blessed our project with an audience over the years.

---

[1] **transonuscribe** – a highly specialized linguist who translates and transcribes vocalizations across alien languages. This profession grew out of necessity during the early days of the Clipto-Terran Alliance, circa A.D. 2142. The title was created by Arvessa Grimmol, the Cliptorgian translator who composed that treaty.

REFERENCE

For the reader who prefers a worldbuilding deep-dive, footnotes have been provided with **IPA pronunciations** and historical context from the *Space Cadets* universe.

For the visual learner, **illustrations** of key individuals, encountered species, and technology are interspersed throughout the text, as are **maps** of each planet visited. Those documents can be found on the following pages:

CONTENTS

1. FREIGHTER 601

March 15th, A.D. 2349
02:47 Interplanetary Standard Time

    Interstellar Commercial Transit 601 rumbled through deep space like a diesel train engine along its trade route. The rumbling was, of course, only audible from inside the ship. Only a fool would suggest sound traveled through space.

    Its thrusters spewed heat and particles from the distortion drive, which leapt the ship from point to point through space along its given route. As it made each leap, the tall red letters of its call sign, *ICT 601*, flecked away from its decrepit yellow hull, crumbling off into the vast abyss. They were barely discernable as they danced past one of the ship's many security feeds, all displayed on a grid of small monitors along the back wall of the grimy, cluttered cockpit.

The ship's two helmsmen did not notice, for they were reclined in their bucket seats at the front of the cockpit. Helmsman Paul, the much bigger, much scruffier of them threw his video game controller to the floor. "Damn it! Can we *please* lower the difficulty?"

In the pilot seat next to him, the mousy Helmsman Phil squirmed, trying to sound casual. "If we do that, we're gonna blow through half the game before we even reach the Barrier."

"We can change it back when we find the dumb relic. I just want to get to the war," Paul protested. "That's why I bought this, anyway. The stuff about the Rebellion is based on *actual* history. I wanna kill some purplebloods," he said, using the common Outer Rim slur for citizens of the Interplanetary Space Federation[2]. Paul even tried saying the last bit with the chewed consonants and rollicking vowels of a classic Terran pirate accent.

Phil frowned at the poor, outdated stereotype. He also frowned because it was bad luck to conjure pirates of any kind beyond ISF borders.

---

[2] **Interplanetary Space Federation** – more commonly referred to as 'the ISF' or 'the Federation,' and considered the larger, wealthier of two multi-planet governments in the known universe. The ISF started as a war-time treaty between the planets Earth and Cliptorgia /klɪpˈtɔɚ giə/. Because of this, that war is commonly referred to as 'The War of Formation,' or 'The Great War.'

FREIGHTER 601

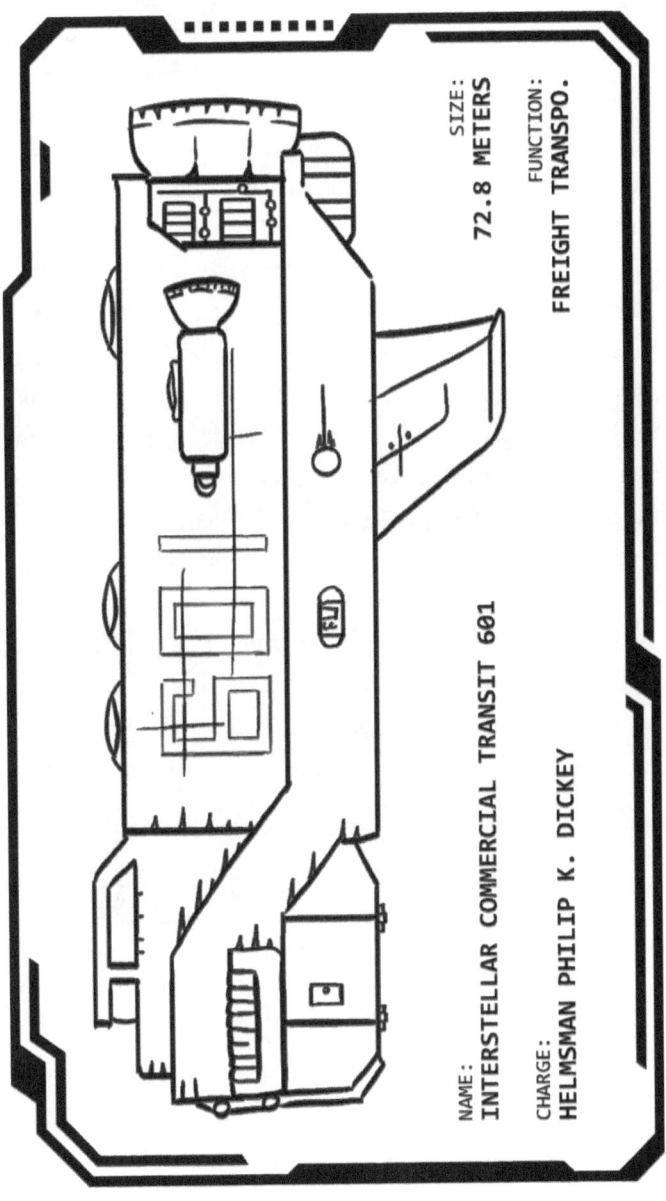

SIZE:
72.8 METERS

FUNCTION:
FREIGHT TRANSPO.

NAME:
INTERSTELLAR COMMERCIAL TRANSIT 601

CHARGE:
HELMSMAN PHILIP K. DICKEY

The Outer Rim[3], especially, was pirate country. Merchants traveled at their own risk. Phil admitted to a morbid curiosity, but he found that Paul seemed to romanticize pirates too much. Phil had gone twenty years among the stars and never had he encountered a pirate attack in person. He was not nearly as eager as Paul to break such a track record.

Phil used his sleeve to wipe the sweat from his game controller. They were trying out a novelty retro game – *The Adventures of Nogylop[4] Smith* – a collector's item nowadays. It was extremely rare: never released within the Federation worlds because it depicted the title character as an Outer Rim war-hero instead of history's first blood-thirsty space pirate. And, allegedly, the whole game had been designed and programmed by other pirates as an anti-ISF propaganda piece.

Helmsman Phil and Helmsman Paul didn't have much in common, save their love of video games, and Paul was always hunting for the controversial stuff when they shipped out on transit runs. It was the only hobby

---

[3] **Outer Rim** – formally referred to as the **Ornaus** /ˈɔɹnɑs/ **System**, consists of five planets, including three inhabitable worlds: Heiznaus, Hierrnaus & Mynaus. Deemed 'the frontier,' these planets were once colonized by the ISF. In A.D. 2238, the ISF declared war on rebels at New Cortallek, their well-established colony on Hierrnaus. The people of the Outer Rim rallied around their commander, Nogylop Smith and by 2245, the ISF agreed to terms of surrender. The rebels formed a new nation, the Free Worlds of the Outer Rim. In honor of their victorious commander, they renamed New Cortallek 'Smith's Pointe' and resurrected a statue of 'their illustrious Pirate Lord' in the center of town.

[4] **Nogylop** /ˈnɑgəlɑp/ **Smith** – keep reading to learn more.

they shared. Being meager in build, Phil was never willing to venture into the unsavory sectors of Smith's Pointe[5] to purchase rare titles, but Paul was a bold ruffian. He was a gruff, thick man, towering well over two meters tall. He had no care at all that the capital port of the Outer Rim was crawling with outlaws. In fact, Phil recalled, Paul bragged about job offers he received while strolling along the Pointe's dockyards.

Come to think of it, Phil was surprised Paul hadn't brought it up yet on their current trek. Phil decided to keep his companion talking. It passed the time, and they had plenty of it left. If they ran out of game before they made port, Phil warned himself, they'd also run out of common ground, making for another miserable trip home. "You don't believe the bit about the Goliathon[6]," he asked Paul curiously, trying to distract the big guy from changing the game difficulty.

"Nah," Paul said, waving the thought away like a phantom stink before his nose. "That's all just folklore – bedtime stories for kids. Nogylop was a clever bloke; I think he made up those stories to rally his troops. How

---

[5] **Smith's Pointe** – capital of both the Free Worlds of the Outer Rim and the planet Hierrnaus, this city is also the region's epicenter for pirate activity. Despite a network of political figures, the governance of this seaside city falls to a Pirate Lord appointed by the clans of cutthroats operating in the area. The laborers, ranchers, and Candolite missionaries of the region are quite free to go about their everyday lives, so long as they steer clear of trouble.

[6] **Goliathon** /gəˈlaɪəˌθɑn/ – it is said that this Candalonian relic grants its wielder immense power. Shrouded in myth, it is unclear whether the Goliathon is more than mere folklore.

else do you raise a pirate army big enough to win a war?"

"I always thought his questing days were more interesting. Any hothead can fight a war – history has proven that – but to risk your whole reputation like he did – that takes cojones."

"You're so gullible," Paul shot back. He set down his controller and cracked open another can of beer. Phil followed his lead, which was unfortunate, for while doing so, neither of them noticed the green stingray insignia load on the console behind them, nor the other cockpit screens switching off one at a time. With a shuddering guffaw, Freighter 601 staggered to a dead halt. The lights cut out, and the engines failed.

Phil felt the familiar tug of zero-G trying to coax his body to float out of his chair. He and Paul grabbed their tattered armrests at the same time.

A heartbeat later, auxiliary power hummed to life somewhere in the floor beneath them, and they settled back into their seats. Auxiliary power restored gravity, and the hiss of cool air told them oxygen levels were also intact.

"What the hell's going on," Paul muttered.

Phil shrugged. He had suspected that Paul wasn't recharging the fuel cells as frequently as he ought to, but they'd had the same problem on their last shipment, and this time they had taken shifts during the recharge. Paul had probably screwed up on his shift. But Phil couldn't *say that* because Paul was three times his size, with arms the size of Phil's legs: arms capable of doing quite a bit of damage to someone like Phil. Phil was self-described as 'slight of frame.' So, Phil opted to keep his companion calm. He'd simply state the obvious and see how far it got him. "The ship's dead."

"How can she be dead?" Paul barked back, adding plaintively, "I double-checked my work: the fuel cells were charged to max before we broke orbit."

Well, Paul hadn't screwed up. Hopefully he didn't think that was Phil's motive. It was, of course, but Phil hoped Paul didn't *think* it was.

Not sure what to add, Phil shrugged again. "I don't know how it's dead, but it is. Look!" Even the distress signal button was out; that meant the auxiliary backup was down, too. He swatted at the distress signal, drumming on it dramatically.

"No," Paul said, shaking his head in agitation. "That can't be right. Maybe something's wrong with the distress signal, but we have auxiliary power, genius, because life support systems are up."

Oh yeah, Phil realized. He was thinking too fast. The talk of pirates had shaken him into a world of old superstitions he'd been raised in. "I'm sorry," Phil offered, laughing awkwardly. "You're absolutely right. We can worry about that later."

There was an awkward silence.

Phil hesitated. He wasn't a certified ship's mechanic. Paul was. Even though Paul had shown him a few basics on their last two hauls, it was not Phil's specialty. He liked the details of a job and was considered a Shipping Technician. His position involved the charting of calculations to maximize shipping volume while

7

considering transit weight limits. There were far more little details and tricks he'd learned in his time on the job, but he'd learned to keep those things internalized for his own private delight. "D-do you want me to get some practice in?"

"No," Paul said firmly. He made no move to get up.

Phil waited another beat, glancing up at the blank monitors around them. "You think it'll try to come back on by itself?"

"Okay, okay. I'll go check it out," Paul's words were tipped with venom.

"Take your tools," Phil risked.

"Thanks, mom." Paul loomed over Phil's seat for a moment as he hefted his tool belt off the creaking, groaning metal floor. Phil didn't bother to look after him. He just listened as Paul observed what Phil already knew. "The auxiliary lights didn't eve–"

He didn't finish, his incomplete thought punctuated by a dull thud. Phil waited in the cold, dark silence, shrinking into his ratty seat cushions. "Uh… Paul?" Phil shivered but forced himself to stand up. "You okay?"

There was no reply.

Phil took two cautious steps towards the door before a figure lunged at him from the shadows, stabbing him in the neck. The pain was sharp and sweet: a dozen pinched nerves in his spine all at once. Instantly, Phil felt his knees buckle, and his body collapsed to the floor. As he choked his last breath, groping at the hole in his neck, he spotted Paul's bloody corpse in the doorway.

His attacker stepped delicately around the murder

scene, avoiding the body, avoiding the blood. Pulling up the sleeve of his ornate maroon jacket, the figure opened a channel on his WristCom. "Murray: restore the freighter's power."

The man's WristCom dinged. "Aye, Cap'n," replied a grumbling old voice with a muddled accent of British origin.

Phil wheezed, feeling half his breath escape through the hole in his throat. It hurt to raise his head, so he let the weight of it press against the cool metal floor. Damn, he thought, where did we go wrong?

"Eldadip, get the cockpit set," his attacker said.

"Aye, sir," a female voice replied from the shadows in the hallway, her dialect carrying those rolling vowels that suggested good Federation schooling. Phil gasped again as the Cliptorgian[7] woman ducked into the cockpit. She was a strikingly graceful and powerful figure concealed within her weathered pirate persona. Though Cliptorgian, her complexion held pigment, and her silver freckles had faded, blotching and bronzing her skin in the light of alien suns.

She tossed her crochet locs back over her shoulder and motioned to Paul's corpse. Two hulking, shrouded figures knelt, bending the man's lifeless body at uncomfortable angles.

---

[7] **Cliptorgian** /klɪpˈtɔ˞ giən/ – originally nocturnal, this mammalian species is strikingly similar to Terrans. Hailing from a societal matriarchy, the Cliptorgians were the first to colonize the Outer Rim worlds of Hierrnaus and Heiznaus but lost both due to the transgressions of invading Candalonians in that region.

"Quickly, now," the captain said, nudging Phil with the toe of his boot. "Activate the freighter's S.O.S. and our trap is set."

As the touch of the pirate's boot-tip grew duller, Phil realized he was dying. He stared up at his killer, revealed only by the faint blue light of his WristCom's little display. The bushy golden beard and tricorn hat were unmistakable… not to mention the pronounced scar above his left eye. That face had been on every dockyard post in Smith's Pointe… the Outer Rim's most wanted outlaw.

As his body choked out its final gust of air, Phil's last contribution to consciousness was: "Sliced by the great Captain Alaborap[8], Nogylop's very own grandson. What are the odds?"

---

[8] **Captain Alaborap** /əˈlæbəˌɹæp/ **Smith** – current leader of the notorious Halogien Stingray pirates. He is one of five pirate leaders on the ISF's 'Most Wanted' list.

2. THE PIRATES

March 15th, A.D. 2349
02:58 IST

Eldadip kept an eye on Captain Alaborap as he sighed, strolling out of *601*'s cockpit. His boots clanked with purpose on the catwalks as he wiped blood from the blade of his cutlass. He was calm and patient, seemingly unfazed by the freighter's S.O.S. alert. The warning rattled over the loudspeakers and down the ship's vast hallways. The captain was unfazed. He was a powerful mind equipped with a fighter's physique. His figure was as striking as his strange personality; a middle-aged human with antique tastes, long, wavy hair and enough brains to fill three freighters like the one they were in. Alaborap changed the channel on his WristCom.

"Argylesox," he barked, "meet me by the emergency

ALABORAP & ELDADIP

hatch on deck eight." The captain turned, leaning into the doorway so Eldadip could see him. "We'll be waiting for you there."

"Aye sir," Eldadip saluted her captain. She couldn't help but notice the subtle nod of approval he gave her before departing. He tended not to give much away in his responses, but Eldadip had learned to recognize when he offered validation. She knew what needed to be done, and, more importantly, she knew *how* the captain wanted it done.

She held her salute until Captain Alaborap disappeared into the shadows in *601*'s upper catwalks. Once he was gone, she let herself stand at ease outside the cockpit doors.

Pockam Lars, the teenager who had just joined them a month or so ago, lingered there with her. He was a thin, scrappy kid who liked to sport a replica Viking helmet that drooped heavily over his smooth forehead. Together, they moved the two helmsmen into one extra-large body bag, then zipped the thing up and set it at the top of the metal staircase leading down into the depths of the freighter. There was no discussion. Eldadip preferred it that way. She broke the silence with the chime of her WristCom. "Oi, Vestonn?"

"Yes, ma'am?" Vestonn's voice was small and warped over the device's small speakers.

"Report to the cockpit," she commanded. "Bring Naughtadargh with you. We've got biohazardous waste prepped for jettison."

After a moment, her WristCom chimed again. "Aye,

aye, ma'am," Vestonn replied. "On our way."

Eldadip rested her hands on her hips, rocking to one side, then the other. Pockam stood nearby, glancing around at nothing in particular. What the hell was the kid doing? She could still see spatters of blood on the floor in the cockpit from where she stood. She nudged Pockam, pointing to the mess on the smooth floor just inside the cockpit doorway. "Aren't you on clean-up duty?"

Pockam said nothing, only nodded with big, dull eyes under the brim of his much-too-large helm.

"The captain doesn't want evidence of the crew's death left in the cockpit," Eldadip warned.

She watched as Pockam's shoulders drooped, but he knelt with his rag and applied more surface cleaner. Cringing, he wiped up the blood. It wasn't long before he needed to pull out a second rag. "Why, exactly, can't there be any blood?" Pockam sprayed the metal floor with his cleaner. He produced a third rag from his mess of supplies and buffed the floor sparkling clean.

"Because whoever intercepts this hulking tin can needs to search it for as long as possible. If they think the crew is somewhere aboard, they'll stay longer." Eldadip didn't bother to hide her exasperated tone. She'd been growing tired of the kid's poor listening skills. He didn't pay attention when the captain was going over plans, then asked too many questions on the job.

Eldadip scrutinized the kid while he cleaned up, then shook her head. The polish was too much. It was obvious to her that one patch of the floor was cleaner than the rest of the ship. "That's enough," she snapped. "Don't make your clean-up so apparent."

Pockam stood, cramming his supplies into a plastic bag. "Clean it up, but not too clean," he muttered to himself. Then, more to her, he said, "This whole job makes zero sense." He backed into the hallway before she could reply. The metal stairs outside of the cockpit rumbled and rang like thunder and bells. Vestonn and Naughtadargh[9] were hustling up the staircase to meet them.

Between Vestonn, a solid, two-meter tall by one-meter-wide stack of human brawn, and Naughtadargh, the 2.5-meter-tall wolfman mutant, Pockam managed to seem even smaller than he already was – fragile, even.

"Bottom decks secured," Vestonn reported. "This was a skeleton crew assignment: just two technician-sailors. There wasn't even a security officer for the cargo bay."

"Wow," Eldadip mused, "cheap shipment."

Vestonn, at least, laughed with mild amusement.

Eldadip ducked into the cockpit and sprayed down the bucket seats with butane. She plucked an electric lighter from the inner pocket of her coat and activated it. The cool blue sizzle of electricity touched the seat fabric. With a spark and a huff of flame, fire leapt across the acrylic cushions, climbing high in mere seconds, and melting the cheaper plastic framework around the control console.

---

[9] **Naughtadargh** /ˈnɑtədɑʒg/ – keep reading to learn more.

Her vandalism complete, Eldadip rejoined her crewmates, stepping out into the freighter's cavernous cargo bay, where eight levels of red metal catwalks lined the perimeter of the cargo ship's yawning cargo bay. She took a moment to survey the other pirates in her charge. That's when she spied the steady red light shining from Vestonn's firearm.

"Vestonn, you oaf, your rifle's armed!" Eldadip disarmed the rifle before she swatted Vestonn on the head with her vintage sea-captain's hat.

The big Terran clenched his chiseled jaw and shrugged. "Don't look at me. Naughtadargh can't keep his paws off."

Next to Vestonn, the hulking wolf-mutant Naughtadargh heaved like a rabid dog. Eldadip squared her shoulders and stared him down. His beady eyes and furry snout curled as he growled at her, but like a submissive pet, he could not hold eye contact with her for more than a few seconds. He was a mountain of white fur and bulging muscle, but after a moment Naughtadargh grumbled in the back of his throat. He didn't even commit to a full growl, then he broke eye contact entirely. His dirty white fur settled along his shoulders and neck.

"I touched nothing," he roared. "It must've been the little boy." He poked at Pockam.

"Hey, lay off, dog-breath," Pockam challenged, straightening his Viking helmet. At one-point-seven meters, his wiry stature was no match for any of the other pirates in the room. His big mouth made up for it.

VESTONN, POCKAM, NAUGHTADARGH

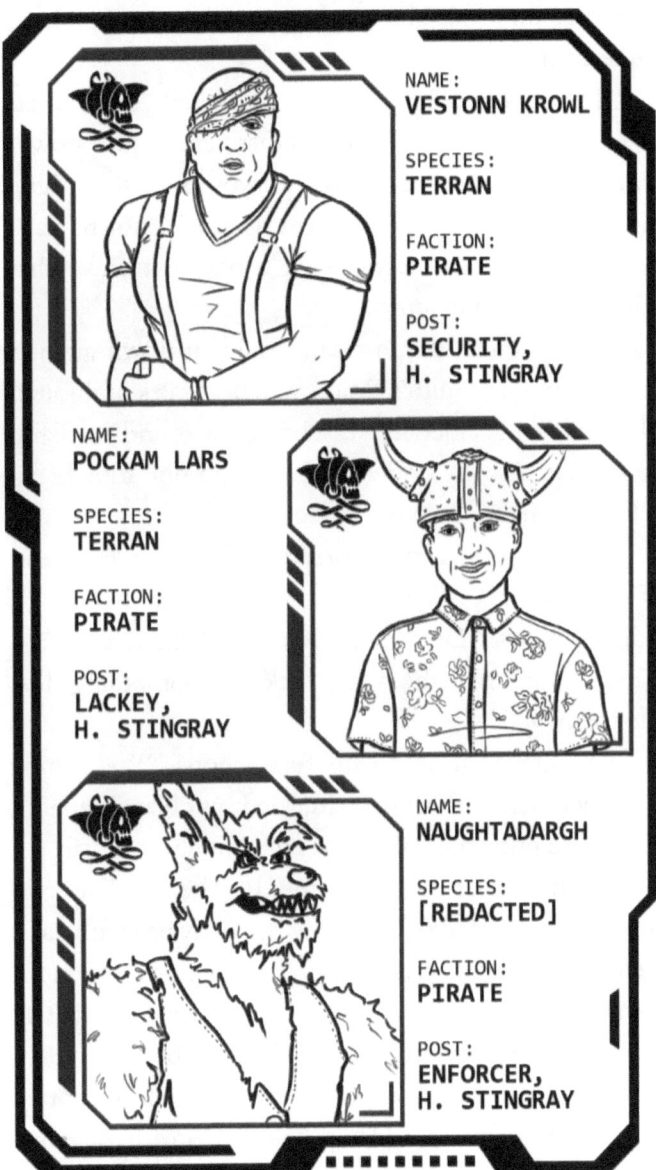

NAME:
VESTONN KROWL

SPECIES:
TERRAN

FACTION:
PIRATE

POST:
**SECURITY,
H. STINGRAY**

NAME:
POCKAM LARS

SPECIES:
TERRAN

FACTION:
PIRATE

POST:
**LACKEY,
H. STINGRAY**

NAME:
NAUGHTADARGH

SPECIES:
[REDACTED]

FACTION:
PIRATE

POST:
**ENFORCER,
H. STINGRAY**

"Don't call me that," Naughtadargh barked, lumbering forward. His black lips curled, baring sharp canine teeth.

"That's enough," Eldadip hollered over their bickering. "I don't care how it happened, just power down your firearms before one of you does something stupid." She shook her head. It was crucial not to have live firearms aboard any vessel; it was a mistake that ended many a pirate crew.

On any given day, a pirate could sit down at their choice of pub in Smith's Pointe and hear tales of ill-fated sailors who'd accidentally discharged a round in-flight. Those tales usually ended with some poor fool being sucked through a hole the size of a coin.

Eldadip took a deep breath and shook her head before continuing. "Vestonn and Naughtadargh, take the bodies down to Deck One. Jettison them if there's a chute. If not, cram them in a locker or something. Just hide them well."

Naughtadargh licked his furry chops. "We'll think of something." Vestonn chuckled as Naughtadargh rubbed the pure white fur of his mutant chest. It was the cleanest patch of fluff on the big beast. The two muscleheads trotted off, hoisting the body bag with ease. Their inflated hulks clattered all the way down the metal catwalks. Eldadip leaned over the worn guard rail, watching them descend into the shadows below.

Further down the hallway, Pockam skulked around a corner out of sight. Eldadip held her breath, listening carefully. It wasn't long before she heard something clank to the floor. She marched down the hall toward the noise. Rounding the corner where she'd lost sight of the kid, she found him kneeling at a storage compartment, holding a beat-up, homemade hot-hacker[10].

"Oi, what do you think you're doing?" She grabbed him under the arm and pulled him to his feet, knocking his Viking helmet crooked. The damn thing was heavier than he was.

"What," he whined back at her.

"You're looting."

"Yeah, 'cause I signed up to be a *pirate*."

"No looting aboard *601*. No damage beyond what's instructed. Captain's orders."

"Yeah, yeah," Pockam said, shrugging off her grip. "It's a stupid order," he said. "And it was Argyle's, not the captain's," he added plaintively.

"Kid, they call him 'The Overpolite Pirate.' What did you expect?" Eldadip emphasized her challenge by crossing her arms. She maintained eye contact with Pockam until he tucked his hot-hacker back into the grime-caked fanny pack around his slight waist.

Pockam may be out of line, she thought, but the kid was right, in a way; he just had a terrible way of expressing it. Their Clipterran[11] Argyle had been calling a fair share of the shots. He'd done some interesting damage... he'd been encouraging the captain's

---

[10] **hot-hacker** – handheld device used for hacking basic electronics and computer systems, such as digital locks.

[11] **Clipterran** /klɪpˈtɛɹən/ – any being who is the result of Cliptorgian & Terran crossbreeding.

increasingly obsessive behavior over Outer Rim folklore. Had the captain talking about the evidence that Nogylop Smith, Alaborap's grandfather, had allegedly tracked down the relic, and it had somehow aided in raising forces for the Outer Rim Rebellion. It was a slippery slope of conspiracy theories and tall tales. Eldadip was fairly certain it was all zirkrum[12]; there was no ancient device that channeled the power of creation. It was just another fun story from those early days of a frontier democracy, embellished to spark hope and patriotism throughout the Free Worlds.

One thing she had seen, which the kid hadn't, was the temple on Heiznaus. She'd gone with Alaborap, Glygorg, and Argyle. Even though the Goliathon wasn't real, she saw the value to be had in charting the old temple ruins Argyle kept leading them to. She'd seen inexplicable things with them in that beautiful pink crystal temple dome nestled in the smooth black rock at the foot of a volcano. The translucent temple stones had jumped and jolted with the occasional bolt of rose-tinted electricity. Whatever that material was, she knew just one block of it would give her enough to buy a ship of her own, maybe even pay a crew for an endeavor or two to get business started. After all, she reasoned, Captain

---

[12] **zirkrum** /ˈzɚ krʌm/ – thought to originate from the root words 'zir' (bird) and 'krum' (feces), this Cliptorgian cuss has no apparent genesis. The most popular theory points to prehistory, when large predatory falcons preyed on the Cliptorgian species during daylight hours. Etymology suggests that the term was meant to declare a nearby predator and fell into use as a colorful curse over time.

Alaborap had confided on several tavern outings that he was interested in his own fleet. Eldadip knew she was captain material, and she had no interest in switching flags. Anyone could claim to be a space pirate. It was quite commonplace. But there was value in being a Halogien Stingray[13]. The kid didn't get that yet.

Vestonn and Naughtadargh came hustling up the stairs again, their collective mass thrumming the skeletal metal catwalks like some subtle percussion instrument. Eldadip let them both ahead of her. Pockam scrambled out of their way, then followed behind. The pirates had to rendezvous with Alaborap and Argyle at Hatch Eight.

"Hey, guys," Pockam called out, rushing to trail the two big bruisers to the rendezvous position. "Don't you think we've been doing too much artifact-chasing? Growing crew… shouldn't we be profiteering?"

Eldadip didn't want morale souring. "If you've got a problem with it, take it up with the captain," she suggested with a pernicious smile. "Otherwise, you just keep your opinions to yourself and stick to the plan while you're on my watch."

Even if she agreed with the kid, which she did not, now was no time to start protesting. They were in the middle of a job and so far, all was going according to plan. What's more, it was falling out just as Captain Alaborap said it would. He had a knack for that. Another perk of sailing under the green skull of his Stingrays.

Overtaking the freighter at their present coordinates

---

[13] **Halogien** /həˈloŭdʒiən/ **Stingray** – keep reading to learn more.

had been crucial. At their current position, the only patrolling vessels were operated by younger, less experienced ISF troops. There was also only one surveillance station within range this far off the tired old transit route. The skeleton crew of *601* had run astray of their neutral transit route after clearing the Ornaus[14] System. It was typical, even of experienced freight pilots. The poor fools had traced the perimeter of Rigel's Belt. Any further and they would have arched the freighter away from the Great Barrier[15]. In a way, Eldadip reasoned, the pirates had spared them.

Eldadip tried to recall the exterior of *601* as she'd seen it from the Stingray's cockpit upon their approach. She had a knack for ship layouts and floor plans, particularly freighters. It was the result of her own days in the ISF Military Academy. A two-year detail as a customs officer had her inside, over, and under every make and model of commercial transit vessel bound for ISF borders and trading posts. *601* had the frame of a 2339 bulk transporter, if she had to guess. Like any other bulk freighter, this commercial transit vessel had a boxy frame. Eldadip had heard once that they were designed with old Terran diesel train engines of the twentieth century. They were built in space, traveled in space, and

---

[14] **Ornaus** /ˈɔš-nɑs/ **System** – the frontier solar system containing the Outer Rim worlds (see 'Outer Rim' for more).

[15] **Great Barrier** – a border comprised of billions of force field emitters networked around the star systems of Cliptorgia and Earth, isolating the ISF from the rest of the universe. The ISF began constructing it in A.D. 2247, after losing the Outer Rim worlds.

were unloaded in space; there was no need for them to be sleek or aerodynamic.

Eldadip trailed her crewmates aft in determined silence, keeping an ear on them. Eldadip's imagination drifted to their own ship, the *Halogien Stingray*, which was clinging to the starboard quarter of the freighter like an angry scavenger. Their vessel had a sleek but stout frame, which, as the captain had explained once, bore a loose resemblance to twentieth-century Warthog fighter jets. It had a heavy, rounded prow and its cylindrical primary engines mounted at aft, riding a tapering tail. The forewings had been reshaped, curving elegantly from the nose, imitating the wingspan of a manta ray, and an upper deck had been added to mimic a Terran eighteenth-century sloop-of-war. The captain had rendered an excellent imitation; she'd had the privilege to see his reference images one time.

Equally distinct was the vessel's pair of telescoping masts complete with solar-charging black sails. With its lime-green-frosted cockpit windshield and unmistakable stingray silhouette, it was a bold and beastly vessel, lavish with intimidating mechanical features that, Eldadip noted, boasted of her captain's ingenuity.

Alaborap waited at the aft hatch where the pirates had boarded. As was customary, he sported Glygorg's[16] speckled green Fallamon[17] shell on his back. Next to him,

---

[16] **Glygorg** /ˈɡliɡɔ͛rɡ/ – keep reading to learn more.

[17] **Fallamon** /ˈfæləmɑn/ – very little is known about this reptilian species due to their distrust of outsiders. Indigenous to the Faylore

the Clipterran Argylesox was fumbling with one of his data recorders. As her contingent joined them, the others pressed in around Argyle, who bumbled in response.

"Excuse me," he said, tapping Naughtadargh. "Oh, sorry," he continued meekly as everyone ignored him. Eldadip tried not to scowl as she observed the half-human, half-Cliptorgian man, with his curling handlebar mustache, dark features, and prominent triangular nose. The genteel Argyle exuded meekness, yet the captain humored it. His defense of the weakling was an unpleasant reminder of recent pursuits. Eldadip considered Argylesox a problem… and she wasn't the only one.

"Captain," Murray interrupted over the Coms, "military vessel in-bound. They're broadcasting a response to the S.O.S."

"Excellent. Send no reply. We're on to Phase Two; move the Stingray into hiding and wait for my signal."

"Copy that. Detaching now, sir." A metallic thump rattled the hull of *Freighter 601*. Somewhere down the vast corridor of shadows, air hissed to crescendo, punctuated with a dull thwop.

"Now," Alaborap said with a confident nod to his crew, "we wait for them to spring our trap."

River Delta on the planet Hierrnaus, these bipedal, shell-backed beings have a one-meter stature and an average lifespan of 220 years. Fallamon are fiercely materialistic and relish in re-appropriating trinkets, antiques, and other luxury goods. Their broods are often found living in barns, scrap yards, and even landfills.

3. THE RECRUITS

March 15th, A.D. 2349
03:13 IST

Twelve A-Kays[18] from *Freighter 601*, the *ISF Yulacki*, Interstellar Ship of the Fleet, drifted in a lazy orbit around a small, beige moon. That lazy moon was reluctantly orbiting an icy planetoid at the very edge of the Ornaus system in the early morning hours of *Interplanetary Standard Time*. From a certain distance, the slender patrol-class military vessel had a silhouette like a crescent wrench with its jaw closed. At least, that was the opinion of the fresh-faced recruit lounging inside the *Yulacki* cockpit.

The young man reclined lackadaisically, his feet

---

[18] **A-Kay** /eɪ keɪ/– the standard unit for measuring distance in space travel. The 'A-Kay' (or 'A.K.)' stands for astronomical knot.

kicked up on the console in front of him. He stretched, knocking his name badge loose. He fumbled with it, his fingers tracing the grooves of the engraving: Midshipman Walter Stanik.

Midshipman was not an impressive title, Stanik thought. Nor was it indicative of his acumen, he told himself. He was eager to have his rank upgraded to something with a little more weight, but he could do nothing to accelerate his advancement. The ISF Military Academy didn't offer advanced placement. Not a single training course could be tested out of... ever. They wanted everyone to have the same foundational training. Stanik wouldn't get to excel the way he wanted to until he was out of academy and climbing the ranks.

But which ranks to climb, Stanik pondered. Where did he see himself in a few years? Maybe gunner[19], he told himself. His aim could use some work, but his attention to detail would more than compensate for it. His mind wandered as he brushed his fingers through the stubble of his closely buzzed crew cut. His attention was fixed on a large screen cycling through surveillance footage. It was just after three, meaning he had less than four hours left on the night watch. Still no transmission from Demaria, he thought, his heart sinking.

As if on cue, a green light blinked at him from the console, and he tapped it with the tip of his boot. "I

---

[19] **gunner** – historically, this was the role of 'quartermaster' aboard Terran seafaring vessels. Expanding duties and advances in automated weaponry throughout the 23rd Century drastically altered the demands of this role, which eventually resulted in a title change.

almost gave up on you." Stanik instantly loathed his phony attempt at nonchalance.

"I told you I'd be here when my shift ended," Demaria Cole's voice flirted back. "Plus, I like to keep you on your toes."

Stanik grinned, thinking about her wavy, cotton-candy pink hair, her crystal-clear blue eyes, and the tattoos she never made an effort to hide. He and Demaria had met a little less than a year ago, just before she had finished her Advanced Basic Training. She was two years older than him, something she occasionally used to placate him. They dated for a while and, in Stanik's mind, they'd had great chemistry, but Demaria still seemed unsure. With the demands of travel and their conflicting schedules, they had stopped dating exclusively about a month ago. It made sense, but he hated admitting it. He still had a year of deep space training exercises, while Demaria had landed herself a semi-permanent gig running a small Coms department for a commercially owned surveillance station. Commercially owned by her father, no less.

"So, how'd your date go?" Stanik asked, suppressing his insecurity.

Demaria groaned. "Don't get me started. Drake is such an ass!" Stanik couldn't help but grin. "He took me to that gross bar down by the dockyard and talked about the *Seahawk* all night. 'I, uh, don't know if I told you this, but, ah, last week the *Seahawk* had a new what-cha-ma-call-it put in.' And he never stops rubbing his head, like he still can't believe they buzzed his hair off." Stanik jerked his hand away from his head, nearly falling out of his chair. He caught himself, crossing his arms and pinning his hands to his side. "Whatever," Demaria carried on, "When do you get back from training exercises? I need a normal date."

Stanik laughed, his ego soothed by her invitation. She'd made no secret that she was still attracted to him, but she continued to remind him that she didn't want anything serious… not while they were constantly apart. "Captain Billie's extended our tour by a day and a half. She wants me to captain all thirty-six hours." He realized too late that he'd let his disappointment creep into his voice. At that moment, he just wanted a date.

"But that's great, right? She's grooming you for a command position," Demaria encouraged, sensing his sentiments through his tone.

"Yeah. Unless I screw it up. But it's smooth sailing so far." He paused, considering how well the conversation was going. He knew she was encouraged when he didn't react insecurely – it's why she insisted on sharing how each date went. Stanik's only interest was Demaria, and she wasn't interested in 'them,' so he simply chose to focus on other things. Eager to prove he didn't mind that she was seeing other people, he did his own impression of Drake. It wasn't the first time. Stanik and his friends went through basic with Drake. He was a simple, oaf-like boy with a country drawl who loved flying machinery. "Gee, I'd rather get back sooner so I can take you to the dockyard, show you my top five favorite ships."

"Walt, I swear," Demaria laughed through the rest of her warning. "Be nice–" An alarm at Demaria's console beeped furiously over their channel and Stanik quickly lowered the volume on his end. "Oh, hey, hold on a sec."

"Alert," he heard the computer report on her end, "S.O.S. – Interstellar Commercial Transit six-oh-one. Alert: S.O.S. –"

"*Freighter 601*, what's your situation? Over." Demaria kept her voice calm and even. "*Freighter 601*, this is *Pan Motion Surveillance Station thirty-three* contacting you in response to an S.O.S. Come in, please. Over." Static garbled back at her. She redirected her attention to Stanik.

"Hey, I'm back. Did you catch any of that?"

"Yeah – freighter with an S.O.S."

"They're only twelve A-Kays from your position. No radio contact, and they're *way* off course. Probably just need to lead them back to Route Zulu. Think you guys can take a look?"

"Oh, this should be fun," Stanik sighed, "Jablon without his complete night of beauty sleep."

Demaria gave a knowing laugh that sent Stanik's heart singing. "Then I owe you one," she said. "I'll log the situation in case it puts you behind."

"Deal," Stanik said playfully, noting her promise. He disconnected Demaria and hit the *Yulacki*'s summons alarm. It thonked like a wounded trombone as it reverberated down the training vessel's main hallway.

STANIK & JABLON

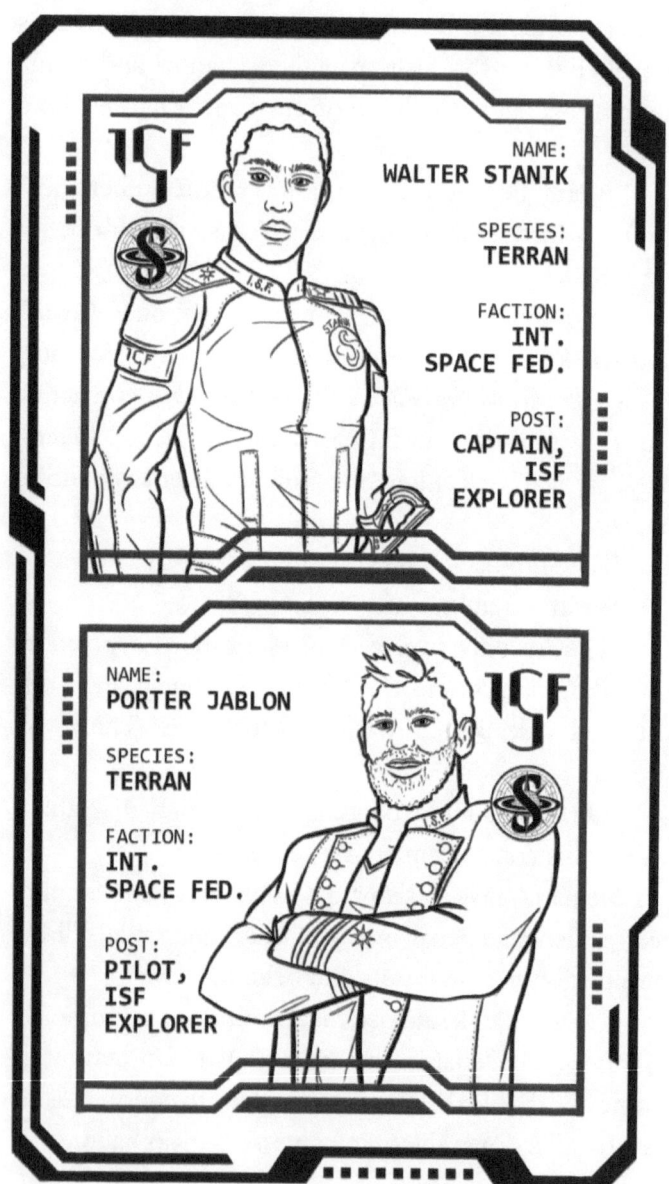

NAME:
WALTER STANIK

SPECIES:
TERRAN

FACTION:
**INT.
SPACE FED.**

POST:
**CAPTAIN,
ISF
EXPLORER**

NAME:
PORTER JABLON

SPECIES:
TERRAN

FACTION:
**INT.
SPACE FED.**

POST:
**PILOT,
ISF
EXPLORER**

X   X   X

"Damn it!" Jablon's voice grumbled from the bunk below. Cliptok's mattress shuddered. She rolled to the edge of her bunk and peered down in time to see Jablon cramming his pillow over his head. He was a burly young Terran with a square jaw and broad shoulders, and he was *not* a morning person.

Cliptok shook the sleep from her head and leapt off the top bunk, landing deftly next to Jablon. She pounced, snatching Jablon's pillow right out of his hands. "C'mon, ya big baby," she teased, swatting him with the pillow, "get up!"

"It's just another drill," Jablon groaned, unwilling to play along. Cliptok shrugged. Jablon could be a real whiner, especially when he was tired. Thankfully, he wasn't her responsibility. She grabbed her metallic black military flight jacket and pulled it over her milky-white Cliptorgian skin. She tried to ignore how dull her fine silver freckles had grown after weeks in space away from the light of a star. A quick brush of her cropped jet-black hair and she was ready to report to the cockpit.

Before she bolted out, she turned and rapped gently on the porthole in the wall next to her.

"Hank, buddy, you up?" Cliptok waited as bubbles fluttered up through the royal blue water sloshing around on the other side of the glass. Hank's webbed yellow hand with its lavender speckles appeared in the porthole, offering a thumbs-up.

That was Cliptok's cue. She bounded out of the

barracks and into the hallway, where the hatch door to Hank's quarters was located. Cliptok grabbed hold of the large metal wheel that served as the hatch's manual lock. She threw her weight into a hefty tug, and the lock turned, clicked, and groaned as the door swung free.

A splash of water puddled onto the floor next to Cliptok as Hank the Hulgarian[20] climbed down the ladder. His bare lemon-yellow scalp glistened under the ship's lights as he hopped over to a pair of mechanical legs called 'hydraulegs' suspended by cables in a corner of the small compartment.

Apart from the lemon yellow of his smooth skin and the wing-like membrane connecting his arms to his torso, Hank appeared humanoid from the waist up. At the pelvis, however, his body tapered into a manta ray tail. Cliptok was from the same planet as Hank – had grown up with him, in fact – but Hank was amphibious. To maintain their physical health during long space voyages, Hulgarians needed a regular soak in brackish water to keep their derma properly moisturized and free of fungal infections. Aboard the *Yulacki*, part of the sleeping chamber had been converted into such a space to accommodate Hank. Jablon had taken to calling it Hank's 'Aqualab'.

Hank was already wearing his black wetsuit when he exited the Aqualab, and so he slithered over to the hydraulegs. Nimbly, he slipped his tail through the belt

---

[20] **Hulgarian** /hʌlˈgɛʒ·iən/ – the sentient, aquatic amphibians of the planet Cliptorgia. Keep reading to learn more.

and harness connecting the legs. With a twist of his 'hips,' Hank activated the legs, locking the belt of his wetsuit into the waist of the metal appendages. Although any fit Hulgarian was fully capable of sitting up on their tail like a cobra, the hydraulegs made working with bipeds much easier, particularly in close quarters on a modest-sized spaceship.

Standing in his legs at just under one and a half meters, Hank reached up into the corner behind him and pulled his helmet down off a charging slot on the wall. Methodically, he ducked his head inside the neon green glass dome and pulled the helmet down, giving it a half-turn to lock it into the collar of his wetsuit's armored shoulders. The helmet activated, drizzling water sparingly over Hank's face, his glowing turquoise eyes sparkling through the subtle shower. Hank gave a sharp nod to Cliptok. 'Race you to the bridge,' his eyes suggested to his lifelong friend. She took off down the hall after him.

Hank sprung ahead by half a meter to start.

No way was she letting a pair of hydraulegs beat her.

They still had a good seven meters of hallway to clear. The *Yulacki* was a long and narrow ship all the way around. Maintenance dragged on in long corridors. Security patrols dragged on through long corridors. Cleaning details especially dragged on and on in these halls, Cliptok thought. She wiped sweat from the corners of her eyes and leapt forward over a loose panel of grating she knew was in the floor just beyond midship. That leap put her ahead, she realized with a grin.

Cliptok hunkered her resolve, focusing on the threshold of the Command Bridge that served as her finish line. Then, she heard the whir of hydraulics behind her and a gasp that indicated Hank's genuine surprise. She chanced a quick look over her shoulder.

Hank's robotic foot had kicked out on him when he ran over the loose floor grate. He was still running forward, but at an angle. His right leg wobbled off on its own accord, like an ostrich with a sprained ankle.

Sensing an impending accident, Cliptok eased up, turned, and caught Hank just before his legs sent him careening into the wall. He grabbed her arm for stability and raised his hairless brow at her through the green visor of his mask. "Too early for a race, I guess."

"Especially when your legs have a mind of their own," Cliptok taunted, swatting at the neural control interface affixed along the beltline of Hank's uniform.

"Yeah, okay. But I'd swim laps around you even if the ISF had mermaid tails for all you bipeds."

"You joke, but it's probably already in development," Cliptok shot back.

They both laughed as they ducked into the cockpit together. Stanik smiled and nodded. They were the first to report.

A few minutes later, Jablon lumbered into the cockpit, his hair sticking straight out where it had been bent and ruffled by his pillow. Behind him, Stanik snapped to attention. "Attention," Walt said, saluting. "Captain Billie on the bridge."

Cliptok and Hank spun around in unison, flashing a

CLIPTOK & HANK

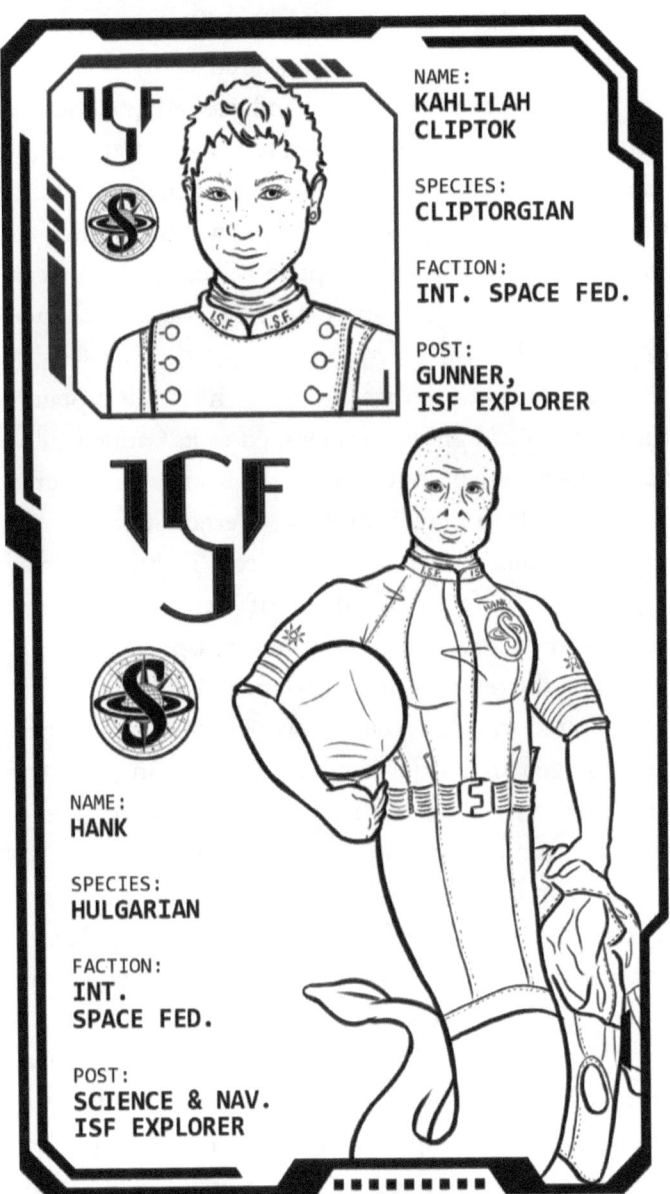

NAME:
**KAHLILAH
CLIPTOK**

SPECIES:
CLIPTORGIAN

FACTION:
INT. SPACE FED.

POST:
**GUNNER,
ISF EXPLORER**

NAME:
HANK

SPECIES:
HULGARIAN

FACTION:
**INT.
SPACE FED.**

POST:
**SCIENCE & NAV.
ISF EXPLORER**

crisp salute as they parted to allow their commanding officer through.

"At ease," Captain Billie reassured.

Cliptok relaxed her stance and clasped one hand in the other behind her back. She remained attentive for Captain Billie. They'd been on the captain's crew for a little over a standard year. The *Yulacki* was their third and final ship assignment with Captain Billie; she'd overseen all three of their deep-space training tours, each one longer than the last.

Cliptok knew she was going to miss the captain's leadership. She'd grown accustomed to it. Captain Billie wasn't Cliptorgian, but her steely resolve and fierce freckles made for an impressive Terran imitation, in Cliptok's mind. The middle-aged Terran woman displayed very few indications of her age, save for distinguished crow's feet and a few whisps of gray hair peppering the temples of her cropped blond hair.

Cliptok wasn't certain how old the captain was. Terrans aged much quicker than Cliptorgians, but the difference was so great that Cliptok admittedly had a hard time comprehending it.

Captain Billie placed her thumb firmly in the cleft of her chin, as she often did when she was thinking. After a moment, she nodded to herself. "Stanik, you're in command. Log this mission as our acting captain."

"Ma'am, yes, ma'am," Walt saluted Captain Billie. Then, with a clap of his hands, Stanik shifted gears, leaning in like a camp counselor about to tell a ghost story. Cliptok suppressed a smirk. Stanik was her bud, but he could be such a goober. "Okay," he said as if he knew her thoughts were poking fun at him, "Here's the situation: *Pan Motion Surveillance Station Thirty-three* is detecting an S.O.S. coming from *Interstellar Commercial Transit Six-Oh-One.*" Jablon made eye contact with Cliptok and raised an eyebrow as Stanik mentioned Demaria's station. Cliptok gave the slightest, sharpest shake of her head. Jablon dropped his gaze.

Stanik pretended not to notice. He kept going, "The freighter seems to have run astray of Transit Route Zulu. At twelve A-Kays, we're the closest vessel and we're being asked to investigate."

"Affirmative," Captain Billie said. She offered a thoughtful smile. "What do you advise?"

"I'm advising routine procedure: we dock the *Yulacki* alongside it and send a boarding party to scope things out. Jablon and I remain stationed in the cockpit. As supervising officer, Captain Billie oversees our boarding party, comprised of Hank and Cliptok."

"Excellent work." Captain Billie gave Walt a sharp salute of approval. "You may proceed," she added.

"Jablon," Stanik instructed, "coordinates have been downloaded to your navigations console. The helm is yours."

"Aye, sir," Jablon saluted. Cliptok watched his hand brush past a wing-like tuft of bedhead jutting from the crown of his head. She suppressed a snicker as he patted at it, trying to press the hair down. It would not oblige. Jablon shook his head and flipped a series of switches at his console. "Overriding autopilot," he murmured, rubbing the sleep out of his eyes. In no time at all, they were off to the edge of Rigel's Belt.

X   X   X

03:32 IST

On their approach to *ICT 601*, Captain Billie had grown skeptical. "Something's off," she kept muttering to herself. Once they drew close to the drifting freighter, Stanik felt a knot of concern twist in his gut. Captain Billie made Jablon circle the perimeter twice before they docked. She noted fresh scrape marks on the hull at aft starboard, which indicated a forced docking procedure. The only movement inside *601* seemed to be the fire flickering away as the cockpit interior burned.

"Stanik," Captain Billie said firmly after studying the freighter through their own windshield, "I'm taking command of this situation."

"Yes, ma'am," he replied, trying not to sound disappointed. "Should I—"

"No time to log it," she said with a half shake of her head. "I'm just gonna get us in and then get us out as quickly as possible."

"What's wrong," Stanik pressed. The captain was acting distracted… unsettled. He'd never seen Captain Billie nervous.

"I won't lie to you," Captain Billie said. She shook her head. "This feels like a trap to me." Stanik's innards bundled themselves together and leapt up into his throat. He swallowed the anxiety and reached for the hilt of his sword. "If I'm right," the captain went on, "someone expects us to board the freighter. But we'll wait them out on the *Yulacki* instead."

The captain thought about her plan for a second before continuing. "Jablon, commence boarding procedures. Stanik, you stay here with Jablon. Send instructions for their highest-ranking crew member to come aboard. If there are people in need, they'll oblige quickly."

Stanik saluted but did not speak or break eye contact. He could tell she was not done yet with her orders.

"When that's done, the two of you secure the cockpit. Hank and Cliptok; you follow me. We'll station ourselves at stern. If someone comes aboard, we'll push forward from aft and cut off their path to the hatch. That way, if they're intentions aren't genuine, we'll be able to claim a prisoner."

"Ma'am, yes, ma'am," the recruits called out confidently and in unison. In that moment, Stanik could feel the extra confidence the captain's plan instilled in them.

Captain Billie paused long enough to look them each over, gave a sharp nod of approval to no one in particular, then marched out of the *Yulacki* cockpit. Cliptok and Hank stayed on her heels, marching forward at attention. By the time the cockpit doors sealed shut behind them with a whisper, Stanik had already typed out the captain's instructions to anyone aboard *Freighter 601*.

The minutes ticked past like hours as Stanik and

Jablon waited quietly at their assigned post inside the cockpit. They had carried out their orders, but no response came from the freighter. The S.O.S. was on loop, an automated alert that had made Stanik's brain go numb while he tried transmitting a response.

Jablon had launched an inexpensive drone-bot to examine the freighter's cockpit windows. They were using it to monitor any movement inside via the robot's live camera feed. A flash inside the cockpit drew their attention.

"Movement," Stanik urged. "Just behind the helm seats." As a flash of light inside the cockpit burst forth, Stanik realized it was merely a clump of insulation igniting in one of the recessed chairs. There was no other movement from the mysterious vessel for a solid ten minutes.

"Walt," Jablon whispered next to the closed cockpit door; he was peering out the window. "Movement at the hatch." Stanik risked a peek down the hallway as the hatch swung wide and a Cliptorgian woman in a green mariner's hat stepped lightly down into the *Yulacki*, her sword drawn. Pirate, Stanik thought. Captain Billie was right; this was a trap.

"There's no one here, Captain," the Cliptorgian intruder whispered over her shoulder to someone waiting in the umbilicus connector tethering the *Yulacki* to *Freighter 601*.

A man with long blond hair and a tricorn hat stepped down into the *Yulacki* behind her. "I can see that," he snapped. Stanik noted the Fallamon shell he wore on his back, the scar above his left eye. The running lights in the *Yulacki* hallway glinted off the blade of his black steel cutlass.

Stanik ducked away from the window as the blonde man peered toward the cockpit. "Just head for the cockpit and stay close," he heard the man instruct. The intruder was quiet, but he did not bother to whisper.

Not ready to pull his pistol from its holster, Stanik let his hand rest on the grip – had to wipe his sweaty palms off twice. If there were footsteps that followed, Stanik didn't hear them, but it was only a few heartbeats before someone tapped the access panel on the other side of the cockpit door.

As soon as he heard it, Stanik hit the switch to raise the door. The door jolted free, ascending into the ceiling with a snap. Jablon and Stanik both struck a fighting stance, pistols out. "Freeze," Captain Billie hollered from the end of the hallway at stern. She pushed in from the shadows, flanked by Cliptok and Hank. They moved quickly to cut off the pirates' escape through the hatch. While Hank and Cliptok had their swords drawn, Stanik noted that the captain had her pistol aimed. She strafed, keeping her muzzle steadily trained on the pirate captain.

Stanik charged his pistol, extending it so it was mere centimeters from the pirate captain's nose. "Hands in the air," he barked at the intruders, "You've got nowhere to go!" Stanik could feel the adrenaline firing through his body. Then, a moment of calm clarity washed over him.

Stanik recognized the blond cutthroat in front of him. This was the infamous space pirate, Captain

Alaborap Smith, whose visage Stanik had encountered in his criminology training. The military academy made recruits study his attack methods. He was one of the top five most wanted pirates in the Outer Rim, and by some strange chance, he was staring down the barrel of Stanik's pistol.

"Come, now," Alaborap Smith sneered pompously, "I don't think you're thick enough to use that onboard."

"Try me." Stanik's challenge was calm and cool. He released his pistol's safety. The pirate's right eyebrow crept up his forehead.

"You're either very brave... or very foolish," Captain Alaborap sneered. With barely a flinch, the pirate flicked a marble-sized object past Walt's face. It skittered to the floor inside the cockpit. In a flash-bang, a cloud of green smoke erupted all around them. Stanik shielded his face with his free hand. As he did, he felt Alaborap kick his legs out. Instinctually, Stanik recoiled, stammering as his pistol tumbled from his grip.

As Stanik hit the floor, he felt the air around him stinging his lungs. He snorted hard to clear his airways, stifled a cough, and rolled over onto his belly. Captain Alaborap had donned a small mask, a device that covered his nostrils and mouth and made his face look like some haunted skeleton's grim smirk. The other two pirates had crammed masks on, too, and were now mustering Jablon against the far wall. Stanik was too far away from the intruders to grapple them to the floor, and whatever he'd just breathed in was still singing through his nerves. He coughed, shaking his head to try and loose the burning sensation from within him.

Control of the situation was lost, Stanik acknowledged in a moment of lucidity. His mind swam through old training modules; Captain Billie ran piracy scenarios with them once every four weeks. 'Mark each and every one of them,' was always her first instruction. 'Burn their faces into your memory – their distinguishing features, their species. Listen for their names. Every detail helps Central Command confirm their I.D. and track them.'

The captain was stony about piracy training. She said it was because the reality of serving in the ISF was that young, inexperienced troops were too often stationed beyond the Great Barrier. That was the end of regulated space. Beyond it, the Outer Rim worlds and the rest of the known universe sprawled out unforgivingly... vast starscapes where pirate attacks were an everyday threat, particularly to ISF citizens and soldiers.

Plus, Stanik reminded himself, Captain Billie had a reputation. Rumor at the Academy was she'd never personally lost a recruit on a training mission, even though she'd been running such missions beyond the Barrier for at least two decades. There were even a few wild stories about her daring rescues. But in a full year patrolling the outer reaches, the *Yulacki* training crew hadn't sighted a single swashbuckler. They'd been lucky... until now, Stanik corrected himself.

Alaborap stood over him, pressing the tip of his sword against Stanik's throat. Stanik could feel the control this man had over a sword, and he dared not even move enough to swallow. He did manage to glance at Jablon in his periphery. His friend was pinned against one of the bare metal walls in the cockpit, held there by the Cliptorgian woman with the green hat and a lanky man with a prominent nose and a curling mustache. The man struck Stanik as odd, with his little rectangular spectacles and his billowy polka-dot shirt.

The acrid green smoke thinned out, and Alaborap plucked his mask from his mouth. The pirates restraining Jablon followed suit. Down the hall, a clatter drew their attention.

In a blur of white fur, a huge creature lunged from the umbilicus, tackling Hank and Billie in one fell swoop. The creature roared like a lion, its hot breath a curling vapor in the cool *Yulacki* hallway.

Stanik saw Cliptok duck away from the attack, adjusting her sword and taking a defensive stance. She did so just in time, for a mountain of a man charged through the umbilicus next, wielding a massive Cliptorgian broadsword[21]. He struck at her, but Cliptok side-stepped. She was limber, and her quick footwork allowed her some advantage. But Stanik gritted his teeth as he watched her struggle against the muscle man's force. The pirate growled at Cliptok as she leapt away from him again. Then, Cliptok countered, locking swords. She pivoted, gave a shove, and the big man fell back with an ugly smile. Stanik noticed the shiny, bubbly

---

[21] **Cliptorgian broadsword** – a hefty, 't'-shaped sword made with a blade of zevver, the glittering purple alloy found in certain mountainous regions of Cliptorgia.

cracks of scar tissue puckering with the pirate's sickly grin.

Just then, a scrawny kid in a Viking helmet leapt out and pulled Cliptok's arms behind her back. She ducked away, using the kid's force to flip him onto his back. Then, she reached for her sword, but the big man pushed forward, knocking her sword away. He twisted her arm behind her back, but he was slow and deliberate about it. There seemed to barely be any force. Then, he said calmly, "You're a worthy opponent. Do you yield?"

Cliptok nodded, her jaw flexing as she forced herself to make eye contact with him. He merely nodded, then saluted his captain.

"We have the Bridge," Alaborap hollered.

It was over just like that. Stanik would barely even consider the *Yulacki* crew's resistance a tussle, he thought. The Stingrays were so... methodical, he realized. So well-organized. They'd anticipated pirates, they'd come up with a plan to spring a possible trap, and yet Stanik was on the floor with a sword-point pressed to his throat. The ISF trainees had been bested in less than fifteen minutes.

"Don't just stand there looking pleased with yourselves," Captain Alaborap sneered. "Clear the upper deck of purplebloods[22]!" There was an arrogance in him, Stanik noted. The *Yulacki* crew, his little band of peers

---

[22] **purpleblood** – a popular derogatory slur in the frontier worlds which refers to ISF troops & citizens. Coined during the Outer Rim Rebellion, this term refers to the claim that Federalists are said to 'bleed purple,' the primary color of the ISF flag.

and his steady-handed mentor, were not just victims of a pirate attack. They were prisoners of one of the most wanted men in the known universe. Survival had to be Stanik's primary focus. He had to absorb every detail he could about these felons, and he had to keep as many of his crewmates alive as he possibly could.

Stanik stared down the blade at his throat… stared at the hilt… found Alaborap's defiant eyes. They burned a sour hazel green, like the smoke that still lingered under the *Yulacki*'s cockpit running lights like sickly, acrid fog. Stanik flashed a grin as the pirate locked eyes with him. A rush of adrenaline coursed through Stanik's veins, sending a shiver through his arms and neck. He'd never stared into the eyes of the enemy before. An unsettling need to exterminate him rushed up to Stanik's animal reflexes like some wild predator.

No, he told himself. He had to stay alive. What did he know about his captors? People said the Halogien Stingray pirates rarely left survivors, only casualties. Was this how he was going to die? His grandma would be devastated. She'd objected to him enlisting from the get-go, but he had wanted to see the universe. That was hard to do from a tiny town on Earth, especially being raised on a teacher's salary. He had argued with her night and day that he'd be fine, that he would likely never see a combat situation, and had even pulled statistics to prove how well the ISF protected its young recruits. His heart pounded in his chest as he realized this might just be it. He had always hoped to be an exception in some way, but not as a statistic. His head spiraled as he confronted his impending death.

He shook himself from that tailspin, unwilling to surrender to such thoughts. Lying there on the floor at sword point, he noted that he was, in fact, still alive presently, and that was enough motivation to keep fighting. He listened for names as Captain Alaborap rattled off orders.

"Argyle, stay with me," Alaborap ordered. Stanik marked Argyle as the man with the mustache and polka dots, who nodded to acknowledge his orders. "Vestonn," Alaborap continued, "lock up the crew and wait for my orders." Stanik saw the muscle man detaining Cliptok give a salute. So, he thought, 'Vestonn' was the bald bruiser with the multicolored, paisley-patterned bandana. It was wrapped taught over the bronze skin of his bald head.

"Eldadip, you, too." The striking Cliptorgian woman with the green mariner's hat grabbed Stanik. She hefted him up off the floor as he struggled against her and twisted his arms behind his back. Stanik made note that she was only slightly taller than him, the stiff brim of her green hat poking into the back of his head as she forced him along. 'Eldadip,' Stanik repeated to himself as he noted the sea salt smell of her aroma. The Cliptorgian woman, Eldadip, had enough fine leather and wool about her wardrobe that it had detained the scent of their last whereabouts. A seaside port, most likely in the Outer Rim... that meant they'd probably come right from Smith's Pointe. That was a helpful detail, Stanik realized excitedly. That could help track their whereabouts!

"Glygorg," Alaborap carried on with his orders, "see to it that we're ready to disembark." Stanik waited. None of the pirates reacted to this order until, with a startling, wet pop, a reptilian head poked out of the Fallamon shell on Alaborap's back.

"Aye, Captain," the Fallamon acknowledged, his needle-like teeth flashing from underneath a leathery red battle helmet. Stanik had heard stories about thugs in the Outer Rim adorning Fallamon shells as armor, but Alaborap was *wearing* his Fallamon crew member. That was... odd. It was also an unforgettable detail. How had that never made it into the stories about this guy, Stanik wondered. Glygorg popped his scaly black legs and arms out of the shell, revealing his one-meter-tall bipedal stature. He peeled his chest away from Alaborap's coat and skittered down the hall, back through the hatch door from whence the pirates had come.

Eldadip, the Cliptorgian woman, and Vestonn, the bulked-up bandana man, roughed up Stanik and Jablon as they forced them out of the cockpit. Stanik struggled well until Eldadip paused, took a step forward, and elbowed him square in his right eye.

Stanik collapsed, stifling a cry of pain, and Eldadip dragged him the rest of the way, leaving Alaborap and the man with the mustache alone in the cockpit.

"Get to work, Argyle," was the last order Stanik heard Alaborap give. After that, the pirate captain's voice was swallowed in the struggling grunts and threats exchanged between the pirates and captured recruits as they proceeded aft, down the *Yulacki*'s main corridor.

X   X   X

Stanik's heart was racing; his anger surged as the pirates tossed him into the brig belowdecks. He growled at them as he stumbled gracelessly forward. They paused only a moment before both pirates looked at each other and burst out laughing.

"Easy, tiger," Vestonn snapped as he activated the brig's locking mechanism. The pirates cackled to each other as the blast door sealed tight.

Stanik tried to swing around and face them, but he tripped on someone's foot and came crashing down into Jablon's gut instead.

"Damn it," Jablon gasped, "it's too early for this shit." In reflex, he pushed Stanik away. Realizing what he'd done, Jablon was quick to extend a hand and help Stanik back up to his feet.

"You boys okay," Captain Billie asked, giving them a once-over for any injuries.

"Fine," Stanik nodded, brushing himself off. "They just roughed us up." Cliptok raised a challenging eyebrow. Stanik ignored the pulpy bruise he could feel swelling slowly around his right eye.

"Good," Billie nodded. She leaned in, encouraging the recruits to huddle up. As they did, she began strategizing in hushed tones. "We need to break out of here. I don't want to let that bastard get away if we can help it," she paused, looking at her young crew. "But your safety is paramount."

"I think I can identify his crew for authorities," Stanik reported quietly. "I was listening to him give orders."

"That's a hell of a start," Captain Billie grinned.

Outside the solid brig door, a WristCom pinged the pirates. Silence fell over the recruits as they tried to hear what was being said. Stanik only heard muffled orders before Vestonn opened the solid metal door, his sword leading the way.

"Line up shoulder to shoulder," he barked, brandishing his blade at the recruits. They obliged, but only after Captain Billie stepped forward.

The big pirate inspected them one by one. His gaze lingered on Stanik's name badge. Even with half his face under a bandana, it was clear the pirate was considering a thought he found puzzling. He rubbed his chin, his fingertips scraping a fine layer of stubble developing there. Stanik watched the pirate's eyes go back and forth between Captain Billie and himself.

"You," the big man said finally. His sword was pointed at Stanik. "Come with me." With one massive hand, the pirate Vestonn yanked Stanik away from his crewmates.

4. GUILTY CONSCIENCE

March 15th, A.D. 2349
03:48 IST

"Get to work, Argyle." Argylesox flinched as Captain Alaborap's command sliced through his cloud of thoughts. He had been playing with the curling ends of his handlebar mustache, trying not to think about what would become of the young recruits who were now at the mercy of the Halogien Stingray pirates.

He couldn't make that his concern. He had to maintain his composure to blend in with the scoundrels. Shaking himself back to the present, he nodded and took a seat at the captain's console, noting the smell of stale vinyl that clung to every millimeter of the old vessel's cockpit. Rapidly, he plunked away on the keyboard, hoping he could hack the system without putting their young prisoners in danger. Three times in a row, the console beeped its denial at him.

His shoulders drooped as the computer responded verbally in a cold and scolding tone, "Access Denied: captain's clearance required."

"Damn." Argyle mumbled, typing in a restart command. Sometimes, upon restarting an older ship console, he'd had luck breaking into the BIOS[23] menu. He plunked away at the keyboard, entering a few known ISF system startup commands.

Alaborap turned to peer over his shoulder, his calm demeanor a threat all its own. "I thought you could get around this garbage," he challenged, doubt in his voice.

"Usually, yes," Argyle had to mind his tone with this man; it was important to keep him hooked on the line. The slightest hint of dissent could trigger Alaborap. "The issue is there are too many fail-safes on a training vessel. There's no way to access these files without the captain's passcode."

"Does it allow you to check the logs?"

Argyle nodded. He understood where his captain's suggestion was leading them. "Yes. That I can do from here."

"So, who's the acting captain?"

Argyle pulled up the ship's logs and scanned the

---

[23] **BIOS** – a Terran computing invention circa A.D. 1975. The acronym is short for 'Basic Input/Output System,' and provides a simplified user interface which allows for the configuration and/or alteration of boot files and system-level firmware. Such features are accessed before a computer boots its primary operating system.

most recent entries. "Here we are," he said calmly. "Acting captain is Walter Stanik."

Alaborap tapped his WristCom immediately. "Vestonn," he demanded, "bring me Walter Stanik."

"Aye, sir. Copy that." The bodyguard's voice was tinny and unimposing over the little WristCom speaker.

Alaborap closed the channel with a chime. "He'll figure it out," the captain said with a small chuckle.

Captain Alaborap sat quietly after that. Argyle had quickly learned that, unless they were trying to answer questions about their quest together, Alaborap had a low tolerance for casual conversation. It made no difference to Argyle, who preferred the company of his own thoughts, even though he considered himself a relatively sociable person. The captain despised small talk, and Argylesox was the first to admit that he was no good at it. Instead, an awkward silence lingered in the air between them until Vestonn marched in, firmly grasping the young black Terran who'd waved his pistol in Alaborap's face upon their arrival. The young recruit, presumably Walter Stanik, resisted Vestonn's hold, to no avail.

"Are you sure you want *him*?" The skepticism was heavy in Vestonn's tone. "His badge says he's a Midshipman. There's that older woman who might—"

"No, no. We want *Captain* Stanik," Alaborap mocked. "What's your pass code?"

Behind him, Argyle heard Stanik spit and turned in time to see Alaborap wipe the foamy glob of phlegm from his cheek, grinning slyly.

Argyle cringed. That was ill-advised, even though he

couldn't help but admire the kid's moxie. Alaborap said nothing. He merely stepped to the side and punched Stanik firmly in the gut.

He grabbed the recruit by the throat, hatred burning in his eyes. "Pass. *Code.*" His demand was guttural, a threat Argyle worried the kid didn't take seriously enough. Alaborap wasn't necessarily a hateful person, but he held the conviction that other beings were merely in his way, and he expected his crew to demonstrate that ideology every time they took a prize or had a run-in with another pirate clan.

In fact, Argyle noted, Alaborap did not have to take action on his own very often; he simply extended disapproval to his crew. They were so scared of him, so eager for his approval, that they'd exact his will ten-fold in hopes of regaining his respect. It was a cycle even Argyle felt himself succumbing to, especially in a moment of adrenaline like the one he found himself in now. Already aboard a government vessel *illegally* with a very specific goal, Argyle felt himself seeking that calm, exacting guidance Alaborap was able to offer under such circumstances.

"Go to hell." Stanik smirked defiantly, unintimidated by Alaborap. Big mistake, Argylesox thought. The kid had just sealed his fate. Without letting go of Stanik's throat, Alaborap kneed him swiftly in the groin, knocking him to his knees.

"I can do this all day, *Captain,*" Alaborap reassured his new punching bag. He cracked Stanik across the mouth with an open hand, and the young man sputtered up blood, but still he shook his head, no. "Tell me, *Captain*, how much conditioning have you had, hmm? Are you far enough along in your training to understand the pain we're prepared to exact on you?"

"Yeah," the young Stanik said helpfully. "It's E. A. – T. M. – E." Argyle suppressed a chuckle. Alaborap rolled his eyes. "I don't... aid *pirates*," the soldier said firmly. That was a first, Argyle thought. He cringed as his captain punched Stanik twice, his right eye and cheek swelling up in a blooming bruise.

Alaborap stepped back, allowing Vestonn to step in and continue the beating. It went on for longer than Argyle was expecting. The kid finally passed out, then seemed to blurt the code out unconsciously. As quickly as possible, Argyle typed in the passcode, provided through the swollen lips of a freshly battered face. The ship console beeped in agreement. "That's the one," Argyle said hurriedly, twirling his mustache around his finger nervously, "I'm in."

"Good," Captain Alaborap scoffed, waving Vestonn away from the kid. "Do you have access to the necessary system files, Argyle?"

"Yessir," Argyle gulped, unable to shake the guilty feeling growing in the pit of his stomach. He had to muscle through it. If he showed the slightest regret or weakness, his whole pirate charade would be for naught.

Alaborap nodded. "Vestonn, we should have what we need in just a few minutes. Go get Eldadip and head back to the freighter. Take the boy captain with you."

"Aye, sir," Vestonn nodded, cracking his knuckles

before dragging Stanik out of the cockpit.

X   X   X

Argylesox fiddled with his mustache as he paced himself half a step behind Alaborap, ready to answer questions or offer advice, as had been his position for the past few months. Behind them, Eldadip and Vestonn dragged the bloodied and bruised Stanik by the collar of his flight jacket. Captain Alaborap was leading them across the base level of *Freighter 601*'s dank, hollow cargo bay.

The empty freighter's belly was cold and dark, and it accented even the rustling of their clothing with a hollow metallic echo. As his mind wandered, Argyle glanced up at the worn red catwalks lining the perimeter of the monstrous room. Their steep staircases resembled the old fire escapes he'd seen in Earth's urban sprawls. The skeletal structures felt like the freighter's ribcage, he noted. He was literally and metaphorically in the belly of the beast. Still, his good nature won out over intimidation, and he tested the subject of Walter Stanik's fate. Leaning in so only Alaborap could hear him, he asked, "How are you planning to deal with the prisoner, sir?"

Alaborap raised an eyebrow. "I'm not taking any prisoners," he said matter-of-factly. Then, he stopped abruptly, turning to face Argyle. "You stay here and deal with young Stanik. Report back to the ship when you're finished."

"What, exactly, am I supposed to do with him,"

Argyle asked, hiding the dread in his voice.

Alaborap passed the buck. "Eldadip," he said. Suggestive orders were one of his tactics. He liked crewmembers who took initiative, and he prompted them occasionally to do so while inferring his intentions or desires.

"Here," Eldadip said, rifling through her pack and producing two metal bricks and a digital counter. "Strap him to these."

"What's the blast radius on those," Alaborap barked.

"One of these is enough to rip the freighter in two. Place them aft of center here in the middle of the hold and they'll blow the whole thing wide open *and* ignite the engines. Even if that doesn't consume the Feds' vessel, it'll cripple it beyond recognition. Should give us some fireworks on the way out." She slapped the explosives into Argyle's sweaty palms, and he fumbled to compensate for their weight against his body. Each one easily weighed two kilos.

Eldadip plowed through her instructions, ignoring Argyle's difficulty with the weight. "We'll need ten minutes to get clear of the blast, so give me a heads up and don't start the timer until you're ready to make a run for it."

With that, she and Vestonn shoved the recruit to the floor, flanking Alaborap as they marched back to the *Stingray*. Safely alone, Argylesox allowed himself to sigh, frustrated with their disregard for other beings. But he knew this was a test, as were most of the tasks Alaborap had given him lately, and he needed to have his pirate's trust. He set Eldadip's explosives next to the battered recruit, who groaned, regaining consciousness. The young man looked up at him through swollen eyes, and Argyle felt tears of regret well up in his eyes. He sniffled, frowning at the scene, then decided he might try to give the young man a chance.

Vestonn had bound the recruit's arms and legs with plastic zip ties, so Argyle reached out and helped Stanik to his feet, careful not to rough him up anymore. He guided the recruit away from the explosives, over to the foot of the catwalk staircase, where he helped him take a seat on the steps. The young man looked questioningly at Argyle, who stood back for a moment, then drew his hunting knife from its sheath on his ankle.

As he stepped toward Stanik, the young man curled up to protect his abdomen and clenched his eyes shut, waiting for the jab. Understandably, he misunderstood Argyle's intention. Instead of sinking the blade into Stanik's gut, Argyle took the knife to the zip-ties and cut the soldier's bondage. It wasn't much, but he couldn't do more without risking his own skin; the Stingray pirates already suspected him of being a softy. He shook his regret, exhaling to clear the maddening flutters of anxiety that quivered in his chest.

As he tinkered with the digital counter, Stanik seemed to muster enough strength to push himself up the stairs to the first landing. The counter's screen glowed to life, its readout blinking: **00:10:00**.

Argyle signaled for Stanik to be quiet, stepping away

as he activated his WristCom. "Eldadip, this is Argyle. We're good to go here."

"Copy that," she responded over the crackling line. "Activate the counter and get back here." Sensing Stanik's confusion, Argyle nodded up to the hatch door in the catwalks: the one leading back to the *ISF Yulacki*. Then, he winked as he saw realization flood the young recruit's face. The kid spat blood onto the floor, then opened his mouth to speak.

Argyle raised a finger to his lips. He shook his head for extra emphasis. Don't make a sound, Argyle warned with every fiber of his being. The young man nodded in understanding and slid himself away from his spot on the floor. With a wiggle of his nose, Argyle activated the explosives counter at his feet before sprinting back to the Stingray. As he pulled the *Yulacki* hatch shut behind him, he saw the young man staggering up the steep stairs. His chances were slim, but at least Argyle had given him the *hope* of survival... that would have to be enough to clear Argyle's conscience.

Swallowing his guilt, Argylesox twirled the ends of his mustache and hardened his fluttering heart. There was no need to kill any of these soldiers, he thought, shaking his head. But his mission was to gain Alaborap's trust. Resisting his orders in favor of a young ISF crew would only raise the captain's suspicions.

Argyle tried not to picture their faces, but of course he had noted each of them. He pictured them screaming, then gasped as his mind conjured images of their flesh melting. Pain clawed at his chest like a desperate critter trapped in a box. If they died, he told himself, their blood was on his hands.

He hated that thought. The guilt of it urged his heart to hammer louder in his ears. If the pirates were this unforgiving with strangers, Argyle worried, how would they deal with him if they found out the truth?

He simply couldn't let that happen, he told himself. Still, his heartbeat louder. Argyle took a long, deep breath. Even though the air was cold and stale, the shadowed solitude of the Stingray's umbilicus connector offered him a momentary comfort before he had to reconvene with the merciless cutthroats he called comrades.

5. COLLATERAL DAMAGE

March 15th, A.D. 2349
04:02 IST

Belowdecks, in the *Yulacki* brig, Captain Grace Billie was working her way along the seams in the metal floor paneling, trying to find a place where she could get a grip on one. She was trying to ignore the nervous energy of her recruits, particularly Jablon, who paced along the walls of the tiny room, swinging his arms forward and back. He possessed an imposing physique, but also a lack of self-certainty in nearly all his body language. Billie made a note to include that in her next progress report.

Cliptok and Hank were watching her with looks of curiosity from their seats on the single metal cot affixed to the back wall. As she felt along a gap in the floor panels, Billie decided to get those two involved. "Cliptok, give me a hand," she instructed.

"What're you doing," Cliptok asked as she knelt next to Billie.

"What's my number one rule," Billie prompted.

"Know your ship," Hank said quickly.

Billie nodded. "Damn right," she said. It was a simple but important fact she drilled into every crew of trainees she had. It was the only thing she quizzed them on repeatedly during their time with her. Though she'd never had such a crucial opportunity to prove its importance before. No time like the present.

"There's an electrical conduit that runs along here," she explained. "If we crack it open, that'll trip security systems—"

"And the turrets do a retinal scan before they open fire," Cliptok interrupted excitedly with the snap of her fingers.

Billie saw Hank's eyes light up behind his hydro-mask as he put her plan together. "If the turrets detect a commanding officer's retinal pattern in the brig, emergency functions will unlock the chamber door."

"Exactly," Billie said with a wink. Somewhere above them, the *Yulacki*'s fuselage groaned.

Outside the brig door, heavy footsteps echoed their way. Billie held up a finger, signaling for the recruits to be silent. They quieted themselves, and Billie could hear the bullying voice of the musclehead pirate who had taken Stanik. "Eldadip, they've got it. Let's go." The big brute's voice reverberated harshly through the ship's lower deck.

Billie listened as boots clanked down the hallway. Then, she noted the singing and ringing of the ladder up to the main deck. The sounds of pirate foot traffic trailed off. In no time, the hallway outside was still. No shifting of gear. No jostling of fabrics. Billie sighed with relief. "Sounds like they're gone," she told her recruits.

Billie gave the floor panel she'd been fussing with a good tug, and it popped free with a clatter. As the automated turret rocked out of its compartment in the wall, Captain Billie raised her head high and stared it down. The security systems chirruped, and a red light scanned the captain's eyeballs.

Then, the brig's hefty locks deactivated with a series of reverberant thunks. Captain Billie pushed the door, and it swung wide. "Good," she said. "Now, let's get the hell out of here."

χ   χ   χ

Back on the *Yulacki*'s main deck, Captain Billie led her crew into the cockpit. "Walt," she called after Stanik, hurriedly scanning the room. Grimtash[24]. There was no trace of the young recruit.

"Captain," Hank jarred Billie from her thoughts, pointing to a corner of the cockpit. "Blood on the floor.

---

[24] **grimtash** /ˈgrɪmtæʃ/ – a Cliptorgian curse originating from root words 'grim' (star) and 'tash' (dust/soot/mess), this ancient planetary slur is used as versatilely as the English word 'fuck.' It is thought to have originally expressed 'nonsense,' such as the Terran terms 'balderdash' & 'hogwash.'

And a few drops trailing down the hallway!" Hank's yellow finger traced the trail of drying crimson droplets.

"Good eyes, Hank," she said, giving the Hulgarian a pat on the shoulder. "They must've taken him." Billie's mind raced. She had to keep the other recruits safe.

If a pirate as dangerous as Captain Alaborap had taken Walter, he likely wasn't coming back. Billie winced at the thought, but she had to work on accepting it. She couldn't risk another of the young beings in her charge, not even to save their mate. Plus, she reminded herself, this group was sharp; they had to be fully aware that their friend Walter Stanik was a potential goner. To keep them calm, and get them out of there, she'd need to distract them… keep their minds busy. They had to be focused on survival.

"All right," she ordered, "Jablon, prepare to separate us from the freighter. Cliptok, search the computers and figure out what they did." Billie took a confident breath and raised her WristCom. "Hank, synchronize watches?"

Hank saluted, then leaned over his console. "System marks Interplanetary Standard Time at oh-four-thirty-two-hours."

"Oh-four-thirty-two, roger that," Billie said, synching her WristCom to Hank's console.

"Captain," Hank started to ask.

Billie cut him off. She knew what the question was. "I'm going after Walt." Her tone was firm and certain. There could be no room for an argument. She hustled a few steps down the hall, then stopped to call out over her shoulder. "Be prepared to leave without me." She heard their protests echoing back to her. "That's an *order*."

Captain Billie couldn't help but grin as she heard all three recruits mutter a defeated, "Yes, ma'am." She continued on down the hall. Reaching for her belt, she felt the hilt of her sword still in its sheath. Good. She raced to the hatch, swung it wide, and climbed through.

The umbilicus to *Freighter 601* wiggled around Captain Billie, and she let the effects of zero-gravity propel her. In leaping bounds, she tumbled through the wriggling tunnel out into the freighter's upper level. She grasped the worn red catwalks and peered down the steep staircase.

On the yellow arrows painted across the floor, she saw streaks of blood and heard the clank of metal. The railing vibrated in response, and Billie's eyes darted from landing to landing, struggling to find the source of movement through the corrugated metal. She drew her sword, but then spied Stanik, bruised and bloody, hoisting himself up the stairs to the third landing. She couldn't help but grin at the recruit's grit. Soldiers that tough, both mentally and physically, just weren't enlisting anymore. It was a point of contention she'd discussed at length with her peers. The crew aboard the *Yulacki* were a refreshing exception, and Billie smiled through her fear as she hustled down the stairs to help Stanik.

Swiftly, she crept down the noisy metal stairs to her trainee. "Hang on, soldier," she whispered once she was close enough to avoid shouting. Crouching down, she examined Stanik, prodding him gently for broken bones. The young man's eyes were swollen, and his nose looked broken. His ankle was swollen, too… sprained, possibly broken, but his arms seemed unharmed. She realized he had been hoisting himself up the stairs with upper body strength before she got to him.

Bruised or broken ribs, Billie noted, watching Stanik wince as she pressed at his sides. Slinging Stanik's arm over her shoulder, Billie heard his mumbling.

"Hnnho," he struggled, "nho thhym." He tried nodding his head towards the stairs but winced with pain as he did. It was enough; Billie realized what he was trying to say. She glanced over the catwalks and followed Stanik's drying blood trail from the stairs to the explosives set out in the middle of the floor. A digital panel glowed angry red digits: 00:03:47.

Billie sighed, taking most of Stanik's weight. The recruit had weakened himself further by climbing the stairs, and his breath was shallow, rasping in Billie's ear.

"C'mon, soldier, you've got a way to go and not much time to get there." Careful not to agitate Stanik's sore ribs, Billie did most of the work, her quadriceps burning as she dragged Walter to the fifth and final level of the catwalk stairs. Billie's thighs burned as she hauled them both, but she pressed on, coaxing her recruit into the trembling rubber of the umbilicus. Such connecting tunnels were a necessary evil to allow safe docking between vessels. The modern umbilicus was fragile, constructed of a malleable wire frame and thick, accordion rubber. They couldn't be too long, or gravity simulators between ships caused issues for crew. They also couldn't be too short, or ships face much higher collision risks during docking procedures.

Momentary relief flooded Captain Billie's system as some of their weight left them back in the freighter's artificial gravity field. That told her they were near the middle of the seven-meter-long umbilicus connector. Billie carefully adjusted her arm under Stanik's shoulders and pushed off the umbilicus floor. They covered two meters in one weightless bound. Excitement rushed through her; she hadn't accounted for the lack of gravity. They were going to make it!

That's when the countdown started chirping ominously behind them, its shrill warning echoing up to her. On digital counters, that usually meant there was less than a minute to go. They had to clear the rubber walkway in that time.

Desperately, Billie kicked hard, springing them off the floor again. They were slowing down... entering the *Yulacki*'s gravity field.

The explosives chirped away their seconds, ringing in Billie's ears. As if in response, her heartbeat thumped in her temples. She couldn't help but count the chirps.

Chirp.

Chirp.

Chirp.

The tempo of the chirping doubled.

Chirp, chirp, chirp, chirp, chirp.

They had less than thirty seconds. Billie's heart seemed to reset to the rapid pace of those awful little warnings. Suddenly, she tasted the fresh, crisp air drifting through the umbilicus tunnel ahead of them. They were only two meters from the hatch into the *Yulacki*. Sweat beaded across her brow, and Stanik's weight seemed to increase in her arms as one of the midshipman's boots snagged on the tunnel framework. Billie staggered with the extra weight, dropping Stanik. They were back in the pull of artificial gravity. "Walter?" Billie shook the young man out of a daze.

Stanik sputtered, peering up at her through swollen eyes. "I – I gave them the code... I'm sorry." The shame was palpable, but Billie didn't have time to address it.

"Come on," she said, trying not to sound frightened. "We've gotta move!" She tugged with all her might, fighting fatigue as they closed the distance to the *Yulacki* hatch door. Behind them, the counter's chirps were shrill. Billie had lost track, but those piercing notes suggested they had–

Before she could finish her thought, the counter expired. Heat swept over them first as the explosion roared with fury through the cavernous freighter. With the last of her will power, Billie was able to hurl Stanik forward, out of the umbilicus and into the *Yulacki* hallway. The cold metal floor jarred young Stanik from his injured daze. Billie saw him scramble to his feet, turning back with horror in his eyes.

"Captain," he hollered, reaching his right hand out for Billie. No, Billie thought desperately, but she had no time to shout before the *Yulacki*'s blast doors clamped down on Stanik's outstretched arm.

Trapped inside the umbilicus connector, Billie felt flames licking over her, felt her flesh cooking. Charged by fear and adrenaline, she did the only thing she could do; she reached up, locking eyes with Stanik, and shoved his arm back into the *Yulacki*. She cringed as she watched patches of Walter's skin slide away from his arm, but she had to free him. Doing so allowed the blast doors to snap shut before the hellfire around her was quenched by a roaring, blinding white light.

X   X   X

In Captain Billie's absence, Hank and Cliptok had hunkered down in the back of the *Yulacki* cockpit, working vigorously at their consoles. From their spot, Cliptok had been watching Jablon. He stood at the helm in front of them, tapping his foot nervously as he fixated on the clock next to the piloting console, shaking his head. "Why doesn't she ping the Coms," Jablon muttered.

Cliptok tuned out his fretting. It wasn't helping anyone, and none of Hank's reassurances had worked yet. Hank had far better bedside manner than she did, so she just kept quiet.

She was scanning the ship's security logs as she had been ordered to. No malware, no tracking... what had the pirates wanted? Then, she spotted the download command. "Oh, I think I've got it! Look at this," she pointed at the line of code on her screen so Hank could spot it faster. "Apparently, the ISF has a classified file code-named *Legend*. It's tagged with keywords Goliathon, Zaremoth, and Candalonian[25]."

"Like in the old myths?" Hank leaned over to read her screen.

"Yeah, look… it says Walt entered his clearance code and downloaded this file."

"Where are they," Jablon asked, his impatience bubbling over. As if on cue, the *Yulacki* shuddered, rumbling around them like an earthquake.

Jablon stumbled, catching himself on the piloting console. Cliptok sprang to her feet, her attention snapping to the exterior viewscreens at the security console to her left. She watched the live feed in horror as *ICT 601* burst apart. The explosion lobbed hunks of metal at the *Yulacki*. The hallway behind them erupted in chaos. Red lights flashed and alarms blared as the ship's calm, cold computer voice reported the damage.

"Hull breach in sector three. Hull breach in sector five," the lifeless female computer informed.

Without a word, Cliptok bolted from the cockpit. As soon as the cockpit door opened, she spotted Stanik on the floor by the hatch. He was sobbing, holding his mangled right arm away from his body. Cliptok's heart

---

[25] **Candalonian** /ˈkændəˌloŭniən/ – much of this reptilian race's history has been lost to time, but information gathered during the War of Formation suggests that they advanced to the stars sixty million years ago. Shortly thereafter, their home world Khandah grew unstable, and they abandoned it to reset their evolutionary clocks on Candalos Prime. There, they established a technology-free life for centuries. Thousands of years later, they reached for the stars again and were enraged to find intelligent life had evolved elsewhere.

sank as she smelled singed hair and saw the melted flesh on the blast doors. She swallowed the lump of disgust forming in her throat before it gagged her. She needed to help Walt.

"Jablon," she cried out over her shoulder. "Hank!" Please let them hear me over this chaos, she thought.

Cliptok kept her attention on the wailing figure of her crewmate curled up and shivering on the floor ahead of her. The hissing pipes and sparking conduits along the hallway fought back, and it took her eons to reach Stanik. He rocked rhythmically, cradling the deformed remnants of his right arm close as he saw her approaching. She was careful not to touch it, but wrapped him in her arms, resting her chin on his head.

She soothed him, matching the rhythm of his rocking, waiting for the chaos around them to subside. "I've got you," Cliptok reassured him, fighting the panic in her own voice. "It's gonna be okay."

6. SCAR TISSUE

"While the four trainees are all expected to recover from minor injuries," the news anchor at *Federation Nightly* relayed, "their mentor, Captain Grace Billie, was not so lucky. The fifty-six-year-old training officer was lost in the attack on *Freighter 601*."

The news reports had been wrong, had even offered Stanik's grandmother, his only living relative, false hope that her baby had gotten away unscathed. What *Federation Nightly* had missed — or, Stanik suspected, hadn't been told — was that he had been admitted to the intensive care unit at the nearest ISF checkpoint along the Great Barrier. He had been in shock because of the damage to his arm, and Hank had done everything in his power to field-dress the wound, but there wasn't much that could be done. Stanik had been prepared for it; he had watched the skin pull away from his right forearm like cheese separating from a slice of hot pizza, had felt the knives of pain in each nerve from his fingertips clear up to his elbow.

Stanik had been a fool to stick his arm in the hatch doors. Thankfully, his friends had rushed to his side. Jablon and Cliptok apparently hauled him back to the *Yulacki* cockpit, which doubled as a lifeboat, where Hank was waiting to jettison everyone to safety. Stanik was lucky he was alive, and he used that fact to steel himself for reconstructive surgery.

March 17, A.D. 2349
11:06 IST

Surgery came and went. When Stanik woke up in the recovery room two days after the incident, he felt tears streaked down his face. His brain felt numb as he watched a MedBot drift along the ceiling until it was directly overhead. "Hello," the MedBot said, flashing a smiley face across the display screen that ran the circumference of its cone-shaped head. "Can you hear me?"

Stanik blinked forcefully, allowing the hospital room to come into focus. "Yeah," he said weakly. "Yeah, I'm here. Thanks, MedBot."

"There is no need to thank me, but I acknowledge and appreciate your courtesy. Dr. Mullig said the procedure went well. 'Even better than he anticipated,' was the phrase used. You are to be on bed rest for the next three days. You are to be eased into physical therapy on the third day, depending on how you are healing."

Stanik nodded. "Understood." His right arm's flesh and bone had been fused to a hagron[26] brace. It was a prosthetic robotic frame designed to aid him in hand mobility, provoking his tendons and muscles to stretch out rather than wither and tighten as they healed and scarred over from the burns.

The procedure was costly, and the military had paid for it, but in exchange they wanted at least another five years of service out of him once he was fully recovered. Being of modest means, and not wanting to spend the foreseeable future crippled, he had signed the documents. He liked traveling, and he wasn't entirely sure what else to do with himself. Besides, the affordable alternative was to have them lob off everything below his right elbow. Stanik knew his body had always been stubbornly right-handed, so he wasn't about to give it up if he had an alternative.

MedBot's speaker played a soft jingle as it read Stanik's vitals. "Does the patient approve of receiving company?"

Oh, shit, Walt thought. Had grandma traveled all the way out here from Earth? She was *not* well enough to be doing that. "Who's here?"

"Your crewmates would like to join you today. Do

---

[26] **hagron** /ˈheɪgɹɑn/ – this pliable onyx-colored metal can bend but gradually restore its original shape. Native to the planet Cliptorgia, it has been used in medical prosthetics for centuries.

you permit it?"

Walt relaxed into his pillow with a smile. "Let 'em in." The door to his room retracted on its magnatrak frame. A split second later, Hank poked his head in. Like a gag in a cartoon, Cliptok poked her head in just above Hank's, and Jablon's face peered in next from above Cliptok's.

Stanik laughed. "Hey, guys! Come in."

Hank led the way, peering at Stanik's right arm as he approached. He pointed to the wad of bandages swaddling it. "Have they shown you the new hardware yet?"

"He *just* woke up," Cliptok nudged Hank with her elbow. "Give the guy a second."

"It's okay," Walt reassured her, "I haven't even thought about it yet... but I do want to see my arm. MedBot, can you unwrap my bandages?"

"It would not be detrimental to your recovery if I unwrapped it briefly for your examination," MedBot replied. "Would that satisfy the patient?"

Stanik noticed that Hank had to suppress an eager smile. He *was* in the middle of earning a field medic certification to diversify his skillset for easier placement on a starship crew, Stanik told himself.

"Yes, please. MedBot, I'd like to see my new arm." The MedBot hummed as it drifted across the ceiling to position itself over Walt's bandaged arm. Two thin hydraulic appendages, each with a fine set of needle nose pincers, reached down and delicately worked Stanik's bandages loose.

"Oof," Jablon uttered as the scar tissue and skeletal metal bracing of the prosthetic were revealed.

Walt's wrist had been broken when the hatch clamped shut on it, and most of his skin was completely gone. Instead, the doctors had grafted skin grown in a lab from Walt's own cells over the burns, but the lab skin was a pale brown that seemed sickly where it had been grafted to the darker natural skin of his upper arm. The extensive damage meant that nearly all of his lower arm had to be encased in a skeletal sleeve of hagron. It was like having a bulky metal glove pulled taught over his own flesh and bone, Stanik thought. He couldn't feel any of it yet... it was just a lifeless branch of scarred, numb cells that happened to be weighing him down. The sensation stirred up some nausea in him.

"Okay," he said. "I think you can wrap that back up, MedBot."

"Affirmative." The MedBot cinched up Walt's bandages. His friends fell quiet, but their uncertainty was deafening.

Finally, Cliptok broke the silence. "I don't know how you feel about it, but I think the new hardware gives you an edge."

"Oh, yeah?"

"Yeah! Good thing, too. You needed something to rough up that Boy Scout image," Cliptok smirked.

The entertainment console on the opposite wall played a jingle and an alert popped up on the viewscreen. "Oh, that's my reminder about the *Yulacki* broadcast."

"What broadcast," Jablon prodded, sounding like a

concerned parent.

"There's a special report tonight," Walt said plainly. He plucked a thin silver remote control from his bedside and the viewscreen glowed to life.

Jablon frowned. "Don't you think that's unhealthy?"

"Different people process trauma differently," Hank chimed in. Jablon's cheeks went rosy. He plopped himself in a chair, then mumbled an apology.

"Hey," Stanik said, trying to soften the blow and, admittedly, playing up the delirium his pain meds were causing, "your beard is looking good." It wasn't just an empty compliment, either. Jablon had tried growing out his facial hair since relocating to Cliptorgia[27]. He'd shared with Stanik back in basic training that, because Cliptorgian men couldn't grow facial hair, he understood that many Cliptorgian women took a liking to bearded Terrans. His stubble only made it a few days before all the new recruits were ordered to clean up and shave. The *Yulacki* assignment had been the first relaxed setting that offered Jablon an opportunity to let it grow. He had even sought permission from Captain Billie, who laughed, affirming that Jablon could do what he wanted with his hair while they were out patrolling the void. "I thought

---

[27] **Cliptorgia** /klɪpˈtɔ˞ giə/ – the second planet in the Cor system is shared by two intelligent species: the mammalian Cliptorgians and the amphibian Hulgarians. Both species continue to develop in the harmony of their symbiotic bond. They strive to live in concert with the natural forces on their planet, even cordoning off their homeworld's entire western hemisphere for preservation.

for sure they'd make you shave it," Stanik added.

Jablon scratched the bushy blonde hairs that blanketed his chin. "They granted us leave, Walt. We've got a while."

"Oh," Hank raised a webbed finger, "that reminds me. Admiral Southerland stopped by, but your surgery ran over, and he wasn't able to stay." Hank retrieved a small, dark case the size of a watchcase from his military pack. Its midnight black metal sparkled when it caught the light of the room. Hank opened it and offered it to Stanik. "It's your new clearance chip and badge. They've acknowledged our bravery with promotions. Congrats, *Lieutenant* Stanik!"

Stanik felt like he was dreaming. The fresh metal badge gleamed under the dimmed lights of the recovery room.

"Wait, is that what that box was," Jablon scooted to the edge of his chair, peering at Stanik's shining insignia.

Cliptok and Hank both raised an eyebrow, nearly in unison. "Yeah," Cliptok said. "Did you not open it?"

Jablon shrugged. "No. Haven't gotten around to it."

"Why not," Stanik asked.

At that, Jablon averted his gaze. "I guess I'm not sure I want to do this anymore." He was jutting out his chin like he did when he was bracing for an argument.

"Seriously?" Stanik had heard stories of soldiers who tucked tail after a traumatic experience, but he couldn't fathom this reaction from any of the *Yulacki* crew... especially not the tough guy who was twice his own size. "We should talk about it," Stanik said firmly to his friend. "Captain Billie saved our lives. We owe it to her."

"Hold up, Walt," Jablon said defensively. "First of all, she saved *your* life. She left the rest of us waiting in the cockpit and we got lucky, plain and simple."

"That is a highly inaccurate statement," Hank said calmly.

Jablon glanced down at the shine of 'Lieutenant' glinting back at him from Stanik's badge. His nose wrinkled in disgust. "I thought we always said, 'No pity promotions.' Isn't that exactly what this is?"

"Hey, man," Stanik sat up, "no one said you have to take it. But after what we just went through, I sure as hell will. And I'll definitely take the pay raise." Stanik's heartrate jumped up and down on the wall monitor above his pillow. His MedBot glowed to life again on the ceiling, its cone-shaped 'face' turning to observe the patient. MedBot worked in silence for an awkward moment, its limbs whizzing and whirring as it shined a light in Stanik's eyes, scanned his vitals, and poked gently at his scar tissue.

Jablon cleared his throat. "Th- there's a pay raise?"

Cliptok scoffed.

Stanik shook his head. "You never study."

Jablon's face morphed into a maelstrom of angry wrinkles. "C'mon, lay off! Not everyone's brain works as fast as yours! Besides, I said I wasn't sure. I didn't say I had decided." He stood, making for the door.

"That's fair," Hank chimed in, ever the arbiter. He crossed in front of Jablon and gestured calmly for their friend to sit back down. Hank turned back to Walt and Cliptok. "We shouldn't attack each other," he suggested in the gentlest, sternest parental timbre. "We've all been through a lot the past few days." Hulgarians desired harmony and collaboration in any conversation. Sometimes, it got under Stanik's skin, but he appreciated it now; his increased heart rate made the right side of his body throb with aching pain.

"Hey, check it out. They've already started the feed," Cliptok said from the entertainment console across the room. She was tinkering with the volume.

She's deflecting, Walt thought. That was always strange to him. Her culture preferred to tackle conflict through straightforward discussion and collaborative resolution. She'd never exhibited those traits in the two years Stanik had known her.

Stanik decided to leave Jablon alone. The frustration was stirring up pain all through his newly repaired arm. "Thanks, Cliptok. I don't want to miss this."

Cliptok turned up the newsfeed, using the voice of media vulture Gorf Nimdok to clear the air. Judging by the feed, Nimdok had slithered his way to the scrapyard where they were hauling in the *Yulacki*. His deep, luxurious voice shared details intimately with his audience like a sexy secret. "The military is being very hush-hush about this attack," Nimdok divulged, "but as you can see behind me here, the *Yulacki* wreckage has been towed in, and we've been informed they plan on investigating the attack further."

"Whoa," Hank marveled, "look at the hull damage."

Stanik didn't have to look. The charred, twisted remains of the *Yulacki* were burned into his memory from the military files he'd reviewed for his official report. He had noted each visible hull breach, the metal shredded and torn like the pages of a damaged book. Each dark hole in that hull marked a different spot where Alaborap had tried to kill him, Stanik told himself. His gut twisted with anger as his memory stirred up the image of Captain Billie's final moments.

It was her eyes. They had glazed over, staring beyond Stanik, searching for anything other than death. Night after night, that look continued to shake Stanik from his sleep, and he'd spend the early hours of the morning wondering what it was Billie saw before her there. Every time, the phantom pains in his arm cried out in agony. To make matters worse, it didn't feel like his friends were particularly angry about the circumstances. Stanik, on the other hand, felt his ears heat up any time he heard the word 'pirate.' It made sense, he supposed. None of his friends had been there when Captain Billie died.

He said nothing to his friends as a screaming bolt of pain screeched through his arm, all the way down to his fingers. Stanik winced, clenching his teeth until the sensation faded. He chose then and there not to avoid the pain. After everyone left, he started clipping and saving the news reels. It didn't help him sleep, but he continued that routine throughout his recovery. Every night, he still heard Captain Billie's screams...

7. THERAPY

Walt stared at himself in the mirror as he gripped the side of his sink. There was a bit of bruising still visible on his face, and the dark rings gathering under his eyes didn't do him any favors. Demaria was coming to see him, and he didn't want to look like a victim. He also didn't want to look like complete shit. There wasn't much he could do right then; he'd been struggling to sleep, and he felt constantly sore. He'd lost muscle mass because exercising made his whole arm throb like a second heart. He didn't feel like himself.

He had his useless hand resting on the sink ledge because he still couldn't move his thumb more than a *centimeter*, let alone grip something or lean on his arm in any way. The weight of the hardware tugged at his shoulder, pinching at the nerves in his neck while he tried to wash his face.

It hadn't started that way. His surgery and the initial recovery had gone off without a hitch. For the first three days post-surgery, doctors buzzed in and out of his hospital room, each time marveling at how well his skin graft was taking to the natural skin of his upper arm, and how well it was growing in around the hagron support brace. They'd download his vitals from the MedBot, nod to themselves, then test the reflexive actions of his brace. Each day, he felt more pangs and needles in parts of his hand and fingers, and each day, he regretted his decision to have it implanted; it had no use yet, other than to cause him pain.

Days four and five saw him start physical therapy. They had been encouraging, with very few setbacks. Hand exercises to wiggle fingers and swivel his wrist seemed gentle and breezy. The only discouraging part was how much of Stanik's hand and arm felt like a lump of dead weight… numb flesh that occasionally woke up and screamed at his brain in agonizing pain. The sensations would slumber again as quickly as they stirred up within him. It wasn't until he was cleared to start the intense physical therapy that Stanik truly struggled to accept the reality of his new circumstances.

On days six through ten, the physicians pushed him harder than he'd ever been pushed before… and that was coming from the guy who'd struggled a bit through basic training. On day eleven of recovery, one of the physicians had finally pushed Walter Stanik to the brink.

As the skin healed, he lost dexterity in his wound. It stiffened into a gnarled, frozen claw. The physician wanted him to make a fist.

"I told you, *I can't*," he snapped back at her during their morning session.

"That's because you're resisting the movement in your mind. Physically, everything is ready to go."

"Really," he shot back. "*Really?* You think *this* is ready to go?" He shook his ugly, hooked fingers at her.

"I do," she said firmly.

"Then you must be a real *quack*," he said, "because I'm the one attached to it, and I'll tell you right now the only place it's ready to go is the Halloween aisle at your nearest Holidaze Warehouse!"

She sighed, then took a deep breath. "Perhaps you should ask the doctor to hack it off, then." Her tone was calm and plain. Stanik knew it was a moment of suggestive therapy, but he was an exposed nerve already, and it felt condescending.

"Why don't I just save him the trouble?" With that, he balled his bad hand up into a fist and punched a hole through the wall. The plaster huffed and crumbled, clumping with crimson blood all over his right knuckle. He jerked his hand back to his chest as if to shield it from some unseen aggressor. That's when he noted the shape of the hole his fist had made in the wall. The hagron braces that ran the length of each finger had left an extra notch above each knuckle, and the outline made his fist look like the pawprint of a grizzly bear, that rare apex predator preserved only in Earth's poshest parks. Long ago, they'd been native to his home in the Alaskan Province.

"Grimtash," he cussed at himself. "I'm sorry! I'm so sorry," he blubbered.

After a split second of silence, his physiotherapist had burst out laughing. "It's okay," she cheered, "did you see that? You did it, Lieutenant! You made a fist!"

Stanik fought back tears. He was ashamed he'd lost his temper. He was ashamed that, when he hit the wall, he was fighting the urge to hit *her*. "I think I need to be done for the day," he blurted out, averting his eyes as he lingered in the doorway.

"It's truly not a problem," she encouraged. "I've seen *far* worse." All Stanik could do was shake his head. He apologized again, more to the gray tile floor than to the therapist, then excused himself.

By that afternoon, he'd received word that he was wanted back at the ISF Military Academy to continue his recovery. No one said anything, but he was sure it was related to his outburst. He knew deep down they were sending him back to counter his deteriorating mental health. So, days twelve and thirteen of rehab were technically spent in transit. That had been his whole day yesterday and the day before. As he remembered his bear paw fist-print again, he wondered what damage it might do to Alaborap's smug fucking face. Start running, Goldilocks, Stanik mused, staring hard in the mirror.

A knock at his front door pulled him from his mind. Demaria, he thought. He splashed some water on his face, then hustled out of the bathroom. It was good to be back on Cliptorgia in his own quarters at the academy. No matter the reason, he told himself, it was a plus. Besides the promotion in rank, it was the only positive thing to come from the *Yulacki* incident.

Walt tapped the lockscreen and his front door slid open. Demaria Cole beamed at him. "Hey," he said, feeling dopey as soon as the word left his mouth.

Demaria said nothing; she simply wrapped him up in a hug. Stanik took a deep breath, enjoying the familiar sweet smell of her hair. They held each other without saying a word, but the moment passed far too quickly for his taste. Demaria released him, stepped back, and gave him a once-over. "You look way better than I was expecting!"

Everyone kept saying that. He didn't feel better, and it just felt like empty encouragement. He'd been hoping Demaria would be upfront with him. Walt said nothing, only shrugged.

"I mean it," she encouraged, tapping the lockscreen to close the door behind her. "How was your day," she asked, gliding into the sitting room where his couch and desk were. Gingerly, she set a ratty orange duffel bag on his desk.

"What's in the bag," Stanik asked.

"A surprise," Demaria said with a mischievous grin as she fell back on the couch. "But let's save it. C'mon, sit with me." He did so. "How was your first day back?"

"Being planet-side always makes me feel... heavy, I guess. I really feel my own density. It's extra strain on the body, and I didn't feel like doing much. I just slept out on the Academy lawn most of the day," he said.

She smiled knowingly. "I had a feeling you might, you reptile."

Stanik put his hands up in jest. "Please, if you're gonna' make those comparisons, at least call me an amphibian. I'd much rather be compared to my Hulgarian friends than a Candalonian."

Demaria chuckled. "Speaking of friends, did you visit with them today?"

"No." He registered her raised eyebrow. "They reached out this morning, I just... didn't feel like it."

"They want to help. And I bet they need to talk."

"I don't want to talk to them right now."

"Why not?"

"Because they can't actually relate. Because they all walked away from that mess. They didn't lose anything."

"They lost their captain, same as you."

Stanik lowered his voice. "Yeah, but they didn't have to watch her die..."

Demaria frowned, her brow bunching with concern. "You watched her die?"

Stanik took a deep breath. "I did."

"You didn't tell me that." At that, Demaria leaned back into the couch cushions, gesturing for Walt to join her. He obliged without hesitation. As he leaned into her arms, it felt better than any painkiller he'd been on. "Tell me everything," she said. She rubbed her fingernails over his scalp, and he relaxed into her embrace even more.

"You want every detail," he asked, holding up his

grotesque limb of mangled flesh and metal.

"Every last bit," she reassured.

He told her the whole story, careful not to embellish it, for she hated braggadocio. That carried them through a good portion of the evening. The clock on Walt's desk read '21:07' before she finally stretched, yawned, and let him go. Her stomach growled.

"You hungry," Stanik asked.

"Yeah, I didn't have a chance to grab dinner."

They ordered food, then Demaria swept across the room and plucked the ratty orange duffel bag off Walt's desk. "While we're waiting," she said, "it's time to give you this." She held the orange bag up eagerly. "I *am* sorry I didn't get here sooner like I promised. My dad swooped in as soon as I touched down. He had a whole slew of 'company dealings' he wanted me to attend while I'm planet-side." She puffed out her face and put air quotes around 'company dealings,' mocking one of her father's favorite phrases.

Demaria's father Damien Cole was the fourth-generation owner and C.E.O. of Pan Motion Industries[28], which made Demaria the sole heiress to the most powerful company in the Interplanetary Space Federation. Her great-great-grandfather had started out as a modest commercial transit provider, building his fortune on weapons shipments to Earth's colonies in the

---

[28] **Pan Motion Industries** – an Earth-based transit company established in A.D. 2107. Owned and operated by the Cole family, Pan Motion monopolize the manufacturing of spaceships and weapons for the ISF as well as interstellar cargo shipping.

Sol system. From there, her great-grandfather had expanded the company to include aerospace engineering. Their military contracts proved beneficial once Cliptorgia stepped out of the shadows and appealed to Earth for help during the *War of Formation*. That would have been nearly two hundred years ago, and since then, her forefathers had built a fortune as the ISF's primary contractor for technology development, aerospace engineering, commercial and citizen transportation, and military defense. Her grandfather, Dallas, had expanded the company's influence even further, pioneering the integration of S.A.I. – Service-based Artificial Intelligence – into starships, and introducing an advanced wave of fully-functioning autonomous robots.

Demaria liked to say they had monopolized every facet of interstellar life. She felt as if her father was spoiled by his power and money, so she sought to undermine him at every opportunity. Walt caught his mind racing and steered himself back to Demaria.

"I wanted to avoid suspicion," she was saying, "so I had to play along."

Stanik sat back. "Avoid suspicion?"

"Yeah," she grinned, her perfect, round cheek bones rising to accent her smile lines. They sparked a sense of mischief and mirth in her pale blue eyes. She unzipped the duffel bag. "Before you take this, I want you to know it was *not* easy to come by. I know how you can be, so just… trust me."

"Whatever you say," Stanik reassured her, nodding emphatically.

Demaria stuck her hand down inside the bag and produced a datapad brandished with the Pan Motion Industries logo. The words 'Confidential Record' were printed in red block letters along every side of the little touchscreen tablet. Demaria set it in his hands.

"What did you do," he asked, unable to mask his concern.

"Relax," she warned him, "I can handle the repercussions… if I even get caught. This," she paused dramatically to turn the device on before she continued, "is a database of every pirate Pan Motion has filed grievances against with law enforcement. Daddy insists on having as much information on all of them as possible. He's even hired private investigators to fill in the missing details for authorities."

"That sounds like your dad," he agreed. "Hates to be bested."

"By *anyone*, the poor, spoiled baby," Demaria added.

"So, what," Stanik asked, worried he already knew her answer to his question, "you stole it?"

Demaria said nothing, but she flashed him a devious smile. She was such a badass, he thought. She had absolutely no regard for the consequences because she knew damn well she could outmaneuver her father, even if she committed corporate espionage. She was a rebel… a punk for social good, and Stanik found that edge to her irresistible. A little dangerous, maybe, but irresistible, nonetheless. She was his complete opposite.

"I hope you plan to wipe our prints off this thing before you put it back," he said.

Demaria shrugged cheekily. "I don't plan on putting it back. I wiped it from company inventory. *This* is now yours."

Stanik shook his head. "I don't know if I feel comfortable holding onto it," he confessed. "What if there's tracking you don't know about?"

"My dad's been grooming me to run his whole operation since I could walk. I think I know all his secrets by now. Besides," she added with a touch of scorn in her voice, "do you really think I'd be that careless with your reputation? Or your *career*?"

"No… I mean, I hope not." He paused for comedic effect. "Did I say something to piss you off? I'll remind you, they have me on a lot of drugs!"

When Demaria laughed at his jokes, it made his heart leap. "No," she said. "Remember what you said to me last week?"

"I remember we talked," Stanik admitted. "But the meds are definitely blurring things together."

"You told me you wanted to fight pirates. I figured you'd want the best study guide available, and I'd be willing to bet this is it!"

Stanik considered the gesture as he turned the device over in his hands. "Could we copy the data to one of my own devices, just to be safe?"

"No, Walt. That would incriminate you more. C'mon, please just trust me?"

He thought about it for a moment, then agreed.

His intercom rang, announcing that their food had arrived. Walt went out to the front entrance to retrieve it, and they sat down to peruse the datapad files while they ate. Alaborap's file was right at the top, so they read through that first, then added Stanik's descriptions.

They worked on his descriptions of the entire Stingray crew as the evening wore away. At some point, they both fell asleep huddled next to each other on the couch. When Walt woke up in the middle of the night, Demaria was already gone. So was her duffel bag, but she'd left him the stolen datapad. He thought their visit had gone well. He even let himself hope they might start seeing each other again.

He was sorely mistaken. That was the last time she visited him in person over the course of his recovery. It didn't stop her from haunting him in the press, though...

X   X   X

April 9th, A.D. 2349
21:04 IST

About a week later, after a particularly successful day working on his finger dexterity in rehab, Walt sat down to relax in the comfort of his quarters. He even used his right index finger to turn on his console, managing to curl his other digits partway under his palm. He kicked his feet up on his coffee table as the late-night talk show *Our Universe* buzzed to life on the screen.

As a public figure, Demaria didn't always slip back into Stanik's life directly. Often, he didn't even know her whereabouts until she'd pop up on some TV network for an interview. That's how she appeared to him next. On his console... on a special debate episode of *Our Universe*. He'd missed her introduction, as well as the host's probing question, but Demaria's response was enough to infer the gist of it.

"Well, I think the biggest concern is how uncharacteristic the attack was," Demaria said. "If Alaborap is hitting military training vessels that close to regulated space, what's to stop him from wreaking havoc within ISF borders?"

"A lot of people," the show's host replied coolly, "myself included, think we're already sinking too many tax dollars into maintaining safe trade with the Outer Rim." The live audience cheered the host from behind the camera. "Taxpayers voted recently to defund the ISF's Piracy Prosecution Program out there. The last thing we want is an increased military presence *outside* our own borders." She'd dyed her hair a pale lavender. On camera, it gave striking accent to her icy blue eyes as the camera zoomed in on her.

"The problem here," Demaria diagnosed instead of offering a direct response, "is that your complacency offers the most dangerous solution; if it ain't broke, don't fix it. But I think the *Yulacki* attack is proof enough that it *is* broken. We have an opportunity to make things safer now: to increase patrols and virtual security measures before the Barrier is severely compromised. Or, we do like you say and we wait. We wait until we've got pirates slipping through that forcefield every day. Is that what you're suggesting?"

She showed up twice more that week on similar

shows, pressing the same safety issues to the public. Stanik appreciated her vigor; he knew she was upset about what happened to him. When Demaria didn't like something, she changed it.

Walt wasn't sure she realized that she was stirring the pot for him, too. He'd gone two whole weeks without a message from a reporter, and then, because Demaria found a few media outlets to market her concerns, it stirred things up again. His first week in the hospital, the media storm did not cease its barrage on the hospital until Admiral Southerland held a press conference. He spent five minutes berating the press on Walt's behalf. Stanik never found a recording of that press conference, but Cliptok had done a pretty good impression. According to her, his closer was, "There's a young man fighting for his life in that hospital, and all *you people* can figure to do is skulk around like buzzards! What an embarrassment. You should be embarrassed!" Surprisingly, that had done the trick.

Then, two days after Demaria's appearance on *Our Universe*, a new recruit tried to corner Walt on academy grounds. He got all chummy and tried asking questions about what Walt wanted to do with his military career. After maybe two questions, Stanik caught on and pressed the kid until he confessed. He'd been approached by a reporter who offered to pay him off for an update.

Instead of an update, Stanik sent the kid back with an offer. He offered to hold a press conference if the nameless reporter would spread the word to local news outlets. It took less than twenty-four hours before the recruit returned to him with a message. "Okay, my contact says he's got everything setup for you. Tomorrow morning, just outside the Academy gates at nine hundred hours. That work?"

"I'll be there."

X   X   X

April 12th, A.D. 2349
08:59 IST

Stanik was true to his word. He showed up fifteen minutes early to the press conference, and he even got a chance to practice gripping the podium.

Word of the press conference was out so fast, Walt got summoned to talk to his superior officers at the Academy at oh-seven hundred that very same morning. Apparently, the powers that be were none too pleased with his initiative, and two military P.R. officers detained him and asked a ton of probing questions. They drilled him on every topic he might address, requesting adjustments and flagging several key words they did *not* want him to use.

It was all grimtash, he told himself. He'd say what he wanted to say, the way he wanted to say it. Clearing his throat, he slipped out through the Academy's curling iron gates and took the podium. Reporters and camera-ops leaned in, jostling shoulders and elbows as they pressed in on one another.

"Thank you all for your continued concern for my condition," Stanik started sincerely. "I've been listening to all the conjecture following our incident on the *ISF Yulacki*, and I thought it might clear things up if I weighed in. As the survivor who served as acting captain when the *Yulacki* encountered the Stingray pirates, I can confirm that our ship was running a routine Distress Call Investigation. Had we been aware of the danger, I have confidence that Captain Billie would not have left the ship in my charge. If there's one thing losing my captain has taught me, it's that we need to do more to protect our soldiers and civilians." His statement was met with grumbles and muttering. He had nothing else prepared, so Stanik opened the floor for questions.

A woman with a prodding eye pushed her way closer to the podium. Stanik was transfixed not by her pupils, but by the intensity of the whites of her eyes. The negative space intimidated him. "As a young recruit in the ISF, has this changed your view of the risks involved?"

The question was strange. Maybe she thought it would lend itself to a good soundbite, but to Stanik it was self-evident. "I mean, I knew it was a risk to begin with," he said, nodding slowly to make sure she comprehended. "That's – that's what we do. The only thing this has really changed is how I want to serve; I've decided to apply to the Piracy Prosecution Program[29]."

"To clarify," the same reporter chimed in, "you're

---

[29] **Piracy Prosecution Program** – founded in A.D. 2249, this branch of the ISF military specializes in pirate hunting. Due to its mercenary lifestyle, the '3-P' program has a reputation for turning good soldiers into paranoid, raving addicts.

saying you're willingly enlisting in a program the ISF has taken extreme steps to defund for the past five years?"

"It's a good program," Stanik said. "Captain Billie was my mentor. She saved my life, but she couldn't shield me from being preyed on by pirates. It's been hard to cope with, and I'm a *trained soldier*. I think there's a lot of honor in the Three-P program." He had found his stride, and he'd still not broken the rules of engagement laid out for him by the ISF, though he was sure there'd be blowback for his claims. He didn't care. "Seems like a logical next step, doesn't it? Find men like Alaborap and make it my job to stop them."

The blowback from Admiral Southerland and the ISF was far more severe than he'd anticipated, and he was forced to sit through four hearings where he answered the same questions as calmly and politely as he could. They threatened to strip away his rank, and to force him along alternate professional routes, but they were ultimately overruled by their own code of conduct. Hank pulled in help from his pod, namely an audacious Hulgarian legal expert specializing in the gray areas of legislature between citizens' rights and soldiers' rights. Fortunately, that ordeal was handled in a matter of nine weeks or so, and the solution was simple; Stanik agreed not to make further public comments. After that, he kept his mouth shut and it all melted away. His interest in the Three-P program was sincere, though, and Stanik spent all his spare time studying up on space pirates with the help of Demaria's stolen datapad.

8. A PIRATE'S LIFE

After his incident with the press, Walter Stanik kept his head down for well over a year. He finished physical therapy, regained his swordsmanship skills, and took whatever assignment was suggested to him. Most importantly, he kept his mouth shut about pirates for a good, long while. But every time he shipped out, he took his Pan Motion datapad with him. The more he read, the more engrossed Walt became. He'd never realized just how dangerous life in the Outer Rim was – never fully grasped the reality of the piracy problem beyond the Great Barrier.

First, he'd learned about all the most influential pirate clans. There were the Blackhearts, who dissolved after the Blackpool Butcher slaughtered them on some haunted Hierrnaus ranch. The Deacons of Devi's End were a group that ran many of the Pointe's pleasure traps, including three taverns and at least a dozen small-time brothels. The Widows Cheng, an all-female cast of cutthroats, struck him as particularly nasty, and the Wayward Bucks were a gang of marksmen and sharp shooters who doubled as militia to keep the Pointe secure during times of crisis. Then, of course, there was the Halogien Stingray clan. Alaborap's clan… shrouded in unbelievable myth and unthinkable lore.

That was the most aggravating part. Even with the Pan Motion files, intel on Alaborap read like some ghastly folktale. There was very little on the man Alaborap Smith, apart from a scant few nightmare tales where the Stingrays had left a sole survivor.

One account said he had materialized out of a poisonous green slime like a bog monster. Another claimed he possessed a ghost ship that disappeared against the blackness of space to prey silently on other ships. Some oaf even claimed the pirate had killed him accidentally, then brought him back from the dead to correct the mistake.

The information collected by Mr. Cole's private investigators was far more concrete. Apparently, the pirate captain was from the New England province of North America, on Earth, where he attended public school until graduating at the age of fifteen. A blurb from local news postings highlighted academic accolades and scholarship offers for 'the boy genius.' A missing person report was filed with local authorities by Alaborap's parents later that same year and would remain an open case for nearly a decade, closed only after Alaborap's first act of piracy catapulted him to infamy.

That was basically all Walt could find, apart from the obvious – Alaborap made port in Smith's Pointe on the planet Hierrnaus[30]; he was the grandson of Nogylop Smith, the pirate-turned-soldier who led the rebellion of the Free Worlds against the ISF; and he seemed a fan of Shakespeare, for he often responded to criticism by citing the poet's more acidic quotes.

Discouraged by this lackluster psych-profile on Alaborap, Stanik turned his attention to other aspects of piracy. He learned as much as he could about their politics; crews maintained a democratic voting system; the clan wars still plagued their homeworld because opposing factions were always seeking control of their planet's Governor. Apparently, there wasn't much in-fighting in present pirate politics, as most of the clans were working together to uphold the peace. Hierrnaus had only just entered an age of prosperity brought about by their current leader, the Jolly Pirate Lord Dimitri Ivanova.

As Stanik dug back into the history, he realized much of it had been authored by Alaborap's grandfather, Nogylop Smith, the first cutthroat captain to prescribe

---

[30] **Hierrnaus** /ˈhiɚˌnɑs/ – the red planet is third in the Ornaus system and boasts two moons, Orcus & Nargal, as well as the most diverse ecosystems and exotic species of any Outer Rim world. It is also home to the largest established metropolis in all the Free Worlds, the gritty seaside capital Smith's Pointe, which is how Hierrnaus earned its reputation as the 'Planet of Pirates.'

the title 'space pirate' to his crew and deeds. He was the real founder of the Halogien Stingrays. Perhaps that gave Walt *something* to poke at Alaborap's psyche with.

At some point in his clandestine, obsessive studies, Stanik's nightmares morphed into first-person experiences reflecting the accounts he was reading. To survive as an enlisted aeronaut soldier was one thing, but his brain shifted, concocting fear and anxiety as he lived out a dozen brutal attacks through the eyes of a helpless citizen, both planet-side and in space. The desperation that thumped at his chest and knotted a lump in his throat served to jolt him from his disturbed slumber, but it was only a temporary relief. As soon as he slipped back into the comfort of his rest, the experiences would rise out of the darkness again.

There was an itching desire deep within him to join the effort against piracy. What better way to spare others the torture he was going through, he told himself. What better way to stop Alaborap? On days when he wanted to give up, Stanik would recall his head physician's words: "Walter, you really are a fighter. Someday that pirate's going to regret messing with you."

It kept pushing him.

Finally, in the late summer of 2350, the horrors in Stanik's dreams mutated into something pleasant. As the plumbing clanked methodically in the wall behind his bed one night, Stanik's brain reinterpreted the sound as the clashing of swords. He found himself in a spacious corridor aboard an unknown but impressive spaceship – or perhaps it was along the ramparts of an old fort – he couldn't tell, and it wasn't important. What was important was his opponent; the blond-haired buccaneer he longed to confront. Captain Alaborap's cutlass swung and jabbed at Stanik, its blade slicing the air with contempt. But Walter Stanik deflected each blow mightily, taunting his adversary.

"You've grown weak," he felt his mouth form the words, and though he didn't hear them come out, he knew he had said them, for he saw the flames of hatred flicker in Alaborap's eyes. Their swords locked, and Stanik seized the opportunity, elbowing the pirate in the face, then tripping him. There, before the Stingray pirates, Stanik kicked Alaborap's sword away, nestling the point of his blade under the cutthroat's chin. "You should have killed me when you had the chance," he taunted.

The rest of the dream passed through him in snapshots, like a montage in some arthouse movie. The Stingrays lowered their weapons, Cliptok tossed him a pair of restraints, and he marched Alaborap up to a podium. He claimed the pirate's sword and tricorn hat for himself, and rode all the way to Europa, where the ISF had their maximum-security prison. He awoke in a haze, convinced that the pompous Captain Alaborap Smith was about to serve the rest of his years mining ice on Jupiter's smallest moon. Then, Stanik woke up. His right arm was inflamed with a rash of needling pin pricks.

Anger, he told himself. His whole body yearned to fight pirates. He had made up his mind for good. He was going to ask for transfer to a Barrier post so he could get himself closer to the Outer Rim. He was going to hunt pirates, and he was going to track down Goldilocks.

X   X   X

November 25ᵗʰ, A.D. 2350
18:15 IST

"Breaking news today," Walt didn't recognize the excitable news anchor. "Authorities have confirmed that the body of the infamous space pirate Alaborap Smith was presented to them by a pirate pleading for his own pardon." The news hit Stanik like a swift kick in the gut. "Bartholomew Higginbotham, former member of the pirate clan The Deacons of Devil's End, presented the headless corpse to ISF representatives this Tuesday, November 22ⁿᵈ. The man claims to have bested Captain Alaborap in a skirmish earlier that day. As proof of the deed, Higginbotham also submitted *The Articles of Nogylop Smith*. The diary belonging to Alaborap's late grandfather is considered by some to be an invaluable historic document. It will be dedicated to the Museum of Interstellar History, and Mr. Higginbotham will be publicly pardoned at a ceremony tomorrow."

Stanik's brain went numb. He felt like he was floating, his cheeks grew hot with anger, and his body felt like it was a million kilometers from his head. One news report and his flame of motivation flickered, dwindling in the howling winds of unrealized revenge.

That night, Jablon took him out for drinks. Stanik sat and waited patiently as Jablon made the same point he'd been making for over two years. It was like listening to a song Walt didn't like on repeat.

"You're just gonna' have to deal with it," Jablon said. "Someone beat you to it. Not like you're the only one who wanted that guy dead." He punctuated his remark with a firm shrug.

The music vamped on the sound system, a vocal screech that morphed into Billie's screams. Stanik fell back into his memories... back into the *Yulacki*, where he was forced to watch the hatch doors clamp shut around his arm.

Jablon snapped a finger, jolting Stanik out of his flashback. "Walt, you still with me?"

Stanik shook his head, trying to let his thoughts go with it. "Yeah... sorry." It was just Jablon and him, he told himself, breathing deeply. Just Jablon and him, seated at the bar, years after the accident... years after the pain. He was safe. But knowing Captain Billie would forever remain on the other side of the blast doors kept life in perspective for Walt.

"Hey," Jablon said thoughtfully, leaning in so he could confide his next thought exclusively to his friend. "Maybe this was fate."

"How do you mean?"

"Maybe this is, like, the universe telling you to let it go. Stop setting yourself up for this... revenge tour you seem to be plotting. Y'know?"

Stanik patted his friend on the shoulder. "You're absolutely right," he conceded, not believing a word of it as he forced the words from his mouth. "Which is why I need to get off this rock." He paid for their round and left before Jablon had a chance to change his mind. Thankfully, things were quiet for Stanik through the last few weeks of that calendar year.

9. PIRATES OF THE OUTER RIM

November 22nd, A.D. 2350
17:18 IST

Captain Alaborap despised November the twenty-second. He knew it in Earth's history as Blackbeard's death day, and he couldn't help but feel particularly unlucky any time it rolled around. 2350 served as a perfect reminder to him. No manner of plotting or planning could have saved him. He'd sailed the *Stingray* all the way to Candalos Prime[31]. The planet was a nuclear wasteland; it had been for nearly two centuries. That was because it had once served as homeworld to the extinct

---

[31] **Candalos** /ˈkændəˌloǔs/ **Prime** – the only restricted planet in the charted systems. During the Great War, the ISF resorted to nuclear attacks, causing the planet's atmosphere to go radioactive. In surrender, the surviving Candalonians fled the galaxy, never to be heard from again.

Candalonian species. The planet had been all but condemned after the War of Unification. There were few regions where the atmosphere wouldn't give a living organism mild radiation burns, and in the severest of sectors, the seas boiled with acid rain that could melt flesh from bone. For all those reasons, Alaborap and Argylesox had been avoiding it. But *The Articles of Nogylop Smith* had confirmed their suspicions, and they'd spent two months or so gathering nuclear shielding, a fortified short-range vessel, and hazmat spacesuits for the necessary crew.

Alaborap sat in the Stingray's cockpit, the windshield tinting the room a rich, soothing green. At least, Alaborap found it soothing. He was seeking any small comfort as he waited for news from his team on the surface of Candalos Prime. His role on that particular mission was merely to wait and worry. He despised the latter emotion, for it meant he had no sense of control over the situation. He'd been unwilling to risk himself or Glygorg for such a mission, but he'd sent Argylesox, along with Vestonn, the kid Pockam, and Naughtadargh. In truth, Argyle and Vestonn were the only two in the group he gave any credit for competence.

Murray, his curmudgeonly old pirate, and Eldadip, his sultry Till[32] gunner, were both off duty. So, it was

---

[32] **Till** / ˈtɪl / – a sect of Cliptorgians who continue ancient education techniques of their planet's past. They are often hired as mercenaries and mediators in socio-political situations throughout the universe. This is because their training emphasizes inward balance: equal reverence of intellectual and martial prowess.

Glygorg and Alaborap alone in the cockpit. They listened for the Com, waiting to hear from Argylesox. Alaborap forced a heavy sigh, focusing on the ticks, tocks, and occasional chimes of the antique grandfather clock he kept in an aft corner of the cockpit. With each clicking second, he considered the mission unfolding on the planet below.

The group on the planet's surface was searching a vast sulfur field for any sign of a Goliathon temple. The search zone was based on coordinates whipped up by map data Argylesox had retrieved from the temple they'd visited on Heiznaus: the very same site that convinced Alaborap the Goliathon was not just some dismissible tall tale.

"Yarh," Glygorg fussed at the helm. "I'm reading their vitals through the suits. Should we check in?"

"Open a channel to Argylesox," Alaborap said patiently. Glygorg had missed Alaborap's previous demonstration. The Fallamon had been on his own rest break earlier. Alaborap watched as his first mate's hook-clawed, lizard-like fingers tapped the Com dial. Whizzing, whirring static crackled back to them both. "I suspect their Coms are down because of the radiation disruption. They have what they need to get the job done, and they have my orders. Fretting will only make the wait longer."

Glygorg nodded thoughtfully, scratching his chin with a spindly claw.

Alaborap tipped his tricornered hat up in back, allowing the front to droop over his eyes. He leaned back in his chair, stretching slightly.

'We do not seek comfort.' His own words rang in his head. It was the third Stingray oath taken by his crew upon initiation. He should have never gotten comfortable.

Alaborap's DashCom dinged. It was a distress call. On his personal line?

Glygorg hopped up into the helmsman's seat and grasped the back of the headrest, peering at his captain with alert red eyes. Alaborap tapped the button in his armrest that patched the line through to the ship's DashCom.

"Vero nihil verius," a wheezing old voice said in his thick Siberian Sector accent. It was Alaborap's old mentor, Dimitri Ivanova. The Latin was Alaborap's frequency passcode.

"Dimitri, what's wrong? You sound distressed." Alaborap kept his deep voice grounded... reassuring.

"We been had, old boy! They been working together!"

"Who has, Dimitri?"

"Dey take your book from under my nose!" Alaborap swallowed the lump forming in his throat. His 'book' was his grandfather's diary: *The Articles of Nogylop Smith*. It contained the history of the Stingray pirates, including strange chronicles and hints about his grandfather's Goliathon quest. He'd left it with Dimitri for safe keeping. The irony stung like a sharp knife.

"Dimitri, who are you talking about?"

"Bah... Bart Higginbot'am," Dimitri sounded like

he was struggling to breathe. "Bastard is... vorking vit' Tah-deus Karp!"

Glygorg growled.

Thaddeus Karp, whose name was too much for Dimitri's accent, was the governor of Smith's Pointe. He'd been appointed by the good citizens of the Outer Rim to oversee the commonfolk politics of Hierrnaus. Alaborap's former captain, The Jolly Pirate Dimitri Ivanova, was the current acting Pirate Lord. He was elected by force to see that the governor did what was best for the pirate clans who drove commerce for the Free Worlds of the Outer Rim. He certainly shouldn't have had dealings with a bilge rat like Bartholomew Higginbotham. People said a lot of disturbing things about Bart, but his nickname said it all: the Weasel Pirate. He'd sooner shoot someone in the ass than look them in the eyes. So, Thaddeus Karp preferred the chaos of weaselly Higginbotham for pirate lord? Alaborap would take great joy in unseating them both.

"Where are you?" Alaborap held his breath waiting for Dimitri's reply.

"Dey got me, old boy," Alaborap imagined the distress wrinkling Ivanova's face. He could almost see the man's frizzy white beard trembling with each gasping word. "I get out, die on own terms, eh?"

"Dimitri, you old fool," Alaborap blurted out, "Clear the line. Call someone who can get to you! I'm not even in the same solar system!"

"Dis is last call," Dimitri said with a cough and a strained chuckle. "I make right call... You get dem back?"

"Aye, sir," Alaborap said, steeling his resolve.

"Goot boy." With that, he listened as his mentor gasped his final breath. Alaborap tapped his armrest and the Com channel returned to his personal device. He pressed record and switched the line to silent. He'd scrub the audio footage for clues to Dimitri's whereabouts later... when he had all his Stingrays back aboard.

Glygorg stared expectantly at him. "What do we do," the Fallamon asked finally.

Alaborap shrugged. He felt numb inside. "What can we do," he asked. "If we leave now, we're at least five days out. Not to mention we'd be unsettlingly light on crewmembers."

After a few more painful minutes of silence, Glygorg tried to strike up conversation. "What do yeh' think Bart will do with the diary?"

"I really don't want to think about it right now," Alaborap barked back. That was the end of the conversation. Ten more creeping minutes passed by, and then the ship's Com speakers erupted.

"Mayday, mayday," Argylesox cried over the Coms. Before Glygorg or Alaborap could jump to respond, they felt the thud of an umbilicus latching onto the *Halogien Stingray*.

"What's going on," Alaborap barked into the Coms.

Argyle was winded, breathing like a marathon runner. Alaborap turned down the volume.

The Gentleman Pirate's voice continued, shaking with adrenaline. "Mission success, but we are abandoning ship! Vestonn needs radiation treatment! We'll decontaminate ourselves and treat him belowdecks. Keep the cargo hold sealed off until my all-clear."

The Com clicked off just as Eldadip and Murray came rushing onto the *Stingray*'s bridge. Alaborap shook his head. "I despise November the twenty-second," he said to no one in particular.

10. SPECIAL ASSIGNMENT

January 10ᵗʰ, A.D. 2351
06:11 IST

Through the chaos of his subconscious, Stanik's alarm clock beckoned him to morning. He rubbed his right arm, where a series of computer chips and fiber optics had been networked in and around his right biceps over time. They were the result of upgrades to his arm brace – sensors that helped with precision and control, further integrating his own nervous system to the robotic prosthetic encasing his arm.

Stanik was out of bed quickly, taking extra care to apply lotion to the weeks-old tattoo just under his shoulder. The ink was simple: just tall, black block letters boldly declaring the message, 'ICT 601.' He'd gone to the parlor to have it done for New Year's. It was Jablon's idea… maybe the first good one he'd had since the news of Alaborap's death.

Stanik's console was quick to greet him. "Good morning, Walter. This is your reminder to meet with Admiral Southerland at oh-seven-hundred hours." Walt's routine was quick and crisp, his body preparing itself for a disciplined stance before his commanding officer.

Stanik rushed out into the warm amber sunlight of Cor[33] and crossed the military grounds. There was no grass on Cliptorgia: only rolling plains of grayish-purple soil dotted with pale green shrubs and dense forests of towering trees. Stanik preferred the protective boughs of the dense Cliptorgian forests, but the ISF Military Academy sat in the dusty purple dunes northeast of Cortallek[34]. The terrain was good for survival and combat training, and nearly all the buildings were dug into the base of the rocky, rolling foothills.

Stanik took a moment to enjoy the quiet view of Cortallek at daybreak. He marveled momentarily at the cumulous white fog shrouding the aquamarine waters of Unity Bay, which stretched out southwest of the ISF Military Academy. All he saw before him were the bay waters and fog, glistening in the gathering daylight. All he could discern beyond that were the towering treetops.

---

[33] **Cor** /kɔɚˈ/ – the star Cliptorgia orbits.

[34] **Cortallek** /kɔɚˈtælək/ – capital city of the Interplanetary Space Federation. It is known as 'the City of Unity' for being both the lynchpin of ISF governance and the historic site where Hulgarians and Cliptorgians first allied their societies in ancient times.

CLIPTORGIA

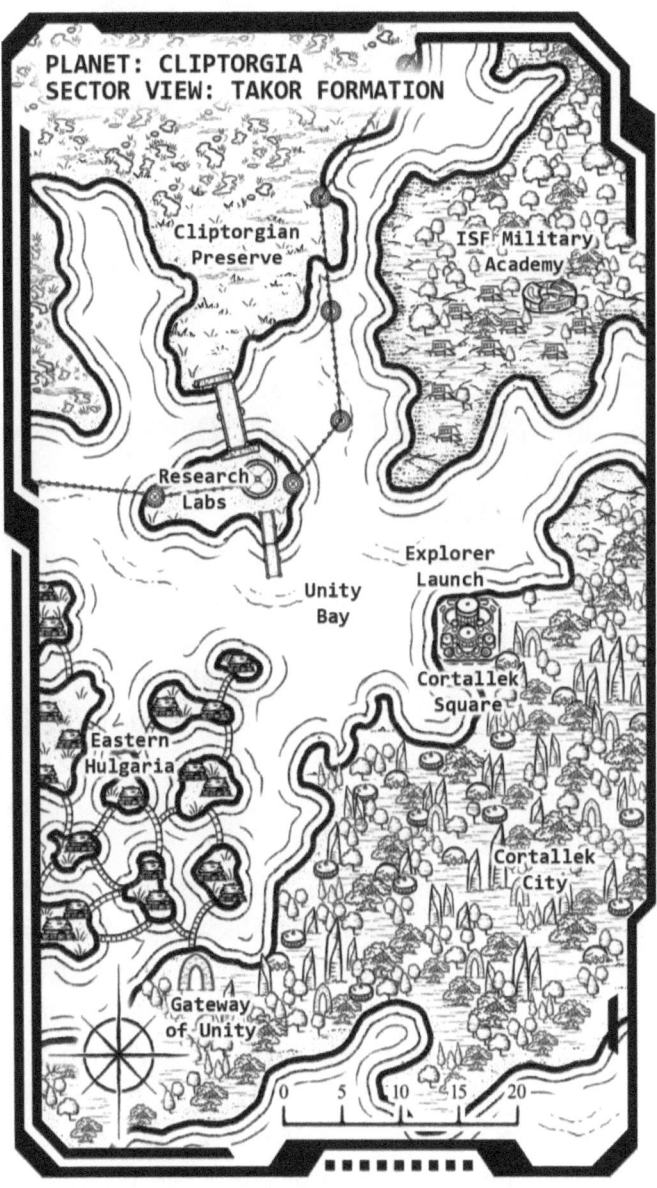

If he didn't know any better, he wouldn't believe there was a thriving metropolis hiding in that fog. But it was there, he told himself, in all its emerald glory.

Stanik drew in a slow breath of fresh morning air, then ducked into the Operations Base, the largest of the wedge-shaped buildings jutting out of a prominent purple hillside. Inside the Evaluations Office, the secretary leaned over, forcing a smile. "Oh, Walt, it's you. Hold on." She pressed her Com. "Admiral? Walter Stanik's here."

Admiral Southerland's slow drawl carried an unusually heavy dose of aggravation. "He's *early*."

"Should I–?"

"Send him in."

The secretary pushed her glasses up the bridge of her nose as she swung her gaze lazily up to meet Stanik's again. "Go ahead, Walt."

"Thanks, Ms. Melnitz." He nodded to her and stepped through the office door as it opened. Stanik leaned inside graciously, averting his eyes so as not to acknowledge how much shorter Rear-Admiral Lionel Southerland was.

His commanding officer was a stout, grizzled military man with a wide potbelly. His wild goatee, once a blazing blond, had long since withered white with his age. "Good God," his voice rattled through Stanik's bones, "don't you have any decency? I haven't even had my coffee." The admiral chuckled, rocking in his chair, and gestured for Stanik to sit. It was his way of telling Walt to make himself comfortable. Either all was well, or

Southerland was trying to make him feel at ease before he pounced.

Stanik studied Southerland, even ventured to make eye contact. Southerland was easy. Uncharacteristically jovial. Perhaps it was all the coffee creamer that soured him. Everyone on campus knew Southerland for his stale-coffee-and-curdled-milk breath. Stanik stuffed the insult down deep.

The Rear-Admiral clasped his hands over the bulging buttons at the belly of his uniform.

"Sorry, sir," Stanik conceded, truly uncertain whether or not he should be.

"I'll manage." Southerland waved away his poor attempt at pleasantries. "Let's talk about your next assignment."

"Yes, sir." So, it was the reprimand, Stanik noted, deciding to get ahead of the criticism. "Permission to speak freely, sir?"

"Granted."

"The Code of Conduct clearly states that in peacetime, any soldier can put in a request to be considered for specific placement. You know that piracy in the Outer Rim is an issue I care deeply about. I only thought—"

"At ease, Lieutenant. You're not in trouble." Even though Southerland barked it at him, Stanik relaxed, trusting that the old man was just cutting to the chase. "I called you here *because* you've repeatedly requested a post beyond the Barrier." Southerland slapped a physical dossier on the table, slid it to Stanik. "Here's the mission brief. You may *not* scan a digital copy for your records. No exceptions."

Walt couldn't believe it. No one he knew had ever seen a *hard copy* of a mission brief. Stanik's heart skipped a beat. The Federation only did that when—

"The whole thing is strictly confidential. I'll cover the basics: it's a new initiative. ISF's planning to launch an open-ended exploration mission within the next eighteen months. The old isolationist approach isn't cutting it anymore. Crew goes out beyond the Barrier, reaches out to new species – starts building alliances. Diplomatic but dangerous. Each officer is to pick their best candidate to compete for the spot. I'm picking you. Mission launch planned for June of 2352. You interested?"

"Yes, sir. Thank you, sir!"

"Good. Go over everything; select a crew and have them assembled and ready for testing Sunday at oh eight hundred. You're excused."

Stanik smiled, turning to the office door.

"And Walter?"

"Yes, sir?"

He heard the old man suck in a wheezy breath. "Don't just pick your friends." Southerland waved him away without a second glance. Stanik let his shoulders droop and retreated to the fresh air of morning.

Outside, Walt found Jablon leaning against a bronze statue. The big guy was surprisingly put together despite the early hour. He winked at two girls as they passed by before noticing Walt.

"So," Jablon urged, "what'd he say?"

"Let's walk." Stanik steered them off the main sidewalk and out onto the purple dirt lawn. "Special assignment. I need to pick a crew."

"Captaining position!" Jablon pumped his fist.

Stanik shushed him, swatting his hand out of the air.

"Sorry," Jablon waved his hands away. "Where are you being stationed?"

"It's an exploration mission. Collect data, scout potential allies. ISF expansion planning. Here's the dossier."

Jablon raised an eyebrow. "A mission brief in *hard copy*, are you kidding me! Whoa, Walt, this is big! This is so cool! It's – it's – not your thing at all, is it?"

"No. But after this, I could get any assignment I wanted. They'd have to station me in the Outer Rim–"

"You've got to let the privateer thing go. You'll end up going nuts, like the Blackpool Butcher." The Blackpool Butcher was a law marshal-turned-privateer who ended up losing it and slaughtered the *Blackhearts* pirate clan. It had happened a few years before Jablon and Stanik were born. Jablon's parents were newlyweds then, and Stanik knew they used to fixate on the deadly tales that haunted Jablon's father as a freight-runner.

"That's the only example of a crazy privateer you have," Stanik scolded.

"Okay, okay. Forget I brought it up."

"Look," Stanik directed his attention to the dossier. "Everyone on the crew has to graduate to Vice-Admiral before mission launch."

"Wait," Jablon cut him off, his face wrinkling. "They're calling it the Space Cadets Initiative?"

"They say it represents—"

"Yeah, I see it," Jablon nodded, reading from the mission brief, "'This mission program acknowledges the ISF's inexperience as we embark on a journey of galactic discovery and understanding.' Gross." He offered the dossier back to Stanik. "This is propaganda. You know that, right?"

"Yes, Jablon. It's *the military*."

"All right, fair. Vice Admiral Porter Jablon definitely has a ring to it," Jablon mused, grinning hopefully at his friend. "That is, if…"

"The qualification tests are on Sunday," Stanik nodded emphatically. "Can you be there?"

"Hell yeah! I mean, y'know, depending on the rest of the crew." Jablon's comment was playful, but Walt knew there was sincerity in it.

"Gunner: Cliptok. Hank in science and navigations, and if you'll *risk* an assignment beyond the Barrier, then you're my pilot." Stanik extended his hand, offering to shake on it.

Jablon hesitated, considering. After half a beat, though, his hand dove in to accept his friend's offer. They shook on it right there. "Done," Jablon said. "What do you think our chances are?"

11. LAUNCH DAY

June 11ᵗʰ, A.D. 2352
09:39 IST

People swarmed in the streets of Cortallek below the winding tracks of the city's skyrail transit system. The skytrain ferried Walter Stanik into the heart of the city, gliding over to a private access track. It weaved a path behind the ceremonial launch pad erected in the middle of Cortallek Square. Stanik tried not to think about the streets full of people below, all gathered to watch the Space Cadets launch. He peered out the far window at the towering trees of Takor Forest.

Cliptorgians had long ago evolved the tendency to design around their planet's natural landscapes, a difference from humans Stanik greatly appreciated. The entire eastern half of Cortallek was essentially a city-forest. Natural, living structures built into the skeletons of dying trees, carefully given new life as a crutch for wild vines to climb and bloom. The streets felt more like a woodland path than a city block, and Stanik always had a sense that he understood the planet and its people better. After all, the city itself was at least a millennium old; it was the site of the first settlement where Hulgarians and Cliptorgians made first contact with one another, forging their Alliance of Cliptorgian Consciousness.

The skytrain eased to a quiet halt and Stanik stood, stepping towards the door. Stanik noticed a woman on the platform outside. Even in the shadows, he could see her strawberry-blond hair. Demaria. She'd switched her hair back to its natural color about a year prior, when her dad passed away. She said it was so the Pan Motion executives would take her seriously. Stanik missed the pink hair, but he admitted the adjustment made her look older.

Instinctually, he adjusted the collar of his royal purple uniform jacket, then combed his fingers through his hair. The smell of grease and engine coolant clung to the fresh salt sea air. Stanik flinched slightly as Demaria put her hands on his waist and swept him around a corner for privacy. He suppressed the urge to resist her touch. During his recovery, he'd grown bitter at her absence, not to mention the empty promises. It was half a year before she revealed to him that her father's health was failing. She'd been shuffled away to assume more responsibility at Pan Motion.

They'd had a few casual rendezvous, and the flame had flickered again for a few short months. Then, Demaria distanced herself again shortly after Stanik's assignment to the Space Cadets Initiative. One of the dropout candidates, bitter with defeat as the first runner-up, suggested to the media that Stanik's romantic entanglements with Demaria influenced his selection for the program. She withdrew from him entirely after that. Now, he regarded her as he would an open flame. He was certain the warmth he felt would burn him as soon as he touched it.

"How do you feel," Demaria asked him, her hands straightening his golden shoulder cords.

Stanik let himself smile. "Pretty damn good," he said with confidence and excitement. "Today, that becomes *my* ship up there. I finally feel like a captain." He saw the hint of sentiment gathering in her eyes.

"You deserve this," Demaria said, searching for his gaze to meet hers. He averted his eyes. For once, it felt like she was seeking his approval. "You earned it," she added, squeezing his hand. It was still there, he reassured himself. Whatever it was that they had, it was still there. And maybe he'd finally be able to do something about it when the Space Cadets buzz had faded away. It would only take a few weeks before the public eye was onto the next big thing. If Demaria didn't respond, at least he'd already steeled his heart. He was the one leaving to further his career. He was the one with a mission to accomplish. Demaria would likely still be single, and still working her ass off, when his mission wrapped up.

"The turnout's really good today," he said, leaning from the shadows to scope out the scene beneath them. The crowd had gathered in Cortallek Square below. They were gathered around the *ISF Explorer*, which was perched on its launch pad like a trophy on a pedestal. *His* ship, he told himself again. That intricate combination of acute curves and bold angles... it was in his charge. It stood poised at the ready, a cross between a tank and an old-fashioned SR-71 fighter jet fitted onto the belly of a speedboat.

Media drones and camerabots hovered around the scene like gnats, obscuring the scene with sensationalism. Bits of their audio feeds zipped in and out of Stanik's ears.

"I'm reporting live at the heart of Cortallek Square where an enormous crowd is gathering not only to show their patriotism, but also to catch a glimpse of the Space Cadets, who will be addressing the crowd before boarding the *ISF Explorer*, seen here behind me. Sponsored by Pan Motion, the ceremony is–" Off that feed zipped, adjusting for a better shot of the crowd.

"It took well over a year of extensive training, Susan, but when I spoke with Captain Stanik last night, he said he was not nearly as nervous as the day they were selected for this mission–" And zip, off that one went.

Yet another live feed hovered near them. "Remember, Tom," Demaria's voice reminded a reporter, "in order to choose the best team for this mission, the ISF conducted several rounds of elimination tests. They elected each potential captain and allowed those soldiers to select their own crews. Never before has a mission been handled this way. It's been a huge undertaking for everyone: the sponsors, the military personnel, and especially the team at Pan Motion–" Stanik liked how she had worked that in. She did get particularly feisty whenever the accusations about Stanik's candidacy surfaced. She still took moments to siphon accurate information back to the public. It made her seem less like a puppet spokesperson for Pan Motion's shareholders.

Another media drone zipped past. "–More evidence being made public regarding the Space Cadets selection process. It has been confirmed that Demaria Cole's father was still alive and running things when the ISF selection committee chose Stanik's crew." That one was on-the-nose. He liked that especially. Stanik was slow to climb up the rear service ladder, which brought him up onto the launch pad.

He found his crew standing around, answering questions posed by some of the drones with amber lights. That meant there were interview privileges attached to the drone's media outlet sponsor. "No light; no questions," the Pan Motion public relations team had said to help them remember.

After maybe twenty minutes of polite camera-flirting, Stanik made his way up onto the *Explorer*'s deck for the main ceremony. Demaria turned around, nodded to him, and he led the Space Cadets out onto the bow of the *ISF Explorer*. It reminded Stanik of a proud purple frog. He made note that that would make a good metaphor to hit his crew with. They should operate the ship like its personality: like a colorful, poisonous frog. Not harmful unless tampered with, not threatening unless cornered.

He shook the thought away as Demaria's smile snagged his heart. She waved, and the crowd below them burst into cheers. Stanik gripped the gunwale as he peered over the edge at the crowd below. The cityscape took his breath away.

Demaria pulled a small silver microphone from her pocket and released it into the air before her. Its little rotors whirred to life, and it hovered up to them, ready to amplify her speech.

Jablon pumped his fist in the air for the crowd, prompting them to roar even louder. Hank stepped forward and Demaria gave him a warm handshake and a pat on the shoulder. His yellow face blotched with purple spots around his eyes as the Hulgarian blushed, mistaking the crowd's cheers as a reaction to his moment. Cliptok simply saluted casually, flashed her mischievous grin, and waved to the cameras.

Finally, Stanik reached out for his handshake. Demaria clasped his healed hand in both of hers. She gave him an affectionate squeeze, her touch lingering before she forced herself to pull away. Stanik's heart sank. She did have feelings for him. Great way to find out, he thought, right before she ships me off world for three years.

Frustration crept in to replace his affection for her. Not exactly how he wanted to go into the mission. Too late, he told himself, just like her feelings for him. He stepped back and smiled politely as Demaria cleared her throat. The crowd settled in below them.

"The unknown can only be discovered once," Demaria stated with levity. "The people who charge into it? They mark our history books. Their names stand out for all posterity. Their actions define our view of the universe, and rarely can someone say, 'I was there.' But today, we're adding four brave soldiers to the history books, and every one of you who came out today to show support? You all get to say, 'I was there!' Ladies and gentlemen, on behalf of Pan Motion and the ISF, I am proud to present the *ISF Explorer* to the Space Cadets! Please join me in congratulating them; the finest soldiers our great 'verse has to offer."

Confetti popped and, stories beneath them, a marching band struck up the Federation anthem. Decorations showered the raucous crowd, and Pan Motion brought in a gravity platform with some contestant who had won the chance to christen the *Explorer* for the ceremony. It had been some sort of consumer loyalty giveaway, but Stanik couldn't determine how old the winner was as the platform came to a halt beneath them. Demaria nodded to the Cadets, ushering them over to the forehatch. The others swaggered across the deck excitedly, but Stanik hung back. Demaria hesitated as a hover-lift rose up to the deck. It was waiting to ferry her down off the ship.

He approached her, but as he closed the distance between them, she rocked back on her heels, admiring him a moment. Then, she stepped onto her lift.

"I'll be thinking about you," he heard her say before the champagne bottle shattered on the bow somewhere beneath them, frothing Terran alcohol across the *Explorer*'s pristine prow. Before Stanik could answer, Demaria's lift carried her out of sight. Walt turned away, descending into his ship and sealing the hatch behind him.

X   X   X

Stanik jogged into the *Explorer* cockpit, where the other Cadets were already strapped into their seats and adjusting their console preferences. Jablon nodded to Stanik, then checked several readouts before tapping a code in on his DashCom. "*ISF Explorer* to ground control; we are ready to initiate launch sequence."

The folksy cadence of their ground operator, Karuhl, replied, "Ground control copies that, *Explorer*. Initiating launch sequence. Please hold." Stanik could hear ground control's adjustments chirp over Jablon's tiny headset speaker.

Walt strapped himself into the captain's chair, aft of everyone else's seats, raised slightly so he could see their consoles without more than a lean and swivel of the chair. It had a gyroscope that fixed it into place, which allowed for the fluid mobility. All he had to do was shift, and the chair followed his movement.

Over the live feed on his own console, Stanik heard the band's drum core strike up a drag on the streets below. The crowd cheered as the hydraulics of the launch pad whirred, adjusting the *Explorer*'s trajectory. Next to him, Stanik heard Jablon take a deep breath. He didn't like dry launches. Most pilots didn't, Walt reminded himself. They were a superstitious bunch.

'We came from the sea, and we should keep it that way,' he'd sat and listened to some of Jablon's peers drunkenly pontificate. Dry-launch was reserved for special occasions and home-world defense drills, but it was considered risky and impractical. Nothing about the Space Cadets launch was practical. It was truly spectacle.

"*ISF Explorer*, launch pad has been extended." Ground control's message was fed through the cockpit loudspeakers. The feedback loop trilled in Stanik's earpiece. "Navigations, please confirm trajectory at your console."

Hank flipped a single switch, the computer tweeted, and he tapped his Com. "Trajectory locked."

"*ISF Explorer*, you are cleared for lift off. Standby to fire all thrusters at my command."

"Standing by," Jablon nodded, tightening his grip on the helm.

"Fire all thrusters in ten, nine, eight…" the countdown was intense. Stanik found himself remembering each of Jablon's complaints about dry launch as ground control rattled off each second.

'What if the boosters don't fire,' 'What if the boosters blow up?' 'How do we know the thrusters will be stable if they're so new?' Jablon's list had been long, and Walt was certain he was jumbling some of them together in his mind. Finally, that ten seconds was over.

"...Three, two, one: blast off." Ground Control affirmed their orders. Walt stared ahead at the cockpit windshield, seeing the rings of Cliptorgia on the edge of the horizon. Jablon fired the thrusters, and the *Explorer* shot off the launch pad. It twisted up into the sky with a whistling shriek. A feverish volley of purple, and white fireworks crackled from the towers around the city square, bursting flashes of color on the trees in the windshield's peripheral.

As thrust leveled them out, the *Explorer*'s nose burned bright, gathering hot flames for only a minute or two before it broke atmosphere. With a whooping cheer, Jablon leaned over and high-fived Hank, leaving the familiar sights and sounds of home far behind them.

12. ARTICLES OF NOGYLOP SMITH

June 11ᵗʰ, A.D. 2352
09:50 IST

The air over Cortallek that morning was alive with the bustle and fanfare of a special military mission launch, which is why no one paid any mind to a nearby alley as Argylesox jumped a fence. His double-breasted frock coat and long dark hair billowed around him as he coaxed his legs into a full-on sprint. In fact, the only part of him that managed to stay perfectly still was his handlebar mustache.

Argyle ducked around a corner, risking a look back as Vestonn and Eldadip bounded angrily over the fence. They stopped to scan the crowd congesting the streets. Finally, Eldadip spotted the gap in displaced onlookers where Argyle had pushed through.

She pointed it out to Vestonn, and both pirates disappeared in the crowd. Unable to track his pursuers, Argylesox slowed his pace. He acted casual, pulling a ratty baseball cap from his coat and slapping it on his head. Then, he slipped into the swarm of people crawling around the ISF launch platform in the city square. The royal purple ship on the pedestal above him had a prominent bow and round belly. It reminded him of a pet bullfrog he cared for as a child.

"Ship's not as big as it looked in the ads," an old-timer critiqued nearby, drawing Argyle back to the present. He kept moving, elbowing his way around to the back of the launch platform. That's where his robot Clackshok[35] would be waiting at their rendezvous point. Clackshok had his belongings tucked away in a Vac-U-Pack. That included a portable cot, a change of fresh clothes, and a few basic camping supplies.

Argyle felt as though he'd finally broken free of a heavy set of shackles. After nearly four years, he was finally escaping the Halogien Stingrays. What better place to desert his post than at the heart of the Federation?

Alaborap had to lie low in Federation space. That had made him the prime candidate to stay aboard the *Stingray* and run the storm machine. The pirates were

---

[35] **Clackshok** /ˈklæk ʃɔːk/ – a model ER-16 android (in Outer Rim slang an 'eric') manufactured primarily for farm maintenance and inventory cataloging. Argylesox salvaged Clackshok from a plantation scrapyard on Hierrnaus in A.D. 2343 and refurbished him as a research companion.

only in Cortallek to steal back Nogylop's *Articles* from the Museum of Interstellar History. They'd faked a storm and a brief power outage to do so on the sly. The museum sat in a pocket of unpredictable weather, including freak squalls that would stir up at random. Their ever-resourceful Captain Alaborap managed to swing a deal with the Widow's Cheng to test a weather-tech machine they'd detained by dubious means.

Argylesox pushed on, getting further from the museum... further from those damnable Stingrays. He took a deep breath. Safety was near.

The crowd was milling about in pedestrian gridlock, which made Argyle antsy. He tucked one hand into his frock coat, feeling for the brown leather-bound diary he had stashed there. Still seated safely in one of his big interior breast pockets.

Good. He sighed, allowed the exhale to calm the butterflies swimming in his chest, and slipped into the shadows of an alley nearby. Overhead, the skeletal frame of the ceremonial launch pad loomed large, dripping unwelcome moisture from random metal joints. Clackshok, his meter-and-a-half-tall robot, flung open a door just a few meters ahead.

The robot beckoned. "In here!"

Argylesox grinned at his clever companion before diving through the doorway. Clackshok yanked it shut just before Vestonn and Eldadip rounded the corner.

CLACKSHOK, DATACOM, ARGYLESOX

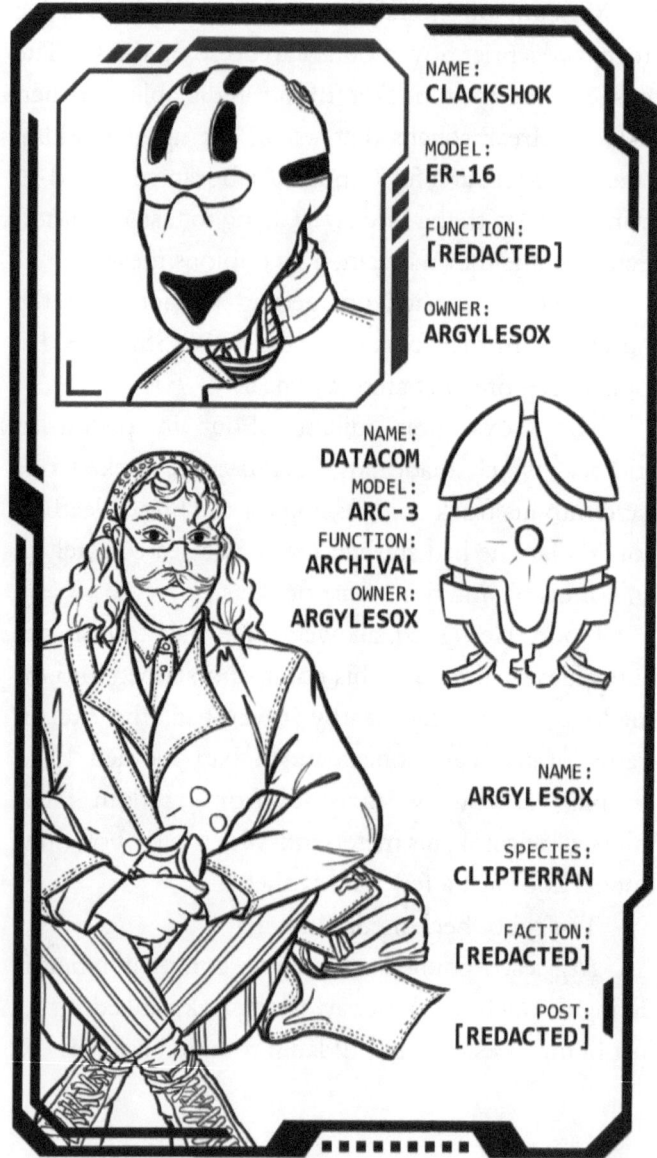

NAME:
CLACKSHOK

MODEL:
ER-16

FUNCTION:
[REDACTED]

OWNER:
ARGYLESOX

NAME:
DATACOM

MODEL:
ARC-3

FUNCTION:
ARCHIVAL

OWNER:
ARGYLESOX

NAME:
ARGYLESOX

SPECIES:
CLIPTERRAN

FACTION:
[REDACTED]

POST:
[REDACTED]

Argyle waited, holding his breath to listen to them. Gingerly, he bolted the thick door concealing them. Then, he produced a small copper tab no larger than a pillow mint and wedged it into the electronic lock. He tapped a button on the thin edge. A small electric burst of blue light shot through the lock, and its keypad died with a whispering mechanical groan.

Outside, Argyle could hear the Stingrays.

"He shook us again." Vestonn grumbled. "Which way did he go?"

"Glygorg?" Eldadip asked, and Argyle heard her tap rhythmically on the Fallamon's shell. She must've been wearing Glygorg, Argyle noted, for he hadn't seen the Fallamon with them during his getaway. He heard the unmistakable suction-cup plop as Glygorg poked his head out of his shell, sniffling like a bloodhound.

"Nyarh," the Fallamon gurgled, "maintenance door on the left."

That was, indeed, the door hiding him, but it would take them a while to figure out how to trip the locking mechanism or hack through. Either way, that was Argyle's cue to keep running.

Deeper in the launch pad's rattly maintenance tunnels, Argyle handed the diary to Clackshok as they ran alongside each other. "Clackshok, here. You hold onto this."

"Yes, sir." Clackshok plucked the book from Argyle's hand. He tucked the diary deep into his black jumpsuit. The neon pink and yellow trim of Clackshok's jumpsuit flashed under the low maintenance lights. It was a bit much, but Argyle didn't have the heart to say anything. Clackshok had chosen the suit for himself after Argyle had installed the robot's first batch of personality enhancers.

Argyle's chest was tight. He hadn't realized how quickly he'd get winded. "Where is this taking us?"

"This should bring us out underneath the launch pad." Clackshok said, rather proud for a robot. Argyle smirked. His personality enhancers were indeed working. Clackshok pointed ahead. "So long as we get past security, we will be able to hide out until things settle down after the launch."

"And blend in with the cleanup crew," Argyle nodded approvingly at his robot.

"Hey, you," a gruff voice echoed down the hall. Argyle shuddered to a halt, pushed Clackshok against the left wall, and ducked into the shadows cast by the absurd framework of piping that ran along that particular corridor.

He peeked around the corner in time to see Vestonn and Eldadip step towards four armed federal guards. Security class, Argyle noted when he saw the twinkle of emerald reflected off their jackets. The pirates raised their hands in surrender. Vestonn ducked, crouching low. As he did, Eldadip raised her hands skyward. Briskly, she flicked her wrists, and mounted pistols flung from her billowing coat sleeves up into her hands. She fired off four silent rounds and the guards collapsed, dead before they hit the floor.

"Zirkrum," Argyle cursed under his breath.

"Captain, here." Clackshok grabbed the bottom rung of a ladder tucked behind the pipes, "Start climbing." Never had Argyle received sounder advice from a robot. Upward they climbed, until Argyle's arm and shoulder muscles were ablaze. It felt like an hour, but it might have only been three minutes. He could not track such things in his current state. Above him, he saw Clackshok duck onto a landing.

"Sir," he heard the robot say, but he couldn't tell if it was the beginning of a glitched statement, or a questioning moment.

"Just keep climbing," Argyle responded, his tone unintentionally sharp. Argyle's feet hit the landing, and he spun around. His heart leapt into his throat as he stared down the bone white fangs of Naughtadargh, who growled low and threatening like some awful wolf. Of course Alaborap sent the mutant, Argyle thought, trying to calculate how best to talk himself out of the situation. Naughtadargh fancied himself Alaborap's bodyguard. Alaborap played along, using the mutant like a guard dog. Argyle hesitated to insensitively call the mutant a pet, though his wet nose and pointed ears made that an easy slip.

The big beast was essentially a wolf-man… a gene-splicing experiment with shaggy white fur. Argyle had very little success ever reasoning with Naughtadargh, for Naughtadargh did not reason, nor did he understand. He was all gut, and his gut had told him for some time now that Captain Alaborap was his pack leader; his protector; his chief. Which is exactly why

Alaborap sent him, Argyle noted.

The wolf-mutant panted patiently, ignoring the saliva that dribbled from his maw. Argyle backpedaled, keeping some distance between them. In turn, Naughtadargh side-stepped, snatched up Clackshok and clenched him firmly in his monstrous right hand. The mutant was far from bilateral in proportions. His right side bulged with extra mass and bulbous muscle. The lopsidedness was particularly apparent in Naughtadargh's hands and feet. 'Mangy,' some rude drunkard had described him at a tavern one night. That sailor drew his last breath the night he uttered that truth.

Naughtadargh held Clackshok out in front of him, snarling and snapping centimeters from the robot's face. "Stop," Clackshok pleaded. Having a friend as realistic as Clackshok usually made things easier on Argyle. In moments like this, though, he just felt awful. He had been forced to keep quiet for the past three years, stuck on Captain Alaborap's crew with little rest and Clackshok as his only confidant.

Argyle had worked so hard to gain Alaborap's trust. He'd revealed the location of the first Goliathon Temple, which was a risky first move. He'd had help from the ISF planting shards of his own research in their system for the file heist on *Freighter 601*. That had been what won the cutthroat captain over. Argyle was not only invited to see *The Articles of Nogylop Smith,* Alaborap had let him hold it the very next day.

"Give the diary back, Argyle!" Glygorg sneered,

rushing in to perch atop Naughtadargh's shoulder. The mutant wolf lurched forward, dangling helpless Clackshok before Argyle, taunting him like a schoolyard bully. Naughtadargh lumbered forward in the dark tunnel, rocking slowly as he shifted his bulk. With his first step, he paused, sniffing at Clackshok's face. His icy blue eyes narrowed as he pinched one of Clackshok's wrists in each monstrous hand.

Argyle shuddered half a step forward. "Don't," he blurted out in protest. Naughtadargh growled in disapproval, his vocalization rumbling through his big, resonant chest.

"Don't do what," he taunted, pulling Clackshok's arms wide. The big mutant yanked and twisted until sparks sputtered from the ripped mechanics. Clackshok howled in shock and, Argyle assumed, some phantom version of pain. Suddenly, Argyle was not proud of his personality enhancements anymore.

I must protect Clackshok, Argyle repeated to himself internally. He knew quite well that Naughtadargh could not read his thoughts, but Argyle had a moment of doubt as the white wolf slammed Clackshok to the ground.

Over and over, the genetic monster beat the robot's frame into the metal floor like a drummer keeping time. He was far too big; Argyle couldn't intervene. He was forced to watch helplessly as his robot friend was ripped apart and tossed aside.

Finally, Vestonn and Eldadip emerged from the shadows behind them, cutting off Argyle's escape.

Naughtadargh swiped an abusive left paw across Argyle's face. His glasses spun wildly off his nose, and he could feel the sting of ripped flesh where the beast's claws had nicked his cheek.

"Give us the diary," Glygorg snapped.

"Fine." Argyle's tone was defiant. He had to give them what they wanted in order to get away. He had to trust his DataCom's scans of the necessary pages in *The Articles*. He had to get the pirates away from Clackshok before he lost the years of research he'd struggled to attain.

Huffing and puffing, Argyle limped to Clackshok's crumpled body. Glygorg scampered down Naughtadargh's back and grabbed Argyle by the pantleg. Argyle unzipped the robot's inner breast pocket and offered the leatherbound book to Glygorg's eager gray claws.

Naughtadargh flinched, raising his monstrous right paw.

Argyle winced, waiting to be scratched again.

"Wait!" Alaborap rushed in from the shadows.

Argyle smirked. The captain still didn't like to be out and about anywhere on Cliptorgia, yet here he was. Clearly, Argyle had made him upset enough to risk it. Check and mate.

Captain Alaborap peered down his nose at Argyle, resting a heavy hand on Argyle's quivering shoulder. He leaned in speaking softly, his voice oozing with menace. "No one steals from me, Argyle."

With one swift motion, Alaborap sank a dagger

into Argyle's gut. Before he could protest, Argyle crumpled to the cold metal floor. Somewhere much further away, he heard himself yelp as the blade plunged into his side, digging around under his ribs.

Darkness clouded in around Argyle, and he found himself thankful he hadn't worn his favorite shirt that day. The last thing he felt was the warm blood his clothes were absorbing. Grimtash, he told himself, I thought for sure I was going to get away.

With that, Argyle dipped in and out of consciousness as if his head were bobbing in and out of water. He waded there, face up, sounds traveling to him lazily. He felt the pirates leaning over him, prowling around his body as something rumbled and hummed, causing the platform to pulsate around them. To Argyle, it felt like an invitation to rest.

Before turning to go, Alaborap's voice bubbled in Argyle's imaginary surf. "To the last, I grapple with thee. From hell's heart, I stab at thee." Argyle recognized the quote. Was that Melville or Stevenson?

Alaborap barked orders at his crew. It was some devious plan to be rid of Argyle's body. Upon hearing it, the Stingrays laughed sharply. Then, as he faded away, Argylesox heard Glygorg the Fallamon hiss, "Bon voyage, yeh' filthy kalaman[36]."

---

[36] **kalaman** /ˌkælə'mæn/ – Fallamon slur with no known definition or translation.

13. THE LEGEND

June 11ᵗʰ, A.D. 2352
12:28 IST

Bound for the Great Barrier, the *Explorer* burned through distortion, the state at which the ship's engines bent time and space along pre-determined clearance routes. The process shortened extreme travel times between established planetary systems. The science was far easier to summarize than it was to replicate, and Stanik struggled with the lofty equations needed to grasp concepts like string theory or general relativity. Hell, even the late Grace Billie used to admit that an effective captain was more likely to understand basic grease-bot repair and maintenance.

As complicated as the quantum mechanics were, distortion only did so much to reduce flight times. The

THE *ISF EXPLORER*

NAME:
ISF EXPLORER

FUNCTION:
MILITARY SCIENCE

CHARGE:
VADM. STANIK

SIZE:
15.5 METERS

first four hours of the journey would take them to the outskirts of their home in the Cor system, then another six hours saw them to the Great Barrier. While they were flying along transit routes, Jablon didn't even have to be at the helm except at the beginning and end of each distortion jump. Stanik let the Cadets spend the first two hours settling into their assigned bunks.

After that time to adjust, Stanik settled himself in the mess hall and invited the Cadets to join him. It was a modest-sized dining area, spartan, as was the rest of the ship, but outfitted with a table for six. Stanik set four mugs out, as well as the fresh pitcher of coffee. One by one, his crew joined him. Hank pulled up a star chart on the wall monitor, and the lights in the room dimmed. Jablon poured himself coffee and sat down across from Hank and Walt. Cliptok took a seat next to Jablon.

"Okay," Stanik said, offering Hank a mug. "We reach the Barrier in approximately six hours. What's our plan from there?"

"Well," Hank said, taking a sip from his mug, "We know we need a wide berth around Hierrnaus to avoid pirates, but Jablon suggested we avoid Heiznaus[37], too."

"Yeah," Jablon agreed. "The locals are boycotting

---

[37] **Heiznaus** /ˈhaɪznɑs/ – the second planet in the Ornaus system, this yellow rock is half the size of its closest neighbor, Hierrnaus. Its only established settlement is the capital city, Tilldalok, which was founded by the Till clan, who defected from Cliptorgia during the Outer Rim Rebellion.

Federalist goods again. They've got some aggressive barricades in orbit."

"Right," Hank agreed. "So, we can get as close to Mynaus[38] as we need, but... wait." Hank held up his hand politely, yet haltingly. Stanik cut himself off from his next thought as Hank cocked his head. Stanik held still for an eternity, but Hank said nothing.

"What is it?" Stanik asked after waiting in silence. Hank held up a finger, careful not to appear disrespectful to his captain. He and Stanik had had numerous conversations about the various uses of Hulgarian Sonar. In their training days, they had developed the one-finger hand-signal as a way for Hank to request the focus he needed while performing it. Stanik had for a long time been interested in what Hulgarians experienced during a sonar read. He listened patiently as the pulsating, chirping noise emanated from Hank's throat and chest.

Jablon and Cliptok leaned in, as if doing so might reveal what Hank was sensing. At least they remained quiet, Walt thought. Hank's bright blue eyes opened again. "Walt... someone else is on board," Hank said warily. "Below decks: at stern."

"The engine room?" Jablon pushed back from the table and hustled to the door. He assumed a defensive stance in the hallway, motioning for Walt to stay behind him. The pilot's efforts to protect Walt

---

[38] **Mynaus** /ˈmaɪnas/ – the fifth planet in the Ornaus system, this frigid planet is supposedly in the throes of an ice age.

extended beyond friendship to sworn duty. Stanik wasn't particularly concerned. Curious, certainly, but whatever was in the engine room, Stanik's gut told him it was harmless.

The door to the engine room slid open and the lights flickered in the green haze of heat put off by the Pimco drive, which was mounted at stern between the ship's primary thrusters. Walt had to step in and peer around Jablon to see what had been disturbed. First, he noticed a symbol resembling a trident in a circle had been carved into several metal surfaces around the room. Next, he noted the shredded torso and left arm of an ER-16 crawling across the mechanics trench like some undead creature. Its rubbery skin was flaked and shredded away at the fingers, where the skeletal metal hand was furiously glitching out, carving the trident symbol into another surface. Finally, Stanik saw the blood. Just beyond the scrap heap, he saw the streaks of blood where an injured stowaway lay in a battered, unconscious lump.

Jablon drew his sword and stepped closer to the lump of stowaway. He poked at it carefully with his sword tip, but it gave no sign of life. Jablon reached out and gave the body a hefty nudge, at which the weight of its shoulder revealed a familiar face. There, in the engine room of the *Explorer*, was the handlebar mustache and triangular nose of the pirate Argylesox. Jablon recognized him, too, because in unison, he and Walt said, "Oh, shit."

Stanik ordered Jablon back to the bridge to initiate

the next distortion jump. He and Hank then carefully relocated Argylesox to the MedBay on stretcher. From there, Hank delicately connected the curly-haired pirate to the ship's Intensive Care MedBot. The robot, a white, cone-shaped automaton, scanned Argylesox twice with one of its spider-like arms. Then, Stanik swore he saw it pause before hovering over to Hank on its ceiling-mounted magnatrack.

"The patient has suffered external tissue trauma, likely from a metal blade," the MedBot's ineffectual voice reported. "The patient has lost significant blood. To stabilize, a transfusion is suggested."

Cliptok ducked her head into the room. "I'll be in the Mess Hall working on this." She hefted a plastic container containing the head and shoulders of the ER-16 robot.

"MedBot, do we have his blood type in stock," Hank asked.

"Approximately," the robot's words weren't cold, but they did clunk around the room.

"Please define that," Hank said patiently.

"The patient is Clipterran. I can match the patient's blood type by first transfusing the appropriate Cliptorgian and Terran samples. It is within my programming to do so."

Hank nodded, then asked, "What are the primary differences in his physiology?"

"The patient's system produces blood at a slower rate. If we simply dress his wounds and let him heal naturally, he has only a twenty-eight percent chance of survival. With the suggested transfusion, the patient has a forty-two percent chance of survival."

"MedBot," Stanik stepped forward, "stabilize the patient. Use the transfusion method to increase his odds of survival and keep him in stasis until I say otherwise."

"Affirmative, Captain Stanik. Allow me at least one hour to finish the procedure."

Walt nodded. "Once you stabilize him, keep him in stasis until I request otherwise."

"Affirmative, Captain." MedBot swiveled back to the pirate, its spider arms reaching for medical instruments.

Walt led Hank and Cliptok back to the mess hall while the MedBot operated on their stowaway.

Stanik made fresh coffee, sipping it as he watched Cliptok and Hank use the dining table to resurrect Argyle's ER-16 robot.

"Cliptok, what exactly are you hoping to do with that thing?" His eyebrows danced with skepticism.

"I want to access its private files. Maybe I'll find something that'll explain why he's onboard."

Jablon sat down with them. "Good luck with that," he said, offering a jumble of wires to her.

Cliptok ignored him, captivated by something on her console. She sat back in her chair. "Huh," she murmured as she read her handheld display. "Interesting."

"What," Hank leaned over, peering at her screen.

"When we were attacked on the *Yulacki*,

remember I said they took files codenamed *Legend*?"

"I remember," Stanik said. "And our stowaway was with Alaborap in the cockpit that day."

"I thought he looked familiar," Hank said.

"His robot's got a subfile codenamed *Legend*."

"Can you pull it up," Stanik asked.

Cliptok didn't say a word, just focused on her pad until an electronic beeping noise chirruped from somewhere down the robot's throat. After a few minutes, the light in the robot's mouth grew as bright as a projector, playing back a hologram recording in miniature on the table before them. The file's audio was low, rendering the Cadets silent as they watched the playback. A file slate popped up:

File Information

Name: Legend
Category: Holoscan
Date: August 11th, A.D. 2348

Underneath that, Walt noticed the animated countdown: 'File playback in three… two… one…'

The pale orange projection flickered, and a board room materialized before them. Stanik traced the beam of light back to the robot's mangled mouth. In the projection, several Federalist executives in stiff suits reclined around a long wooden conference table. Earth wood, Stanik noted. The fancy stuff.

Before them, Argylesox lined up a few handheld devices on a podium. He fiddled with a white device the size and shape of a jumbo chicken egg. Stanik recognized it as a DataCom; a handy little device used by teachers and researchers for intense archiving and documentation. Argyle's face was defined by wire-frame glasses, his impressive mane of hair tucked politely into a ponytail. Stanik watched Argyle peer down the bridge of his nose. He smiled at the unamused faces staring back at him.

"Thank you, members of the research board for selecting this project." Hologram Argyle hesitated before going on. "I realize the controversial subject matter makes this–"

"Please, Mr. Sox," interrupted an older man shaped like a beach ball, "keep to your presentation."

"Right. Sorry," the video flickered as Argyle regrouped at the podium with a gulp of water. He nodded to the men and women situated around the table and tried again. "I'm sure many of you know the Legend of the Goliathon," the flame of a fireside story flickered in Argyle's eyes as he waited for them to respond. They, however, seemed to be waiting for a punchline. Still, Argyle pressed on. "I'm sure you have. It makes a fascinating bedtime story." He chuckled, perhaps at himself. His deeply tanned cheeks bloomed. Had he embarrassed himself with his joke?

Stanik studied the holographic replica of the strange man. He seemed too genteel to have ever been wrapped up with the likes of Captain Alaborap.

The hologram of Argyle pushed on with his presentation. "The legend of Goliathon and

Zaremoth[39] is arguably all that survives of the Candalonian race. You've undoubtedly heard some variation, but the truths within hold great historic significance."

The lounging board members shifted, offering no response save for two coughs and a sip of coffee.

Argyle pressed on. "Millions of years before life on Earth or Cliptorgia developed consciousness, the Candalonians, our hot-tempered reptilian brethren, evolved.

"From the beginning, Candalonian theology acknowledged the existence of other intelligent lifeforms. Their monotheistic deity Kahl was viewed as what we might describe as a wise, old dragon living in the stars. Seeing themselves as a reflection of this god, they held fast to the belief that they were Kahl's favored race. Their 'proof' of this was a pair of sister relics they claimed were left in the universe for their exclusive use. The Goliathon, a device to convert energy into matter, and Zaremoth, to convert matter into energy. Surviving records suggest that, throughout history, the Goliathon was more coveted, for with it, the wielder could summon armies, erect kingdoms, or even generate whole worlds, just as Kahl did.

---

[39] **Zaremoth** /zəˈɹiməθ/ – nearly all knowledge of this item is lost, save that it is referenced in The Legend as the Goliathon's sister or counterpart. It is unclear whether it is a relic or structure of some sort. Allegedly, the Candolite Church has withheld details about Zaremoth for centuries, but there is no concrete evidence to support this theory.

"Such as these stories go, the Candalonians grew overconfident... prideful... elitist. Witnessing the folly of his Candalonians, Kahl wiped away both relics, hiding them away in the farthest reaches of the universe. Ever the riddle maker, Kahl did leave a series of trials that only the wisest soul might withstand.

"While the tale has outlived the Candalonians, few people believe the legend of the Goliathon holds any truth. Now, xenoarchaeology has proven that Candalonians abandoned technology roughly sixty million years ago, once they successfully colonized Candalos Prime. None of the surviving records referencing the Goliathon predate that historic event. I propose that this is because Candalonians of the first age somehow fabricated both devices, and it wasn't until the second age that the relics somehow took on religious significance. I could be wrong, of course... but what if I'm right? What if it's out there?"

The Cadets had huddled around Clackshok's body, listening intently to the holoscan playback of Argylesox's strange board meeting. Jablon slapped the table. "Well, that settles it," he said, "this guy's certifiably insane." He slumped back down into his chair.

Stanik scanned the rest of his crew, but they were quiet. Cliptok's eyes shifted back and forth between the ER-16 scraps and Stanik, but she said nothing. Hank's chin was jutting thoughtfully as he leaned against the jumble of wires he had running from the robot's body to the ship's console.

Reaching over Jablon, Walt tapped the screen above their table and pulled up a security feed of the MedBay. Argylesox was strapped to the ICU bed, surrounded by glowing green monitors. The MedBot hovered over him. Its many arms whirred around his body, tending to his wounds. The Cadets watched intently in total silence for a while.

"I think it's important to remember he's a living being," Walt said firmly... almost with an air of paternity.

Jablon sucked in a short breath, about to speak. Before the pilot mustered a syllable, however, Clackshok's body erupted in a sudden fizzle of smoke and sparks.

"Whoa!" Hank ducked away. Stanik waved his hand through the smoke as a compartment in Clackshok's chest popped open, revealing a DataCom. Stanik plucked the device out of the compartment.

Jablon sat forward, trying to see it without getting too close. "What is it," he asked.

"It's a DataCom," Walt explained. "My grandmother had one for teaching history." Jablon wasn't one for details, so Stanik kept his description simple. "It's an old research device. Archives documents. Probably the source of all the robot's files."

"Can confirm," Cliptok said, showing them her handheld's blank screen. A message along the bottom read: Missing File Reference.

Walt pressed the DataCom's activation button, a

subtle indent for a thumb along the egg's equator. It honked a quick warning at him. Stanik read the message. "Private Property of Argylesox."

Cliptok typed that into her handheld. "According to our database, he's entangled with the Piracy Prosecution Program."

Something in Stanik's gut snagged on that detail. He wasn't sure if that was a good thing or a bad thing. "So... what," Stanik asked. "He's with the ISF?"

"Was," Cliptok corrected. "According to our database, he was dishonorably discharged three years ago."

"What cause?"

"The details are classified, but the date..." Cliptok slumped back in her chair.

"What," Stanik pressed.

He watched Cliptok hesitate again before giving in. "He was discharged on March sixteenth, 2349... immediately following incident six-oh-one."

"I thought he looked familiar," Hank said gravely. It had been a good while since Walter Stanik thought of Captain Alaborap Smith, but in that moment, confronted with the crippled apparition of Argylesox, it was all flooding back to him. The strange man who had cut Walt loose that day had somehow ended up nearly dead in his engine room. He was unsure what strange twist of fate plagued them as he watched Argyle's body onscreen. Stanik listened to the stowaway's heart monitor, watching for the rise and fall of his chest. Before he mustered a response, a notification pinged over their WristComs. Jablon was the first to read the notice. "We're exiting distortion. Coming up on the Great Barrier," he reported.

The mission, Stanik told himself. Stay focused on the mission. Argylesox wasn't going anywhere. "Everyone back to the bridge," he ordered calmly.

14. BLAST FROM THE PAST

June 11th, A.D. 2352
20:10 IST

The Explorer's engines whined to a stop, allowing the ship to drift towards the Great Barrier. This wasn't the first time the Cadets had seen that glowing blue patchwork of force fields, but it still struck Stanik with awe. He watched from the cockpit as the rippling blue walls of light stretched out into space above and below them, emitted from silver towers the size of skyscrapers. The resources it took to conceal the allied systems of the ISF astounded him. Along the surface of the nearest tower, a tunnel passage opened a hefty pair of bay doors, and the *Explorer* was towed inside by a pneumatic arm. The whole ship rumbled around them as the Barrier's automated arm locked into their starboard forehatch. Stanik stood, leaning to watch through the windshield as they were ferried methodically inside the Barrier passage. For maximum security, the ship passageways were designed to imitate boat canal locks on Earth. Walt had taken the tour on his first trip out to the edge of regulated space.

He sat back, waiting as Jablon handled the helm for the procedure. He tapped his DashCom. "*Gateway 15-93 Sierra*," Jablon transmitted, "this is *ISF Explorer* requesting Barrier passage. Clearance code oh-one-nine-bravo-eight-three-one. Over."

"Clearance confirmed. Please hold," the automated voice responded to Jablon.

"Thank you, kindly," Jablon said back, grinning at Stanik. The system did not reply. The machines rarely did.

"Told you," Jablon said smugly.

"I'm sorry," Cliptok cut in, "I don't believe any of us doubted you. Or did someone actually take you up on your stupid bet?"

Jablon said nothing, just leaned back in his seat and flashed a grin Walt's way.

Cliptok's jaw dropped. "Why?" She managed to form the word in two syllables.

"I did it to shut him up," Stanik said.

Jablon shrugged. "That's fine. A bet's a bet, though. You still owe me." He had tried to make bets with the crew as to whether they'd get to talk to a real person during passage. No one was going to take him up on it, namely because he was right: it was damn near impossible to convince anyone with a pulse to live and work along the Great Barrier. A few desperate souls did it, but not many. In truth, Walt made the bet to give them a bit of extra fun. He had secretly hoped a mission of their caliber would be afforded the chance to talk with a living soul before crossing the border into harsher territories.

Inside the first lock of the Barrier passageway, two robotic arms equipped with security scanners hovered past the cockpit windshield. They swiveled away over the top of the new vessel. A few moments later, the computer pinged Jablon's DashCom again. "Scans complete. You will be moved to the next compartment until clearance is confirmed. Please do not activate your ship's distortion drive."

"Roger that," Jablon answered the system. Ahead of them, the lock doors slid wide, and the ship was handed off to another pneumatic arm, which pulled them gently into a new lock.

The lock doors behind the *Explorer* groaned shut.

Passage doors in front of them slid open, revealing the stars of unregulated space. The pneumatic arm hoisting the ship adjusted its position.

Jablon's Com pinged once more. "Thank you for your compliance," the computer voice instructed. "You will be propelled away from the Barrier. Await verbal confirmation before activating your distortion drive. Your compliance is necessary."

"Aye, aye," Jablon said sarcastically.

The pneumatic arm unfurled, lofting the *Explorer*

out of the Barrier lock. Jablon unlocked helm controls, gripping them tightly. He turned to face them all with a big, dumb smile. "Welcome to the frontier," he said.

Cliptok rolled her eyes at him. "We're still in civilized space," she said.

"Are we, though?"

"Jablon, the Free Worlds still count as civilization," Hank said firmly.

Jablon merely shrugged.

The stars before them seemed disinterested in their passage, but the fierce and icy glow of the Barrier forcefields seemed to stare them down as they pushed ahead into the rugged frontier of the unorganized territories. These included the Ornaus system, the Candalos system, and the Zebu system. Stanik remembered there was a Pan Motion replenishing station some thirty A-Kays from their current position. Until Incident 601, that had been the farthest he'd ever trekked into unregulated space.

That had been during Walt's time on the *Yulacki*; Demaria had even traveled out to meet him there. Stanik wondered how many of the unorganized systems Demaria had been to. She always argued with him about Hierrnaus. She admired the red rock and the white sage west of Smith's Pointe. The Pointe was the center of everything for the Free Worlds. It was the center of commerce, the center for politics, and the center for tradespersons. And the beating heart central to all that civilization was piracy.

Stanik knew the port city was named after

Nogylop Smith; he'd helped the rebels capture it from the ISF over a century ago, in 2239. Alaborap made port there, which meant their stowaway, Argylesox, was also all too familiar with Smith's Pointe.

Jablon's DashCom dinged, pulling Stanik from his thoughts, which had drifted with his shifting view of the stars. "*ISF Explorer*," the computer said, "you are clear of the Barrier. Please activate distortion and make your desired jump within the next fifteen minutes."

"Roger that," Jablon said into his dash. "Over and out." He tapped the button to close the channel. "Ladies and gentlemen," he announced to them like a carnival barker, "as of oh-eight-thirty-one IST, we are officially in unregulated space." The group cheered, exchanging high-fives.

The Cadets all helped Jablon prep the ship for another distortion jump. They had two six-hour jumps before they'd arrive at the outer limits of the Free Worlds. That gave him plenty of time to interrogate their unexpected guest. Stanik waited patiently as the *Explorer's* distortion drive catapulted the ship into subspace. Walt let things quiet down in the cockpit before he decided to go check on Argylesox. "Stay sharp, everyone," he said as he stood, trying to sound encouraging. "Now that we're in unregulated space, two of us should always be on cockpit duty. Until we're through the Outer Rim, we're at risk."

Jablon nodded quietly in agreement.

"Jablon and Hank," Stanik continued, "Take the first watch. Cliptok, you should rest up. We'll switch with them in two hours."

"Aye, sir."

Walt took two steps aft to the cockpit door before Jablon spoke up. "Where are you going?"

Stanik stopped in the doorway. He did not turn around; the captain didn't need to. "I want to find out who our stowaway really is." With that, Walt made his way back to the mess hall, where he continued to sift through the files on the DataCom: maps of planets, dig sites, and nearly fifty pirate profiles and crime records.

Stanik lost himself in a firsthand account written by Argylesox about Bartholomew Higginbotham. Bart was the pirate who killed Alaborap back in 2350. He'd been granted amnesty by the ISF; they dropped his piracy record in exchange for Alaborap's headless body and the historic *Articles of Nogylop Smith*, his grandfather's personal diary. According to Argyle's records, Alaborap and his crew were off hunting the Goliathon in the Candalos system when that all happened.

Stanik's heart raced. Was Alaborap still alive? He kept reading. A pirate-turned-politician by the name of Thaddeus Karp got himself elected governor of Smith's Pointe, and Bart had been helping him. In exchange, they aimed to appoint Bart as Pirate Lord. The man they needed to oust was the jolly pirate Dimitri Ivanova. Argyle denoted Captain Ivanova as Alaborap's close friend and mentor.

That wasn't in the Pan Motion records, Stanik thought. He would have to add it later. He brought the datapad with him anticipating a few opportunities to add to his own pirate files.

He kept reading, trying to keep track of the names. Argyle and Alaborap were off in the Candalos system when Dimitri died. They only learned of Alaborap's alleged death from Federalist news feeds a few days later. Alaborap decided to play along with the death, allowing the Stingrays to function incognito ever since.

Stanik sat back, blinking to give his eyes a rest from the screen. He was also a bit numb. The new information was exhilarating, but Walt wasn't sure if it should be. Alaborap was *alive?*

Stanik sat stooped in his chair, letting that sink in. His body was sedentary as stone while emotions hammered at his brain. The man he had always intended to capture was still out there. The drive that had propelled him through service after the *Yulacki...* it was all still there... all still possible. He double-checked. Sure enough, the file he had open was tagged with the category 'Alaborap' and had entries dated from 2348 to present day.

Before he realized what he was doing, Walter Stanik pushed back from the dining table and marched down the hall to the MedBay. MedBot swiveled over to greet him. "Captain, good news. Patient vitals have been stabilized," its quirky electronic voice reported.

Before Stanik could collect his thoughts, he blurted out, "MedBot, wake up the patient. Now." He wanted to talk to this Argylesox.

"Affirmative," the MedBot spun back to Argyle's

body, zapping him with one of its prodding limbs. Argyle yelped, jolted back to consciousness.

Walt had no idea what he wanted to say. He hesitated as Argyle's eyes went wide. Walt let him get his bearings.

Finally, Walt asked calmly, "How're you feeling?" He crossed his arms, being sure to keep his distance from the stowaway. He didn't need the pirate to be afraid of him; he was aiming for imposing and quiet.

"Damn," Argyle tenderly sat up, inhaling raggedly. He touched the wound in his torso gingerly, then blinked before he slowly surveyed the room. "Where's Clackshok?"

"The robot? He didn't make it," Stanik kept his tone neutral. He saw how quickly the gears in Argyle's mind were turning. Then, without warning, Argyle hopped off the table, twirling the ends of his mustache.

"His body – take me to his body," he managed to request and demand all at once.

Walt held up his hands, indicating Argyle calm himself. "I have your Vac-U-Pack right here." He reached for the bedside cupboard and opened it, revealing Argyle's sealed supply kit.

"My gunner found it tucked into your robot's jumpsuit"

"Hmm," Argylesox muttered. Walt wasn't sure if the sound was meant to be words. Then, Argyle sighed. "May I still see what's left of his body?"

"Sure," Walt said. "Follow me." Anything to make him more cooperative, Stanik told himself.

He led the stowaway Argyle down the hallway to the mess hall. The console still displayed file readouts from the DataCom.

"You hacked in," Argyle asked, his shoulders sinking as he stepped inside the room.

"This is my ship," Stanik said firmly. "When I find a stowaway unconscious in the engine room, I want to know why."

"Stowaway?" Argylesox shook his head. "Where am I?"

"You're aboard the *ISF Explorer*."

"Ah, the Space Cadets," Argyle realized aloud to himself. "I suppose congratulations are also in order." The pirate held out his hand.

"Oh, we've met," Walt said, ignoring Argyle's handshake.

"Yes," Argyle said, wincing as he stretched his wounded torso. "Yes, I'm sure we have. But you'll have to forgive me, I'm not yet sure where. I travel quite a bit."

Stanik said nothing. He let the silence hang until Argyle carried on. "How far out have you gone? Where are we?"

"We just passed through the Barrier. We'll hit the Outer Rim before we make our next jump." No harm in sharing that much with him, Stanik thought. Argyle couldn't do much with the information.

Argyle thought on that for a moment. Absent-mindedly, he plucked the electrodes off his chest and disconnected from MedBot's EKG. That told Stanik he was familiar with ISF med-tech, which meant this wasn't the pirate's first trip to a military MedBay. Finally, Argyle spoke again. "Er... I don't suppose you're making a supply drop on Hierrnaus?"

"Not a chance," Stanik shook his head. Argyle took a step, then grabbed blindly at the pain in his side. "How's your side," Stanik asked.

"Huh?" Argyle responded, glancing up at him, as if he found the question distracting. "Oh, fine. I'll be fine," he said, waving the thought away. Then, after a moment, he politely prodded with, "Could I convince you to make a drop at Smith's Pointe? I could pay you; wouldn't take long to collect a few debts I'm owed there."

"First off," Stanik said patiently, "I'm not taking a ship this expensive anywhere near Smith's Pointe. Same goes for Tilldalok right now."

Argyle nodded in understanding. "Right, the boycott."

"Second of all, payment won't be necessary. I feel I owe you one... even if you don't recognize me."

Argyle nodded, a meek smile forming under the curls of his mustache.

"I'm willing to find a safe port to drop you off," Stanik continued. "Somewhere reasonable.

Argylesox was far too genteel to be any kind of real threat. However, Stanik reminded himself, it was important to temper his expectations. "My crew will gauge the pirate activity when we pass through and go from there."

"If it's pirates you're worried about, then take me to Mynaus," Argyle blurted out. "That's where I need to end up."

"Like I said, we'll see." Stanik had to keep Argyle talking. If he agreed to anything outright, he felt he might lose his leverage in the situation. "In the meantime, help me understand something; why did I find you bleeding out in my engine room?"

"Oh, yes. *That…*" Argyle took a deep breath. He opened his arms in calm surrender. "I'm a xenoarcheaologist. I've been trying to track down an old artifact, and I've had to make some shady business deals. It's an unfortunate truth to my line of research."

Stanik narrowed his gaze. The pirate was lying. "We checked; you're in ISF records."

Argyle nodded. "That's true. I do privateer work for the ISF." He leaned in. Stanik followed. "My current work top-secret." Argyle dismissed that fact with a wave of his hand, as though he didn't want to bother Stanik with the details.

"I read your file," Stanik challenged, his voice stern. "You were discharged three years ago. So, tell me another one."

"Captain, please trust me," the desperation in Argyle's voice was bubbling over. "I'm handling a delicate matter. Just drop me on Mynaus so I can continue my work."

"Who are you working for?"

"I don't work for anyone—"

"This holoscan was taken three months ago,"

Stanik interrupted, tapping an image of Argyle and Alaborap. "You make a habit of spending time with dead pirates, or is Alaborap an exception?"

"There is an explanation."

"Let's hear it." Stanik demanded with a raised eyebrow. A shot of adrenaline fired through his system as he raised his voice at the stowaway.

Instead of shouting back or squaring his chest, Argyle raised his hands in surrender. Somewhat exasperated, he pointed to his DataCom on the dining table. "May I?"

"By all means," Stanik was polite but brusque. He wanted to seem reasonable. Gesturing for Argyle to use the console, Stanik stepped aside to allow the pirate space. Argyle nodded and sat at the console hardwired to the DataCom.

Argyle activated the DataCom, rapidly pulling up files and whipping them around on the screen as he divulged his story. He even lowered his voice, as though Stanik was suddenly a confidant.

"Well, for starters, the reports about Alaborap's death were false – as you've already gathered, I'm sure... and I was working with him, but undercover for the ISF. I needed to gain access to this." He magnified a series of hand-written pages and isolated them on-screen for Stanik to examine. "These are pages from *The Articles of Nogylop Smith*. Are you familiar?"

Stanik nodded intently. It had been in Demaria's pirate files. "Yeah. It was his personal diary, right?"

"Correct," Argyle pointed at him excitedly.

"Isn't that in a museum?"

"Was," Argyle corrected him.

"Oh?"

"I, uh… have it on good authority that Alaborap stole the diary back."

Stanik was distracted, and so he did not catch Argyle's hesitation. He was flipping through the diary's pages on the DataCom. He stopped, spying a sketch of a trident in a circle. "That's the symbol your robot carved all over my engine room."

Argyle scratched his chin. "The mark of the Goliathon… really?" The lanky Clipterran paused, seemingly lost in a torrent of thoughts.

"The legend of the Goliathon," Stanik heard the disbelief in his own voice. He had never felt a true appreciation for the word 'incredulous' before. Maybe Jablon was right; maybe Argyle wasn't right in the head. "That's really what this is about," he asked, trying to sound interested. He failed, his tone giving away his cynicism.

"Yes." Argyle blinked, impervious to skepticism.

"No wonder you were decommissioned." Stanik scoffed. Shit, he hadn't meant to say that out loud. He couldn't help it, though. The story seemed bogus.

Argyle simply smiled politely in response. If he was bothered, he didn't let it show, but Stanik bowed his head in apology. "No offense," he added weakly.

"Look," Argyle instructed like a veteran professor, "All these holoscans were taken at Candalonian archaeological sites. I've discovered a series of temples that lead to the Goliathon. I've been to two of them, and I know where to find the third, but Alaborap isn't far behind me. That's why I need to get to Mynaus."

"I find it hard to believe that someone as cunning as Alaborap is chasing a fairytale," Stanik shot back. Argylesox made him feel like an unfocused student again. He wanted to remind the pirate that he still didn't believe the whole story. Parts of it were coming into focus for him, though.

Argyle met his gaze. "Knowing Alaborap's after it should be your assurance that it exists. I know it, Alaborap knows it, and I have to get to it before he does." He pointed at the console behind Stanik. Argylesox had pulled up an image of Captain Alaborap in his long maroon coat studying a wall of Candalonian hieroglyphs in a strange, pink room.

Stanik couldn't think straight with Argyle's piercing eyes challenging him. He dropped his own gaze to the floor. Argylesox made sense. Then there was the file they'd stolen from ISF records, Walt reminded himself. It was codenamed *Legend*, and it had topic tags for Goliathon and Zaremoth.

Stanik studied Argyle's demeanor as he considered the story. It seemed to check out. It certainly made sense of those details from the *Yulacki*. Walt made his decision. "If I drop you on Mynaus," he bartered, "I want any information you have on Alaborap's whereabouts."

"Why the interest in Alaborap?"

"March fifteenth, 2349. The attack on *Freighter*

601? I assume you remember that?"

"Yes," Argyle's face dropped into a heavy frown. "Yes, of course I remember."

"Then you understand my interest in Alaborap."

Realization flooded Argyle's face. His eyebrows begged for forgiveness. "Oh, yes! *You!* How could I–? I'm sorry– I... I'm very glad you made it out of there," Argyle said with a firm nod of sincerity.

"My captain didn't," Stanik fired back. He worked the fingers of his bionic hagron arm absentmindedly.

Argyle took notice of the gesture. "Ah," he said, folding his arms behind his back as he began pacing the room. "So, it's revenge?"

"This isn't revenge. He killed my captain." Stanik defended his statement.

Calmly, Argyle replied, "An eye for an eye... sounds like vengeance to me. Just be warned, Captain. Revenge clouds a man's judgement."

Stanik groaned in frustration. Why did he suddenly feel the need to justify himself to this pirate? "It's not like that," Stanik insisted. "If he's still alive, I want justice.

"Call it what you will," Argyle shook his head.

"Don't dismiss that! He killed my captain... he almost killed me!"

"Yes," Argyle said. "Alaborap's a dangerous man."

"Which is why he should be stopped!" Stanik might have sounded like an aggravated teenager, but he didn't care. Indignance fluttered in his heart.

For the first time, Argyle raised his voice. "Do you really think no one's tried?" His right eyebrow punctuated his challenge.

Of course not, Stanik thought. He knew better. But Argyle's indignation made Stanik think maybe the mustachioed pirate had something against Alaborap, too. "He's the one who left me for dead in your engine room, Captain Stanik. I'm all too familiar with the threat he poses."

So, there it was, Stanik thought. He pressed Argyle for more. "Do you know where he'll be?"

"I don't, Captain!" Argyle let the full weight of Stanik's title hit, and it caught him off guard. "And given the day I've had, I'd prefer to keep my distance from him for the foreseeable future." Argylesox sighed. "Look, I don't mean to get upset. Alaborap has Nogylop's book back, which means he's free to pursue its Goliathon clues without me. Depending on how he interprets them, Alaborap could be headed anywhere."

"Grimtash… I'm sorry, too. I just thought…" Stanik waved away the idea, trying to get a handle on himself.

Argyle allowed their silence to linger a moment. "If you came with me," he encouraged, "we'd undoubtedly cross paths with him." He twirled the ends of his mustache.

Walter Stanik hesitated. He couldn't leave a mission like this. Even if it brought down the most notorious pirate in the Outer Rim? No, he told himself. Not now. "I can't," Stanik shook his head. "But I will keep you ahead of him." Walt activated his WristCom and pinged the cockpit. "Jablon, come in."

"Copy you," his WristCom warped Jablon's voice.

"Jablon, at the next jump, I want you to redirect course for Mynaus," Stanik ordered. He winked at Argyle, who bowed to gesture a silent 'thank you.'

"Copy that," Jablon hesitated. "I'll calculate the adjustment and log the command."

Stanik closed his WristCom channel. Immediately, Argylesox grabbed his hand and shook it emphatically. "Oh, thank the 'verse," Argyle said, "thank you, Captain. We should keep in touch. I always like to repay a favor."

Walt had to suppress a laugh. "It's no big deal," he reassured his strange guest. "C'mon, I'll show you to the spare cabin." He unplugged the DataCom from the ship's console and handed it back to Argyle. Then, he led Argyle aft to the spare cabin, which was tucked in a corner at the end of the *Explorer*'s main hallway.

"Nearest grooming compartment is across the hall from you," Walt said. "Should be soap and fresh towels if you'd like to shower."

"Thank you again, Captain."

"Don't mention it," Stanik replied coolly. "Just prep those Alaborap files for me."

Argylesox nodded in agreement.

Trusting that all was in order, Stanik reported back to the cockpit and sat with his crew. He tried to be open with them, answered their questions plainly. Jablon wasn't keen on Argyle being allowed to roam around. He kept a live security feed of the aft hallway open on his console.

Cliptok was quiet on the subject, but Hank asked a few questions about Argyle's health and demeanor. Stanik answered him honestly so they could all hear him say it again. "I think his story is credible… I'm still piecing some of it together, but it makes sense of a few things regarding Incident 601." Walt waited a beat, but no one interjected, so he pressed on. "Dropping him on Mynaus barely puts us off course and it solves our stowaway predicament without a headache," he reasoned.

"I'll take Mynaus over the inner worlds any day," Cliptok chimed in softly. That sounded like one vote.

Jablon crossed his arms. "I don't want to deviate course. Let's drop him at a trade depot or something."

"That's no good," replied Stanik. "A ship like this is going to draw a lot of attention at a frontier depot. Especially since the *Explorer*'s been all over the news for the launch. A peaceful Federalist mission marooning a pirate at a backwater trade depot would make the news circuits all too quickly. Dropping him on an unmonitored planet slightly off course gives us plausible deniability in the rare event we're spotted."

"Point well-made, Captain," Hank nodded. That secured two votes… and Hank tended to be the voice of reason, which usually helped Jablon along.

"What's this guy doing?" the pilot complained, tapped a stylus on his console. Stanik peered at the video feed. Jablon was watching security footage for the camera overlooking Argyle's cabin. "He hasn't left his quarters this whole time," Jablon huffed.

"He's probably still sleeping." Before Walt could remind Jablon that their stowaway was recovering from a stab wound, the door to Argyle's quarters opened and they watched as he pattered to the mess hall. Jablon changed cameras, and they spied Argyle as he brewed himself a cup of coffee.

In that moment, Stanik saw something in Argyle's physicality that reassured him the stowaway was no threat. He was scholarly. His quick and quirky movements, his intentional but polite way of speaking all reminded Stanik of his grandma's colleagues. He seemed like a soul driven by curiosity. He was more historian than hijacker, Stanik suspected... more of books than buccaneers. Then there was the DataCom archive: even if Stanik thought it was a crackpot theory, Argyle's interest in the Goliathon was *clearly* academic.

On Jablon's screen, Argyle stirred creamer into his coffee. He sat hunched in a corner, staring off into space as he sipped the hot beverage. "Well," Stanik said, "the scary man made a coffee. Should I lock him up now?" Walt snickered, shaking his head.

Jablon wrinkled his nose and waved Stanik's taunts away. "Fine," he said. "You're right; he's fine. It's still smart to keep an eye on him." Fortunately, he didn't have a chance. Argyle retreated to his room with the coffee and wasn't seen again for nearly ten hours, when the *Explorer* was closing in on Mynaus.

15. SMITH FAMILY SENTIMENTS

June 11ᵗʰ, A.D. 2352
21:04 IST

Captain Alaborap's Halogien Stingray drifted up to the Great Barrier. Thrusters helped position the ship in front of one of the smaller sections of the force field. The Stingray waited.

In the cockpit, Alaborap stood at the helm not far from Glygorg, who rocked like a parakeet on his hanging control perch situated to the right of the captain's chair. Vestonn stood dutifully off to their left, his hands held at ease behind his back. He watched intently as Glygorg and Alaborap hacked the Barrier.

"Yarh, Captain," Glygorg sputtered, "I pinpointed this grid's network frequency for ye'. Isolated it here."

"Excellent," Alaborap said. He held out a hand.

THE *HALOGIEN STINGRAY*

NAME:
HALOGIEN STINGRAY

FUNCTION:
SWASHBUCKLING

CHARGE:
CAPTAIN A. SMITH

SIZE:
18.2 METERS

"Let me have your console a moment." Alaborap waited while his stout first mate detached the touchpad from his perch and held it out.

In one fell swoop, Alaborap plucked the touchpad from Glygorg's outstretched claws and plugged it into his own console. He injected the ransomware he'd programmed years ago and closed the interface with a tap of his thumb. Ahead of them, a triangular segment of blue forcefield shuddered, morphed to an angry cherry red glow, then flickered out entirely.

"Murray, initiate a quick jump," he commanded his pilot.

"Aye, sir," said Murray from his seat ahead of them at the helm. Alaborap's pilot was a pear-shaped old man with quivering jowls and deep red mutton chops salted white and gray with age. His black domino mask, though it concealed a portion of his face, was not enough to shroud his sour demeanor. He tapped a command into the helm console, and the Stingray lurched forward. Through the windshield, the blinking lights along the Barrier's dark watchtowers were drawn out into erratic pen lines. The blue forcefields twisted like wire. The stars ahead of them wiggled and warped, as if shaken at the bottom of a glass. After only a few seconds, Murray yanked the ship's break lever, and the Stingray's distortion drive cried, sputtering them to a relative halt again.

Captain Alaborap held his breath a moment. He pulled up the Stingray's stern security feed, where he could clearly see the sprawling, unnatural border imposing on the freedom of space travel, courtesy of the ISF. Just like anything else, it was about control... control and the politics that resulted. He grimaced for the sheer catharsis of the gesture. What an ugly monstrosity of tech, he thought... and an utter waste of digits[40].

The Barrier glowed to life again behind them on the feed from stern, and Alaborap allowed himself to breathe again. That was the confirmation he needed; it meant his code had removed itself from the system.

"Jump coordinates set for the Candalos system," Murray grumbled.

"Proceed," Alaborap muttered half-heartedly. He was tired, and he wanted to sit in his thoughts for a bit. The journey from Cliptorgia to the Barrier had taken them twelve hours. It was the price they paid for traveling in stealth; transit routes were off limits, so distortion jumps were riskier... they required more calculations. Murray and Alaborap had managed that feat once again, but as always it left the captain feeling drained.

He yawned, stretched his arms out, then sat back in his chair. His right hand fell on his grandfather's diary. With a satisfied grin, Alaborap opened *The Articles of Nogylop Smith* for the first time in a long while. In seconds, he was lost between its pages again.

---

[40] **digit** – the official, fully digital currency of the Interplanetary Space Federation. It is also the primary currency used in the Free Worlds of the Outer Rim, despite that system having its own forms of established currency.

The *Stingray* crew was self-sufficient, and, barring an emergency, they knew better than to interrupt Alaborap if he was reading. He'd used the boy Pockam as an example not long after they embarked on their Goliathon trek. The kid had interrupted him while he and Argyle were reviewing the diary. So, Alaborap shut the kid in the airlock for forty-eight hours. No one else stooped to interject when Alaborap was immersed in his grandfather's notes.

Despite the undisciplined teen, though, the current Stingrays were highly competent... perhaps even Alaborap's finest accomplishment as a captain. They were even more competent when he had Argyle aboard. Alaborap sighed. The poor bastard would be dead by now. He hadn't wanted to kill Argylesox. It broke his streak: two years since he had last ended a life. He didn't enjoy killing. There was something inherently nasty in it. He felt that life was to be cherished: lived to the fullest. Depriving any creature of that put a curse on the soul, or at least it did his.

Killing was also unavoidable. Survival was by its very nature red in tooth and claw. It was therefore necessary for Alaborap to get his hands dirty, but he did so sparingly. His most useful tactic was to demand it as a show of loyalty to ship, captain, and clan.

Every once in a great while, though, the veil had to be lifted. His crew needed to glimpse his ferocity, otherwise he might lose their allegiance. If he preached 'kill or be killed,' he had to kill on occasion. The alternative was death, and he did not intend to die any time soon.

Argylesox had known that long before choosing to get in the way. Regrettably, his absence left an intellectual void, Alaborap noted.

Flipping through *The Articles* in search of the page he wanted, Alaborap considered his crewmates: Next to the captain's chair, Vestonn stood at ease. He no doubt awaited Alaborap's next order. The big man was always willing to pitch in. Glygorg swung from his perch, the dish-shaped chair creaking as the chains holding it handled the Fallamon's weight. Glygorg was an excellent first mate. He had sharp senses, he was a cunning judge of character, and he anticipated everyone's needs, Alaborap's most of all. Seventy-five years of wisdom before the mast perched right next to Alaborap. How fortunate he was. Though their perspectives were worlds apart, he shared a bond with his stout, loyal reptile.

Glygorg had sailed with Nogylop, too. He'd met the man at the height of his military career. According to the diary, Glygorg had been approximately nine years old when his clutch was attacked by an ISF invasion force. Nogylop saved the clutch from death and nursed an injured Glygorg back to health. Then, he gave the Fallamon freedom to return to the forests or carry on as a Stingray. Luckily, Alaborap thought, Glygorg chose the Smiths.

Eldadip lounged at the combat console behind two joysticks. Her gaze was fixed to her screen, and Alaborap heard her console emit the familiar monotonous blips of the weapons diagnostics program. Her diligence was perhaps her best trait as quartermaster– er– 'Gunner,' Alaborap corrected himself. Occasionally, he let his brain get too wrapped up in antiquated nautical terminology. It was important to keep up with the times.

Feeling the pages of his grandfather's diary was comforting, and Alaborap allowed his mind to drift into memory. The book and he had come a long way together, after all, and it felt good to have it back in his possession, to feel the pebbled texture of the thick, hand-bound pages. It was unlike any book or notebook Alaborap had ever come across, and the heft of it seated in his grasp took him back to his first discovery of the dear old thing…

Alaborap Smith had been a very discontent eight-year-old; a boy of medium size and medium weight with a bland haircut and no notable lineage. To make matters worse, he had been cursed with adultlike intelligence at an early age. As a result, he found most social interactions with peers to be… unnecessary. He would often find himself adding mental narration as though he were a great British documentarian of old, like Attenborough, watching animals. It didn't help him navigate interactions with other children any better, but it reduced his social stress significantly.

His father, Clifton, was and always had been a lawyer. As far as Alaborap knew, his father wasn't a very good lawyer, always settling silly problems for bland, quarrelsome creatures: civil suits, domestic disputes, and familial fallouts. When people asked, he'd simply say, 'Dad was big on karma.' The family was big on debt because of dad's do-good spirit.

Alaborap's mother never seemed to notice. He assumed it was because she was just as dull. He'd always preferred time alone, namely because the boy Alaborap Smith had no friends. He attributed this to the fact that no species of child was interested in a mediocre blond boy with boring parents who were satisfied to live a life in the shadows of obscurity.

His father spent vacation time in their meager backyard, the whole family suffering for his travel anxieties. Alaborap had been raised in Federalist territory during a prosperous time, when other children were catching interplanetary cruises from Earth all the way to the Great Barrier. Luxury star cruises had been at their peak in Alaborap's childhood, but his parents always pointed to the latest starship mishap as a reason not to trust such services.

Whenever Alaborap asked if his parents would consider even a terrestrial vacation, they'd smile and tell him to read a book. It finally came to pass that he had read every article of text in his house. Some of it, he enjoyed, but some of it was for one purpose: spite. He had cooked up a retort that he knew would outmaneuver them, hopefully prompting a shift in their approach. After three years of nonstop reading, the day had finally come to use his perfect retort.

Knowledge was young Alaborap's favorite weapon. One of the first things he learned, for instance, was how to tell exactly where both of his parents were in their house at any given moment. He did this by sitting in the basement-level game room and listening to the creaks and groans in the floorboards. His young imagination had reasoned that it was because the house predated the War of Formation. This, of course, was a young boy's fancy, for the house had been built in 2304, only five years before Alaborap's birth. It was simply a noisy house. Perhaps it was protesting the mediocrity ensconced within... then again, perhaps it was just made of cheap materials. Regardless, Alaborap knew precisely where his plain, dull father was in their house that early October evening.

Alaborap listened as the floorboards whispered his father's location. The *thawunk* on the ceiling behind him told Alaborap what he needed to know. That was his father's recliner opening up. Quietly, he crept up the basement stairs, passed through the evening shadows of the first-floor hallway, and crossed into the study. There sat his father, in his leather lounge chair, recliner out... right where the house said he'd be. Alaborap rolled his eyes as his father spoke calmly to his Speak-and-Solve calculator, one of the only technological devices present in the household. The calculator's irritating robotic voice recited a large number back to Clifton as it hovered over his left shoulder. Alaborap held his breath as he hid in the hallway shadows, watching his Poindexter father fuss. While he waited, he glanced over at the fireplace, allowing his distaste for his parents to fester as his father's humidifier bubbled and brewed under the mantle where a fire should have been. Alaborap knew then that he could not let himself become like them. To do that, he had to travel. To travel, he unfortunately needed his parents.

He stepped out of the shadows and into plain view in the doorway. His father didn't respond, so Alaborap cleared his throat.

"Oh, my! Son… I didn't see you there. You know we aren't supposed to sneak up on each other, especially when we're managing finances."

"I realize this, father, but I have an urgent request."

"And what might that be?"

"I have never seen the surface of another planet, let alone most of the one we live on. I want to go on vacation."

"Well, you know what mother and I always say…" This was it, the moment Alaborap was ready for; that most intolerable of excuses was about to escape his father's lips for the last time. It seemed to happen in slow motion, and Alaborap cringed as he watched the ripple of his father's upper lip, where the few stray hairs he'd missed shaving bobbed up and down. They appeared to be cheering for Alaborap's imminent victory.

"There's no better vacation than the one you take between the pages of a book." His father formed the words with a tense smile.

Alaborap sighed lightly, inhaled and, with the slightest hint of condescension, stated his rebuttal. "I know, father, but I've read every vacation in the house."

At last, his father looked up at him, cocking both head and eyebrow in a most peculiar fashion. "Really? Every last one," he inquired.

"I started with *Fallamon Fun* and ended with the owner's manual for your Speak-and-Solve."

"Prove it," his father challenged him. Alaborap presumed it was the first time his parent had ever challenged anyone in his entire life. He was wrong, of course, but he had never seen his father in the court room. That would never change.

"Speak-and-Solve, calculate the five most popular family vacation spots among Federalist citizens and display percentages in a pie chart."

The Speak-and-Solve complied.

"You could have seen me doing that," his father argued.

"You've never used that function," Alaborap stated plainly.

"Well, maybe you're ready for some more mature 'vacations.' Why don't you read *Colonizing the Outer Worlds?*"

"The ISF loses in the end."

"Don't just dismiss that. It's your nation's history! Billions of beings were affected by the outcome of the Outer Rim Rebellion."

"It was pathetic. There's no reason the ISF

should've lost that war."

"It's amazing what a difference one misguided person can make in such matters," his father scoffed.

Alaborap was perplexed. "What does that mean?"

"I think the Outer Rim beat us because the pirates were able to organize. That was all done by one man."

"The pirate Nogylop," Alaborap said with a sharp nod. He wanted to prove he'd actually read the book.

His father cringed. "Yes, him. Very good. So, what I'm saying is, history proves that man was cunning and… and intelligent… but instead of using his big brain to solve problems, he used it to start a war." His father waved some unseen thought away. "Why don't you read some of my classics? They're on the shelf in my room," Clifton Smith said, forcing a smile.

"I already read those," Alaborap informed him, trying to reassert the fact that he had read every printed word in the house.

"What about *The Great Gatsby*?"

"A droll example of twentieth-century class privilege."

"*Lord of the Rings*?"

"Lengthy and lacking resolution."

"*Don Quixote*?"

"Please reference my previous statement."

"*The Complete Works of Willi–*"

"Yes." Alaborap was proving his point. His father studied him over his horn-rimmed glasses, skimming the recesses of his memory for other titles. *Typical*, thought Alaborap.

"You read *all* of Shakespeare?" Alaborap only glared in response. "Did you like any of it?"

"*Richard III* and *Hamlet* stand out most," Alaborap said honestly. "I have also come to believe that *Hamlet* is a brilliant work of biographical fiction by Edward de Vere, Seventeenth Earl of Oxford."

His father blinked slowly. "What?"

"It would take too long to explain," Alaborap sighed. He had, indeed, enjoyed the Bard. The mastery of language, the written *sparring* of contemporary writers... it had been an eye-opener to history as well as to the English lexicon. He also thought it quite clear that a man of court should have to closet his works behind a pseudonym during Elizabeth's reign. History proved that much to be true, especially if the writings contained a noble's most personal affairs and feelings. That was a fun 'vacation' that had lasted over a year.

"Well," his father finally said, "I think your mother has a box of books tucked away in the crawlspace... why don't you try some of those?"

"Fine," said Alaborap. He teetered away feeling somewhat defeated. They were probably all romance novels with pictures of muscular Cliptorgian women rescuing their fragile males from vicious Candalonians.

It didn't matter. Alaborap was bored and he needed something to do. Perhaps if he got into the raunchy literature, his parents would finally be flustered enough to acquiesce. He climbed the last of the stairs to the second floor and made his way for the last few stairs up to the crawl space.

Alaborap unlatched the door to the crawlspace and tapped the lighting panel on the outer wall. The doorway measured a meter-squared, which made absolutely no sense to Alaborap, because it opened into what was practically a narrow office room. He liked it inside the mysterious crawlspace, but he wasn't usually allowed in it. It was uncharted territory... full of unrifled drawers and keepsakes. In a sense, it was the most interesting part of his parents, and it was all tucked away so he couldn't access it.

His father had just given him a free pass to snoop around, and he intended to capitalize on the opportunity. He figured his parents would hide anything of extreme intrigue in the attic, so Alaborap trudged through the pond of sentiments and, after squeezing behind an antique dresser, found himself underneath the attic door.

The overhead light was dim in the office-sized room. Alaborap had to squint to find the chain for the attic door. He tugged on it again, harder this time. The door rattled angrily, the rust on the hinges protesting in squeaks. It wouldn't budge, not without an attention-drawing ruckus. Reluctantly, he shimmied out from behind the old dresser blocking the way when something peculiar caught his eye. In the corner there was a short tether of rope fed into the floor. Alaborap blinked. That couldn't be. He contorted his arm around some boxes and tried to tug at it, but it seemed stuck, so he squeezed into the corner, using his whole body to shift a dusty chest of drawers. The antique honked in protest as he pushed it several centimeters, dragging the legs. Alaborap got down on his knees and tugged at the rope again. The floorboard it was attached to swung upward, revealing a secret compartment.

Without a second thought, he plunged his arm down into the little hole and felt around until his hand closed on a very thick book. It felt like it was wrapped in cloth and covered in grime. He fished it out slowly, trying not to make any noise. Once he'd retrieved the book, he inched back to the crawlspace door, where he knew the streetlights outside were leaking through the hall window. He turned off the crawlspace light and closed the door behind him.

With a deep inhale, Alaborap blew the dust off the dingy cloth. It was tattered and black, and it smelled musty and stale. Carefully, he unraveled it, letting the dirt and cobwebs tumble quietly to the floor. A sliver of streetlight on the floor caught the tattered cloth, revealing a green skull and stingray tail emblazoned on the cleaner side.

The book was heavy in his hand, made of fine, firm brown leather and wrapped shut with a black ribbon. Alaborap tilted it into the light to examine the cover. The title *The Articles of Nogylop Smith* was stamped neatly across the face in gold calligraphic letters. His heart skipped a beat. Why was such a significant item in the home of his very insignificant parents?

There was no other text elsewhere on the cover,

nor on the binding, but when Alaborap opened it up and the pages breathed a sigh of relief, they revealed elegant, curling, hand-written words. That meant it was probably one-of-a-kind, perhaps left by the home's previous owners?

He bolted for his room, clutching the most incredible artifact he'd ever come across under his arm. Alaborap slipped through his door, slowly easing the knob so it would click soundlessly into position. He knew his parents would bother him about what he'd found, so he locked the door. It was still necessary to have a cover story. He loaded his favorite book, *Historic Human Ascension, Volume III: Magellan and the Edge of the World*, onto his nightstand console. Next, he turned the screen of his watch up to full brightness and hunkered down under his covers. The light from his watch, which he always wore facing inward, illuminated the Preface on the first page.

'It is true that much of the Federalist populace, and therefore most of the known universe, calls me a pirate. A villain, a cutthroat, an ingrate. But to the good people of my home, I am their defender: their voice.

'I embody the best they have to offer. We are, most of us, alien to our home worlds. That's true of all denizens in the Free Worlds, save for Fallamon, and we all understand the imposition we place on the natural forces of those planets... but Federalists do not. They have ravaged our homes and abused our people, poisoned our waters, and littered our streets for far too long. I am seeking reimbursement for these multi-generational crimes. What I have taken from them, I have distributed generously among the Free Worlds. The Federalists want to prove me a mad man, and I'll give them proof enough! By revealing my true nature between these pages, I hope to state my case. Here is your mad man! Here is my story.'

That very night, Alaborap read all one hundred and eighty-two pages of Nogylop's records. It was only after all that that he flipped back to the front and found the dedication: 'For my son Clifton, and for familial posterity.' Young Alaborap froze, a chill running through his bones. Clifton was his father's name.

Was Nogylop Smith his grandfather? At the time, it seemed too good to be true. Young Alaborap was nervous to wish such an interesting curse on his bland parents. But it made sense, his youthful reason had insisted. His father had no living family, and he never spoke of his childhood. What's more, Alaborap's father never talked about his parents. His mother hadn't been in the picture, and he said his father was 'there, but never present.' There weren't even photos of the man, and the only explanation his father ever had was, "He was a selfish old kook who wanted nothing to do with his family!" Fortunately, Nogylop's explanation in *The Articles* did end up offering Alaborap the other side of that story…

Captain Alaborap leaned back in his chair, removing his nose from the diary. He rubbed his temples, removing himself from his distant memories. His gaze drifted out the cockpit windshield.

"Coordinates set for a jump to the Candalos system, Cap'n," Murray growled in his muddled Cockney accent.

"Good," Alaborap said. "We'll have pinpointed a specific destination well before the second jump.

"Very good, sir," Murray saluted. He turned back to the ship's wheel, bustling to pull levers and press buttons at the helm. The Stingray's distortion drive kicked in, and the world through their windshield warped the distant stars beyond into erratic lines like neon signs. Murray cleared his throat. "If you're all gonna' be 'ere by thee 'elm," he said softly, "I'd quite like a meal break, Cap'n."

"Sounds good," Alaborap reassured him with a nod of approval.

Murray saluted again as he shuffled past them to the cockpit exit. He was a grumbly old goat, but he valued the Stingray, and he was thorough about its maintenance and upkeep. He'd also been the first man to join up with Alaborap and Glygorg. Their pilot claimed to have led a relatively normal life before Alaborap came along. He'd grown up on Hierrnaus, worked as a mechanic in the dockyards of Smith's Pointe from the age of sixteen, and even inherited his father's scrapyard.

After his father passed, however, Murray sold off the scrapyard and retired. The only thing he ever said about his home life was, "truly awful, sir." He often suggested that perhaps he had run away from a partner

MURRAY & GLYGORG

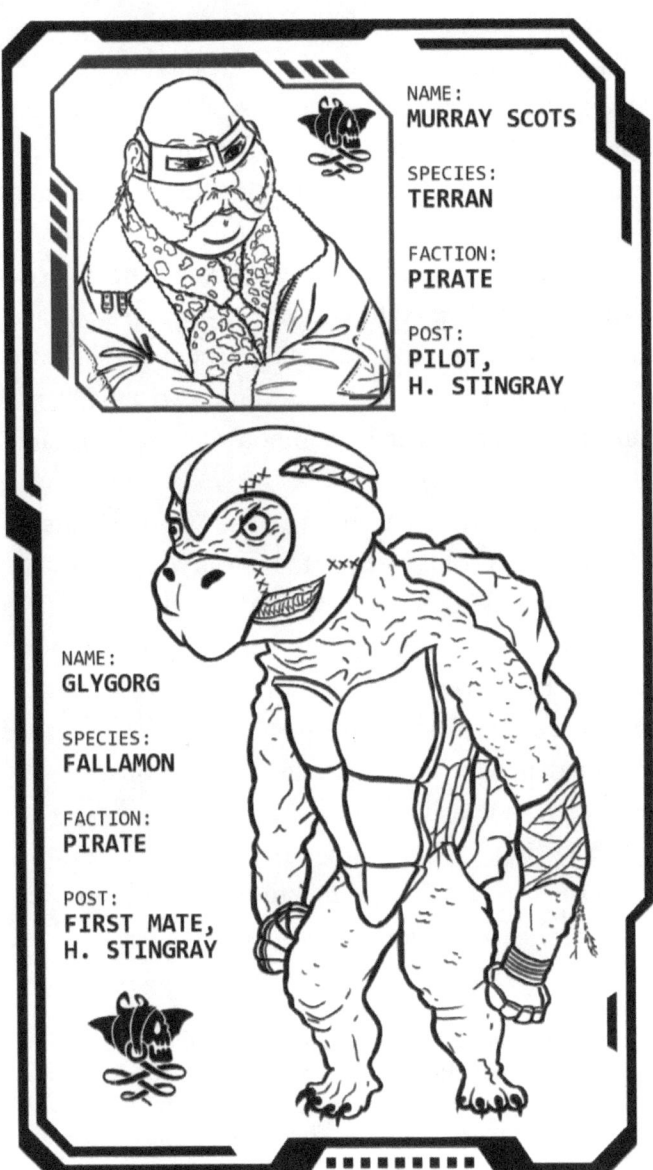

NAME:
MURRAY SCOTS

SPECIES:
TERRAN

FACTION:
PIRATE

POST:
**PILOT,
H. STINGRAY**

NAME:
GLYGORG

SPECIES:
FALLAMON

FACTION:
PIRATE

POST:
**FIRST MATE,
H. STINGRAY**

of some kind. Whatever it was, it led him to the city taverns, which led him to drink. The day Glygorg came calling with news of a young Captain Smith was the day Murray claimed to have found his true purpose. All his boredom, all the depression of mundanity was swept away. Or so, that's how Murray told it, if enough alcohol pulled at his heart and his tongue.

Alaborap tapped the diary page he'd been inspecting and turned to Glygorg. "Nogylop's passage says, 'If the scent is lost, seek judgment in the shadows of Candalos Prime.' There are only two inhabitable satellites in that system: the moon of Forgrasia[41] and Nabdok 731[42]."

Vestonn cleared his throat. "Sir? Wasn't Forgrasia a Candalonian colony before the Great War," he asked.

"Yes, indeed," Alaborap nodded like a satisfied schoolteacher. Vestonn was applying his history lessons. He'd been raised as part of the Till Vanguard on Heiznaus. They were genetically farmed and modified human males brought up like Spartans to protect the colony in Tilldalok[43].

That was a particularly nasty sect of Cliptorgian tribalism, he noted, remembering how brainwashed Vestonn had been, struggling to choose his freedom

---

[41] **Forgrasia** /fɔɚˈgɹeɪ̆ʒə/ – keep reading to learn more.
[42] **Nabdok** /næbˈdɑk/ **731** – referred to as 'Nabdok Seven-Thirty-One', it is the only life-bearing asteroid in the Nabdok belt, which sits within the Goldilocks Zone of the Candalos System.
[43] **Tilldalok** /ˈtɪlˌdulɑːk/ – capital city of the planet Heiznaus, a planet belonging to the Free Worlds of the Outer Rim.

when Eldadip and Alaborap offered it. The Till hadn't taught him anything beyond the methods of a trained assassin... well, Alaborap corrected himself, they'd taught the man to read and speak. Despite that upbringing, Vestonn had an innate curiosity, and Alaborap had been working to free the man's mind in their time together on the Stingray.

Alaborap stood, arching his back. His whole body was stiff from hunching over his book. Typical, he thought. Stretching out his legs, he shifted over to Vestonn's console. "What else do we have on Forgrasia?"

Vestonn tapped through a few prompts. Then, he proceeded to rattle off key points as he skimmed the text before him. "Orbits the gas giant Cyntune[44]. Atmospheric conditions for carbon-based lifeforms, flora and fauna alike..." He trailed off, reading ahead. The next paragraph made him grunt. "Says here the ISF ignored making any claims to it after the Great War until August of 2190. Then, they claimed it, had it scanned and surveyed, and sold it to the Velirno family in February 2191. Apparently, the family's died off, but the whole rock's held in the Velirno Trust."

Alaborap read the information over Vestonn's shoulder. "Is it inhabited?"

The big man leaned back, crossing his massive

---

[44] **Cyntune** /ˈsɪntjuːn/ – a large, gaseous planet in the Candalos System with an atmosphere comprised of ammonium hydrogen sulfide and helium.

arms. "Unless there's a research group from the Velirno Institute camped out somewhere, it'll be Stingrays versus the great outdoors."

Alaborap nodded sharply. "The wild doesn't stand a chance."

"So," Glygorg chimed in, "we make for Forgrasia?"

"I'm resolved to start our search there," Alaborap said, drumming his fingers on his armrest. "What say you both?"

Glygorg growled, his chest and neck fluttering with the noise. "Nnno complaints from me, sir."

"Aye," Vestonn bowed slightly, his colorful bandana wrapped tight over the awful scars around his right eye and forehead. "It makes the most sense to me, too, sir... based on the evidence at-hand."

"Well done, Vestonn." Alaborap clapped his hand on Vestonn's shoulder before turning to his first mate. "Glygorg? Push the Forgrasia NAV file to Murray's console."

"Nyarh," Glygorg saluted, "yessir."

16. MOUNTAINS OF MYNAUS

June 12th, A.D. 2352
08:31 IST

The *Explorer*'s mighty purple hull gleamed in a glimpse of light from the sunny side of Mynaus. As the snowy planet overwhelmed their windshield, Stanik went to retrieve Argyle from his quarters. There, he found the long-haired man napping in the armchair next to the bed. He seemed not at all embarrassed by this, and Stanik couldn't help but notice the fresh new button-down Argyle was wearing. It was a silky red shirt sporting poet sleeves and more than a few ruffles. Thankfully Argyle's navy scarf and beige frock coat muted the shirt's punch bowl pigment.

They walked in silence to the cockpit, Argyle cracking his fingers and neck as they went. When they ducked onto the bridge, Mynaus loomed in the windshield. From space, the planet looked like a marbled pearl of white and lavender, with blotches of dark blue ocean peeking through the cloud cover. The big, old planet technically straddled the Ornaus system's Goldilocks Zone, making it home to frigid, icy biomes. Stanik's brain raced for Mynaus facts from his academy days, but they were elusive, slipping away as he beheld the wild planet with reverence.

Older humans said Earth once looked as dramatic. Stanik believed it. He'd grown up rapt by the tales of his grandparents and their friends: tales that remembered a stunning green and blue orb. But Earth was grey and brown, the atmosphere soured like a worn piece of wood. Mynaus, by comparison, looked like an uncut royal gem, its natural colors swirling together as massive white clouds roamed over its jagged tracks of land.

"Argyle, have Hank help you set coordinates for a drop point," Stanik said with a gesture toward Hank's starboard console.

"Oh," Argyle smiled awkwardly, as if he were uncertain how to react. "Thank you." Hank nodded in acknowledgement, and Argylesox shimmied between the consoles. Like most military vessels, the *Explorer* cockpit was a bit cramped.

Argylesox didn't seem to notice. "Hank," he said, wasting no time at all, "if you'll accept the patch request from my DataCom, I can upload my NAV file directly to your console."

MYNAUS

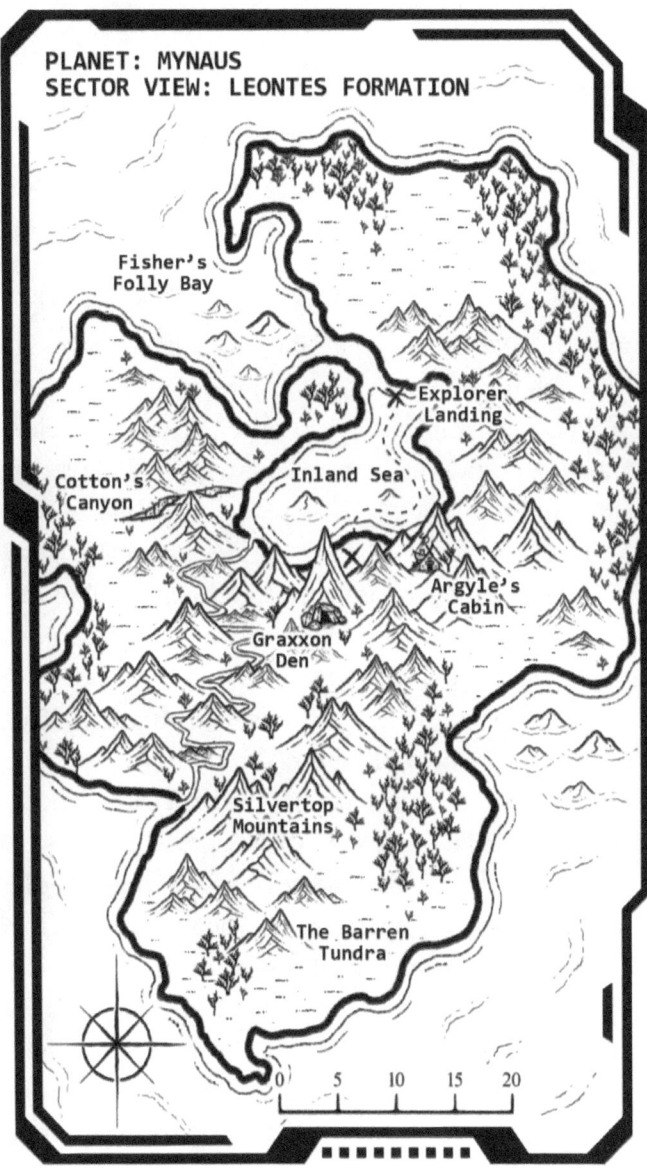

"Sure thing," Hank said. In moments, he had the map pulled up.

"There," Argyle pointed to a large body of water along a moderately sized landmass in the planet's northern hemisphere. Hank zoomed in on that continent. "Best place to land is the inland sea on the largest continent."

Hank worked quickly on the request. In seconds, his console dinged with notifications. "I've got atmospheric readouts," he said. "Kicking a suggested flight path to your console now, Jablon."

The helm dinged in response. "Got it," Jablon nodded, adjusting his grip on the wheel. "Everybody hold tight."

The cockpit rattled, bucking like a wild animal as Jablon dropped them into atmosphere. The hull of the ship withstood atmospheric burn, but only after its nose glowed yellow with heat stress.

It could be worse, Stanik told himself. The *Yulacki*'s blunt snout had burned red hot the one and only time he and Jablon had to dock it. That had been just after their first tour with Captain Billie.

Walt smiled at the memory of his mentor. He allowed his captain's chair to buck and wobble with the *Explorer* as their ship soared down into the billowing white clouds of a raging blizzard. The fierce shift in temperature jolted the cockpit anew and the hull sizzled outside.

"Atmosphere's pretty harsh here," Cliptok warned as she strapped herself into her seat.

"Yes. But I have shelter," Argyle said. "And I can hitch a ride with some fur trappers when I'm through."

"Zero visibility and I've got no readout in this storm," Jablon reported. "Sir, get Argyle in the spare seat and strap yourself down while you're at it," he shouted, fighting the helm's kickback as a snowstorm hammered the ship.

Stanik nodded, pointing Argyle to a well-cushioned bucket seat built into the aft-most wall of the cockpit.

"Argyle," Stanik had to shout over the orchestra of cockpit warning sounds. "You know how to work a T-Clamp?" He pointed Argyle to a well-cushioned bucket seat built into the aft-most wall of the cockpit, right behind the captain's chair.

"Aye, sir," Argyle snapped a quick salute, then braced himself along the ceiling rails as he shimmied safely aft. Stanik waited to see that Argyle's safety belt was clamped in before securing his own.

"Sorry for the chop," Jablon said. "Wind shears are nasty here."

"Let me help," Hank chimed in. He closed his eyes, emitting a powerful burst of clicks and coos that sang through Stanik's torso. There was even a distinct hum as Hank's reverberations passed through the *Explorer*'s gadgetry.

Feeling Hulgarian sonar travel through the body was odd. It rumbled through the bones in vibrating shocks, some more intense than others. The further an appendage was from Stanik's brain, the more the sonar felt like pin pricks. After two or three minutes of sustained sonar, Hank started calling out navigational adjustments.

"Right twenty degrees rudder," he instructed Jablon. "Mountains off the port bow. Hold your altitude here."

Stanik cautioned a glance behind him. Argyle was beaming like a kid on a field trip. "Hulgarian sonar," he mouthed to Stanik quietly. "Very nice." Stanik wondered where the hell Argyle was going to find shelter. He believed the pirate wouldn't have asked to come to Mynaus without a game plan, but traveling in this weather was dangerous, especially without the right equipment. It just so happened the *Explorer* had the perfect all-terrain vehicle for that task, and the blizzard created a perfect excuse to try it out.

"Cliptok," Walt said confidently, "activate the POD's pre-launch systems."

"Sir?" Cliptok's brow wrinkled with disapproval. He nodded firmly to her, mindful to separate himself as their commanding officer. "I will not simply drop Argyle off in the middle of a storm." Stanik turned back to Argyle. "You said you had shelter; where is it?"

"About a day's hike southwest," Argyle said. "Maybe a little longer in this storm."

Stanik smiled. "How long in a POD?"

"A what," Argyle asked.

"A Planetary Observation Dinghy," Hank added for clarity. "We call it the 'POD' for short."

"It's an all-terrain vehicle," Stanik offered.

Argyle nodded. "Oh, well… say… forty minutes? Yes, forty minutes, I should think. Maybe an hour, if there's a downed tree." He thought a beat longer, then sighed. "This means I don't have to camp out until daybreak," he said warmly, nodding at the snowflakes swirling outside the windshield.

Mynaus's gravity twisted Walt's stomach as the *Explorer* descended over the icy blue waters of the Inland Sea. The waves rolled high in the surging storm.

Jablon pulled up on the helm, raising the ship's nose. The cockpit dipped back nearly forty-five degrees as the ship's belly eased into the water. The sea's friction grabbed at them all too quickly, and the *Explorer* lurched, skipping across the angry waves like a thrown pebble.

Stanik watched patiently as Jablon rode each pebble-skip. After three gut-torquing hops, the *Explorer's* belly settled into the dark blue waters. Jablon sped them in a wide circle to test the rudder after the rough landing. Then, he aimed the *Explorer* at the rocky beach.

Argyle cleared his throat, speaking loud enough for Jablon to hear him up at the helm. "Excuse me, Jablon? My coordinates will run you aground now, but the rising tide will free you up in the next ninety minutes or so."

"Copy that," Jablon said. The *Explorer* groaned to a halt on the rocky shore as he ran it aground.

June 12th, A.D. 2352
09:04 IST

The *Explorer* lowered its hatch onto the frost-bitten beach outside, presenting Stanik's landing party with a ramp down out of the vessel's belly. Walt swore he could hear the metal crunching and scraping on the rocks as the ship listed in the surf. He ignored it, sitting back in the passenger seat as Cliptok roved the POD down out of the cargo bay. The vehicle was a compact transport with thick, rutted tires and a rear-mounted turret gun. Its boxy frame was painted in a reflective finish that warped light and color around the vehicle's chassis, providing a mirror-like camouflage for any environment. The paint job was experimental, something Pan Motion was still cooking up in a lab for widespread military use.

The POD's wheels churned in several meters of thick white powder. Stanik watched in his rearview mirror as the *Explorer* disappeared in the billowing plumes of snow behind them. The wilderness all around was blanketed in layers of crisp, white powder, and a forest of leafless purple trees sprawled up the slopes of jagged mountainsides.

The skeletal purple trees were, Stanik remembered, a favorite topic of Hank's. They were called arborspongia and were, in truth, a species of polyp, like the sea sponges of Earth's coral reefs or the grovak[45] anemone of western Cliptorgia. Stanik marveled at their twisted branches, which reached for the sky like gnarled fingers. Their trunks glistened in their headlights, calloused against cold winds. Despite the snow whirling around them, none of the polyps in the forest held frost on their branches, save for a few fallen trees that were clearly dead. Somewhere in the annals of his memory, Stanik remembered that this was because the tree-polyps of Mynaus produced their own heat, and that doing so melted the snow, allowing them to absorb the moisture. That's why their hides glistened. The blizzard was a feast for the forest.

Hank had spent a great deal of time studying them. He could go on and on about the plant's potential medicinal applications. Thankfully, Stanik noted, Hank wasn't with them.

Inside, Cliptok steered through the storm, bouncing the POD up the slope of the nearest mountain, where the trees closed in. "Hard to believe anyone actually lives out here," she said as she peered ahead through the whipping wind.

"Well," Argyle offered, "the climate has encouraged some interesting animal hides. And a few months' discomfort is worth the price they fetch. I've turned in a few myself."

"Huh," was Cliptok's only response. A gust of

---

[45] **grovak** /ɡɹɑˈvæk/ **anemone** – a species of Cliptorgian saltwater invertebrate, most commonly white or pale purple in hue.

wind howled, tugging the vehicle sideways and chattering in the icy branches above. Cliptok righted course, correcting for the drift. They rode patiently up the pass as the POD's windshield wipers marked time. Stanik found himself studying the patchwork of leafless branches jutting up into the swirling snow, casting shadows like spindly fingers.

"There it is," Argyle pointed, shaking Stanik from his trance. The captain followed Argyle's finger to a little wooden shack nestled between two boulders.

"Your next clue to the Goliathon is in some mountain man's home?" Cliptok harassed playfully.

"Oh, heavens no," Argyle chuckled, "I built this!" The strange man produced a fur cap from his Vac-U-Pack and pulled it snugly over his long hair.

Cliptok steered up to the shack and Argyle hopped out, creeping carefully around each side of the cabin. He even stooped inside cautiously, and finally Stanik realized he was making sure the shack was bereft of drifters. Convinced there were none, Argyle proceeded to heft several cords of firewood inside from a snowdrift on the westward-facing wall of his weather-beaten shelter.

"Jablon, do you copy?" Stanik tapped his WristCom, adjusting the settings. "Come in, Jablon?" Static hissed back at him, changing only in pitch and whine.

"We can't make it back in this," Cliptok warned. She was right. They had no way to signal Jablon in an emergency. "I can't see more than two meters ahead."

"He never would've made it on foot," Stanik said. They had saved Argyle's life.

Cliptok nodded slowly… skeptically.

"Plus," Stanik ventured, "we have all this equipment and we've only field tested it once. This was a good opportunity for a low-risk field test."

Cliptok turned to him, a storm of severity sweeping across her face. "We're not going after Alaborap," she said.

"I never said we were," Stanik blurted out.

"I know," Cliptok shot back.

"Okay," Stanik said. He hated his own bratty tone.

"Know your ship, honor your crew, uphold your mission," Cliptok said gently. She was quoting Captain Billie's three rules for success aboard an ISF vessel.

"Approach outsiders with compassion," Stanik replied with another lesson from their late mentor. The conversation stood still, snagged on subconscious motives. Stanik wanted to help Argyle. What was the harm in driving the man up a mountain?

Cliptok shook her head. "Never mind." She said to shake the awkward silence. She reclined her seat enough to see out the rear window.

Stanik wanted to re-establish communications with the ship. Otherwise, he'd have to sit with Cliptok longer. He busied himself, firing up the POD's DashCom. It, too, gurgled static at him. He needed to increase its range. Most military vehicles were equipped with a transmitter extension. There was nothing in the glove box, and no com-tech in the utility drawer under his seat. "Where's the transmitter extension," he asked.

"This system doesn't need one," Cliptok said, "Signal booster's built in." She had requested the vehicle specs long before their first and only field test a few months back. Walt had attempted to learn it all himself, but Stanik trusted Cliptok's familiarity with the equipment over his own. He didn't, however, trust the equipment to help them navigate back down to Jablon's position… not without coms.

Admittedly, Stanik also wasn't quite ready to let Argylesox out of his sight. His opportunity to hang around presented itself easily enough.

They sat with the vehicle running interior heat for a good fifteen minutes or more before Argyle poked his head out of the cabin door. He pulled his furry cap on as he approached them, patting the hood of the POD. Stanik could see the worry lines frozen on his face. He opened his door so they could hear each other.

"Everything okay?" Argyle had to shout over the howling winter winds.

"Can't reach Jablon, and storm's got navigations on the fritz. Can we wait it out here?"

"Of course," Argyle opened his arms wide, as if he intended to offer hugs of welcome to them both. "Come in, please!"

Inside the drafty cabin, Argyle plucked a kerosene lantern from a rickety shelf and lit it. Doused in lamplight, the shack's timbers came alive with shadows. They danced across a multitude of furs nailed to the walls.

Argyle grunted as he tugged a bookshelf away from the wall, revealing a rocky cavernous tunnel. "Last time I was here," he explained, "I excavated some old Candalonian artifacts in this cave. I constructed the shack to conceal it. Lucky thing, too; my visit was cut short by some nosy ruffians. I should've known Mynaus had a temple... You'll excuse me if I get right to work?"

"Don't let us hold you up," Stanik encouraged. Cliptok rolled her eyes. Walt pretended not to notice.

"I'll leave a lantern for you," Argyle said, setting one out on a dusty side table for them. "There are a few books around here somewhere. Oh, and some canned meat, if you get hungry," he said, pointing to an open cupboard above a small sink. His thoughts trailed off after that. It seemed as if he lost his way in their social interaction, distracted by whatever it was he was after. He did manage to nod politely before he ducked down into the mysterious cavern. Then, Argyle paused in the doorway and turned back to them. "Or you can join me, if you like," he flashed his savvy grin. With that, he shuffled off, slipping quietly into the depths of the mountain.

Stanik lit the lantern and ducked into the cave. "Walt," Cliptok snapped. "What're you doing?"

Stanik stopped, turning back to her. Playfully, he raised an eyebrow. "What?" he chided, "You'd rather stay here and eat canned meat by lantern light?"

Cliptok simply shook her head and climbed into

the cavern after him. He held out the lantern to her as a peace offering, which she took, shoving him playfully as she did.

The Cadets followed Argyle quietly for a time before the cave narrowed into a cramped tunnel. The next twenty minutes of their journey was spent clawing through that tunnel on hands and knees. Thankfully, it gave way to a spacious subterranean passage. They were free and walking upright again when their lantern light roved across the rocky ceiling. Movement overhead attracted Cliptok's attention and she stopped, raising her lamp.

"Hey, Argyle?" She directed her light to a patch of lumpy orange moss that quivered as it clung to the rocks above. Cliptok gently raised the lantern as high as she could, and Stanik noticed a good portion of the light shining through the moss. It jiggled in response, and its phosphorescence glowed a sunny orange in the dark passage.

"Fantastic," Argyle whispered. "Everyone keep an eye on that." He rubbed his hands together. "Be ready... now, Cliptok, lower your light nice and slow."

Cliptok followed Argyle's instructions. As soon as she doused her light, the moss wriggled along the ceiling. Stanik and Cliptok stood frozen for a second, unable to comprehend. The moss traversed craggy ceiling freely. As it tumbled along, more moss joined it, writhing around stalactites. It jumbled into a single mass, then wobbled deeper into the cave.

"Follow that moss," Argyle exclaimed.

17. SHADOWS OF CANDALOS PRIME

June 12ᵗʰ, A.D. 2352
10:30 IST

The Halogien Stingray thundered to a stop not far from the gravitational influences of Forgrasia. The little blue and yellow marble was a moon of insignificant size orbiting the gas giant Cyntune. Pale, yellow clouds scurried across the brooding gas giant's cinnamon-colored surface.

They had made it to the Candalos System. Glygorg's thoughts wandered as he watched over their pilot. Old Murray prepared calculations to drop the ship into Forgrasia's atmosphere. They slipped into the shadows on the dark side of the moon, and Glygorg pressed the command to retract the *Stingray*'s telescoping masts. The whole cockpit rumbled as the mainyards retracted into the masts before the masts themselves withdrew down inside the ship. They had not been easy to outfit, and the metal mesh singed along the edges during distortion jumps, but the solar-powered distortion drive made the *Stingray* even more formidable during getaways. Alaborap's crew only made port for repairs and relaxation.

A heavy thud carried through the ship, informing Glygorg that the masts were stowed successfully. Murray swiveled his chair around to face the rest of them. "Strap in, ye' black'earts. Stingray's ready for atmos."

Alaborap strapped himself in at his console, as did Vestonn. Glygorg's harness was mounted to the wall above their heads, just next to his perch. He locked himself in, suspended from the ceiling, and scanned the others in the cockpit. "Cockpit personnel secured," he grumbled.

Alaborap tapped his WristCom. "Naughtadargh?"

"Aye, sir," the mutant dutifully answered.

"Strap yourself in. We're landing."

"Copy that," Naughtadargh purred. Alaborap nodded to Glygorg.

Glygorg, however, raised a scaly eyebrow at his captain before he hit his own Com. "Yarh, Pockam," his raspy reptilian voice barked, "slap a lid on the stew and grab a seat."

Alaborap's cheeks bloomed. He forgot the kid again. Glygorg shook his head. In the captain's defense, Pockam was not memorable. But that's why Glygorg was First Mate. Fallamon memory was significantly sharper, even with forgettable faces.

"Aye, aye," the kid affirmed from the mess hall.

"Ship-wide personnel secured and ready for drop," Glygorg announced. With that, Murray typed in a command at the helm. The familiar lurch in Glygorg's stomach told him the *Stingray* was easing out of orbit.

Heat rippled through the cockpit as the flames of re-entry licked across the *Stingray*'s windshield. Glygorg gritted his teeth as the ship's cabin pressure adjusted, attempting to reduce the anvil of G-force pushing on the pirates' chests. When he was ship's apprentice, Glygorg had made the mistake of questioning the need for cabin pressure adjustments. The first mate, a sly old roly-poly named Ryan Turnbuckle, was so annoyed by Glygorg's brashness, that he shoved the Fallamon into an escape pod below decks and sealed it up before takeoff. Without the ship's countermeasures for pressure and G-force, Glygorg had pissed himself and shelled up in self-defense. Nogylop eventually found him curled up inside his body's natural armor.

The *Stingray* shuddered to a halt, dipping Glygorg's perch forward as the ship touched down in the waters of Forgrasia. Splashing into the midnight blue sea, the Stingray rode the surf towards the shore of the moon's rosewood sand beaches. The pirates unstrapped and, following their captain's lead, everyone grabbed their munitions and clambered up on deck.

Right away, something about the place made Glygorg uneasy… like he was being watched by some unseen predator. The air smelled like salty sea wind and mulled wine… perhaps with a hint of orange rind. Apart from the hooting of nocturnal birds, there was only natural serenity. Despite the promise of paradise, Glygorg's instincts fluttered uneasily as he surveyed the shadows along the shore. Perhaps it was just the night, he told himself.

Glygorg leaned over the bulwarks as the *Stingray*'s belly dragged in the sand, easing to a halt in shallow surf. The gangplank lowered on its own, slamming into the foamy waters. Everyone was silent, taking in the peaceful vista.

Alaborap was staring off into his own thoughts. Glygorg sidled up next to his captain. "At least ye' got the book back," he said, trying to lighten the mood.

"That only gets me so far without the files from the second temple," Alaborap sulked.

"Spineless gragg[46]," Glygorg shook his head. "I never trusted him." Alaborap nodded, a private admission to Glygorg that trusting Argylesox had been the captain's folly. He sighed, perhaps ready to admit those things verbally to Glygorg. Before Alaborap could say anything, a shrill, blood-curdling shriek broke the serene night air. It was carried to them on the wind from beneath the Forgrasian forest's golden canopy. In the sliver of cinnamon nightlight cast by gaseous Cyntune, the goldenrod trees ahead of the pirates shivered and shook. A flock of birds squawked, fleeing

---

[46] **gragg** /ˈgɹæg/ – a bottom-feeding eel of the Faylore River Delta, commonly fed to hatchling Fallamon.

FORGRASIA

an unseen threat amidst the trees.

Glygorg perched himself on the *Stingray*'s port bow taffrail, staring off into the trees where the birds had just taken flight. The shoreline was deceptively pleasant, but why? Another fresh breeze kicked up and… yes… there was a foul smell he detected on the wind. It was faint, but putrid. What was that?

With a shift in the breeze, the scent was carried right to him from the foreboding foliage ahead. It was the acrid stank of ape shit. Glygorg huffed a wet burst of air from his nostrils, clearing the scent from his olfactory. He turned to Vestonn, who positioned himself defensively in front of Alaborap, peering into the darkness.

"What the—" Vestonn started, but Alaborap shushed him, leaning forward.

Glygorg listened intently. Even though the surf was calm, gently lapping at the base of the gangplank, it was hard to hear anything over the seaside breeze. It bawled in his ears and he could hear nothing else.

For a moment, all was deathly quiet as the critters of the forest hushed all conversation. Stillness hung in the air as the pirates peered up the beach.

Silently, Alaborap urged his crew down the gangplank, weapons drawn. No sooner did boots touch sand than a flood of crazed Neanderthals burst forth from the timber. The terrible beasts were caked in mud, making the whites of their eyes and gnashing teeth stand out in sharp contrast to the night. Glygorg noticed that the ape-like aggressors all seemed to share an identical bulky build and ratty reddish-brown beards.

"Dah," Naughtadargh growled as the beasts swept over them. The big mutant plowed forward to meet the attack. The Neanderthals swarmed around him, biting and scratching at his powerful arms. Their nails dug into the furry pirate, and their bites tore away chunks of his fluff. "Blasted things," he howled, "Let me go!" He writhed like a wounded Raffe[47], trying to shake the devils off.

"Grimtash," Alaborap cursed, ducking as one of the ape-men vaulted over his shoulders and tackled Eldadip on its way to the ground. "What in the name of–" Alaborap was cracked on the back of the head before he could finish his perplexed question.

Glygorg snarled as he struggled against the Neanderthals, trying to get to Alaborap. He watched as the brutes overwhelmed the unconscious captain, dragging him away up the beach.

The dirty apes kept coming. More of them grabbed at Glygorg, and he writhed in their arms, trying to break loose. He watched helplessly as they dragged Alaborap into the woods. Their prize hostage in hand, the Neanderthals scattered, disappearing in all

---

[47] **raffe** [ɹeɪf] – a girthy quadruped dubbed 'the miracle beast' by Outer Rim denizens. Though zoologists compare them to ornithischian dinosaurs of Terran prehistory, raffe are kept as livestock, much like Terran cattle. Unlike cattle, their rapidly decaying waste and modest dietary needs make Raffe far less taxing on an ecosystem... if one can forgive the smell.

directions just as quickly as they'd swarmed the beach.

Pockam sprang to his feet and rushed after the main group, firing his pistols aimlessly. "Captain," he wailed, rushing to the tree line. Five cavemen popped back out of the foliage one at a time. They circled, each swiping at the wiry young pirate, who flailed wildly. The cavemen closed in, yanking at Pockam's limbs. They knocked him over, grabbing ankles and wrists. They ripped and tugged like wolves on a flank of fresh meat.

Finally, the screams of lackey Pockam Lars were cut short as the beastly men ripped him apart. They cackled, swinging his dismembered legs at each other like clubs, dancing in the spurts of blood. It was the most savage thing Glygorg had seen an animal do. He bared his teeth in a fit of rage.

"Nyargh, devils! Come back here," Glygorg barked. He lost control, incensed by the barbarism of it all. He skittered up the beach, but Eldadip grabbed him by the shell before he could get very far.

"Glygorg, don't," she pleaded, "we can't afford to lose you, too!" He hated being the smallest. Particularly, he noted, because he was also the eldest crewmember by nearly a century.

Glygorg let his anger go as he heard the concern in El's voice. Two more breaths and he was able to settle himself. His anger simmered and cooled, and he nodded respectfully as he saw Naughtadargh hoist old Murray to his feet.

"What thee 'ell was that?" Murray rubbed his jaw.

"They took the captain," Eldadip said.

With Alaborap gone, command fell to Glygorg. "Yarh," he growled, "and we're goin' after him." Everyone stood there, still shaken from the ambush. "Grab yer' gear... now," Glygorg snapped, spurring them to action. He sent Eldadip to recover flashlights, and Vestonn was charged with retrieving one of the captain's bandanas. Alaborap always tied his hair back with a bandana. Glygorg needed a sample of the captain's scent so he could track him through the forest.

18. RIDDLES IN THE DARK

June 12th, A.D. 2352
10:31 IST

"Follow that moss!"

At Argyle's command, Stanik took off down the winding cavern. Cliptok kept pace at his side. Thankfully they could stand upright, otherwise they'd have lost the moss. It tumbled away ahead of them, caught in some invisible current.

"It's been suggested," Argyle huffed, "that the Candalonians would use migrating moss to find their way when exploring. Like a trail of breadcrumbs, only they could condition it to migrate along certain routes. And it's not indigenous here."

They raced down the winding cavern until it spilled out into a cobblestone chamber where the orange moss rippled all over the coffered stone ceiling. The three of them came abruptly to a halt as they rushed into the chamber. The room was dome-shaped, though parts of it were barely visible underneath the migrating moss. A crooked limestone podium stood sentry in the middle of the room. Three metal figures caked with dust and grime sat atop the angled pedestal.

"Oh, wait," Argyle said, "before we touch anything…" he pulled his DataCom from one of his frock coat's many side pockets. After a moment of fussing with the device, it emitted a series of orange lasers that fanned out, tracing the room. "Perfect," said Argyle as the DataCom dinged in his hands. "Now to business." He held his device in front of a series of hieroglyphs, and an orange beam of light ensconced the writing. "Uh huh… yes. Yes, I see." Argyle lost himself in thought, hemming and hawing in a tone of profound understanding. Finally, the quirky gent spoke again. "This is High Rohzka[48]."

Cliptok, who was surveying the symbols around the chamber, turned to face them. "Which is what?"

"Yes, forgive me," Argyle said. "High Rohzka is an ancient Candalonian language. It's a predecessor to Rohzkarra[49], which was spoken by most Candalonians of our modern era."

"I see," Stanik said. "So, High Rohzka is like Old English or something?"

---

[48] **High Rohzka** /ˈrɒzkæ/ – keep reading to learn more.

[49] **Rohzkarra** /rɒzˈkæ ræ/ – the modern Candalonian dialect.

Argylesox considered that a moment. "Sure," he said finally. "Though, grammatically and culturally speaking, a Latin-to-English comparison might be more apt."

"Ah, yes," Cliptok said with her nose in the air.

"Unlike Latin, there're very few records available for translating High Rohzka. But, thanks to Nogylop's notes… and a bit of my own savvy, the DataCom can decipher a good portion of these markings." Stanik watched as Argyle tinkered with his device. It projected a keyboard onto a stone ledge, where the scholar typed out his desires. The DataCom's display flickered before offering translations.

Argyle unfolded a pair of bifocals retrieved from a coat pocket and fixed them over his ears. He twirled the ends of his mustache as he read the translation aloud for everyone:

"The test is in The Fall
Leave your pride behind.
Only a humble heart,
shall be left untouched.
For all others,
The beast awakens."

They stood in silence for a moment before Argyle sighed in admiration. "What a pretty poem," he added.

Cliptok and Stanik exchanged a questioning glance, and Cliptok crossed her arms. "Poem, huh?"

"Well, yes," Argyle shrugged. "But certainly not in translation."

Stanik approached the crooked podium, gently

blowing cobwebs off the stone figures there: a long claw, a mushroom, and a leaf. "I suppose we have to choose," said Argyle. "Only one will grant us passage."

"No," Cliptok interrupted, "I don't think so."

"Oh?" Argyle leaned in, genuinely intrigued.

"The riddle suggests singularity," Cliptok reasoned. "*One* with true wisdom shall be left untouched." Stanik grinned. Cliptok was getting involved. It was hard not to. "And look around," she gestured to the empty stone chamber. "Where would we put the piece we choose? I think we have to *leave* one figure and *remove* the other two."

"Ah," Argyle nodded, "yes. I think you may be on to something" He sounded like an impressed schoolteacher.

"So, which one do we leave," Cliptok asked.

"Well," Argyle continued, "in Candalonian theology, the claw, the leaf and the mushroom were all tied to kahl'ep."

Stanik leaned in. "Which is…?"

"A Candalonian cedar tree of great spiritual significance." Argyle leaned in, divulging his studies like a campfire ghost story. "In their sacred text *The Book of Kahl*, the Wisdom Tree was a kahl'ep tree. The Betrayals, those sins which prompted Kahl to take the Goliathon away, all involve the Wisdom Tree… and the story is referred to as The Fall from Grace."

"The 'fall' in the riddle," Cliptok exclaimed.

Argle hovered a finger over the stone carvings. "The claw symbolizes a cautionary tale about pride. A

Candalonian pack elder thought he could do better at answering prayers than Kahl. He spent days tearing away at the bark of the Wisdom Tree with his claws to drink its sap. It was believed that doing so would grant him Kahl's omniscience. Now," Argyle carried on, "the story of the mushroom symbolizes the fungi that grew on the Wisdom Tree. Once every few years, the Candalonian pack elders initiated young warriors by sending them out into the wilderness on a spiritual quest. The warriors' task was to retrieve a mushroom from the Wisdom Tree. We think it was eaten to induce spiritual visions. The fungi took years to ripen, and there was never enough for every warrior. Often, initiates would fight to the death over a season's portions. On one occasion, a smaller initiate knew he stood no chance against his brethren. He ventured out early and scraped the tree clean of fungi, saving only one bite for himself. While he succeeded in becoming the only warrior initiated, his pack's defenses were severely jeopardized, and a rival group whipped them out." Argyle paused, studying them a moment. "I haven't lost you, have I?"

"You're good," Cliptok urged. "So, the mushroom represents greed. Got it. C'mon, what about the leaf?"

"In the story of the leaf, a Candalonian high priest felt Kahl had neglected the Candalonians in favor of other creations. The high priest took the ruffage from kahl'ep and traveled far and wide, convincing Kahl's creations to eat the medley. I should point out that consumption of the Wisdom Tree in any way was sacrilege. To make matters worse, the high priest did this with the hope that Kahl would denounce his other creations. But Kahl is all-knowing, so things didn't end well for the priest. It's an interesting bit of text. I cite it often, as it seems to be the oldest reference to interplanetary travel intertwined with theology."

"Okay," Stanik said as he digested Argyle's tales, "so the three sins were pride, greed, and..."

"Envy," Argyle said. "The leaf represents envy."

"The passage emphasizes humility," Cliptok pointed out, "and pride is arguably the opposite. We've already been told to leave our pride behind."

"It's got to be the claw." Stanik decided.

"You sound so sure," Argyle mused.

"All three of those stories has a common thread: each character serves himself first – the ego..."

Argyle gave a sharp nod of approval. "Which also checks out with Candalonian theology. Religious texts display a tendency to layer multiple meanings into one statement," Argyle added.

"So, we agree?" Cliptok looked at them hesitantly. I should remove the leaf and the mushroom?"

Argylesox nodded confidently and Cliptok reached out for the podium. She stopped herself just before her fingers touched the carvings. "What happens if we're wrong?"

Argyle considered this. "Eh," he said with a shrug.

Cliptok's hesitation dissipated. She shrugged, procuring the leaf and the mushroom.

Stanik jumped aside as a circular pattern of stones in the floor glowed pink. They shifted at his feet, grumbling as they descended, forming a spiral staircase.

Argylesox's face melted into a big, stupid grin. He took a few steps down the stairs then stopped, glancing back at Stanik and Cliptok. He raised an eyebrow, smug satisfaction supplanting his characteristic humility. "Impressive for a fairy tale, don't you think?"

19. THE VELIRNO ESTATE

June 12th, A.D. 2352
10:52 IST

Water dripped patiently... ominously. The sound of each drop reverberated off stone in the dark.

A torch crackled. Shadows danced off the stone ceiling as they mimicked each leaping lick of flame.

"Captain, can you hear me?" A soothing, baritone British man's voice prodded at the darkness of sleep.

Wearily, Alaborap opened his eyes and sat up in a gloomy stone dungeon. He blinked, his pupils dilating, bringing into focus the stocky man who stood before him. Though the stranger seemed to linger in the shadows, Alaborap could make out his yellow smoking jacket, which matched the colors of the Forgrasian foliage. The stranger's spectacles caught the light from his torch, flashing in the dark like a predator's eyes. As he leaned forward, the flame revealed his face. His features were identical to those of the cavemen: a robust, fair-skinned human with a slight gap between his front teeth and a well-groomed reddish-brown beard.

Yes, Alaborap recalled, they attacked us on the beach. He turned, wincing as he irritated the residual pain from that blow he took to the back of his head If this man shares a visage with the beasts, he practically struck me down himself, Alaborap thought. The stranger delicately extended a hand, but Alaborap refused the help, pushing himself to his feet instead.

"I do apologize for the hostile welcome, Captain Alaborap." He knew who Alaborap was? That was… odd, considering how most of the 'verse still thought him dead. "My subjects can be a bit vicious… and dim-witted. But they keep me safe. And you *are* trespassing."

Alaborap was not about to be kidnapped *and* wrongfully shamed for it. "I was dragged here," Alaborap shot back pointedly.

"You misunderstand," the stranger smiled with an intensity that made Alaborap uneasy. "You've been trespassing since you entered orbit."

"You… own this planet?" The question escaped Alaborap before he could correct himself.

"Oh, no. *Moon.*" The stranger sang the word moon, as if savoring the sound of his voice for the first time in a long while. "Planet sounds so large: so expensive," he joked like some country club purple-blood.

"Moon," Alaborap nodded wryly. "Of course."

"But yes, I do own it," the stranger pressed, as if desperate to make casual conversation.

"Who are you," Alaborap said accusatorially before the stout little man could locate his next whimsical thought.

"My name is Beniti Juan Velirno. Please, whatever you do, don't use the Juan. It... *irritates* me."

"Certainly," Alaborap replied to humor his host. He thought the Velirnos had all died off. He chose not to say so to avoid pushing buttons.

"Now," Beniti scooped up the conversation, "if we're playing twenty questions, let me have a turn... what could you possibly be doing with this, hmm?" Beniti plucked *The Articles* from his smoking jacket, waving the diary over Alaborap the way a teacher might with class-disrupting contraband. The fact that he had an interest in *The Articles* at all was cause for alarm. Alaborap tried to brush off the book's significance.

"It's merely sentimental. Nogylop was my grandfather. All I know of him is what's on those pages." An innocent-enough plea, Alaborap commended himself.

"Ah, yes," Beniti said casually, flipping through the diary's pages. "Except, you see, that doesn't make sense either."

"Oh?" Alaborap wasn't expecting that.

"No. In fact, the pages you have marked... they

all reference the Goliathon. Which makes me wonder if you aren't retracing granddad's footsteps?"

"That's a fool's errand," Alaborap forced a derisive laugh, hoping it would conceal his lie. It didn't, and he cringed inside as Beniti raised a speculative eyebrow.

"Captain, please. I can smell a bluff from a mile away. Your secret's safe with me. Besides," his smile morphed into a devious grin, "I'm not giving this back until I think you've been honest with me." Beniti waited for a reaction from Alaborap, who refused to bat an eye. Seeing the futility of his prodding, Beniti sighed, his voice going flat. "Walk with me, Captain."

The stately man led Alaborap out of his stone chamber to a long, elevated walkway that stretched before them, running up to the back of an illustrious mansion. Alaborap recognized the white stucco walls framed by dark timbers, and the sturdy stonework of the foundation.

"Tudor style," Alaborap observed politely. "You have fine taste."

"Ah," Beniti's eyebrows danced up his forehead, "you know your history."

"Not as well as I should," Alaborap said honestly, "but I have always found the European Renaissance fascinating." When molding an exceptional bluff, Alaborap had found it quite efficacious to share small, personal truths. Most sentient beings did, after all, possess some ability to detect a lie.

Beniti sighed longingly. "A time when faith truly

drove things."

As they strolled along, the yellow leaves of the Forgrasian forest stretched out to their left Ahead, a wooden water mill creaked on the side of the mansion as it rotated in a babbling brook.

Alaborap peered over the railing to their right, where acres of lawn behind the mansion formed a zoo-like enclosure. The building behind them seemed to be a stable of sorts for the vicious cavemen. They seemed far less threatening as they cavorted around a tire swing dangling from a twisted tree.

"This is truly quite a treat," Beniti said warmly, gesturing to his fortress around them. "We don't often have visitors, and usually, when we do, my clones have mangled them to a point where I can't really have a conversation with them." The old man chuckled, but Alaborap knew a threat when he heard one.

So, the Neanderthals were actually clones of Beniti, Alaborap noted. That explained the resemblance. It also explained why he'd been carried back to the estate. But the clones had singled him out... how had they known to kidnap him?

They approached a thick metal door leading into the mansion, which jolted open as Beniti approached. He held out his arms, presenting a sterile white lab with floor-to-ceiling gene sequencers. Alaborap understood basic genetics but didn't have nearly enough know-how to be properly impressed with Beniti's state-of-the-art 'God machines.' Knowing the value of Federalist science equipment, Alaborap had stolen a few, reselling them to buyers in the Outer Rim. Equipment like that was for people who wanted to grow things like Naughtadargh.

As he took it all in, Alaborap reached for a small black pile of sand on a nearby table. Swiftly, Beniti swatted his hand away, smacking him sharply as if he were a child. "Mustn't touch anything, Captain. This is my laboratory. I like to keep busy: keep my mind stimulated. It is important that you look only; do not touch." In the same breath, Beniti took a pinch of the sand between his fingers, rolled it around, and then blew it out the door.

Alaborap stored this detail away because it struck him as altogether odd.

They left the lab behind. A short hallway spilled out into a ballroom with parquet wood floors and gold chandeliers. A well-groomed clone in a black bow tie tickled the keys of a grand piano.

Beniti sighed again. Everything seemed blasé to him. "You may recognize the baroque and rococo influence in this wing. The rest of the house is like this, save my library and study, both of which lean more into Victorian influences."

Alaborap nodded politely. He had only recognized the Tudor architecture because of his childhood affinity for Shakespeare. Those memories felt so far gone… not unlike the Elizabethan Era, he mused.

Beniti shook his head. "I often think I put in too many rooms…" His eyes glassed over as his thoughts drifted on that statement. After an awkward silence, he rejoined the conversation. "Ehr– Would you like some tea?"

"No," said Alaborap flatly. He had no desire to sit around.

"Well," Beniti said sounding perturbed, "I'd like some. This way, please." With that, the man called Beniti disappeared around another corner of his seemingly endless abode.

20. THE TEMPLE

July 12ᵗʰ, A.D. 2352
10:53 IST

Deep within the mountains of Mynaus, Argylesox descended the spiral stone staircase ahead of the Cadets. In the lamplight, his eyes were mad with excitement as he turned to help Walt and Cliptok step down into the temple. A cylindrical stone pedestal sat at center, lined up perfectly with the temple's capstone. Stanik estimated six meters between that highest point in the ceiling and the floor beneath their feet. Dirt and cave muck had long since caked over the temple floor, but a faint pink aura still glowed... in the stones. Each temple stone pulsated from within, gently humming with ripples of pink light.

Four Candalonian statues framed the 'corners' of the circular room. Each statue held a weapon out, as if offering it to the center pedestal.

"This is... this is incredible," Cliptok said through an awe-struck smile. Her voice echoed back to them as she touched the glowing walls.

"Impossible," Stanik agreed.

The pink light pulsated in a way that made Walt think of a heartbeat. In a way, he supposed that was fitting. After all, he couldn't shake the feeling he was in the belly of a beast.

The pulsing glow stopped, leaving only the weak illumination offered by the party's lanterns. Cliptok thrust her light upward, and the Candalonian statues frowned with disapproval in the wild shadows. The air was crisp, but warmer than it had been outside... and it was still. Serene, even.

A shockwave burst from the center of the chamber. As it passed under them, a force rippled through the room, knocking the trio to the ground. Stanik threw out his right arm to brace himself before he hit. It had become a habit. His brace cracked against the stones; a jolt of pink electricity throttled his arm. His whole body went numb, except for his pulse thumping in his head. The pink electricity jumped between his fingers, reaching like little lightning bolts. The stone he'd landed on was cracked, but it glowed a brighter pink than the others around it.

"Whoa!" Stanik held his arm up, keeping it away from his face.

"You okay?" Cliptok brushed herself off.

"Fine," he said, "the stones just zapped my arm."

"How electrifying," Cliptok quipped.

"Magnificent!" Argyle said with a laugh as he twirled into the middle of the room, holding out the DataCom and drinking in the scene. The DataCom chirped in his hands. "This temple has full power!"

"Power? What's going on here," Stanik asked.

"Admittedly, I need more data to properly understand it, but from what I've deduced, each stone is like the cell of a biomechanical network. And the presence of an electrical current, such as the DataCom here, wakes the network up. In the past, it's taken me several tries. But here, I'm already downloading information to my DataCom!" Argyle considered the room around them. "Something about the colder climate must have kept this temple intact. The previous temples were drained, and I was barely able to get the data. But this one has readings consistent with what I'd expect to see at full capacity!"

The DataCom beeped an alert from his hands.

"There's the file I need to find the next temple," Argyle beamed. The roseate stones faded, and the spiral staircase withdrew into the ceiling, revealing a dark tunnel as their only exit.

"No turning back, I guess." Cliptok shrugged, stepping cautiously into the tunnel. Stanik stayed close behind her.

21. JUDGEMENT

June 12th, A.D. 2352
11:01 IST

Alaborap rolled his eyes and followed Beniti into a sitting room where two winged armchairs were nestled under a large and arching window. Beniti motioned to the chairs and Alaborap sat, trying to exhibit respectful obedience for his host – captor – whoever this eccentric was. He leaned back in the tall, stiff chair and watched a clone wearing a fancy black vest light the candelabras strewn excessively around the room.

"Mmbah," Beniti commanded.

Mmbah the clone snapped to attention with an inquisitive grunt, still holding the burning match. As he turned to face them, the flame reached his finger, and he flicked the match on the floor, squealing in pain. He stomped his foot like a child, then popped his finger into his mouth to nurse the little burn. Beniti hustled over to stamp out the tiny flame.

"Tea, Mmbah," barked Beniti.

With a huff, Mmbah pattered away, his bare feet slapping across the fine wooden floors. "Yes," Beniti rubbed his hands together. "Now then. The diary." He sat next to Alaborap, his fingers feeling the cover of the book. He thought for a moment until, with a reminiscent sigh, Beniti drifted off into some memory. "He asked me to come with him, you know."

Alaborap blinked. He suspected they were talking about Nogylop now, but he couldn't be sure. His throat was dry, and he regretted turning down the tea, but he also refused to accept food or drink from a stranger. There were enough sane people in the 'verse who wanted to kill him. He cleared his throat politely. "You, uh... knew my grandfather?"

"If the scent is lost," Beniti recited from memory, relishing each word like a benediction, "seek judgment in the shadows of Candalos Prime." His sickly grin crept up his face, twisting in the jumping candlelight. "I am that judgment."

Blast it all, Alaborap thought. Argyle had been right all along... the 'Shadows' passage was a trap.

"I didn't just know him, dear," Beniti boasted, "I pledged him into the Order." The Order? Alaborap's mind raced. He had to mean the Candolite[50] Order. They

---

[50]**Candolite** /ˈkændəˌlaɪt/ – keep reading to learn more.

were a group of monotheistic zealots who bought into Candalonian scripture, which claimed the extinct reptiles were God's chosen race. The Order had cropped up as a group of Candalonian sympathizers organized themselves after the Great War. The group started by lamenting the war's nuclear devastation and demanding repentance for the sins committed by Federation forces. After a decade of repeated terrorist attacks on ISF landmarks, alongside threats of mass genocide, members and associates of the Candolite Order were expelled from the Federation.

Not to be deterred, the sanctimonious bunch fled to Hierrnaus, where they practiced in secret until the Rebellion kicked off. Then, they'd crept out of the shadows, allegedly bankrolling some of Nogylop's military efforts, which earned them enough respect to properly found their church. They hadn't shown any outward aggression in roughly 150 years, but they were a bizarre sect, shrouded in rumors of odd ritual killings and self-flagellation…

If what Beniti said was true and Nogylop had been pledged into the Order, it would have required a devout commitment to the faith. That new fact gave Alaborap a small, powerful headache. Perhaps his grandfather hadn't been so sane.

Beniti took a deep, dramatic breath, the kind reserved for soap opera performances. "Yes, your grandfather and I were close," he whispered, half to himself, half for Alaborap's benefit. His eyes landed on a collection of picture frames perched on a dresser cattycorner to them. Beniti stood, reached over, and plucked one of them from the display. "Here," he offered the photo to Alaborap. "This is a picture of he and I on the day of his confirmation."

In the photograph, Alaborap's grandfather was no older than twenty-four, but strangely, Beniti looked very much the same, or perhaps in his mid-fifties. The Beniti before him now was not a day over sixty-two. That couldn't be right, Alaborap thought. He was forty-two and his grandfather had passed over a decade before his own birth. Nogylop had been in his late sixties when he died, meaning the photo was easily eighty years old.

"You haven't aged much," Alaborap said with a raised eyebrow. It was not a point he minded challenging his host on.

"The miracles of modern science!" Beniti raised triumphant fists, chuckling. There were all sorts of procedures for people to keep up their appearances. Perhaps this fellow was a Centennial: one of those wealthy old farts who'd lived well past one hundred thanks to prosthetic organs and outlandish medical procedures. He was quite spry if that was the case, and showed none of the strange, puckering hairline scars that indicated surgical alterations. But if he was a Velirno, he was certainly wealthy enough to afford such luxuries.

Alaborap offered the photo back to his host, who waved a lazy hand in the air. "Oh, no, no. Keep it. My gift to you."

"Thank you." Alaborap nodded awkwardly and tucked the frame in his lap.

"Think nothing of it, dear." Beniti's voice was charming and warm. It made Alaborap's gut churn. "It's important to know where we come from: to stay connected to our past in some way. Otherwise, one hasn't a true sense of self." Beniti stared off for a moment, pursing his lips thoughtfully.

Fine china clinked from the other room, announcing Mmbah. His big, brutish hands rattled the delicate dishware as he nervously delivered it to his master. The diffident clone bowed his head as Beniti rescued the dainty teacup from his housekeeper.

"Ah, lovely," Beniti encouraged. "Thank you, Mmbah." Alaborap detected a hint of frustration as Beniti patiently sat back and took a sip. Instantly, his lips curled, and he seemed as if he might wretch. "Mmbah?" A thunderstorm brewed in Beniti's throat. "You know very well this tea is wrong." Clearly, they'd been over this before. "Come here," Beniti said slowly, punching each word through clenched teeth.

Obediently, the clone Mmbah returned to him, head hung low. Beniti stood, drew a sword from behind his chair, and turned back to his trembling clone. Clenching the hilt of his sword, Beniti swung it twice in a circle with great control before slashing down at Mmbah. The blade came down on the clone's right shoulder and the beast crumpled to the ground, howling. It did not fight or run, just wailed and whined in pain as Beniti ripped his sword from the wound and swung again, cleaving the fallen clone into chunks. Alaborap stared in horror as Beniti hacked away at Mmbah's body.

The clone's blood spurted, a jet of it sputtering onto the pirate's cheek. Captain Alaborap felt his heart jump, and a flood of nervous adrenaline fired through his system. He gripped the armchair, his eyes darting around the room for anything he might repurpose in self-defense. Could he duck behind his chair in time to save himself?

Beniti sighed heavily, as if he'd just finished a day of honest physical labor, which seemed to expel his rage along with it. He flicked a handkerchief from his breast pocket and offered it to Alaborap, who snatched it and immediately wiped the clone blood off his face.

Beniti procured another handkerchief from a chest of drawers at the far corner of the room. He stepped lightly around the pool of carnage soaking into his floorboards, dabbing blood from his forehead with the kerchief.

"So many interruptions tonight," his voice cracked as he waved the words away like a pestering gnat. "Oh, look," he bemoaned, glancing down at his robes, "I've gone and stained my smoking jacket." He used his handkerchief to dab at a cluster of droplet-sized bloodstains on his shoulder. When it refused to out, he sloshed saliva around in his mouth before spitting a wad of it into his handkerchief. "Human saliva... good for heavy stains... chocolate, red sauce, red wine... blood. Especially blood." The strange man blinked, as if confused by the scene before him.

Beniti turned, frowning at Alaborap. "Where was I?" He spied the diary, which he'd set on an end table out of Alaborap's reach. "Oh, yes! If you're here, with this book, it's no secret to me you're after the Goliathon." He knitted his brow. "Why?" There was no mistaking his challenge. He hoisted the question like a jousting lance, then leaned forward, prying for secrets in Alaborap's eyes.

The captain had to give Beniti something, that much was clear. Plus, his own search for the Goliathon sounded crazy enough that it just might work on this unnervingly erratic man.

Alaborap maintained eye contact with Beniti Juan Velirno and prepared for the performance of a lifetime. To get away, he suspected he would need to win Beniti over. Apparently, the man had admired his grandfather, which was a plus. To add to the appeal, he did something rather risky. "I'm not a Candolite... according to the church. But I share my grandfather's beliefs."

"Of course, you do," Beniti admired. So far, so good.

It was a big lie; Alaborap was not a Candolite sympathizer. In fact, he'd been trying not to question his grandfather's judgement throughout the conversation. Alaborap continued, his voice low, divulging. "The ISF will push into the Outer Rim again, and I believe that day's coming soon. My concern is for the citizens... the good settlers and pilgrims who have built their lives in the Free Worlds. Someone will need to step forward and organize a resistance, just as Nogylop did. The Free Worlds need war machines and fire power. There's no way to summon those kinds of resources without..." he let himself trail off, unwilling to finish his hopeful thought.

Beniti peered expectantly over his glasses. "Without what, dear?"

"A miracle." The word stung in Alaborap's mouth. He wasn't sure he believed in such things.

Beniti sighed in admiration. "You are very much like him." Suddenly, the strange old man stood, clapping his hands together. "I have decided to help you."

Alaborap winced. He did not need this person involved. "I don't think, given your age—"

"I appreciate your concern, Captain, but I'm a bit of a sportsman, and I keep in peak physical condition." As Beniti spoke, he stood, crossing back to his dresser in the corner of the room. He stripped off his smoking jacket, standing casually nude before Alaborap. "You needn't worry about me." The old man's stocky muscular physique was impressive.

Alaborap averted his eyes. Not because it made him uncomfortable, per se, but given all else, he did not need to watch the man disrobe. Beniti procured a pair of satin gold bikini briefs from a dresser drawer, stepping daintily into them.

"You could easily lead me astray," Alaborap argued politely, all too willing to use his distrust of the man as a bartering chip.

"You trusted your grandfather enough to come here," Beniti questioned coolly. He seemed to savor the bite in Alaborap's defiance.

"Clearly," Alaborap conceded with a nod.

"You must realize, then, that he trusted me enough to leave those instructions. My judgment is swift, Captain. If I didn't think you were trustworthy, you'd already be dead." His wicked smile carved ugly wrinkles into his face. "But if you continue on, I come with you. Please. That is my only condition."

In the moment, Alaborap couldn't help but be amused. The man was threatening him politely and offering a mannerly apology practically in the same breath. Alaborap couldn't believe it. He was seldom left speechless, but he had to admit he was uncertain how to respond. Thankfully, he didn't have to.

As the captain shifted in his chair, grasping for words, gunshots cracked open the silence of the night. From a window in the adjacent hallway, Alaborap heard the percussion of gunplay bouncing around outside, the pop-pop-pop ricocheting off the mansion's stone foundations.

"Walk with me," Beniti snapped. His casual familiarity evaporated instantaneously, like a man about to take the stage as one of Shakespeare's tragic, brooding kings. He gestured sharply to the hall, leading the way out onto a balcony the size of a tennis court. As they approached the balcony's wooden railing, Alaborap noticed the finely pruned gardens that sprawled out before them two stories below. The golden leaves of the Forgrasian forest lined the lawn on three sides. A dozen clones screeched, romping up the lawn from the surrounding forest.

Alaborap's pirates charged in from all sides,

unleashing a maelstrom of munitions on the savage Beniti clones.

Floodlights switched on one after another, casting stark white beams into the shadows of the forest. The change in lighting made the whole estate feel like it was confined within the walls of a prison. Alaborap's skin crawled. His pirates shuddered to a halt in the glaring light, their intrusion revealed. Up on the balcony, Beniti cleared his throat. His satin gold briefs sparkled in the floodlights.

The pirates turned their attention to the balcony. Alaborap saw their raised eyebrows as they noted the nearly naked man standing with their captain. Ignoring them, Beniti grunted viciously, his diaphragm heaving under his bare, barreled chest. With this vocalization, six-dozen clones poured out of the forest and surrounded the pirates like a squadron of soldiers.

The Stingrays nervously steadied their aim.

Alaborap gripped the balcony rail. He watched Eldadip; she was his best shot aboard the *Stingray*. Her reaction would tell him if she had a clear shot. He eyed his gunner; she was, understandably, squinting in the floodlights.

Alaborap turned, locking eyes with Beniti, who did well to keep Alaborap between himself and the pirates. No clear shots.

"Let's not have our men hurting each other," Beniti projected into the courtyard, proclaiming like some opera star for the benefit of everyone on the lawn. "After all, you have so few!" He cackled at his own joke.

"Announce our partnership to your crew and let us continue this expedition."

Beniti extended a hand to Alaborap, awaiting a response. The captain was cornered. If Beniti's clones obeyed his commands, none of the Stingrays were safe. And they certainly weren't getting away on their own terms. The moon of Forgrasia was Beniti's. If he knew about the *Stingray* landing, he'd know how to thwart an escape.

Alaborap's mind raced. He could feel the hopeful gaze of his crewmembers, awaiting some ingenious manipulation he might employ to get them out of this predicament. There was no desirable outcome. His knuckles cracked, and he let go of the railing. Alaborap's next move was going to leave the Stingrays extremely vulnerable.

22. THE BEAST AWAKENS

June 12ᵗʰ, A.D. 2352
11:03 IST

Argyle drank in the details of the temple one last time, savoring the moment. There were times when he doubted himself greatly, and he tried very much to make up for it by appreciating moments like Mynaus. In one final scan of the room, he spotted a crude charcoal drawing of a furry quadruped on the keystone over the arched exit. That wasn't original. All the other artwork featured Candalonian hieroglyphs inked onto the stones.

Sensing that he might be falling behind, Argyle ducked through the doorway and followed the rocky tunnel as it arched to the left, widening into an exceptionally large cave. A touch of cool white daylight was spilling in from the mouth of the cave, which was nearly wide enough to fit the Cadets' ship through, Argyle marveled. His eyes adjusted to the stunning morning light, and he saw that the cavern opening was obstructed by a large black mound. As it heaved up and down, towering before his companions, Argyle cussed under his breath.

The Cadets stood paralyzed a few meters ahead, where the cave opening overlooked another craggy mountainside to the southwest. Snow was falling lightly, whirling around them. Their breath billowed in the cold morning air. Argyle stepped up behind the Cadets, resting a trembling but gentle hand on each of their shoulders.

"It's a woolly-haired graxxon[51]," he whispered.

Except for its humped back, which was very bison-like, and its curling ivory horns, which were very ram-like, Argyle had always likened the graxxon to an enormous Schnauzer. After all, it had a pronounced canine-like snout with thick whiskers that grew long like a beard around the face. It also had a stumpy little nub of a tail. Argyle estimated the specimen before them was easily thirteen meters long. Thankfully, it was in a deep slumber. Its intermittent snoring rumbled up the mountainside, shaking the smaller pebbles at their feet.

"Just move quietly," Argyle advised.

The party's breath was shallow, hanging in the cold air as the heat left their bodies. The morning sun shined

---

[51] **graxxon** /ˈgɹæksɑn/ – mammalian megafauna native to Mynaus.

WOOLLY-HAIRED GRAXXON

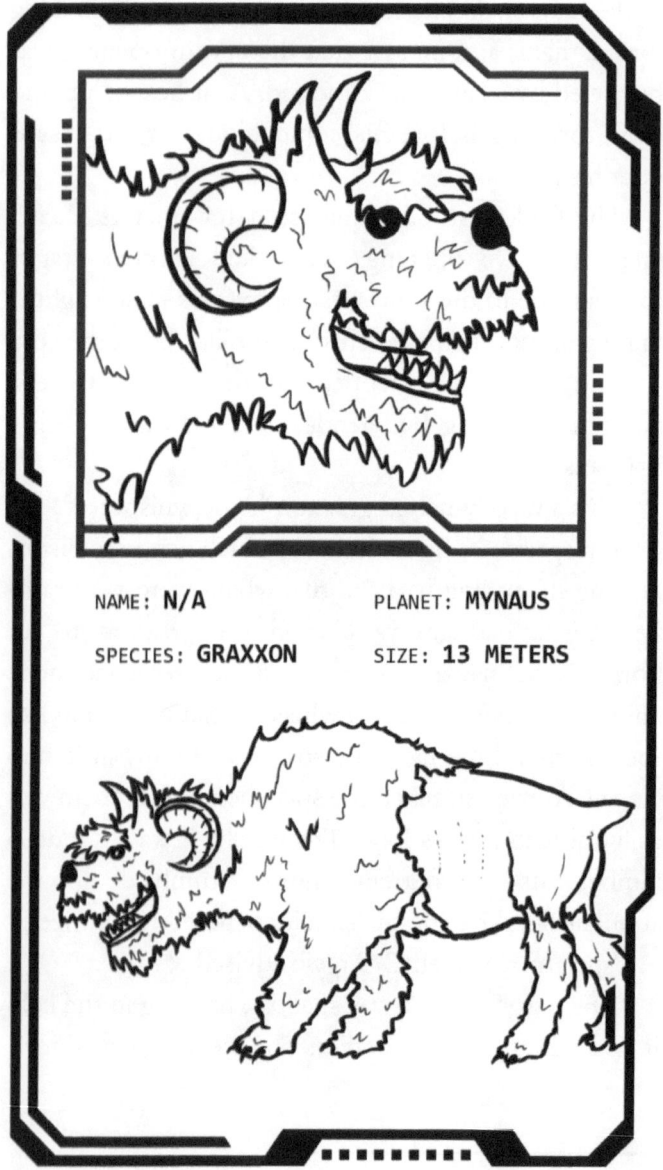

NAME: **N/A**   PLANET: **MYNAUS**

SPECIES: **GRAXXON**   SIZE: **13 METERS**

at their backs from behind the mountain, casting wild shadows in the gully ahead. They weren't even halfway up the mountain, but Argyle was able to look out over the sprawling hills and snow-covered arborspongia forests of the Silvertop Mountains to the south.

Behind them, the graxxon's lungs drew air, growling like an old combustion engine. As they edged along the icy rocks, Argyle realized how much of the cave entry had been scraped bare of any foliage, leaving them in a rocky channel with the snoring apex predator. This was no doubt the graxxon's den, Argyle thought as he spied the grooves cut into smooth rock by massive claws.

Cliptok pointed out a low point along the sloping ramparts of mud and ice, pulling herself up and over the ridge. She turned and offered a hand to Stanik, aiding his quiet climb. Argyle brought up the rear. He felt fortunate to have ended up on this trek with a group of specialized explorers. The lengths he'd gone to in the past had led him to some difficult personalities, and they were not all adept at dealing with life-or-death situations. And when allies *were,* he reminded himself, they were also secretly plotting against him. He thought of those prospectors who had stolen his supply crates and dumped him on Mynaus the last time. That mishap had given him a chance to find the cave and construct his cabin

Argyle got a little lost in his thoughts, as he tended to do. It caused him to misjudge his final step up the slope. The frozen terrain cracked under his weight, knocking loose a brief shower of rock and ice. He managed to fling himself forward, caught by Cliptok.

The mishap was not quiet, for Argyle let out a surprised yelp as his friends leapt to his aid. By the time he had landed on his companions, the graxxon's deep, raucous snores cut out, supplanted by a weary growl. The creature's wet nose sniffled. As the beast inhaled, wind whipped up, swirling around the explorers.

"Run," Argyle yelped, springing to his feet. "Now!" The command snapped his friends into action.

Cliptok was quickest, turning to the northeast and ushering them up over a rocky ledge. "The POD should be back this way," she said. They ducked into an outcropping of the planet's distinguished purple arborspongia for cover and rounded a second rocky ledge that jutted at them from the slopes above. Then, Cliptok pointed down the snowy slopes to their left. "There it is!"

Sure enough, Argyle could see the all-terrain vehicle. It was still nestled next to his cabin, seven meters downhill. The ground sloped gently, and Cliptok covered the distance by dropping into a slide and luging down the powdery slope.

Stanik and Argyle followed her lead as the graxxon crested the hill behind them. Several arborspongia snapped at the trunk with a dull, wet fwap as the agitated predator clambered forth from its resting place. It roared as it shook off the brambles tangled in its thick tufts of fur, stepping wide before it could climb out of its gully.

By then, Cliptok had reached their vehicle. She swung open the door and initiated defrosters. Then, she fired up the engine. Argyle could see the wheels spinning in compacted snow, groping for traction. The snow receded slowly from around the wheel wells as Cliptok cranked up the defrosters, and finally the POD rocked forward. Cliptok kicked the vehicle into reverse, reeling up the hill towards Stanik and Argyle.

In a panic, Argyle jumped in the rear-facing seat and slammed the door shut behind him. He strapped himself in as Captain Stanik hopped in the passenger seat.

Cliptok gunned it. The vehicle careened down the mountainside, seeking the cover of the purple forest they'd passed through the previous night.

"Argyle," she barked, tapping something in on her dash, "you're in the hot seat. Grab those turret controls."

Oh, grimtash! They had no idea what a terrible shot he was. Dutifully, Argyle wrapped his hands around the turret handles.

"Jablon, come in." Stanik was frantically trying to raise the *Explorer* on the DashCom. The speakers cackled interference back at them as their tires slid aimlessly across a patch of ice. The ground thundered, a reminder that the graxxon was still in pursuit. Stanik repeated his message while Argyle worked to find the safety on his turret gun.

The graxxon pounced, its teeth clamping shut less than two meters away. Finally, Argyle found a latch on the underside of the gun. He pulled down hard, and the turret swiveled into position. The chamber hummed, glowing green.

Stanik's WristCom chirped, and he repeated his call for help. Jablon's voice broke through the interference.

"You never answer my calls," he teased his captain.

"Not now, Jablon," Stanik's voice was tense as he watched the graxxon bearing down on them. "We need immediate evac."

"Copy that," Jablon switched gears immediately. "Keep your signal open and I'll come to you."

Argyle watched the graxxon stumble into a snow drift. It twisted violently to pry itself free. Cliptok sped down the mountainside, creating her own switchbacks. Finally, the vehicle crossed into the thick forest of gnarled purple sponge trees. Shadows from their bare branches stretched out, obscuring a good deal of the bright morning sun. Despite the densely packed trees, there was a clear but narrow game trail through the forest. Their chariot fit easily, and Cliptok put some distance between them and the thundering graxxon.

"Hey, Argyle, feel free to *use* the turrets at any point," Cliptok said.

"Aye," Argyle said. "Couldn't find the safety." However, Argyle was of two minds. On the one hand, he knew the graxxon could outrun them, but on the other hand, Argyle had always made it a point not to harm the endangered species he encountered in his travels. Big, beautiful specimens like that were growing scarcer due to poachers...

The POD pitched and weaved on a patch of ice, drifting as the graxxon lunged at them from the right. It forced its hulking, furry frame through the trees, tearing them up by the roots. Argyle jumped. Reflexively, his hands squeezed the triggers before him. His shots fired wide and collided with a snow drift, vaporizing the precipitous substance on impact.

The graxxon closed in again, swatting with a massive black paw and missing their rear bumper by less than a meter. Argyle jumped with a start before squeezing the triggers again and firing off another volley. His shots arched wildly in all directions, but not a single one found its mark in the graxxon's flank.

"Argyle," Cliptok exclaimed, "that thing's the size of a barn!"

"Yes," Argyle agreed defensively. "And?"

"How are you not hitting it," she shouted. He was hoping to scare the beast off and spare it any pain. That was no longer an option.

Cliptok kept her left hand steady on the wheel, reached back with her right hand and grabbed the turret controls. She focused on the path ahead but glanced back and forth between her driving and her aim, following the bounding strafes of the apex predator behind them.

The graxxon snapped and Argyle cringed, closing his eyes. Cliptok fired, her shot hit the graxxon, and a burst of blood erupted from its right eye, sprinkling down onto the snow in a sudden shower of crimson. The beast dropped back, howling in pain, but it continued its chase.

Just then, the *Explorer* roared in overhead.

"Whoa," Jablon chimed in over the WristCom. "What the hell did you do?"

"Just get ahead of us and open the hatch," Cliptok barked. "And fly *low*."

"Okay. Copy."

With that, the *Explorer* pulled ahead of them. The forest opened up, and the *Explorer* dropped low over crisp snowy plains. Its hatch slid open slowly.

"Check your seatbelts," Cliptok warned them.

"What?" Argyle panicked. He couldn't see ahead of them. Behind them, the graxxon's massive teeth clamped shut again, chomping at the vehicle's rear turret. Argyle shouted in fear, twisting in his seat.

Cliptok veered to the left. The *Explorer* was riding dangerously low, its loading ramp hanging open like some flying garage. Cliptok hit a snow drift, shooting them into open air. The hangtime made Argyle's stomach flipflop twice before their wheels slammed down in the *Explorer*'s cargo bay. Their momentum was too much, and the vehicle tumbled over, rolling twice before two robotic arms reached out from the ceiling amidships and locked the whole vehicle down. Before the cargo hatch sealed them in, Argyle saw the graxxon pounce angrily one final time, stumbling face-first into a snow drift. Then, he felt the ship climbing back into the stratosphere. Argylesox smiled; the Space Cadets had not left him behind.

23. CLEARING THE FOG

June 12ᵗʰ, A.D. 2352
11:27 IST

Stanik and Cliptok didn't wait for Argyle. They flung wide the doors to the POD and rushed above decks via the narrow spiral staircase in the corner of the cargo bay. Argyle chuckled to himself as he clambered out of the big bucket seat behind the vehicle's turret gun. The *Explorer*'s lone docking bot zipped over, light on its treads as it hooked a winch to the POD's bumper. Argyle ducked away so the bot could work, shaking snow from the furry flaps of his ushanka. He hung it on a peg next to the supply lockers to dry, along with his frock coat. His hosts had not stopped to remove their snow gear, so he pressed on quickly, taking the spiral stairs that twisted up to join the *Explorer*'s central hallway at midship.

Though he'd lost sight of his military detail, he was able to follow their excited voices... not to mention the trail of melting snow... into the galley. There, Stanik and Cliptok were recounting their adventure to Hank. Their boots and winter coats dripped freshly melted snow in puddles all around. Argyle stepped carefully around them to take a seat at the black granite dining table.

Argylesox pressed the DataCom's only button. In response, the device beeped a friendly tune and shined its orange wireframe menu at him. He scrolled through the list of recent files and pulled up his new prize: the third temple's reward file. He relabeled it to match the others.

"Hey, how exactly does that work?" It was Cliptok. She was leaning over Argyle's shoulder.

He blinked, looking up from the DataCom's projection. "Pardon?"

"Back there, you said the temple gave you data," she said. "How so?"

"Well," Argyle shifted, clearing his throat. It was a valid question, and not one that he had spent enough time studying. "I'm admittedly unclear on *how,* namely because it's not the focus of my research, but each temple seems to contain an energy field, and that energy field contains digital information. I've got functions programmed into the DataCom which detect and download the data. That info is scrambled when the DataCom receives it, but I've long since devised a few functions to unscramble the data and resurrect each temple's intended file. I refer to it as a 'Reward File.'

After all, this data seems to be the end result of activating each temple. Each one is a map, which the DataCom can now translate for me. That required quite a bit of work, I can tell you."

Cliptok gave him a playful nudge. "You must be good with code, then, huh?"

"Not particularly," Argyle said honestly. "That's part of why I joined up with Alaborap. I needed his help with the reward files."

"Wait a minute, you told me you were with him to gain access to clues hidden in *The Articles*," Stanik said firmly.

Argyle made sure to nod slowly and patiently. "Yes," he said, "both are true." No matter the means, he told himself, he had done it. Now, just by running a few commands, the DataCom had a set of coordinates and a 3D map of some unknown continent on an undisclosed planet. His third such map. A thrill rolled off his shoulders as he leaned over his device.

"Oh. Hello, again," Jablon said sarcastically as he strolled into the galley.

"Hello," Argyle responded politely, still swimming in his thoughts as he examined his new map. He refused to 'ego-jockey' with men like Jablon. Nor did he blame the young man for being annoyed. Stowaways were tricky business for Federation military vessels.

Jablon turned to Cliptok and Stanik, a bird with ruffled feathers. "Where have you been?"

"We found the temple," Cliptok exclaimed.

Jablon crossed his arms as the DataCom trilled in

Argyle's hands. He fumbled to mute it quickly, trying not to further aggravate the situation.

'Rendering complete,' the DataCom's readout reported. 'Multiple options found.'

"Oh," Argyle murmured aloud, "well, that complicates things." He couldn't help himself. He hadn't encountered this issue yet, though he suspected he would eventually.

"What is it," Stanik leaned in, studying the DataCom's projections. He motioned for Argyle to set it back on the dining table to share with them. Argyle obliged.

"The maps I've retrieved from the temples are over sixty million years old," he explained to the Cadets, "meaning the continents on these planets have no doubt changed significantly. So, when I retrieve one of these maps, I have the DataCom programmed to cross-reference the map with life-bearing planets. It runs projections for the shifting of tectonic plates and recorded weather erosion to scan for potential matches. So far, my calculations have been spot-on... only one result per map. But this map has two potential matches. Zebulon 5[52]... or Nabdok 731."

"Unfortunately for us, you can't just stop and ask directions," Jablon sassed, adding an insincere shrug.

Argyle met his challenging gaze with a raised eyebrow. An uncomfortable silence hung in the room for

---

[52] **Zebulon 5** /zɛˈbjuːlɔːn/ – the fourth planet in the Zebu system, Zebulon 5 is the only life-bearing planet orbiting the star **Zebu** /zɛˈbuː/.

a beat, until Argyle realized Jablon was wrong… again. He *could* stop and ask for directions because Pontiac Jones was on Zebulon 5! "You, sir, are brilliant," Argyle said, waggling his index finger at Jablon. "I need to go to Zebulon 5!"

"The furthest we're taking you is Smith's Pointe," Jablon said sharply.

"Jablon, we're going to Zebulon 5," Stanik commanded, his shoulders back.

"What?" Jablon's patience snapped, his voice cracking with his question. "Have you lost your mind?"

"No. There's something to all this," Stanik said. "Understanding the mystery behind the Goliathon would make our mission historic. It's a worthy discovery for this team."

"Oh, please," Jablon shot back.

"Look," Stanik said intensely, "a lot of this is weird. To be honest, I don't know what to believe, but I do know this; we were just inside a temple. The whole thing was like– like biotech or something. It was a whole dome of crystal stones, and they were generating their own electricity. There was no apparent source for it. That was very real. Cliptok and I both saw it."

"Can confirm," the gunner interjected.

Stanik kept pressing. "Whatever's at the end of this trail Argyle's on, it's potentially dangerous." The captain paused, lowering his voice as if confiding in them all. "We all know Alaborap's chasing this thing, too," he warned. "We have to help Argyle."

Jablon shook his head. "We can't just desert our

mission because you're hoping to snare Alaborap!"

"Jablon, it's out there," Cliptok argued. Apparently, he'd made a believer out of her. Argyle kept his mouth shut. It would be a breach of etiquette to get involved.

Jablon snorted, pushing away from the table. Stanik stepped up to challenge his growing insubordination. "Do I need to make it a direct order?" Argyle saw Stanik raise an eyebrow. He was threatening his pilot. Jablon stared him down, but his cheeks bloomed. He was clearly rattled by Walt's confrontation.

"They do have the map," Hank offered gently. It seemed to diffuse the tension.

Jablon groaned, rubbing his forehead. "Fine," he sighed, slowly. "I'm in." He turned to Argylesox and huffed. "Are you sure it's on Zebulon 5?"

X   X   X

June 13, A.D. 2352
23:58 IST

A crack of lightning cut across the gustful grey skies of Zebulon 5. The spring rains poured down on Argyle and his companions, drumming the planet's vast and mighty conifer forests. A dense fog hung low in the valley beneath them, shrouding their destination below.

The Cadets had landed the *Explorer* in the Grod River, which ran through the Great Plateau, a sprawling shelf of land that cut the continent in two. They were on the plateau's ledge, preparing to rappel down the smooth white rock face. The region they were traveling through didn't have a winter with snow, instead it was subject to torrential downpours and excessive flooding in spring. Prepared as they were with fine equipment, Argyle wasn't confident enough to navigate the lowland bogs this time of year. Instead, they had hiked to their destination atop the plateau.

Their intention was to drop in on the outskirts of the campsite Argyle needed to locate, avoiding the marshlands altogether. Perhaps he would have risked it if they'd still had access to the POD. Unfortunately, the vehicle was banged up in the Graxxon escape, so it was out of commission. The Cadets were stuck covering the distance from the Grod River to the plateau's edge on foot. It was a mild hike at best, Argyle reasoned, especially for soldiers, but Captain Stanik had ordered them all to a six-hour rest once the ship was anchored. It had been a wise choice, especially considering the elements. Rain and cold had battered them from the moment they stepped foot on the planet's surface.

The smell of happy wet pines whirled through the wind and rain, cracking a smile across Argyle's face as they trudged southeast to the edge of the plateau. Stanik and Cliptok ignored the elements, pressing on as Zebulon 5 squished under the tread of their boots. Hank slithered comfortably across the grass, his derma glistening with moisture. He carried his animatronic legs over his shoulder, folded neatly into a pack, his humidity helmet clipped to the side. His sonar even purred a little as he slid next to Argyle and inquired about the weather. Argyle was happy to oblige, sharing what he could before they found the plateau's ledge.

There, Argyle clapped his hands together, flinging rainwater from the tips of his fingers. "From here, we have to climb down," he informed his friends.

Cliptok swung her pack off her back and worked to unzip it, retrieving several climbing winches along with carabiners, hooks and rope. The climbing winches were military tech. Argyle took one of the sleek metal cannisters and fit it over his climbing lines. The device would lower him automatically via a series of rubber buttons, allowing him to control his descent.

The Cadets worked as a team to get everyone dangling over the sheer, smooth side of the plateau. Dangling against the bare cliff, the wind kicked up. Rainwater swirled up along the rock wall, pummeling them with blasts of whistling wind.

Jablon drooped, frowning like a wet cat as he turned his shoulder against a surge of driving rain. "Are you *sure* we should be on Zebulon 5," he shouted.

"No," Argyle hollered back cheerfully as he slid over the edge, tugging on his line. Cliptok had outfitted him with a spare set of gear from the ship's inventory. He kicked gently away from the white rockface, focusing his attention on the task so as not to be distracted by Jablon's negativity. Light-heartedness was the best way to counter a critic. "This is process of elimination, really. I'm sorry! At least here I can ask directions."

"From who," Jablon barked.

ZEBULON 5

PLANET: ZEBULON 5
SECTOR VIEW: OGGLADONIA

Lantern Light
Swamp

The Great
Plateau

Explorer
Landing

North Rock
Tunnel

Grod
River

Oggladon
Mining Camp

Paw Print
Lakes

0   5   10   15   20

"The Oggladons[53]," Argyle said.

The Oggladons were a simple species, foragers underground, and they had a gentle, supportive society. His father and Pontiac used to pay visits to them when Argyle was a teenager. His father had charted much of the planet's natural history... and Pontiac had made the whiskey. Whenever the Zebulon system came up, it reminded him of Pontiac, and whether by fate or chance or dumb luck, he'd heard not long ago of some old prospector selling the 'finest whiskey in the Free Worlds.' That could only be Pontiac Jones.

Pontiac was an accomplished frontiersman; a loner who preferred to lie low and live off the land, no matter which star that land was orbiting. He'd trained in the Piracy Prosecution Program at the height of its success, and somehow his undercover ISF status was still completely unknown in the Outer Rim worlds. And, most importantly, he was an old family friend. He had started out as hired gun and research companion for Argyle's father, Cotton. A great outdoorsman himself, David 'Cotton' Sox was and always had been Argyle's intellectual role model.

The wanderlust was from his mother's side. The Cliptorgian side. She had trained as a pilot in the ISF, and during her service, she took an interest in celestial meteorology. Her ideas were the result of years making observations at the helm of a starship. She made the career shift into science, met Argyle's father on a

---

[53] Oggladon /ˈɑɡlədɑn/ – keep reading to learn more.

research project, and the rest was family history. His father spent his days ranging over life-bearing planetary frontiers while his mother was in orbit, conducting her studies from their research vessel. Argyle remembered two smart, young people who seemed very much in love. His mother coined the 'Cotton' nickname as a loving riff on their surname, and his father had laborious metaphors comparing his wife to a guardian angel because she was up in orbit during his field work, ready to swoop in if he had an emergency.

Unfortunately, the angel's wings proved waxen one day when Argyle was no more than seven years old. They had been on Hierrnaus when they lost her. She'd dropped them on Oberon[54] for a two-day father-son walkabout. Her climb into orbit was cut short by a faulty booster rocket. They had watched the resulting black smoke streak across the sky just before nightfall.

Losing Argyle's mother sent his father spiraling. They quickly discovered how disorganized his father was without a research partner. The man would forget supplies, forget how to use his tech instruments, and he'd grow frustrated and blame his shortcomings on Argyle's inexperience. Tensions boiled over when Argyle tried to throw hands with his father at the tender age of nine. Within a week, his father hired Pontiac Jones as an expedition leader. "What we really need is someone else who can tackle the survival stuff," his father had

---

[54] **Oberon** – a smaller, sparsely settled continent just south of the equator on Hierrnaus.

informed him excitedly. "This will be a learning experience for both of us. I always let your mother handle those things, so I don't know what I'm doing. And you are far too young to handle those details. I can't be upset with you. From now on, I'll be hiring someone to handle that." That someone ended up being Pontiac Jones. The grizzled frontiersman wasn't just an excellent addition to their expeditions; he proved to be the balance their father-son relationship needed to keep tempers cool.

For seven grand years, Argyle had spent his adolescence rough-and-tumbling through every unknown corner of the known worlds with two capable survivalists. That all ended after Argyle turned sixteen, when his father passed from complications brought on after an untimely stroke. It was, in Argyle's mind, a dumb way for such a daring man to meet his end.

Before the end of his days, Cotton Sox had charted most of the Outer Rim, categorizing nearly three hundred new species of animal life. He did half of that groundbreaking work with Argyle and Pontiac in tow, and the three men formed a fraternity together. Pontiac stepped in to see that Argyle got up on his own two feet, suggested certain methods for monetizing Argyle's survival skills, which he'd practically honed since birth. Pontiac was good at making a buck, and he hired Argyle for all sorts of wild schemes. Hell, that credit helped Argyle refurbish their old ship, the *Demon Stork*, and get it space-worthy again. Once Argyle was in his mid-twenties, he and Pontiac went off and had their own adventures, crossing paths not once in well over a decade. But then, before joining up with the Stingrays, Argyle had tried to hire Pontiac to help him with the Goliathon. They'd gone to the Heiznaus temple site together, but when Pontiac realized what Argyle was chasing, he refused to accept any more job offers. Hopefully Pontiac wasn't still sore about all that nonsense.

Suddenly, Argyle felt solid rock beneath his feet. They had reached the base of the plateau. Argyle detached from his climbing rig and offered help to the others as they descended around him. Jablon's eyes kept darting back up the façade of white rock. Argyle suspected he was concerning himself with the empty *Explorer*, anchored in the river on the plateau above.

"The ship should be fine," Argyle noted, hoping his reassurance would subdue the pilot's fretting. With that, he took the lead, moving them slowly northeast. He squinted through the driving rain as he edged along the base of the plateau. "Watch your step," he warned over his shoulder, "and try to take steps on rock. These lowlands get marshy, and we run the risk of falling into a bog. Have any of you ever experienced the moors of England... on Earth?" He assumed they knew where England was, but he was used to clarifying. They all shook their heads. "Well then, never mind. But I can assure you, the ground here is very similar. Lots more trees, of course. I'm speaking of the boggy terrain."

Argyle worked his way along the sheer, smooth rock of the plateau, stepping only where there was rock until he spotted the warm glow of a soft light through the heavy fog. Pointing to it, Argle held a finger to his lips, signaling for the Cadets to stay quiet. They crept up next to him as the scraping sound of someone shoveling dirt drifted to them across the willowy, grey mist.

"No sudden movements," Argyle whispered. "Just follow my lead."

The fog rolled away as he eased the group forward, revealing the source of the light. A lantern came into clear view, hanging in a three-meter-wide cave dug out of the base of the white cliffs. The light source swung gently as flurries of khaki-colored soil cascaded past it. Argyle cleared his throat and uttered the Oggladonian whinny for 'Excuse me.'

To the others, he was sure he sounded like a buffoon, imitating horse grunts and snuffles. They would understand soon enough. In the burrow, something honked and grunted in response. That honk was actually a hardy, "Who's there?" posed by the Oggladon. The unseen creature grunted as it turned around in its burrow.

Argyle hesitated. He was unclear how to ask his next question. He also couldn't remember how to say his name properly in their language. Instead, he clicked and whinnied at a different pitch, forming the sounds for, "Forgive me, we are outsiders. I squawk bad." Close enough.

A snort and a high-pitched neigh replied for them to stay where they were. Argyle let his shoulders relax before the Oggladon poked its head out of the tunnel, covered in a thick layer of dust and cobwebs.

Most Federalists had never seen an Oggladon, and Argyle marveled at what they were thinking as the equine-like being emerged from the dark, batting its friendly green eyes. The creature was full-grown, standing nearly two and a half meters tall from head to hooves. Its hide was a rich walnut brown, shaggy and scattered with clumpy balls of grime.

Argyle caught Jablon gawking at the alien. It used the thin, muscular forelimbs that grew on either side of its mouth to remove a leather miner's cap from its head. His father had described these as mandibles, as they were short and had limited function compared to other species. Regardless of the limitations, each forearm had two dexterous fingers and one opposable thumb: evolution's greatest treasure.

The Oggladon dipped its head low in a bow. Then, it bent its front legs low. Doing so revealed its bumpy pink tadpole tail to the Cadets. The Oggladon must have been around forty years old, Argyle estimated. He based this on the number of callouses that speckled the being's torso and neck. The more patches of hair had worn away and calloused, the longer the creature had been working in the mines.

"That gesture is a formal greeting," Argyle informed his companions with a smile. He bowed and snorted to the Oggladon. Once that ritual was complete, the Oggladon spoke again. 'Welcome; I am Grunt," she used a feminine form of the pronoun 'I,' which is how her gender was revealed for Argyle. She whinnied and clicked again. Argyle worked the translation as quickly as he could. 'We have a troupe elder who can speak like you.' She meant in English. Pontiac had taught the Oggladon troupe elders enough English to help them negotiation with the ISF. They always had at least one fluent, English-speaking Oggladon on the continent.

Argyle snuffled excitedly, then added a click for emphasis. He hoped he had used an exclamation that simply meant 'I'm excited,' but Grunt's short snort of a laugh suggested he had accidently said, 'I'm flatulent.' The two snuffles were horribly similar.

Grunt led them into the forest along a well-worn trail amidst the towering pines. The Cadets stared at Argyle as he made horse noises to the Oggladon. To try and diffuse their incredulity, he decided to share what he knew of these wonderful creatures.

Argyle excused himself from Grunt's side, falling into step with the Cadets. "The Oggladons are natural miners," he said eagerly. "Their primary nourishment is a species of grub called vron[55] that can only be found deep below the planet's surface. This whole continent is no doubt riddled with mines dug by Grunt's troupe."

Jablon scoffed. "His name is Grunt?"

"Roughly translated, yes, *her* name is Grunt." Argyle nodded pointedly, looking down the bridge of his nose.

Cliptok grinned. "And where is *she* taking us?" She jabbed Jablon with her elbow as she asked the question.

"To the Oggladon mining camp!" Argyle winked at

---

[55] **vron** /vɹɑn/ – keep reading to learn more.

the Cadets. "Excuse me, will you," he asked. "I believe we're getting close."

Captain Stanik gave him a nod of approval, and Argylesox jogged up next to Grunt again. He attempted the customary Oggladonian phrase, "Tell me about yourself." Not only was this considered polite in their culture, but it also distracted Argyle. Let the Cadets placate their pilot, he told himself. That wasn't his responsibility, thank goodness.

OGGLADONS & VRON

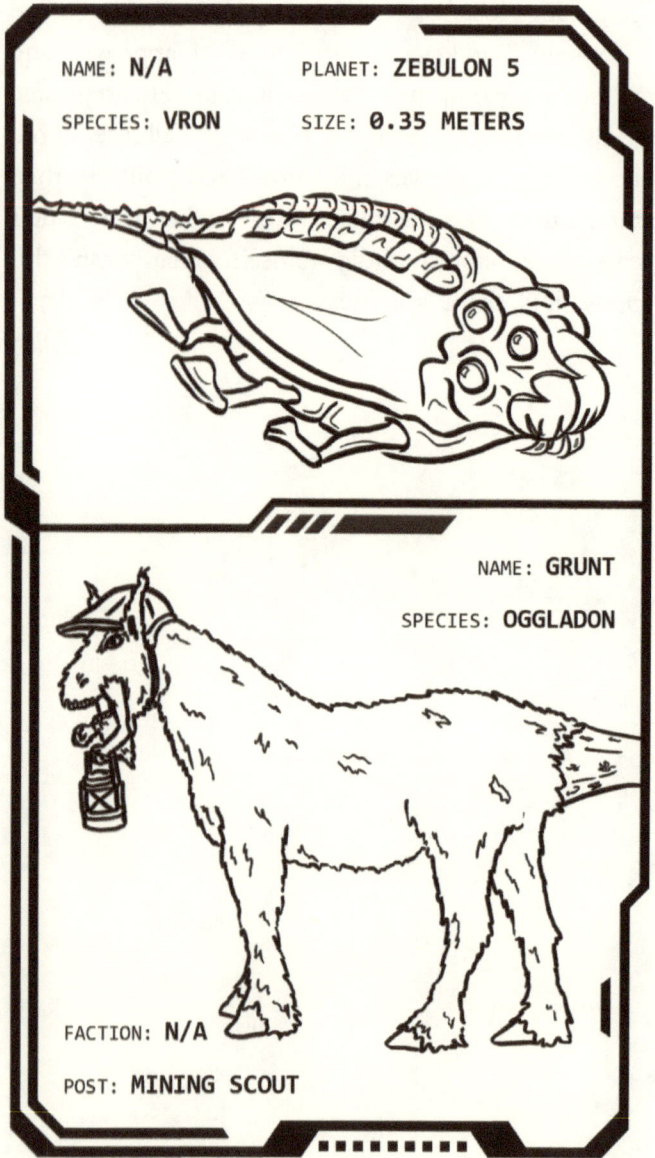

NAME: **N/A**

SPECIES: **VRON**

PLANET: **ZEBULON 5**

SIZE: **0.35 METERS**

NAME: **GRUNT**

SPECIES: **OGGLADON**

FACTION: **N/A**

POST: **MINING SCOUT**

24. MINES BENEATH THE PINES

June 14, A.D. 2352
01:44 IST

The Cadets followed Argyle and Grunt into a muddy clearing. Stanik held back, pulling aside a thorny bramble to allow his crew ahead of him.

Jablon gagged as he stepped into the clearing. "What's that smell," he groaned. Despite the fresh, chilly air and the zest of wet pine, the small clearing they'd stepped into seemed poisoned with the fecal reek of barnyard manure. The source of the smell became evident as their party passed by a narrow trench dug into the ground at the other end of the clearing. There, mounds of feces were soaking up the rain and fouling up the air. Stanik assumed it was an Oggladon latrine.

"Well, no wonder it smells like shit," Jablon scoffed.

Argyle shot an aggravated look back at them.

"That's enough," Stanik warned him. Fortunately, Stanik suspected that Grunt did not understand English, otherwise the alien creature might have taken offense. As happy as he was to have his best friend on his crew, Stanik had to admit that he'd created a challenge for himself when he ignored Southerland's advice. His friends kept him in check, but he wasn't confident that was reciprocal.

Grunt guided them to a mound of boulders that had toppled from the plateau's edge. The Oggladon stepped up to a tangle of red, leafy vines that cascaded over the stack of jagged rocks. She ducked her head, using her neck to pull aside the thick red curtain of foliage. It revealed a tunnel. Stanik ducked under the ruby vegetation, stepped through the short tunnel of rock, and gasped at the view as he stepped out into the rain again.

Before him, nestled at the base of the white cliffs, an Oggladon settlement wallowed in the khaki-and-butterscotch-streaked mud of Zebulon 5. Lichen and moss clung to the soggy timber of every rickety building. Situated in a three-acre clearing amidst the towering pine trees, the village was comprised of rickety lean-tos, pavilions, and cabins, all organized around a grand longhouse at the center of everything. The open structures covered deep wallows in the ground, and everything was made of roughly cut timbers. There were clear trafficways woven through the town, where the mud was freshly trodden with scattered hoofprints.

Grunt led the way through camp. Stanik noticed she

was guiding them to the center building, which gave the impression of a town hall. It was made of felled conifers, and moss grew happily up its bark-encrusted sides, which made it look as if it had risen out of the planet's crust.

To his left, Stanik counted five caverns dug into the base of the cliffs. In the mouth of the nearest one, he spotted a wooden mining cart filled with squirming baby blue footballs. Stanik smiled to himself. There was something he hadn't thought about since he left home. He'd played for his high school team, the Juneau Huskies, for two years. He'd loved every minute of it, but they lost his grandfather during the winter of his junior year, and, after the funeral expenses, Stanik had to pick up a part-time job to help the household. That was also about the time he got serious with his education, improving his grades enough to qualify for military service. Sports were extracurricular, and new recruits didn't have time for extracurriculars, especially those who sought a post aboard a starship.

Stanik frowned, shaken from his nostalgia as one of the blue footballs in the cart rolled over, revealing a pincer-like mouth and an unsettling number of vacuous black eyes. The squirming blue footballs were alive. With this realization, Stanik spotted an Oggladon exiting one of the mining caverns. It pushed a minecart ahead of it, the gondola brimming with wriggling blue football bugs. Was that why they had the mining operation?

Grunt pranced up to the longhouse and swung wide a creaking wooden door as wide as a gate. They followed her inside, where Stanik found himself in the middle of a spacious, single-room structure. A bonfire roared at the center of the room, its flames dancing at least three meters high. His eyes adjusted, and Stanik saw that the center of the roof extended up in a short, hollow column. Smoke and embers rushed to escape the building through slats under the capped, chimney-like extension.

Stanik stepped close to the big fire, rubbing his hands as the orange flames provided relief from the damp and dreary elements outside. Grunt was whinnying and clicking at two Oggladons who sat roasting the blue football critters on metal skewers a few meters away. Grunt turned and bared her teeth at the Cadets in a poor attempt to smile. She rolled a log up to the fire for them to sit on. Argyle bowed to Grunt in thanks, and the bipedal outsiders all sat. Stanik was sure to offer a nod of acknowledgement to the other two Oggladons in the room as he did.

Picking up on Stanik's cue, Jablon waved awkwardly. Good. Stanik appreciated his friend's attempt at respect. Grunt plopped her bottom on the ground, propping herself up on skinny legs. She reached into the crate next to her and snatched up one of the blue critters with her mandible hands. Stanik was fascinated. He had not considered interacting with transient quadrupeds. It was a difficult adjustment, but it was important not to let such physical differences become barriers to conscientious allyship and understanding.

Argyle nodded as Grunt snorted something to him, then he leaned over to Stanik and the Cadets, twirling his mustache. "Grunt says Hinny here is the Oggladon troupe leader. And he speaks English." Argyle nodded to the larger, greyer of the other two Oggladons at the fire. "Is that right, Hinny?" He raised his voice for the aural benefit of the alien.

With a cough, the larger, greyer Oggladon sitting opposite them bobbed his head. "Yes," he nodded, tasting his words for a moment. "I spake de' Anglish." There was a nasally honking to the Oggladon's voice, but it stirred with a bassline rumble from his broad chest.

The Oggladons were magnificent, Stanik thought. No amount of textbook reading could have prepared him to meet these creatures in the flesh. "How do you know English," the captain blurted out incredulously.

"He has a damn good teacher," said a gravelly-voiced man behind them. Stanik turned to see who this newcomer was with the rich Appalachian drawl.

"Ah, yes," Hinny gestured with his mandible hands, "this is Po–"

"Pontiac Jones," Argyle cheered, hopping to his feet. "I was hoping you'd still be out here."

"Of course, I am," Pontiac said. "What're you up to? You look like hell."

25. WHISKEY REBEL

June 14, A.D. 2352
02:18 IST

"Well, I was here to ask for help, actually," Argyle explained.

"No shit," Pontiac grunted.

"Yes," Argyle's voice quavered with uncertainty. "And these are my... uh, well... colleagues? I suppose. Pontiac Jones, meet the Space Cadets."

At the introduction, Stanik gave a nod and stood, ready to extend his hand. Pontiac did not step closer. He lingered there between them and the exit a moment. "A pleasure," he said, tipping his wide-brimmed hat to them.

Stanik wasn't quite sure how to regard old Pontiac Jones. He was a burly man with a bushy black beard and a voice like gravel. He was dressed like a nineteenth century frontiersman, complete with the leather boots and gambler hat. He was carrying two small rodent carcasses, slung casually over his shoulder. It took Stanik a moment to realize that underneath Pontiac's khaki cattleman's jacket, he wore a ratty black Hawaiian shirt covered in pink and orange flowers.

"Hinny here'll make sure yer' properly fed," Pontiac offered. "Don't mind me; I don't have the stomach for those damn bugs, so I'm left ta' scrounge for vermin."

"Pontiac have no taste in good food," Hinny lamented. Stanik sensed it was an old argument between friends. "Come," Hinny said confidently, "try Vron. Try it!"

"Oh, don't mind if I do," Argyle chimed in, wiggling his fingers with anticipation. Hinny ripped the thorax of his Vron apart and extended it to Argyle, who delightedly scooped the blue shell from Hinny's hand. He ripped a strip of steaming white meat from the blue shell and slurped it down.

"I'll try it," Cliptok said, politely extending her hand. Argyle handed her his helping, and she plucked a modest bite from it.

As she bit down, the bug meat crunched between her teeth. The sound was sickening to Stanik, and he noticed Cliptok discretely gag. She tried to swallow a bit of it, covering her mouth with her hand. Stanik tried not to wince.

Grunt whinnied at her.

"Grunt vonders dat you do not like da Vron," Hinny translated eagerly.

Cliptok swallowed the rest of the bug meat. "Oh, no," she lied politely. "It's good. It's just... different." She managed to drag the word 'different' out into four or five syllables.

Grunt honked and whistled, her back leg tapping the ground as she did. Stanik smirked. She seemed to be laughing.

"Grunt says she no like your food neither," Hinny said, punctuating the statement with a little laugh-honk of his own.

Argyle and the Cadets joined in, as did the other Oggladon at the fire. When the moment had passed and silence settled in again, Hinny leaned in close, giving Argylesox a stern once-over.

"So, you are here vhy?" Hinny's discerning stare was calm but expectant. Stanik felt an earnest pressure to be open and honest with the Oggladon elder. He found the alien's demeanor endearing, right down to the crow's feet wrinkling the corners of its big, hazel-green eyes.

Stanik cleared his throat. "We're here to help Argyle," he said with a quick nod. He didn't intend to pass the buck but felt it best that Argyle address the question. After all, it was his idea to visit.

Argyle didn't seem bothered. "We're trying to find a temple," he told Hinny. "Humming, glowing pink rocks... or dangerous traps in old stone structures? Have your troupe members encountered anything like this?"

"Damn it all to hell," Pontiac interrupted. "I shoulda known you were still chasing that old myth." The frontiersman rolled his eyes before cracking open a flask. Argyle hesitated a beat too long. "I know that face... you damn well are! Yer' daddy must be rolling in his grave."

"Is that whiskey I smell on your breath, Pontiac," Argyle challenged. "You're not out here disregarding interplanetary treaties, now, are you?"

Pontiac's face flushed red with embarrassment. "Don't play that game with me. We've both got plenty of bad habits."

Argyle nodded patiently. "We do. So let sleeping dogs lie. Don't get on me about my research. Just talk to me. I need your help, old friend."

"Sure. Fine. Hey, y'know, you're right. What do you need? I'm listening."

"Do you still have the *Stork*," Argyle asked the older man cautiously. Stanik had studied Outer Rim slang as a part of his extended education. He recalled that lots of people on the frontier planets called their ships 'birds.' Stanik guessed that's what 'the Stork' was. Besides, there was no reason for Pontiac to have a Terran bird with him. "I'd like you to give it back now," Argyle continued.

"No way in hell. I saw that ride you came in on."

"That's the Space Cadets' ship," Argyle explained. "I was... err... detained and—"

"He's a stowaway," Jablon chimed in impatiently.

"But not intentionally," Argyle clarified.

"Look, I told you once, I'll tell ya again," Pontiac interrupted before they could start bickering. "If I let you use that ship to go chasing yer' damned conspiracies, your daddy would haunt me 'til Kingdom come!"

"I'm surprised he's not haunting you already! He hated letting you anywhere near that bird when you were sauced," Argyle snapped.

At that, Pontiac sighed heavily. "I ain't giving that ship back… but I'll tell ya what I know." Stanik was right; this was about a ship. Pontiac turned to the English-speaking Oggladon. "Hinny, you remember where the old mines collapsed?"

Hinny nodded emphatically.

"Argyle wants to see the fire rocks," Pontiac said.

Argyle sat up straight. "Fire rocks? What does that mean?"

Pontiac raised a hand, signaling Argyle to keep calm. "There's an old mine shaft a few-hours' hike from camp. I've seen a few shards of that pink crystal, same as we saw on Heiznaus."

Hank and Cliptok gasped, nearly in unison. Argyle laughed, stammering before he finally blurted out, "that's fantastic!" He leaned over to Stanik and whispered, "I swear, you Space Cadets are my good luck charm!" Stanik couldn't help but smile.

"I vill not go dere," Hinny said. The Oggladon shook his head and snorted. "For long time, my kin were getting hurt. Is dangerous place."

"I helped raise this one," Pontiac said proudly, stroking his beard. "He can handle himself."

"No," Hinny said gravely.

"Well," Jablon said, clapping his hands on his knees. "Argyle's all set, so we really should be going–"

"Jablon," Stanik warned.

"What? Argyle has help here, and here's where he needs to be! We still have a mission that does not inv–"

"Hold your tongue soldier," Stanik said sharply. "That's an order."

Jablon slouched, making himself small from his spot on the log.

"Hinny, c'mon," Pontiac spoke over the Cadets, "No one knows those old mines like you. If you took 'em right now, I bet you'd be back by sundown. Won't take more'n a couple hours for them to poke around." Pontiac looked to Argyle for confirmation.

"That's right," Argyle nodded emphatically.

"Plus," Pontiac paused, taking a swig from his flask, "you can scout for Vron nests while you're down there."

Hinny raised a shaggy eyebrow. "You have news?"

"My scout team up on the plateau sent word yesterday. They say the ground is real soft above North Rock Tunnel. Lots of bahgwalla[56] chutes, too."

Hinny snorted, his nostrils flexing like eyebrows. With another snort, Hinny hefted his wide hips up off the soil. "I vill do dis," he said. "Is you ready now?"

Argyle glanced considerately at the Cadets. Stanik jutted his chin confidently and nodded. Argyle smiled. "Yes. Yes, I believe we are! Thank you, Hinny."

"Come along," Hinny instructed with a snuffle. "You follow me. Is short valk. Ve must heads to Nord Rock Tunnel." Before he led them on, Hinny stretched

---

[56] **bahgwalla** /bæg'wæɫæ/ **chutes** – a wild reed indigenous to Zebulon 5 which only grows in patches of loose, well-aerated soil.

his bumpy tail out, shaking off some dirt before ducking out of the shelter. "Pontiac," the Oggladon groaned through his thick accent, "if ve are not beck by sundown, bring de troupe guard and come find us."

The frontiersman nodded, patting his quadrupedal friend on the haunches. "As always, you have my word, Hinny. But you'll be just fine with these folks."

Stanik ushered his crew out behind Hinny, then followed them as Argyle hung back in the doorway with Pontiac. From the corner of his eye, Stanik saw Argyle clasp Pontiac's hand firmly. "Thank you," he said sincerely.

Pontiac grinned. "Don't mention it."

"Good to see you." Argyle said. He offered a smile before he jogged out to the group. Hinny was trotting ahead of them, headed into the pine forests.

Pontiac waved goodbye from the longhouse. "When ya get back, we'll all have drinks on me," he called after them.

X   X   X

June 14, A.D. 2352
23:12 IST

There was no conversation as the Cadets kept pace behind Hinny, who gingerly pranced around the increasingly steep terrain. Stanik had been relying on Argylesox to fertilize the polite banter with these creatures, but he seemed quiet as he toyed with the settings on his DataCom. After ten minutes spent deep in the sounds of the afternoon pine barrens, Jablon shattered the calm.

"How much further," the pilot called out as they clambered up a stack of boulders gathered at the base of the white cliffs.

"Not far. Keep moving," Hinny called back down to him from the top of the boulders. If the Oggladon was annoyed, he hid it well.

"Hinny, when did you first discover the fire rocks," Argyle wondered, glancing up from his DataCom projection, which glowed like a torch in the dreary rain.

"Oh, long ago. Long ago. Vhen I vas small, all us little ones vould go dere to be bravest." He tipped his head to one side. "Argyle?"

"Yes?"

Hinny made a series of honks and whinnies in Oggladonian speech. Argyle snorted something back, and Hinny bobbed his head in agreement.

"Once," Argyle interpreted, "when Hinny here was just a colt, one of his older cousins accepted a dare to dig down and retrieve one of the rocks. Naturally, Hinny and the other children gathered to serve as eager witnesses."

"What happened," Hank asked.

"De tunnels closed in around him, gloweeng angry like a rash in the ground…" Hinny came to a dramatic halt. He turned to them, his hazel pupils severe and wide as he raised an eyebrow of warning to them. "He died… so be most careful."

With that, Hinny rolled a human-sized boulder aside to reveal the partially collapsed mouth of a cave. "Here," he said to them, "Nord' Rock Tunnel. Inside. Come, 've are close. Inside old tunnel." Hinny's little mandible hand reached for a rusty lantern hanging in the mouth of the cavern and lifted it off its hook. Lighting the rusty old thing, Hinny led them inside.

They went forty paces or so before Hinny halted, his mangy haunches wobbling in front of Stanik and the group. The Oggladon shimmied around so he could face them in the narrow space. He pointed to a small hole burrowed into the cave floor near their feet "Dis hole, here. You go down. Is tiny, but you vill fit, I think." Then, prancing at some shattered pink stone shards, he added sadly, "I vould dig for you, but dere are fire rocks. So, I vait here for you." He bared his incisors at them, a very horse-like attempt at smiling.

Argyle sidestepped the pink stone. He crouched, scanning the shard of stone with the DataCom. "No good," he said to himself. He plucked the specimen from the soil and sealed it in a little sample case. "I'll lead the way down," he reassured them. He swung his legs into the burrow-like hole, then shifted his weight onto his hands so he could dangle his legs straight in. The eccentric privateer smirked. "Wish me luck," he said. "And think small thoughts." With that, he took a few big exhales and slipped down through the narrow hole. Stanik watched as Argyle's bandana disappeared into the subterranean void.

After only a moment, Argyle called up to them. "There's a ledge down here, and a much deeper cavern below. Come down one at a time... then have Hinny lower your packs down."

Stanik nodded to Cliptok and Jablon, who both unstrapped their gear and set it next to the hole. Hank shrugged and slipped in the burrow tail-first. Hulgarians had a slightly smaller frame than a Terran or Cliptorgian. Proportionally, when they were provided a pair of legs, the natural height of a Hulgarian was just over a meter and a half. Hank was lean, his body slender with muscle, so he slipped right through as soon as he folded up his winglike arms.

After Hank disappeared, Stanik heard Argyle yelp. Then, both explorers started laughing. "I deserve that for not getting out from under there," Argyle said between their chuckles.

"Heads up," Cliptok warned them. She shimmied down the hole. Jablon required Stanik's assistance. He was a thick man, and he got stuck at the chest. His bust was broader than the opening, but Stanik had him raise his arms over his head and then helped push him through.

Before his turn, Stanik decided to pass the supply packs down himself. He'd noticed Hinny pawing nervously at the dirt, and he didn't want to ask anything more of the Oggladon elder.

Stanik handed the last pack down to Cliptok. "Got it," she said. "All clear and ready for you," she said.

Stanik sucked in a deep breath, holding his belly and chest in, and he slipped through the narrow cavity.

Cliptok had a flare lit, holding it over her head for a moment before she tossed it over the ledge. They watched it tumble further than ten meters down before Stanik saw it ricochet off a dome of stone.

"Oh, yeah," Cliptok confirmed playfully, "Break out the climbing gear, boys." She grabbed her pack from the pile and worked to unravel her bundle of rope, spikes, and clips.

"Here," Jablon said, kneeling close to the ledge, "give me the rigging hooks." Stanik was pleased to see him pitching in. The extra wilderness training they'd had for the job was always Jablon's favorite part.

They set to work securing the hooks and dropping lines before they helped Argyle ease over the edge. Stanik nodded for Jablon to follow next. Stanik watched Jablon and Argyle as they rappelled carefully. After they were a good four meters down, Stanik went next. He wanted to be close by when Jablon realized just how real Argyle's stories were.

They descended in darkness for a good stretch of time before Stanik spotted the flickering red light from Cliptok's fizzling flare. The hellish light shined through the temple's crystalline stones, but the stones themselves were dark, bereft of energy. The flare had fallen through a gaping hole where part of the structure had caved in on itself.

Argyle used his legs to maneuver himself into the temple through the hole. He stopped his descent and locked his line so that he dangled above the room. It appeared nearly identical to the temple they'd explored on Mynaus, save for the damage.

Cliptok and Hank dropped in last, and Hank gasped

in awe. "Hey Hank," Jablon said, swinging his light around. He pointed to the lone statue of a Candalonian ready to pounce, all its claws extended for a kill. "Check this guy out," the pilot said playfully, pointing at the stone-carved predator.

Dangling in the center, Argyle scanned the fragmented stones with his DataCom. "I'm not getting an energy reading from this temple," Argyle said. "But if the temple's dead, there's no way to get our next clue." Argyle rotated ever so slightly as he sat in his climbing harness. "Think. Think. Think," he muttered to himself. "There was pink stone above, so maybe... no, no, no. That's probably not part of the temple. It was more likely one of the tests or traps." He waved the DataCom around slowly for a moment. "Is there no way to make the uplink?"

Stanik retracted his line, drawing closer to the ceiling. He reached out to the iconography of a Candalonian and brushed away the years of grime. A rosy spark jolted from the hagron on his fingertips into the temple stone. The spark zapped him, and he jerked away.

"Argyle," Stanik called out. He inspected his hand for burns or singe marks, but there were none. On the temple stone, the hieroglyphs shuddered to life. The simple silhouettes depicted Candalonians bowing before bright rays of light, surrounded by swaying palms.

Argyle retracted his line until he was hanging next to Stanik. "Oh, thank goodness! There may be enough here..." Argyle lifted the DataCom out and two crackling bolts sizzled from the stone to the spark tip of the DataCom. The device hummed in Argyle's hand, then beeped successfully. "Just enough," Argyle cheered.

Next to them, Stanik felt a pulse as Hank flexed his sonar momentarily. The navigator was silently awestruck, feeling the stones, tracing the structure with his eyes. Below them, Jablon panned the room, his legs dangling like a child. "This is unreal," he chuckled. "I'm sorry I doubted you, Argyle! Just... *wow!*" His glee was cut off as Hinny's growls echoed down to them.

"Argyle?" the Oggladon cried out. He sounded so far away. Argyle shushed the Cadets and listened in silence. "Stay back," Hinny barked. "Argyle," he pleaded. Gunshots rang out, shattering the party's mounting mirth with a cry of agony and a hefty thud. The Cadets stared at each other in disbelief. Had Hinny just been killed? Did the Oggladons have guns? Argyle simply bowed his head.

"Argylesox?" A deep, authoritative voice hollered, firing contempt with every syllable. The hairs on Stanik's neck prickled, firing goose pimples down his arms. He'd know that voice anywhere: Captain Alaborap.

Suddenly, Hank's line was yanked, and the Hulgarian wriggled like a fish on a line. Two more tugs, and he was pulled up out of sight. Argyle's line wrenched next. He reached out and grabbed Stanik's hand. Walt felt Argyle plant the DataCom firmly in his palm. "Get there first," he pleaded. The twinkle in his eyes dwindled like a struggling flame. Before Stanik could respond, Argyle was hoisted away from the group.

26. NORTH ROCK TUNNEL

June 14, A.D. 2352
05:13 IST

Up on the ledge, two familiar Stingrays shoved Hank to the ground. He recognized the Till woman, Eldadip, and the musclehead whose name escaped him. They forced Hank to the ground and held him at swordpoint as a stocky bespectacled man peered down into the precipice. His blue cape and decorative white military jacket gave the old man a Napoleonic bearing.

Beyond the newcomer, Hank saw the furry mutant Naughtadargh yank Argyle up over the ledge. The beast roared, holding Argyle by his hair. He slammed the genteel pirate into the dirt at Alaborap's feet. Alaborap pulled him up by the lapels. "Well, this is disappointing," the pirate said plainly. "Your luck seems to have changed the minute I cut you loose."

Hank watched the stocky Beniti pace along the ledge. He peered over, searching the darkness below. "You have trespassed on sacred land," he hollered, spittle spewing from his lips. "Surrender yourselves!"

"Just cut their lines, Beniti," Alaborap sighed. "I only need Argyle."

"No! We mustn't sully the temple with the blood of the unworthy," the man called Beniti demanded.

The pirates all had eyes on Beniti. While they bantered, Hank seized his moment to act. Eldadip wore a bandolier of military standard-issue grenades. Each one had a red neutralize dial on its underside. A quick quarter-turn, and the wielder could disarm it.

Hank took his chance. Laying prostrate, he kicked his hydraulegs out, then let his mind go blank. The legs glitched, losing his brain's signal, and the hydraulegs jerked, unfolding to their default upright position, just as he intended. Eldadip turned to react, her sword raised, but Hank already had his hand around one of her explosives. He yanked it so hard he ripped the leather ties, and Eldadip stumbled to the ground. Hank pulled the grenade's pin, squeezing the safety lever tight. He held it high as the Till woman cussed to herself.

"Nobody move!" His throat was dry, and his voice cracked. The musclehead lunged, but Hank sidestepped before planting his metal knee firmly in the pirate's groin.

The big man squawked in pain. He threw a wild arm that cracked Hank in the neck. Hank crumpled to the ground; his legs had failed to reboot after his silly trick!

The strike knocked the grenade from his grasp, and it tumbled over the rocky ledge to the temple below.

"No," he shouted. Zirkrum! What had he done? His breath snagged in his chest, and he waited a lifetime for the bang. Finally, the grenade exploded. Its thunderous crack rattled Hank's teeth as it shook the bedrock.

"Grimtash," Alaborap cussed. A shower of soil tumbled from the cavern ceiling like water spilling from a leaking roof.

"Cave-in," the beefy pirate yelled. "Pirates, move!"

"Not without Argyle," Alaborap demanded.

"I've got him," the big guy assured. "Just move!" With that, they were gone.

Jablon struggled to pull himself onto the ledge. Hank dove to help him up, then Jablon rolled onto his belly and grabbed Stanik's line. Hank reached over the ledge and took hold of Stanik's jacket, hauling him to safety.

All three of them lunged for Cliptok's line. Six meters lower, she clung to the rockface, trying to shield herself from tumbling gravel. Her fingers strained for a grip. Another shower of stones spilled over her shoulders, and she slipped, swinging away from the wall. Her harness jolted, dropping her lower. Hank's heart dropped with her. In a final cascade of Zebulonian shale, he lost sight of her. "Cliptok," Hank called desperately. Her name rattled back to him as North Rock Tunnel enveloped them.

27. DIGGING DEEPER

June 14, A.D. 2352
08:18 IST

Muffled sniffles and scraping penetrated the darkness. Something damp and quivering brushed against the tip of Stanik's nose as he dipped back into consciousness. He came to his senses slowly as the dirt tumbled away from his face, putting him up close and personal with an Oggladon's wet, flaring nostrils. The creature gently brushed more dirt away with its mandible hands, its lantern flickering on the ground next to Stanik.

The world around him crawled. Time dragged its tail at a snail's pace as Stanik forced himself to get his bearings. He rolled over, coming face to face with Hinny's lifeless body. His gut twisted up into his throat as he noted the entry wounds from a firearm at the base of the Oggladon's neck. He had to look away when his gaze found the poor creature's dead-eyed stare. He swallowed, suppressing the gathering lump of nausea in his throat. How would the troupe regard them after losing Hinny?

Wincing, Stanik tried to push himself up onto his knees, but his arms and legs were too weak, made sore by the crushing tonnage of ground that had piled on top of them.

The Oggladon who had uncovered him lowered its head, slipping its little arms under his armpits. Then, with a surprisingly muscular flex, its mandible limbs lifted him gently to his feet. Walt hooked his arm over the creature's mangy orange hide. The Oggladon took half his weight, helping him limp out of the deformed mouth of North Rock Tunnel. His four-legged savior led him to a small campfire burning under the starry evening sky of Zebulon 5. There were several wooden casks of water stacked nearby.

Stanik forced himself to sit up on the wet, mossy ground as Jablon trudged over somberly, covered in mud. Behind them, Pontiac offered a pail of water and a wet rag to Hank, who took it, bowed with gratitude as was Hulgarian custom, and went about soaking his hands and tail.

"They can't find Cliptok," Jablon said quietly to Stanik, as if to protect Hank from overhearing. Stanik frowned, watching as Pontiac helped two Oggladons sift through the mud.

"They found us," Stanik said after thinking about it

a moment. "Don't forget: Argyle said these guys were natural miners. We've got that going for us."

Pontiac ambled up next to them, tugging the brim of his hat to greet them. "Hey boys," he said softly, "not sure what all you remember, but yer' Hulgarian friend there says Argyle was taken by pirates?"

"That's right," said Jablon. "The Halogien Stingrays." He growled their name through gritted teeth. With that news, the old prospector took a swig of whiskey from his flask.

"Not the first time he's dealt with Alaborap," Pontiac said, half to Stanik and half, it seemed, to himself. "And I understand she's probably a ways down, but I told the Hulgarian I'm pretty confident we can find yer' fourth crewmember. We just haffta dig a little deeper." He took another sip from his flask.

Good, Stanik thought. He was unwilling to accept the loss of a crewmember… and unprepared to mourn the loss of a friend. Ignoring his aches and pains, Walt staggered over to help the others dig. As he did, the Oggladons shuffled away from him the way a pedestrian might avoid wandering too close to a feral cat.

Jablon rolled his sleeves up and latched his fingers into the grooves of a meter-round boulder. "What's wrong with them?" He nodded to the Oggladons, who kept side-eyeing the Cadets and softly snorting amongst themselves.

"Isn't it obvious? We got their elder killed," Stanik whispered. "We're bad news."

X   X   X

June 14, A.D. 2352
16:00 IST

They scoured the cave-in for hours, until the stars burned brightest in the early morning sky over Zebulon 5. Stanik took a moment to appreciate the view, enjoying the dusty tendrils of the Milky Way that swept across the darkness of space. Sol, his birth star, was out there, as was his home star, Cor. He could never find them without instruments to calibrate everything. There was no light pollution on Zebulon 5. Nothing obscured the stars, save the vignette of pointed pines his spot on the ground provided. It was a brief escape from the sinking feeling in his gut: the one telling him that Cliptok was gone.

He trekked a few meters over to the water flagons to placate his intensifying thirst. Two young Oggladons scampered out of his path. He paused; were they afraid of him or something? Maybe. They probably associated him with the death of their leader... and the death of one of his own. His grief sloshed wildly in his gut like bilge from a rusty bucket.

He poured a cup of water, swigging it down fast. The cups were more like bowls for a human, and he had to slurp it from the side like the remnants of a bowl of soup. An approaching Oggladon scoffed, watching him from a safe distance.

"Sorry," Stanik said, trying to be nice. "My mouth's not designed for lapping." He laughed gently at his own joke. The Oggladon snorted, and one of its ears twitched. Hastily, Stanik grabbed a second bowl of water and took it to Jablon.

"Here," Stanik offered, "take a breather."

"Thanks," Jablon said as he pulled another rock away and wiped sweat from his brow. The two of them sat together and watched as Hank patiently focused on the task at hand. He helped an Oggladon roll a boulder away from the dig site, his mechanical feet sinking into the mud as he gained leverage.

Jablon took a drink of water, then leaned over. "He hasn't stopped moving since they dug him out," he said quietly to Stanik.

Before Walt could offer an answer, Pontiac Jones strolled over to them, removing his hat as he ducked into their circle of confidence. His shoulders drooped. Stanik had a sick feeling. He already knew what Pontiac was going to say as he watched the older man fiddle with the brim of his hat. Then, he said it. "Boys," he sighed gently. He had the bedside manner of a well-trained nurse. "I don't think we're gonna' find her." Stanik slouched as the weight of that truth landed on him. "I can keep the Oggs digging," Pontiac reassured. "When we find her remains, I'll personally fly 'em to Hierrnaus and make sure they wind up in Federalist custody."

"Is there anything we can do to make this better," Stanik asked, gesturing to Hinny's body, now wrapped in a knitted blanket.

"I'd leave it be," Pontiac said quietly. "It's a relief they're not blaming me, honestly. Not that you should jump in front of that pistol for me."

"We kinda deserve it," Jablon said.

"Nah," Pontiac said. "If anything, I blame Argyle." He suppressed a snicker as he realized what he'd said. Then, he sucked in a shuddering breath as tears gathered in his eyes. "If you somehow manage to save Argyle, tell him to get in touch with me, okay?"

Without hesitation, Stanik reached for Pontiac's hand and shook it firmly. "You have my word," he said. "Thank you for helping with the mess."

Pontiac chuckled lightly. "Been doing that since Argyle was a preteen." He nudged Stanik, urging him to enjoy the joke. Stanik smiled at the thought of a preteen Argylesox mouthing off to gritty Pontiac. Their laughter subsided, and Pontiac turned back to the Oggladons, redirecting dig efforts to a new spot.

Jablon waited, perhaps allowing the sentimental moment to subside. Then, softly, he asked, "What about Hank? He won't stop unless we make him."

Jablon was absolutely right. Stanik nodded. "I'll talk to him." He clasped his hands on his knees, pushing himself to his feet. How could he ask Hank to give up on their friend? Cliptok was resilient. Having grown up with her, Hank knew that better than anyone. Walt took a minute to steady himself, swallowing his own grief. He would mourn later. He had to show strength for his friends... he had to be a captain for his crew. Reluctantly, he crossed the clearing and knelt next to Hank, feeling the boggy ground squish under his knees.

Stanik laid a heavy hand on Hank's shoulder. The

Hulgarian stopped digging. "Hank," he said, unsure what exactly what he wanted to say. "If we haven't found her by now…" he trailed off, unwilling to speak the rest. Somehow that made it reality. If they didn't say it–

"I know," Hank said. Silence lingered a moment before, in a hushed tone, he added, "it really is my fault, Captain. I grabbed that grenade."

"You are not to blame, Hank." Stanik said firmly. "And the man who *is* just got away. Just took what he wanted and flew away. Like he always does." As Stanik formed the words to comfort Hank, he realized he couldn't blame himself either… not fully. Had he pressed his crew to go along with Argyle?

Yes.

Did part of him want to catch Alaborap?

Yes. He had to admit that. He owed that to Cliptok. He wanted a shot at Alaborap and Cliptok knew it. She tried to say as much on Mynaus.

But she believed Argylesox. She pushed Jablon to go to Zebulon 5 as much as Walt had. Plus, he thought, if he'd known the pirates were so hot on their trail, he wouldn't have stuffed his whole party into North Rock Tunnel. In fact, he probably would have had Cliptok stay back with the *Explorer*. Maybe then, she'd still be okay.

Stanik felt his grief mutating into hateful determination. Someone had to get in Alaborap's way. Someone had to stop him. He wiped out anyone who got in his way, and he showed no remorse while doing it. To him, it was all just collateral.

Walt looked back at Hinny's corpse.

"We can't do anything else here," Stanik realized as he said it aloud to Hank. "But if we leave now, I think we can stop him." At that, Stanik held out the DataCom for Hank to see, brushing away the grime. He braced for rebuttal from his cool-headed navigator.

"Okay," Hank agreed, holding back tears. His gaze started on the DataCom, but then his bright turquoise eyes met his captain's gaze. "Let's get the son of a bitch."

They tried fruitlessly to thank the Oggladons, then reported their departure to Pontiac. They had to press on after Argyle and the pirates.

Grunt guided them back to the spot at the base of the plateau where they'd first met her. The trek back was awkward, and even after they'd parted ways with the stone-faced equine, the Cadets climbed to the *Explorer* in relative silence, dogged by a cloud of grief.

28. THE AQUA STAR

June 14, A.D. 2352
18:18 IST

"I suggest letting me hook the DataCom up to my NavCon," Hank was saying as they marched into the *Explorer* cockpit. The Hulgarian wanted to get right down to business. Stanik didn't mind. They'd dwelt in a somber silence the whole hike back to the ship.

"Makes sense to me," Stanik affirmed. The NavCon was Hank's navigations console, which would give him more functions when examining the DataCom map files. With that, Hank popped open a small panel on the side of his NavCon and fished through a variety of cable interfaces. Finally, he pinched the end of a thin, single pin plug and slipped it up into the bottom of the DataCom.

"Do you have to hack in again," Jablon asked.

"Nope," Hank said proudly. "Cliptok and I granted the *Explorer* systems access when we hacked in before. Hank turned the DataCom on. It chirped immediately, projecting a map above it. The same map detail appeared on Hank's screen. "Objective complete," Hank read aloud from the data. "I don't understand." Confusion wrinkled the navigator's yellow brow.

"What?" Jablon leaned in, peering over their shoulders at Hank's screen.

"The next map is of Heiznaus," Hank said, pointing to the newly acquired map atop a list of files. "But the DataCom registers information from a temple there. See?" He pulled up a file much further down the list. "Argyle's got the holoscans saved in here, as well as notes on the location."

"Then, he's clearly already been there," Jablon reasoned.

Stanik nodded. "Can we be certain of that?"

"Argyle's data is fairly consistent," Hank said. "He has a wireframe scan of each temple interior, some photos, and a document with his written notes." Hank opened the Mynaus data, pulling it onscreen for them to see. Then, he pulled up the data Argyle had on Heiznaus.

"Yeah," Jablon said. "And look at the dates on the Heiznaus files. They're all from 2347."

"Interesting," Stanik said, leaning over his own console as he reviewed the info. "That suggests that the maps collected from each temple just create a circle of clues…"

Jablon frowned. "You don't think the Goliathon and the first temple are both on Heiznaus, do you?"

Hank shook his head. "No. I get the sense we can't think of this linearly. Each temple gives a clue to another temple. What does that tell us?"

Jablon shrugged, but Stanik thought he knew what Hank was getting at. "It means the clues create a circle," he said.

Hank nodded. "Which suggests to me that its designed so someone can pick up the trail at any location and still get to all four clues."

"Or maybe," Jablon mocked, "it's supposed to be a dead end. Maybe there is no mighty Goliathon."

"C'mon, Jablon," Stanik said with a sigh. "You saw the temple. Do you really think it's just a tall tale?"

"That temple doesn't prove the Goliathon exists, it just proves that temples exist. For all we know, they're part of the hoax!"

"In what world is anyone going to this much trouble for a hoax?" Stanik tried not to sound annoyed.

"It sure feels like they've got us chasing our own tails. Maybe *that's* the point? Like, uh… a test of faith, or something."

"Let's consider the alternative for a little longer," Hank urged. At least he was being helpful, Stanik thought. And Jablon wasn't fighting them at every turn anymore.

"Hey Hank," Stanik pressed on, "can you bring up all four maps at once?"

Hank nodded emphatically, tapped his console, and

moved the files around. "Let me make copies for our own records first," he said. "We can alter those as needed and preserve Argyle's originals"

"Excellent idea," Stanik agreed.

On Hank's console, the maps rearranged, dancing around each other as Hank tinkered. He pulled up the file properties, which the console superimposed over the cartography. He studied one, then pressed another button and the maps reformatted as three-dimensional hemispheres.

"Oh," Hank said, surprise lifting his voice an octave. He typed again, and the hemispheres produced longitude and latitude distinctions. Another keystroke produced a sequence of numbers dancing along the longitude lines.

"What," Jablon asked eagerly. His energy was suddenly childlike, his feet jittering in place.

Hank laughed, giddy with excitement. "There's a mapping algorithm in the charts!" He pointed at the command console, zooming in on the numbers. "This is brilliant!"

"What are we looking at here," Stanik asked calmly.

"Each map contains one fourth of the equation, the same way a genetic code consists of the four nitrogenous bases. You need the complete sequence of all four nitrogenous bases to understand or replicate a complete genome. So, too, you need the four components, one from each of the temple maps, to complete the cartographic code. When you run the code embedded in these longitude measurements, it produces a fifth file."

"Another map," Jablon practically squealed.

"I hope so," Hank said with a nod. "I'll run this code and see what the output file looks like.

Stanik tried to contain his amazement. Were they on the precipice of their mission's defining discovery? He thought of poor Argyle, yanked out of the race so close to the finish line. Stanik had grown fond of their mustachioed stowaway and his seemingly limitless understanding of the natural universe. Hank's console pinged them again, calling Stanik back to the present. Adjusting his focus made him feel lightheaded, caught somewhere between overwhelming elation and an anxiety attack.

"Here it is," Hank announced. Onscreen, the four maps dissolved, replaced by a star chart littered with Candalonian symbols. Hank turned back to the DataCom. "Thanks to Argyle's hard work," Hank explained, "I can translate some of the Candalonian."

The symbols onscreen shifted, morphing into English before Stanik's eyes. At the center of the chart was a little blue planet labelled *Laciport*[57] orbiting a relatively small sun, *Zirkulon*. The DataCom zoomed in on Laciport, displaying its watery surface. From what Stanik could tell, the only landmasses were islands of every size and shape speckling its equator.

"Laciport," Jablon tasted the word for the first time. "Where's that?"

"It's not a known system," Hank confirmed as he checked the data on his own console. "One planet and

---

[57] **Laciport** /ˈlæsɪpɔ˞t/ – no existing data.

a red dwarf sun," He pulled up his star charts to cross-reference their new data. After a moment, he added, "that doesn't match anything on our charts. No references to inhabitable planets around a dwarf star."

Stanik made a copy of the Zirkulon star chart and transferred it over to the DataCom: a complete set of files for Argyle… just in case.

"Let's see what the NavCon has to say about it," Hank said. Stanik could hear the determination in his voice. They were close, and Hank was a problem-solver by nature. The resolute Hulgarian entered a few more calculations before his console blipped in confirmation. "The system just flagged a solar system, but… no, that can't be. ISF charts say that system is a binary star with no orbiting planetoids."

"It's also labeled as a blue dwarf on our charts," Jablon added. Stanik could tell his friend was buying in.

"Well, that checks out," Hank reasoned. "These maps were made nearly sixty-three million years ago. That red dwarf would've burned off most of its hydrogen supply by now." The Hulgarian leaned back, stretching his wing membranes by moving his arms up and down. Walt had learned years ago that meant Hank's mind was working through a problem. "Most of the planet's surface is covered in water," he said finally. "It could be an aqua star."

Jablon huffed. "Which is what, exactly?"

Hank's eyes were fixated on the new map. He toggled the zoom, studying it while he spoke. "Theoretically speaking, it's a star system with one star and an orbiting body of comparable size within the planetary region. The planet's surface is almost completely covered by water, which reflects the star's light at an intense level. So, from a great distance, the system looks like a dim binary star."

"Or this whole thing's just a wild goose chase," Jablon sang, his incredulity creeping back in.

"How far," Stanik asked his pilot.

Jablon crossed back to the helm and ran the calculations. "If these coordinates are right and we plot a clear path, I can get us there in just under nine day-cycles," Jablon confirmed with only a hint of doubt.

Stanik nodded. "In the meantime, we can figure out how we're going to locate the Goliathon once we're there."

"I may have a solution," Hank chimed in again. "On Mynaus, when we were navigating the snowstorm, I noticed an energy pattern in my sonar that I've never encountered. I sensed it again when the Zebulon 5 temple was reactivated."

"That's excellent," Stanik said, his spirits lifted. The trek was going to be long... plenty of time alone with his thoughts. Plenty of time to be haunted by the loss of two good people. He smiled weakly at his friends. "Hopefully we can manage without Argyle."

29. REACQUAINTED

June 14, A.D. 2352
19:25 IST

Argylesox drifted back to consciousness, feeling the cold, corrugated metal floor that dug into his back. He lay crumpled there in a heap, unwilling to move. Green light shined up at him through the floor grates, bathing everything in an unnatural lime light. Rusty shackles scratched at his wrists, and he knew he was chained up in the *Stingray*'s brig. Alaborap had sent him down here to lock up a prisoner more than once in the past, but he'd never experienced it for himself. Alaborap liked to do things old school, and he was smart enough not to rely on technology to detain his foes.

Argyle's hope sank. Once you were in the *Stingray*'s brig, you weren't getting out without a classically trained locksmith or a damn fine magician. From his time aboard, Argyle recalled the brig being belowdecks, between the engine room and the cargo hold. If he *could* get free, he knew the lifeboats were close. They jettisoned from the keel, near the bow. But then, they were activated by an alpha-numeric code, and the only crewmembers privy to it were Glygorg and Eldadip. Alaborap didn't trust anyone else. Grimtash, Argyle thought. The saying was true: when the *Stingray* captured you, you stayed captured.

Argyle sat for a moment, considering his surroundings. He couldn't feel the engines rumbling, so the pirates were likely orbiting Zebulon 5. His shackles were attached to chains that hung from the ceiling, but fortunately for him, those had been left slack. Behind him, a porthole offered a breathtaking view of Zebulon 5, confirming his deduction. The stunning jewel-tone greens and blues reminded Argyle of outdated pictures of Earth, before the atmosphere had browned. Something on the ceiling shifted, and Argyle raised his heavy head. A twinge of pain rippled down his neck and he recoiled.

Glygorg crept out of the shadows, dangling from the rafters. "Yarh, he's up," the Fallamon spat his words like venom, swaying slowly as he leered down at Argyle. Glygorg's red pupils glinted in the dark chamber, burning like hot coals in a dying fire.

Alaborap unlocked the brig with a key, stepped inside, then slammed the barred door shut. As he approached, Argyle sat up, smiling weakly. If this was the end of the road for him, and likely it was, he wasn't going to go out quietly. "You look exhausted," he provoked his rival. "But then, I would be, too, if–"

Without a word, Alaborap hefted the diary in both hands and cracked it across Argyle's face. Argyle gasped, his cheek stinging. He felt the pain bloom under his right eye, and before he could react, Alaborap took two more swings. The leather cover cracked like a whip. Alaborap turned away, checking the binding of the book for damage. He shook his head, turning back to Argyle. "I give credit where it's due, Argyle. You played me for a fool."

"Haste is blind and improvident." Argyle prodded, stealing a modicum of joy from the aggravation Alaborap exhibited. It was his father's favorite quote, coined by Earth's ancient Roman historian, Livy.

"Three years," Alaborap scowled. "You maintained your lies for three years?" Technically, three-and-a-quarter, Argyle thought. "Now I want the truth." Alaborap loomed, standing over him. "Where's the last temple?"

Argyle had never seen Alaborap this enraged, but he refused to let that scare him into cooperating with the cutthroat once more. He'd already made that mistake. Despite his stroke of luck with the Cadets, he feared it was finally time to close out his tab of good fortunes. Might as well have some fun with it, he thought, trying not to panic.

"Men have sacrificed reputation, family… *everything* trying to find this relic. What have you sacrificed?"

"Patience, for one," Alaborap sneered.

"Well, then, I supposed we should congratulate you! The great Captain Alaborap has managed to keep his patience with the rest of us lowly laymen." Argyle couldn't stop himself. "And I think you're angry with yourself, because you're finally realizing how much you relied on *my* expertise."

"You were always quick to cast stones, Argyle," Alaborap growled. "I never liked that." He gave a sharp nod to Glygorg, who jumped from his perch in the rafters and grabbed at Argyle's chains, yanking him off the ground and snapping the shackles taught. Glygorg's counterweight yanked Argylesox up to the ceiling, where he dangled by his arms, prone to the pirates.

Alaborap drew his sword, circling. "I think you've mixed things up inside that busy brain of yours. Your right is no greater than mine. How much of your research was copied from my family's work? How many ships have you lost? How many crewmen have you left for dead?" Alaborap closed in, so much so that Argyle could smell the fresh Zebulonian wilderness still clinging to his beard. "When I found you, there wasn't a sailor in Smith's Pointe who didn't want you six feet under! You needed my protection just as much as you needed my book." The point of Alaborap's sword prodded at Argyle's ribs, drawing blood from his healed stab wound. Argyle gritted his teeth, bearing the pain and stretching out his torso in hopes the blade would miss his vitals. As he tried to inhale again, he yelped. The blade probed at his innards. Either Argyle was already hallucinating from the pain, or Alaborap was so close that his beard hairs tickled Argyle's nose. "Where's the last temple," Alaborap glowered.

"That was it," Argyle blurted out in a tremulous gasp. He cried out again as Alaborap worked the blade around between two ribs. Argyle gritted his teeth as the pain fired past his rib cage, sizzled in his lungs, then rocketed up his spine. He gasped for more breath.

"I'm not going to kill you. Not yet, Argyle. You're coming with me; so, draw this out all you like. But I won't ask again."

"I've been to all four temples," Argyle spat the words out through labored breath. Alaborap withdrew his sword from Argyle's flesh.

"Name them," he demanded.

"Heiznaus, Candalos Prime," Argyle had to gulp for air before he could go on, "Mynaus… and this one, on Zebulon 5." Alaborap glared, raising his WristCom.

"Beniti," he barked into the Com, "the four temples; Where are they?"

"Apart from this one?" A strange British man's voice replied. The transmission was crisp and clean. The genteel voice responded with perfect diction, "Mynaus, Candalos Prime, and Heiznaus. Why?"

"Never mind," Alaborap told the man.

"Who was that," Argyle challenged.

"Never *mind*," Alaborap snapped. "Where are the maps from the last two temples?"

"You followed the 'Judgment' passage, didn't you?" Argyle sneered as he said it, taunting the pirate between ragged breaths.

"Where are they, Argyle?"

"You've made yourself the fool," Argyle lamented. His blood was warm and slick against his shirt. He tried to ignore it, just like he'd ignored the 'Judgement' passage, an excerpt in Nogylop's book referencing the shadows of Candalos Prime. He'd also convinced Alaborap that it was a trap. But he had never explained why. The obvious answer to that passage's riddle was the moon of Forgrasia. It was a private property, held in trust by the Velirno Estate. Even if Argyle died, he needed Alaborap to be wary of entanglements with the Velirno Estate.

"Spare me your lectures," Alaborap snapped back as Argyle's mind raced. Too forceful, Argyle thought, desperate to get his message across.

"Fine. But if I'm right, and you followed that passage, we'll all be cleaning up your mess."

"I'll be sure to hand you the mop," Alaborap barked. Argyle wasn't getting through to him.

"Put down your ego and hear me out," Argyle huffed through his screaming pain. "If you followed that passage, then there's only one question you should be asking: Who is Beniti Juan Velirno?"

"The files, Argyle!" Alaborap's nostrils flared.

Argyle smiled triumphantly. "I don't have them," he stated plainly. "If you'd paid attention, you'd know the DataCom makes the uplink with each temple. But I don't have it; I gave it to my companions. So, if you want it, you'll have to go dig it up."

"I am not foolish enough to camp out here, digging for days so you can buy yourself more time," Alaborap jeered. Good, Argyle thought. Alaborap wasn't convinced, which would buy the Space Cadets more time.

It was only by the most unfortunate of chances that the *ISF Explorer* zipped away from Zebulon 5 at that very moment, glinting in the rays of Zebu. Argyle saw it plain as day out the port window.

"Cap'n," Glygorg gurgled from the rafters, "Ship just broke atmos." The leering Fallamon had been so still that Argyle had forgotten about him.

"The Cadets just launched from Zebulon 5, Captain," Vestonn chimed in over Alaborap's WristCom. "I've got a visual."

The Stingray must've been trolling the location of the cave-in from orbit, Argyle realized, otherwise they'd have never seen it.

Alaborap rushed to the window, watching as the *Explorer* sailed away. His face reddened with rage, even in the lime green light of the brig. "Murray," he erupted, shouting into his WristCom, "Space Cadets off the port bow. Follow that ship!" Moments later, Argyle felt the *Stingray* break free from Zebulon 5's gravity. Grimtash, he thought. The pirates were going after the *Explorer*.

30. THE HUNT

June 24, A.D. 2352
15:50 IST

For ten full day-cycles, Alaborap had conducted his crew as they traced each of the *ISF Explorer*'s distortion jumps away from Zebulon 5. The only way to do so was to track heat signatures from the ship's burn-off via solar sensors. It was easy to lose sight of a target, and the pirates couldn't afford to get too close, or they might alert the Cadets to their presence.

Murray dogged the Cadets' bulbous purple ship, and Alaborap supervised Vestonn as he traced the vessel's jumps. All went accordingly. It wasn't their first time tracking prey.

In shifts, Alaborap allowed each crewmember to rest, to recharge with food, and to stretch their legs.

Murray was old and low to the ground, so he preferred not to move if he could help it. He ate a bowl of ramen at the helm, and took power naps in his seat, relinquishing steerage control to Alaborap when he did so.

As a result of the great distance, the entire Stingray crew was extremely well-rested by the time they drew near a blue dwarf star and a lonely planet orbiting close to it. There was a great asteroid field that created a cloud of defense around the system, and Alaborap estimated the small blue marble of a planet was no bigger than Mercury and about the same orbital distance from its star as Venus was to Sol.

They watched the *Explorer* navigate a few jumps through the asteroid field. "This is interesting," Vestonn said. "On the NavCon, this is listed as a binary star."

"A fine way to keep a planet hidden," Alaborap nodded.

"They're definitely closing in," Murray noted. "If they're busy navigating all this," he added, waggling his plump finger at the asteroids out their windshield, "they won't see us creeping up behind 'em. Shall I dive in, Cap'n?"

Alaborap shook his head. "Hold here," he instructed. "Argyle said he's been to all four temples now. That means the Cadets helped him track down two in less than a week. We barely accomplished that in two *years*. They're tracking the relic somehow. There's no alternative. And we're going to keep them alive until they lead us right to it." Alaborap wasn't sure that was the best move, but it saved them quite a bit of effort. Knowing their destination still left him an entire planet to search. Which, he reminded himself, was why he hadn't killed Argylesox.

His plan took shape in his mind as he watched the *Explorer* zig and zag through the perilous field of rocks. Their pilot was clearly skilled, but flight simulators could only do so much. Alaborap let himself pace, his boots thudding across the cockpit's imitation wood planks – a luxury few outlaws knew.

He would not kill the Cadets. Instead, he would disable their vessel, stranding them on the planet. That way, in a worst-case scenario, he still held the ultimate bartering chip: a space-worthy vessel. Besides, the soldiers aboard the *Explorer* were practically children, plucked from the Federation's bosom with limited real-world experience.

"Glygorg, Vestonn, Eldadip? Take up gunner stations. Eldadip, take the starboard wing, Glygorg the port. Vestonn, go get Naughtadargh – you two are on charger duty." He nodded, dismissing them to their assigned battle stations.

Next, he eased himself into Eldadip's chair and primed the targeting system. "Murray," he finally said as the *Explorer* cleared the last big asteroid in the field of floating rocks, "time to close in on our prey."

31. THE ZIRKULON SYSTEM

June 24, A.D. 2352
15:50 IST

To pass the time in transit, Stanik had Hank help him make ready their weapons and repair the POD. Although the map of Laciport was covered in water, it was dotted with islands and Stanik anticipated they'd need all tools at their disposal. Fortunately, exploring an uncharted, inhabitable planet was what the *Explorer* had been outfitted for. The POD had amphibious capabilities, including a feature for water submersion, albeit at depths that could not exceed twelve meters in Earth-like gravitational conditions. It was exciting, and Stanik and Hank went about preparations with a true sense of adventure. Except for the Graxxon chase, they hadn't really used the gear since their field tests three months earlier.

Hank activated the VOCTAE system, and the overhead maintenance bots danced across the ceiling, running scans of the POD's chassis, and sending spindly arms down to check tire pressure, shocks, and brakes. Versatile-Onboard-Cybernetic-Technologies-for-Automotive-Engineering was cutting-edge, a system of networked 'bots that synced with the *Explorer*'s diagnostic systems and managed all the vessel's tune-ups and repairs. Stanik was certain it would evolve into an everyday necessity aboard commercial vessels, but for the time being, it was a system only equipped on the Federation's newest military vessel. Thank goodness, too, as it turned out the POD needed fitting for three new shock absorbers. No doubt thanks to Cliptok's heroic stunt-driving, he told himself.

Stanik watched as a complement of cat-sized robots entered the bay from compartments along the sidewall. They zipped over to the POD, climbing smoothly around the front driver's side wheel, working in concert to replace the first shock absorber.

Once the POD repairs were underway, Stanik and Hank worked in the cockpit to keep Jablon company, relieving him when he needed a break. Hank redirected his focus to the map of Laciport. Every so often, he would blow bubbles through the water trickling inside his helmet. Any time he did, he'd follow the thoughtful noise up with a new theory on which island chains might harbor secrets about the ancient relic they were after.

Stanik let everyone sleep, but only one at a time and

in four-hour shifts. It seemed to do the trick, and towards the end of their journey, Jablon even returned to the cockpit after an hour's rest. He said he wasn't tired. Shortly after he settled back into his spot at the helm and shifted the *Explorer* into manual, the NavCon startled them all with a trilling alert.

Hank checked his console. "We're entering the Zirkulon system now. System is dead ahead."

"Head straight for our target," Stanik commanded.

"If you're wrong, we're gonna' burn up before I can even say, 'I told you so.'" Jablon warned him.

"Steady as she goes," Stanik affirmed.

"I'd recommend easing up," Hank chimed in. "Asteroids ahead."

Stanik looked up, watching as misshapen rocks cast shadows across their windshield, drifting in a lazy orbit, creating a loose outer shell around the Zirkulon System.

Jablon turned around to Hank. "Hank, you got me," he asked.

Hank nodded, tapping lightly on his touch panel. "Just get me a little closer," he affirmed.

"Everyone strap in," Stanik reminded them. He buckled his harness, opting to take Cliptok's chair rather than sit in the middle at his assigned post. Somehow, it made him feel closer to her. They had to pull this off, he thought, or she died in vain.

Calmly, Hank guided Jablon, who guided the *Explorer* through the asteroid field in a series of short, skillful distortion jumps. It took them quite some time to pass through, though Stanik didn't keep track. It was long enough for him to pace the cockpit several times, until he realized his fussing was a distraction. Stanik sat down, drumming his fingers on his armrests.

The ship finally stopped lurching, and for just a split second, Stanik felt the reality of their weightlessness as the ship's axis adjusted.

"That's it," Jablon said as Stanik felt the *Explorer* adjust one last time. They'd cleared the asteroids. Ahead, the windshield displayed the glistening, watery surface of Laciport, their mystery planet. The Zirkulon sun, which was indeed singular, broke moody red light across the edges of the planet's sphere. Hank opened his eyes and smiled at the sight ahead. Stanik breathed a sigh of relief as he saw Hank relax in his seat.

"Projecting a descent path," Jablon exhaled. His console pinged, and Stanik could see the descent path charted out on Jablon's monitor. Good, Stanik thought, one less thing to worry about.

The cockpit shuddered, breaking Stanik's concentration. The alarms blared in his ears, triggering memories of the *Yulacki*'s demise. A sharp pain shot up Stanik's right arm, from his fingertips up to his neck. He took a deep, sharp breath and pushed his panic back down. "What the hell was that," he barked over the racket.

"We've been hit," Jablon yelped. He corrected course, jerking the helm wildly. Stanik buckled into his chair, watched as Hank did the same, then gave Jablon the go-ahead.

"Evasive maneuvers," Stanik said firmly. With a

sharp nod, Jablon latched his safety harness.

Stanik activated the rear viewscreen to find the *Halogien Stingray* closing in on them. Both ships barreled toward Laciport. The little planetoid danced in a close orbit with its blue dwarf star, reflecting its brilliant light into space. Jablon weaved, throwing off the descent path with each buck delivered to them by the *Stingray*'s guns.

"Walt," Jablon bellowed over the rattling cockpit. "Can you take the rear cannons? Let's give 'em a reason to back off!"

Right! Stanik grabbed the joysticks and fired immediately. The *Explorer*'s rear guns blazed, rattling their chassis as they hurled a cacophony of deadly light at the *Stingray*. Both ships cut down through Laciport's flawless blue sky, their dogfight flashing in a fountain of morning fireworks. The Explorer's guns whirred, and Stanik aimed again. The charge shorted out and the cannons drooped. Stanik swatted his controls. "C'mon, I've got a perfect shot!"

Hank swiveled around. He had moved to a secondary gunner post at the back of the cockpit. "System's non-responsive! What the hell's going on?"

"The guns! They just *died*," Stanik said. His voice chiseled the air with frustration.

"Mine, too," Hank groaned. The power in the cockpit flickered. Belowdecks, the engines screeched.

"Warning," the computer warned, "Power Failure Imminent." The *Explorer* nosed into Laciport's atmosphere, a green flame danced across its bow.

"Damn," Jablon shouted, "we've got a major power

drain somewhere!" The ship was in free fall. Stanik could feel that fluttering sensation in his chest as gravity tugged them closer to the sea. He had one option left to keep them alive. He swallowed, trying to clear the lump in his throat, and gave his final command aboard the *ISF Explorer*. "Abandon ship!"

32. NEW WORLD

June 24, 2352, A.D.
16:04 IST

Walter Stanik gripped the handrail running along the sides of the *Explorer*'s open cargo bay door. His stomach lurched with each jet stream their pilotless ship sailed through. They were in free fall, at the mercy of a new planet's winds. Jablon had locked the helm up so the ship would fly straight. It sagged in the air, and the tip of its starboard wing shattered off a promontory of lava rock. The Cadets were knocked around as the vessel careened towards sandy beaches below.

"Now," Stanik yelled, and all three of them flung themselves from the dying purple ship. They toppled out of cargo bay into thick, humid air. As the wind battered his face, Stanik pulled his ripcord. His parachute billowed into the sky above him. Stanik felt the chute take his weight as the pale grey fabric unfurled from his pack.

The *Halogien Stingray* was still in hot pursuit, but Stanik heard its guns whine, unable to release another blast. Deterred, the *Stingray* swung away like an agitated vulture as the proud *Explorer*'s plummeted into the sparkling surf of a long, thin buffer island just southeast of the two large islands they planned on searching first.

The *Explorer* slammed up onto the beach, gouging a crater into the shoreline. Sand showered down in plumes before the proud vessel settled in the surf, blackening the nearby trees as something in the bow exploded. There, it sat and burned, doomed to decay slowly in the tide pools of paradise.

A gentle sea breeze carried all three of the Cadets over the smoldering wreckage. Stanik had to watch helplessly as his two-hundred-million-digit ship threw a beached barbeque. The flames caught overhanging palms, torching them in seconds. The smoke sent some local winged creatures screeching off into the hot midday sky. He could not guess their true color, for they looked inky black under the strange, indigo daylight of Laciport. The ferns and wildflowers sprinkled through the jungle popped in day-glow pinks, oranges, and yellows. The dried-out palm fronds stood out most, for they glowed a surreal and insistent sapphire in the light of the blue dwarf sun. With Zirkulon burning bright in the sky, Stanik was reminded of his high school haunt, 'Cosmic Bowling,' a dingy old four-lane spot that used blacklights and neon décor to mask the decrepit, smoke-stained bar and lobby.

Not far from him, Hank pulled the latches at his waist, and his hydraulegs folded up into a cube, popped free, and shattered the calm waters below like a falling star. When he was a safe seven meters above the water, Hank swatted the button to retract his parachute. He dived gracefully into the water with barely a splash.

Three meters above the water, Jablon and Stanik finally retracted their chutes. Stanik tried curling up in a cannonball before gravity plunged him into the silky tropical waters. It was like a warm bath, and he took his time kicking back up to the water's surface. He wiped the salt water from his eyes and started treading his legs. Hank zipped through the clear waters, diving to Jablon, who had not yet made it to the surface.

Once he'd ferried Jablon over to Stanik, Hank patiently helped his Terran crewmates onto the beach before returning to the depths for his robot legs. Having an amphibious crewmember was already proving quite the advantage, Stanik thought as he watched Hank drag his hydraulegs up into the fine, powdery sand next to them. Seeing how bright blue it seemed in the daylight, Stanik knew it must be as white as powdered sugar.

Hank's tail glided him forward, slithering up the shore to them. Stanik had always likened the snaking tail and upright posture to that of a cobra. "Anyone injured," Hank asked.

LACIPORT

PLANET: LACIPORT
SECTOR VIEW: RELIC ISLAND FORMATION

Stingray
Landing

Danube
Camp

Explorer
Crash

0   5   10   15   20

"I'm good," Walt said with a nod. "You?"

Hank gave a sharp nod. Walt figured his friend was fine based on how speedy his movements were. He sat and locked his waist into his hydraulegs.

Jablon coughed, spluttering salt water. "I'm good," he said, rubbing his hair to work out the seawater.

Stanik watched the sky, listening for the whine of the *Stingray*'s engines. All he heard was the chittering of birds and the buzzing of insects. "We better get off the beach," he said, wary that he'd hear the pirate ship circling back. "Here, Hank," he handed Argyle's DataCom over, "give us a heading."

In Hank's hands, the DataCom beeped, selected the map of Laciport, then zoomed in. Hank closed his eyes, faced north, and his Hulgarian sonar rippled from his forehead, cooing and clicking as it penetrated the jungle palms.

"We're close," Hank reported as he opened his eyes and studied the map again. "See these two islands making the hourglass shape? Energy signature's real strong. It seems to be coming from up north." He held out the DataCom and stepped into the shade of some nearby palms, but the orange light of the device appeared dull and brown in the intensely blue sunlight. "We're on this buffer island, so we should move to the northeast tip before we try to cross to the main island. It won't be easy, and we're going to have to swim, but we can make it."

On they marched, Hank's legs cutting through the underbrush. He trampled a narrow path for Jablon and Stanik to follow as they pressed uphill through a jungle thicket. "We're going to hike west across the island until we find a river, and then cut north," Hank explained. "The map shows this confluence of two rivers near the center of the island." He pointed it out to them. "They form a much wider river that continues north. We can follow that all the way to our destination island."

They reached the highest point of the buffer island as Hank finished. From their position, Stanik could see the hourglass islands stretching north of them. The nearby shores were jagged, most of the view blocked by looming lava rock peaks wreathed in heavy fog.

The heat suckered Stanik's uniform to his chest as he perspired. The air was thick with humidity, repressing his movement but soothing his raw throat. His nostrils still held the smoke he'd inhaled from the *Explorer*'s flame-out. The smell had seeped into his olfactory until he could taste it, so he welcomed the humidity to cleanse his pallet. A breeze kicked up through the towering palm trees as Hank led them down the steep slope to the tip of the islet, where a strait of lazy water severed it from the main island. Stanik pushed some palm fronds away and smelled the salt air again as he stepped out onto the beach. Hank came to a halt next to him. The Hulgarian pulled tangled vegetation out from between the ankle sockets of his hydraulegs, then unlatched them and hopped down. They folded back into a pack with the press of a button, and Hank slung them over his shoulder and slithered down to the water's edge. "Let me scout the waters," he said.

Jablon and Stanik waited at the surf's edge. The

distance across was no more than eight meters. Hank dipped beneath the surface. When he popped up again, he was on the opposite shore. His translucent green helmet visor practically shined electric lemon in the strange ultraviolet sunlight. He raised a glowing lemon hand from the water and flashed them a thumbs-up. "Everything looks clear, but there's a pretty strong undercurrent. Let me come back for you both."

Hank ferried them through the treacherous current one-by-one. They were able to walk most of the way, but in the middle of the waterway, the sand beneath them gave way to smooth, loose rocks, and they had to slow their pace. It took twice as long as they anticipated, but finally, the Cadets splashed out of the narrow channel.

"Let's hold our position here," Stanik said. He wanted to give everyone a moment to catch their breath. Hank also needed a beat to strap his legs back on. They were on the main island now, at the base of a rocky ledge. To the south, Stanik could see the volcanic mountain range drop suddenly to the bay in a series of sheer, black cliffs of hardened lava. There was no coastal bench they could traverse. They were going to have to climb.

To the north, the vibrant jungle foliage swayed in a gentle sea breeze, covering almost every millimeter of land. Though he had the impression of wild pops of verdant, colorful wilderness, the blue dwarf sun on Laciport threw a deep, indigo daylight. It was an ultraviolet paradise.

Stanik turned east, facing the sea. To his right, the islet they'd come from curled south, and he could see smoke billowing into the sky from the *Explorer* wreckage. Stanik had been so preoccupied with the trek ahead he hadn't bothered to look back.

The branch of a thick tree creaked overhead, where it hung over the stony ledge above. Stanik thought nothing of it until a red mango-like fruit bounced off Jablon's head with a sharp crack.

"Ow! What the—" Jablon shielded the crown of his head instinctively with one hand, then drew his pistol with the other. His aim strafed across the jungle canopy.

"Easy, Jablon," Stanik warned. "If you fire into the trees, it could give away our position to the Stingrays." Stanik suspected the pirates would head for the *Explorer* crash site first. He wanted as much distance between his crew and the smoking shoreline as possible. He surveyed the branches of the powerful tree, then froze up as soon as he realized they had a spectator.

There, dangling from a branch, a Candalonian cocked its head inquisitively atop a curving neck. In the indigo sunlight, the creature's scaly skin appeared the color of black licorice. Stanik blinked. "No way," he gasped. He must be the first person to see a living Candalonian in nearly two hundred years! Back home, they were long gone. Then again, he reminded himself, the Cadets were a long way from home.

He studied the reptilian being, careful not to make any sudden movements. It was about a meter and a half tall, with a pointed saurischian snout and two triangular crests, one protruding from each scaly brow. Its long, skeletal hands and bird-like feet gripped the low-hanging tree branch like birds' feet, and a thick ruby tail provided balance, swaying from side to side to counteract the Candalonian's shifting weight. It cocked its head, peering at each of them individually.

Stanik was held at bay by its big, friendly eyes. They seemed only to harbor an affable curiosity for the Cadets. ISF history made them seem so deadly. That's when Stanik noticed the claws. Despite its kind, gentle features, the reptilian creature was equipped with a natural predatory design. The razor-sharp talons of its feet, the powerful tail... and those needle-like teeth. Stanik felt generations of misunderstanding bubble up inside him. He hoped he might do better. After all, the Candalonian species was suddenly back from extinction.

Delicately, Hank scanned their visitor with the DataCom. The Candalonian stared, cocking its head as Argyle's device scanned a thin orange beam of light up and down its body. Perhaps it understood.

When the DataCom's scan ceased, the Candalonian chirped at them, beckoning with long, spindly fingers. Then, the lizard-like biped leapt to an adjacent tree, swinging away on a vine. Stanik didn't stop to think as he stumbled up the rock face after it. They'd just made a groundbreaking discovery... and it wanted them to follow it.

33. THE RIVER

June 24, A.D. 2352
16:04 IST

Time suspended in the *Stingray* cockpit as the pirates bombarded the Cadets. Alaborap found it often did. Perhaps it was the thrill of the hunt. Any time they closed in on prey, time seemed to slow to a crawl, offering him plenty of opportunities to adjust. Alaborap's tactic was to hit hard and fast, like the Terran birds of prey he admired in his boyhood.

The *Halogien Stingray* whistled through the sky. The *Explorer* had only managed a few volleys of defensive fire, but one of those grazed the Stingray's port engine, making it harder for Murray to stay on course.

"Captain," Eldadip hollered over the cockpit alarms, "cannons aren't holding a charge!"

Murray cracked open a circuit panel, rewiring his console with one hand as he used the other to fight turbulence at the helm. "Just lost port engine two, sir," he shouted, his spluttering accent all but gone as he projected over the roaring guns.

"Power draining," Eldadip reported.

"Murray, get us in the water!" Alaborap ordered. He pointed to a wide river that cut a glistening runway through the island beneath them. Satisfied with his decision, Alaborap leaned back into his chair and gripped the armrests of his seat, bracing for impact. He forced himself to buckle in, something he rarely felt the need to do.

The *Stingray* dipped, dropping closer to its watery landing strip. The sagging port wing must've been drooping lower than Murray anticipated, because it splintered palm trees, cutting short their otherwise graceful touchdown. The ship's proud white keel sloshed into muddy brown water and shuddered to a halt. Alaborap waited to feel his ship settle in the river's current, then signaled for everyone to meet him above decks. "And Naughtadargh," he ordered into his WristCom, "bring Argylesox with you."

The pirates filed out onto the deck at the bow. As they did, Naughtadargh emerged from the stern hatch, dragging the bloodied Argylesox in chains. Beniti and a faction of his clones trudged out demurely behind Naughtadargh's furry white flank. The mutant grumbled as he approached Alaborap. "I had to kill one of his clones. He is not pleased."

"I assume you had good reason," Alaborap offered, unfazed by the news.

"Found it snooping around the brig," Naughtadargh snarled the words more than said them.

Vestonn leaned close to the captain's ear, keeping his good eye on Beniti. "I can waste him right now," he assured them quietly.

"You just stick to the plan," Alaborap instructed. He'd been contemplating Beniti's usefulness, since the Cadets had guided the pirates almost effortlessly to their destination. There was still a whole planet to search, though, and Alaborap had implored Vestonn to try and win over the old Candolite. They had both observed the timorous approach Beniti took when socializing with Vestonn and Naughtadargh, as if he recognized their physical prowess as a force more intimidating than any of his 'experiments.' There was a chance they'd need to reference Beniti's Candolite knowledge, and Alaborap would use Vestonn to apply the necessary pressure. Vestonn nodded, though it was clear from the way he worked his jaw around that he would've preferred bloodshed. Alaborap peered up into the trees, where Glygorg had already skittered from the ship's rigging up into a towering mangrove. At least, it looked very much like a mangrove tree, Alaborap corrected his Sol-centric perspective. "Glygorg," he called up, "can you see the wreck from here?"

"Yarh," the Fallamon barked back, "Black smoke to the east. I can follow it and sniff them out from there."

"Good. Find them, and when they bed down for the

night, mark their coordinates and report back."

"Aye, Cap'n," the reptile saluted.

Eldadip stepped up. "Belay that, Glygorg," she interjected.

"What is it," Alaborap turned to her. It wasn't often that his crew contradicted an order, meaning there might be cause for concern.

"Try Glygorg on your WristCom," she said. Alaborap did so, but his device only tweeted glibly.

"Is your WristCom off, Glygorg," Alaborap asked, fearing he already knew the answer. He watched his first mate fuss with the tech on his wrist. The khaki-colored nylon stood out in stark contrast to the Fallamon's pebbly black and orange scales.

"It's on, sir," Glygorg nodded back, "but it won't let me ping you, even from here."

Eldadip nodded glumly. "Mine's doing the same thing, sir," she confirmed.

"Well," Alaborap watched the clock tick away on his WristCom's display. "My clock's still working. Is that the same for all of us?" A chorus of, 'Aye, sirs' ping-ponged from one pirate to the next as they checked. "Then we spread out in twos and sweep the jungle for a temple. It's sixteen-twenty-three now. We'll give ourselves four hours to search. Return to the ship by twenty thirty hours."

He cut Glygorg loose to track the Cadets alone, knowing the nimble Fallamon would cover more ground in the trees, and Murray was ordered to stay with the ship. Alaborap paired Eldadip with Vestonn and chose

Naughtadargh as his own partner. Not only did the wolfman have the second-best nose on the crew, but Alaborap wanted to keep a close eye on Argylesox. That left Beniti and his twelve clones.

Beniti willfully sent his clones out on patrol with the same instructions, at which point Alaborap was satisfied they would have no trouble from the mysterious man. Still, he felt the need to be cautious. "Remember," he commanded everyone's attention, "our hunt here is for the Goliathon. I want the entire island searched by sundown. And if anyone stumbles across the Cadets before Glygorg, I want them brought back alive! Clearly, they can track the Goliathon temples; we need to know how."

Glygorg swung off through the branches like a monkey as the clones dispersed into the jungle. Alaborap marched down the gangplank and headed north, stopping at the edge of the rainforest to watch Beniti's blue cape swish away into the palms to the west. Then, he nodded to his crew to continue their ten-minute performance.

Naughtadargh grabbed Argyle's tether, dragging him close. He growled, dousing the prisoner in his foul breath. The mutant smirked as he watched the human's nostrils recoil from the stench. "You get to stay with me," he purred sadistically. Argyle averted his eyes.

34. DISCOVERY

June 24, A.D. 2352
17:18 IST

"Whoa, Walt," Jablon called after his captain. "Hey!" Stanik seemed to ignore him, charging deeper into the jungle. With a grunt and a groan, Jablon pushed forth into the dense foliage. A palm thwacked him on the face, the humidity sticking it there for a beat longer. The pilot stopped to peel it away, unable to determine which way his pursuit should continue.

"Jablon, this way," he heard Hank call out somewhere to his right. Jablon hurdled a fallen palm, shoved a patch of ferns aside, and finally found his companions. Stanik paid little attention to them. His eyes were roving the treetops, searching for their discovery.

"What are you doing," Jablon begged.

"That was," Stanik's breath interrupted him. He was still winded as he tried to speak. "It was a Candalonian!"

"Really?" Jablon scratched his head. "I thought they'd be taller."

Hank shook his head. "You never studied."

Jablon rolled his eyes. "Okay, sure, but that's ancient history. No, this is about wilderness survival, and I remember that course. We're not supposed to split up!"

"There!" Stanik pointed, dashing into a thicket of giant ferns.

"Damn it," Jablon shook his head. Walt was acting impulsively. Not a good time for it.

Hank patted Jablon on the shoulder. "Let's try to keep up," he suggested, then ran off after Walt.

The underbrush rattled as Jablon's pulse thumped in his temples. He focused on his steps, ignoring the thick, humid air that clung mercilessly to his skin.

"Over here," Hank called from a dozen paces away. They were spread out too far. It might have bothered Jablon less if it weren't for the pirates. He knew they'd still be looking for the Cadets. If they carried on like this, it'd be stupidly easy to track them down. He didn't want to die so far from home. They might not have a choice, he told himself. Their ship was gone; its beautiful, sturdy frame crumpled in a sandy crater like a giant aluminum can. His nerves churned his stomach at the thought. Unless they could hijack the *Halogien Stingray*, they were probably doomed to live out their remaining years on this unknown rock, pitted against nature. Terrans hadn't been tested in *that* kind of survival since the Free Worlds were settled. Hell, even in those circumstances, there were traces of Candalonian technology for settlers to make use of, or the promise of other vessels touching down. Laciport would offer no such hope.

Jablon caught up to Hank and sighed with relief as he saw Stanik double back to join them. Hank was already reaching out slowly to wave to the Candalonian, which was hanging from a sturdy branch.

The lizard-like biped relaxed, then pulled itself up and perched atop the branch instead. It stared back at them through vertical slit pupils framed by striking orange irises. The gaze was unsettling, crocodilian even, though it didn't make Jablon feel as if Hank was in any danger. The pilot stumbled slightly, snapping a twig under his weight. He froze as the Candalonian squawked at him, pointing.

Stanik shot him a glare and Hank shushed him viciously.

"Sorry," Jablon whispered back sarcastically. Stepping on twigs in a jungle was damn-near inevitable. When the Cadets turned back to the creature, it was gone. The branch above was still rocking up and down, disturbed by the Candalonian's weight.

"Where'd he go," Stanik asked. The jungle was still, the chorus of alien critters hushed to a soft buzz. The Candalonian was nowhere to be seen.

Suddenly, the creature pounced out of a tree and landed on the ground behind them, holding its arms wide to announce itself. The Cadets spun around, and Jablon drew his pistol again.

"Jablon, don't," Stanik warned. Jablon stole a glance at his captain, and the Candalonian cocked its head. It blinked, then lashed out with lightning speed and swatted the gun away, catching the weapon as Jablon recoiled.

"Hit the dirt," Jablon shouted. The Cadets followed him to the ground.

The Candalonian examined the weapon, pulling the trigger several times. The creature examined the pistol from every angle, then offered it back to Jablon with a shrug.

"It's not working," Hank observed.

"Lucky for us," Stanik retorted scornfully.

"I'm sorry. He's fast," was the only defense Jablon could scrape together. As he said it, he noticed the creature's cracked right crest, reminding him more of a dinosaur than a lizard now that they were up close and personal.

The lizard man pointed to the Cadets, holding its hand flat as if to suggest a flying ship. Then it beckoned them with its tail.

"Look," Stanik said, "he wants us to follow him." Jablon nodded and followed them once more into the jungle. They were all together; that was safer.

Jablon followed dutifully behind his captain. "What makes you think our new friend is a *he*," he whispered, remembering his mistake with Grunt on Zebulon 5.

"Well," Stanik replied, "I've read that the females were often bigger, just under two meters tall. Given that this guy's only a meter and a half, and given the bright markings that accent his horns, I think it's safe to assume he's a 'he.'"

"I concur," Hank added. Even though the others weren't looking, Jablon stopped himself from rolling his eyes. He hated when his friends talked down to him. But he had to separate his friends from his crew, so instead of sending his eyes for a spin, he simply gritted his teeth.

X   X   X

Through the midday heat and the fading indigo glow of afternoon, the Cadets followed their Candalonian, who swung through the trees freely, glancing back occasionally to make sure the slow-moving mammals were still with him. Jablon was thankful for the quiet that had settled over the group. It seemed like that was the heat of the day, and even their dinosaur ally slowed its pace.

Thunder rumbled in the distance, and five minutes later, they were trudging through an afternoon rainstorm. The heavy drops pattered the canopy above, relieving them all from the heat, if only for twenty minutes. Then, the rain yielded, substituting a foggy mist in its stead. Jablon took a moment to appreciate the cool breeze cutting through the trees.

A warning chirp from Hank's pistol disturbed the silence. The navigator fiddled with his firearm, checking its settings, checking the safety. He pulled the trigger, then shook his head in defeat. "Captain, look at this."

Stanik moved up next to the Hulgarian, who handed over his pistol. "I don't get it," Hank said.

"What is it," Jablon picked up his pace so that he was directly behind them. He was taller, so he could see over their shoulders.

"We all had fully charged pistols," Stanik said, passing Hank's pistol to him. The charger blipped, flashing angry red digits: 0%.

"So, none of the guns work?" Jablon feared he knew the answer before he asked his question.

"No," Hank said, "all the power cells are drained." He showed them his own pistol charge: 0%. After a beat, he added, "How's the DataCom?"

"Still has power," Walt said. "But I'm switching it off until we need it." Stanik held the power button until the device shut down, and the flaps and antennae protruding from the device retracted, turning the DataCom back into a seamless egg.

"What do you think is causing it?" Jablon meant the question sincerely.

"We're looking for a device that turns energy into matter," Stanik said. Where does it get that energy?"

Jablon couldn't help but scoff. "You don't actually think—"

"Yeah," Stanik cut him off, "I do."

Jablon sighed, letting his shoulders sag.

A few paces ahead of the Cadets, their Candalonian guide dropped from the trees, landing in a cluster of ferns. The alien led them to the bank of a wide jungle river. There, the Candalonian's living situation was like an amateur archaeological camp. Holes had been dug all around, and crates and planks were organized into makeshift tables. Each table was cluttered with metal trinkets, tools, and mechanical objects.

"He's got a ship," Stanik said, nodding downriver. There, a mottled navy-blue vessel was moored to a quaint jetty of rocks and timbers. It was covered in barnacles and rust, and the name '*Blue Danube*' was chipped away on the bow.

Jablon's stomach did a somersault. "Someone wanna tell me how his ship has an *English* name?"

As they stepped into the clearing, Hank's legs locked up, the blue lights on his hips blinking out. Hank lost his balance, nearly toppling backwards. Jablon reached out to catch him. "Whoa, buddy, you okay," he asked, helping Hank gently to a bed of moss on the forest floor.

Hank shook his head. "The atmosphere must've finally drained them."

"Well," Jablon said, stooping a bit so Hank could reach his broad shoulders, "hop on." Hank uncoupled from his hydraulegs and swung himself up onto Jablon's back.

The Candalonian skittered up to the hydraulegs, his eyes wide with excitement. He pointed to the legs and motioned to himself. Then, he pointed to Hank and held out his hands, presenting the Danube.

"Hey, Hank," Stanik nudged, "I think he wants to trade you."

"Does the ship work," Jablon asked skeptically. Hank contemplated for a moment, and then pointed to the ship, imitating engine noises. He used a flat hand to mimic flying.

Hank nodded.

The Candalonian pointed to the sky and frowned, shaking his head. He bent down, splashing a puddle with his spindly fingers, then nodded emphatically.

"It's transportation," Hank reasoned. "I guess I can't say no to that." He hesitated. "It's not really a fair trade, though."

Jablon shrugged. "He seems happy." The Candalonian hopped around Hank's folded legs, curiously poking the hydraulics and tracing wires with his needle-thin claws. Then, in one swift movement, he swung his tail out in front of Hank and, in turn, clasped Hank's tail with both of his scaly hands. Trying to follow the Candalonian's lead, Hank wrapped both his hands around the reptile's tail.

Jablon chuckled. "I think you just shook on it… the Candalonian way." They all laughed together as Hank and the creature released each other's tails.

Then, the reptilian stood before them and bowed. He sat them around a rectangular wooden table. The furniture's unfinished edges scratched at Jablon's arms and back as he settled in.

Their alien host served them all distilled water from a makeshift purification system. It was one of many practical contraptions the Candalonian had cluttering the campsite. They drank their water from little dried out gourds. Purified, the water was crystal clear and refreshing, especially in the muggy post-rain bog. The air was so thick with humidity, in fact, that it felt as if it were pressing against Jablon's chest when he drew in a deep breath.

Next, the Candalonian prepared a stew of herbs, vegetables, and fungi. He proudly leapt about his garden, making a show of gathering all the ingredients.

"I don't think he's ever had guests," Hank mused. The meal was exactly the sustenance Jablon craved after their day-long trek through the jungle; it made him feel clean, even ready to exert more energy. The hike inland had proven a test of their endurance, and they'd passed. The night would bring relief from the heat.

They helped clean up after the meal. Stanik leaned in as he brought the bowls to the riverbank, where Jablon was rinsing everything in the fresh, running water. "We should keep moving through the night. We've got to stay ahead of the pirates."

"Agreed," Jablon said quietly. "Plus, Alaborap's smart. They're probably just as well-rested as we are after a ten-day flight. They'll probably press on searching."

"Hopefully they're not searching for us," said Hank.

Jablon shrugged. "My guess is they think we went down in the crash," he said. "They never circled back and their ship was practically untouched in the dogfight. If they were looking for us, they'd have found us by now."

"We can only hope," Stanik said.

"There's also the possibility that their ship was drained of energy," Hank pointed out. "I suspect that may be why the *Explorer*'s guns died on us."

"That's a fair point," Stanik nodded. "All the more reason to press on."

The three of them tried to explain their departure to

the Candalonian, who squawked excitedly and boarded the *Blue Danube* behind them. It slithered up to the helm before Jablon realized what was happening. "We may have misunderstood the bargain," he said cheekily to his friends, "but I'll take the evening off."

"Hank, which way are we headed from here?"

Hank's sonar cooed and clicked, then waited as the pulses returned to him. "The energy pattern's still coming from north-northwest. This must be the eastern-most river. And the current will take us north." He pointed north for the Candalonian, who chittered excitedly and fired up the *Danube*.

Overhead, the Zirkulon sun was preparing to set to the south, beyond the rocky black mountains tracing the island's southern shores. As the star's ultraviolet rays grew pale, a silvery-white aurora formation snaked through the sky. It restored enough of the color spectrum for Jablon to feel like he was under a yellow star again.

Good, he thought, it was about time things started working out. Of course, he wouldn't have thought that if he'd only checked the trees overhead. Across the river, hidden in the fronds of a massive palm, Glygorg the Fallamon dangled from a branch. Having heard everything, he grinned. Without a sound, the spying Stingray swung away stealthily under the cover of twilight's stretching shadows.

35. NIGHTFALL

June 24, A.D. 2352
20:05 IST

There was no moon on Laciport, but the silver light of an aurora formation sparkled in the sky, glinting off the Stingray's black sails. The *Stingray* creaked as it rocked gently in the river's current. Alaborap watched from the ship's stern as Beniti and his clones marched out of the jungle. He didn't realize how much Beniti's absence had let him breathe until his chest tightened up at the sight of the man and his egotistic entourage.

"Everyone else has experienced power drain in their firearms," Alaborap offered. "What say you?"

"We'd noticed," Beniti patted his holster.

"We're stuck using swords," Alaborap nodded. "Only useful thing we discovered all afternoon."

"Nyarh," Glygorg called, swinging down from the trees like an acrobat and planting his feet squarely in front of his captain. His little lungs heaved under his chest's protective shell. "Captain, if ye' want to catch the Cadets, ye' better get moving."

"All aboard," Alaborap called. "We move out immediately." He beckoned everyone below decks. "Glygorg, meet me in the cockpit."

X   X   X

At their stations, Alaborap consulted Glygorg further. "What else do you know?"

Glygorg was still huffing and puffing as he ticked off information on his fingers. "They're using the Hulgarian's sonar to track the relic. They're just a few kilometers north, using some crummy boat for transportation; we can overtake them!"

Alaborap nodded. "You clever old lizard. I owe you a scotch." They'd bet on whether or not the Hulgarian was tracking temples after the Zebulon 5 fiasco.

Murray fired up the engines and raised anchor. The air had sizzled all day with electricity. It reminded Alaborap of standing on the brink of a lightning storm. The *Stingray* rocked, shuddering forward into the strong current of the wide river. Amphibians chirped in the primordial haze of late evening. Alaborap had returned above decks when they spotted the Cadets' vessel silhouetted on Murray's screen as it rounded a bend in the river ahead. Alaborap waited at midship, relying on the silver serpent of light in the night sky to see the Cadets' ship ahead. He wrinkled his nose at a troop of clones hanging from the *Stingray*'s rigging. The ship gained speed, sailing into darkness as the river narrowed and the shadows closed in around them.

Dripping with sweat, Eldadip ignited green flares along the deck, illuminating the suffocating wall of twisting tree trunks that closed in around them. "Captain, look! In the trees." Eldadip pointed overhead.

Instinctively, Alaborap wrapped his hand around the hilt of his sword as he followed Eldadip's index finger. The mammoth branches that extended over the great river were littered with sleeping Candalonians. The reptiles slept in those creaking boughs like stone gargoyles guarding an ancient castle.

"Candalonians," Alaborap whispered with his next breath. He needed to be careful not to wake the creatures. What a discovery, his mind chided. He signaled for his crew to be quiet so as not to disturb the monstrous biological treasures.

"God be praised," Beniti gasped, stepping up next to him. Alaborap rolled his eyes

Eldadip took a step back. "Think they'll attack?"

"They're sleeping," Vestonn whispered.

Beniti stepped forward. "Aren't they beautiful?" He did not look to the pirates for a reaction. He was preaching to a congregation of one.

Eldadip shook her head. "I think they're creepy, perched up there like gargoyles."

The *Stingray* built up speed in the sturdy night wind.

CANDALONIANS

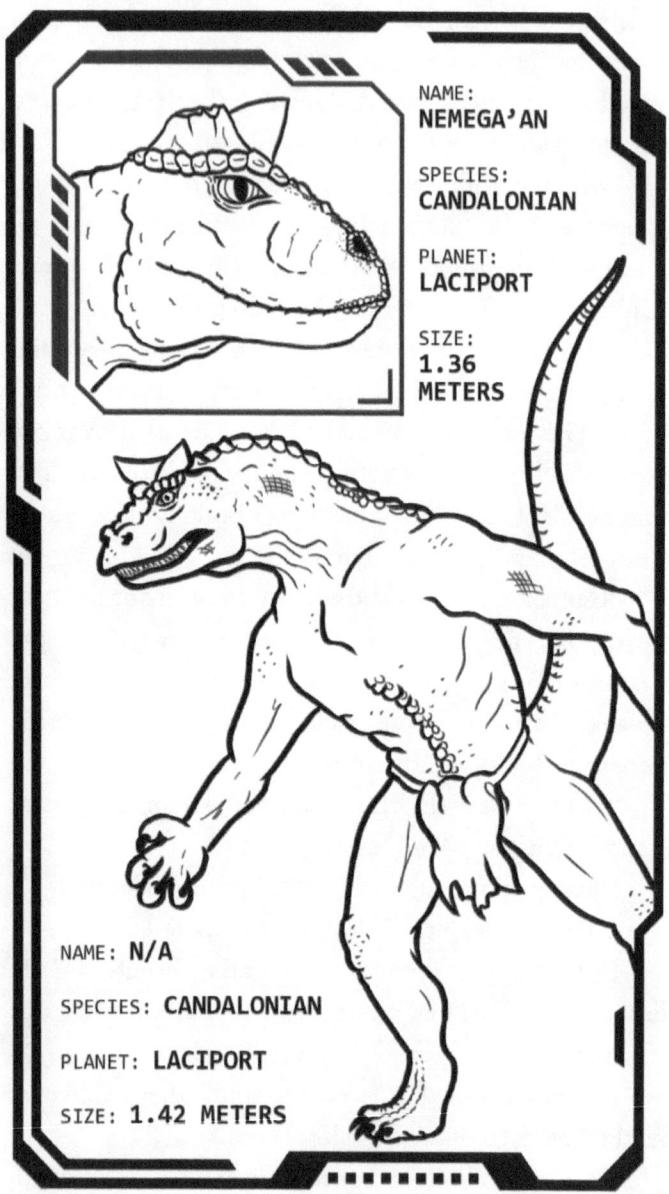

NAME:
NEMEGA'AN

SPECIES:
CANDALONIAN

PLANET:
LACIPORT

SIZE:
1.36 METERS

NAME: **N/A**

SPECIES: **CANDALONIAN**

PLANET: **LACIPORT**

SIZE: **1.42 METERS**

Its masts started slapping against low hanging palms. The rustling branches stirred the Candalonians, who croaked and roared, blinking at the green flares flickering along the deck of the *Stingray*.

Thud. Thud, thud. The slender reptiles dropped one by one to the deck of the *Stingray*. They hissed in unison, then lunged, despite Beniti's loud, repetitive prayers.

Drawn slowly back to the realm of the present, Beniti saw the Candalonians swarming around them and smiled. He growled an order at his clones, who all lowered their guard, slouching, and showing no resistance as their reptilian assailants slaughtered them. Alaborap noticed how Beniti centered himself in a pack of his clones for protection before giving his sacrificial command.

Alaborap drew his sword as a Candalonian pounced at him, claws out. He sank the blade deep into the creature's clawed forearm, and it rolled away into the water. "Don't harm them," Beniti reprimanded everyone, "they're the chosen race!" The night air was alive with Candalonians; the lizards rained down mercilessly to the *Stingray*'s deck. Beniti gurgled at the few clones who raised their fists in resistance. Passively, even reluctantly, they accepted death as Candalonian claws slashed through their ranks like a scythe through wheat stalks.

Despite Beniti's protestations, the pirates defended their ship generously, hacking apart the Candalonians who made it onboard. Finally, the trees over the river gave way and no more Candalonians could launch themselves at the *Stingray*'s deck.

"Wait," Beniti cried out over the din. "Stop!"

Eldadip and Naughtadargh ignored him, skewering the last Candalonian onboard, which was loping around on one leg. Beniti turned to Alaborap, his sword drawn. Beniti pushed aside his clones and approached the pirates, side-stepping their gore, practically frothing at the mouth. His wild gray eyes burned with accusation. "You are no Candolite!" Beniti spat the words.

Alaborap met Beniti's sword with his own. "I distinctly recall saying I was not."

Beniti wiped a dribble of spit from his goatee. "You said you held the same beliefs as your grandfather!"

Alaborap felt the horns of his wicked grin curl up his cheeks. "Oh, that? Yes, I believe, as he did, that the ISF will try to reclaim my home system. It needs defending." He chuckled. "I'm sorry if you misinterpreted that," he taunted the zealot. Alaborap relished in outmaneuvering others. It gave him quite a rush.

Beniti lunged at Alaborap. The pirate had wanted to take a swing at Velirno since waking up in the old man's dungeon. The feeling was apparently mutual. They parried back and forth across the deck, throwing weight around and dodging swinging fists. By driving their footwork, Alaborap forced Beniti out onto the port wing of the ship. His opponent was aggressive, not used to defending, and Alaborap was overcome with a rush of pure joy. "Be gone, thou damned and luxurious mountain goat," he chided. He'd had the quote ready since they arrived on Zebulon 5.

Beniti looked dumbfounded. He had no idea Alaborap was quoting the Bard. Typical, Alaborap thought. But disappointing. Few people really appreciated his humor. No matter. It was time to deliver the knockout blow. Alaborap flourished his sword over his head, overwhelming Beniti with a flurry of downward strikes. The old zealot stumbled to the edge of the wing. Alaborap threw a kick, planting his boot firmly into the stout man's gut. The eccentric Beniti lost his balance and toppled overboard.

Alaborap turned to his crew, a warrior's rage awakened within him. He clenched his jaw, channeling the power he felt into commands for his crew. "Get these filthy clones *off my ship*," he bellowed. His crew rallied with a cheer, their swords liberated to slice and shove. Seeing this change in the pirates, many of the clones dove overboard after their master. Those who failed to were battered, gutted, and helped into the dark river with a swift kick.

The pirates cheered, jeering at the clones who bobbed in the water behind them. Alaborap did not participate in the celebration. He wanted to be ready; they weren't in the clear yet. Eldadip joined him at the Stingray's stern, watching the jungle canopy downriver writhe with the hoots and growls of more Candalonians. "Uh, Captain," she uttered. "Trouble ahead, sir."

"Everyone belowdecks," he ordered. "On the double!"

36. THE *BLUE DANUBE*

Further north, the *Blue Danube* rumbled up the Waltz River. That's what the Cadets had chosen to name the body of water once they had experienced its lazy current. Hank thought it would also be a fine reference to their vessel, which, it turned out, they had not traded for. They had merely paid the Candalonian for a charter.

Stanik shook his head as he gripped the port gunwales, listening to the ship's struggling motor. He leaned in the open doorway, letting the cool night breeze rush past him, freshening the stale air in their vessel's little cab. Jablon was at the helm, which was butted right up against the narrow windshield of the *Danube*. The Candalonian was supervising him.

Stanik was curious as to the ship's significance. They were on an undiscovered planet, and yet an allegedly extinct creature had traded them Federalist technology for a half-operable vessel with a classical Terran name stenciled on the hull in English. He wished he'd realized sooner; he could've questioned the Candalonian survivalist. The drooping palms and mangled mangroves sped past along the riverbank as Stanik pondered the origins of their chariot.

Jablon made an adjustment at helm and sighed in admiration. "I gotta give Chirpy credit, this thing handles nicely."

Hank raised an eyebrow. "Chirpy? Really?" Stanik recognized Hank's challenging tone. Jablon was subconsciously assuming their language barrier with the Candalonian gave him permission to treat the alien as inferior. Like most Hulgarians in the Federation, Hank worked continuously to break down the prejudices that sentient beings, particularly mammalian bipeds, brought to the evolutionary table.

"What? It's catchy," Jablon's tone was ornery, ringing with self-celebrated ignorance.

"Hey," Stanik interrupted. Not only was he saving them from a bickering match, but he was trying to discern what it was he suddenly thought he was hearing. Under the constant chortling of the *Danube*'s noisy engines, there was some other guttural sound that was gnawing at Stanik's attention. He had the distinct impression that, if they could cut the ship's engines for a moment, he'd hear the angry barking of dogs traipsing through the tangled ferns along the riverbank.

"Do you guys hear that?" He stepped out onto the

Danube's deck, scanning the trees. With the melodious chug of the ship overwhelming his ears, Stanik barely detected a faint hooting cry. He glanced over the engines at stern. Bearing down on them, swarming with Candalonian warriors, was the *Halogien Stingray*. The big black ship had sails full of wind. Those sails were crawling with scales, tails, and teeth.

Stanik turned back to the bow of the barge. Scaly limbs swooped down from overhead. Their aggressors were swinging to the ship on leathery vines. Stanik ducked back inside the cockpit, dodging gnashing claws and teeth. He used his hagron arm to shove a Candalonian out of the doorway, its claws clinking harmlessly off the prosthetic's smooth metal. The claws drew blood, but he felt nothing. "Alaborap's behind us," Stanik reported as he slammed the cabin door shut.

"Not sure that's our biggest concern," Jablon warned, pointing to a series of cracks spiderwebbing across the windshield. Scaly fists pounded the glass.

"Shit," Stanik muttered.

The Cadets watched helplessly from their little cabin as the reptiles swarmed over the *Danube*'s rusty old deck. One Candalonian pressed against the windshield and did a double take as it noticed Chirpy inside with them. Stanik shivered. There was so much intellect in their movements, but Candalonian bodies were built to kill. The reptile aimed its pointed snout and outstretched claws. It snarled, lunging nose first like a missile. The beast collided with the glass and flopped backwards with a yelp.

"I wish I had a gun," Jablon said through gritted teeth. Bang! Thump, thud. Candalonians threw their bodies at the glass. The reinforced windshield bent inward with a crunch as it slowly gave way.

"They're trying to get in," Stanik shouted, balling his hands into fists. "Be ready!" With a final gut-wrenching crunch, the windshield burst free, shards of glass splashing to the deck like fast-falling ice. Snarling Candalonians sent reaching limbs through the broken windshield, black needle nails scratching at the Cadets.

Two impacts shook the Danube, one right after the other, and the Candalonians ceased their deadly writhing. The reptiles panicked, chittering to one another as they skittered over the side of the ship. Some grabbed vines and swung away, others splashed into the river. Stanik stole a glance out the window at stern, where he saw the Stingray firing harpoons at them. He ducked away from the small windows, rushing for the helm as the friendly Candalonian panicked, abandoning the ship's wheel. The creature flung the cabin door open and leapt overboard. "Hey," Stanik called after him, taking the helm.

Jablon stepped up and took the wheel from him. Stanik watched through the broken windshield as the last reptilian tails finally cleared the deck, and he saw that the river spilled out into a narrow channel of water ahead. Beyond that, he saw the white sand beaches of another island.

An explosion at stern rattled the *Danube*, knocking the Cadets onto the glass-covered floor again, but there was no fire. Nothing had exploded, he realized. The pirates had run into them. Metal grinded, and ahead of him, Stanik saw the *Danube*'s hull bend and warp.

"They're running us aground," Jablon bellowed.

The bow of the *Danube* pitched skyward as the *Stingray* rammed it over a cluster of jutting rock. The Cadets tumbled helplessly around the *Danube*'s cabin. Stanik's stomach lurched like he was on some awful carnival ride, and he shielded his face as beautiful, sparkling shards of glass sliced through the air around them. Then, Stanik slammed into the starboard wall of the cockpit and everything went dark.

37. CAPTURED

When he came to, Stanik felt like everything around him was floating in molasses. Definitely concussed, he reasoned, feeling the bump that had bloomed above his left eye. He had dreamed about trying to save a beached whale. He remembered that, but not where they were.

He could see Jablon and Hank. They weren't moving. Stanik tried to get up. He had to check on his friends. His shoulders ached; his pulse throbbed in his head. Behind him, he heard boots crunching across the broken glass. The pirates were coming in.

The Cliptorgian woman was the first pirate to reach them. Eldadip Till, Stanik thought as his brain grabbed her name from Demaria's stolen files. She peeled Hank up off his elbows. He hadn't managed to sit upright on his own, and his head lurched back. Stanik couldn't even protest.

"I've got the Hulgarian," Eldadip called to her comrades as they filed into the room. Stanik watched as the musclehead Vestonn nudged Jablon with his boot. The pirate looked older, and the left half his face was shrouded by a lavish, multicolored paisley bandana. "What about the others," the big man asked.

"Take 'em all," the grizzled Fallamon Glygorg ordered. Stanik knew him as Alaborap's first mate. Also, his oldest accomplice… literally. Glygorg was by far the oldest member of the Stingray pirate clan. Stanik's cognitive mind was racing through its catalogue of pirate facts despite his throbbing headache.

The pirates bound the Cadets' hands with zip ties and dragged them away from the *Danube*'s twisted deck. It seemed to take a while, but time was still creeping by. Then he felt the cool night breeze rush past his face and something in Stanik's brain clicked. Time ceased its slipping by, and the details of the Laciporean night were sharp – the gentle tide lapping this new island beach, the chorus of nocturnal creatures vamping overhead, and the varying glimmers of purple light reflected from the sky.

Vestonn Krowl was the scarfed pirate. Stanik remembered his face, but not the scarf that obscured at least half of it. There wasn't much on him, but Stanik was happy to find all these factoids filed away in his mind. His goal was still to operate in the Outer Rim. The more he could study the Stingrays firsthand, the more capable Stanik fancied he'd be when it was time to bring them each in, even if he had to do it one by one.

Vestonn mustered Stanik and Jablon down off the beached *Danube*. As his eyes adjusted, Stanik saw Alaborap and his furry mutant waiting down by the surf. Stanik's chest grew buoyant with hope as he realized that the hairy beast was dragging a chain linked to the shackles of Argylesox. The pirates hadn't killed him. That boded well for the Cadets. Stanik remembered the DataCom. He used his arm to check that the device was still zipped up in his inner jacket pocket. It was there.

Argyle made eye contact and smiled weakly as the Cadets were marched up to Alaborap. The privateer frowned, no doubt noticing Cliptok's absence.

Eldadip pulled out her sword, an elegant black cutlass, and held the blade steadily to Hank's neck. "Give us a heading. Now!"

"What," Hank asked wearily.

Glygorg smacked Hank in the helmet. "Don't play dumb," he gurgled. "Sing your little song, Hulgarian." Damn, Stanik thought, they knew about the sonar. He didn't know how, but the pirates had figured them out.

Hank glared at Glygorg. "No," he insisted.

Alaborap nodded. "I thought as much. Naughtadargh?" Naughtadargh was the beast's name, Stanik noted. The only record on him was the rumor that Alaborap sailed with a beast of unknown origin.

Like a well-disciplined dog, Naughtadargh bowed to his captain, his ears tucking back subserviently. He lumbered up to Stanik and grabbed him by the collar. Behind the beast, Argylesox staggered to keep some slack on his chain, which was looped around

Naughtadargh's waist.

Naughtadargh pried Stanik off his feet, wrapping a big meaty paw around Stanik's ankles, and the other, oddly smaller hand, stretched out Stanik's arms, grasping at his wrists. The beast's coat was greasy, like a big dog in need of a bath. Stanik tensed up, dodging Naughtadargh's fowl breath. The stench of raw meat and dried blood wafted up to Stanik from the wolfman's gaping maw. The monster's razor-sharp teeth pricked anxiously at Stanik's neck.

"Don't do it, Hank," Stanik ordered, trying to lean away from the furry beast's wretched mouth. Naughtadargh growled, flexing his jaw ever so slightly. Stanik clenched his teeth, bearing the pain as dozens of teeth needled at him.

Stanik felt the warm trickle of blood race down his back. Hank winced, and Stanik could see from his friend's expression that Hank was about to disobey his order. Walt felt another trickle of blood dribble down his shoulder. Hank shook his head in defeat. Walt had to admit he was thankful for Hank's decision. Now was not the time for self-sacrifice. He wasn't going to die because he was at the mercy of pirates. Cut down trying to escape them, maybe, but not helpless, and certainly not at Alaborap's whim.

Hank closed his eyes and his sonar pulsed and chirped its strange, intrusive song. "North," Hank told the pirates bitterly. "We need to head north."

"Very good," Alaborap said. "Naughtadargh?" The wolfman snorted, releasing Stanik in a flurry of saliva.

RELIC ISLANDS

PLANET: LACIPORT
SECTOR VIEW: RELIC ISLAND FORMATION

Goliathon
Temple

Shipwreck
Forest

Stingray
Landing

Danube
Camp

Explorer
Crash

0   5   10   15   20

Walt touched his neck gingerly, but an irritated shove from Naughtadargh made him stop.

"Eldadip, Vestonn; clear us a path," Alaborap ordered. Eldadip brushed her thick locs of hair from her face and pulled out a machete. She headed for the tree line. Vestonn joined her, hefting a massive axe. That left Alaborap, Glygorg, and Naughtadargh to guard the Cadets.

"Murray," Alaborap called back to his portly pilot, who stood on the deck of the *Stingray*. "Give us an hour on foot, then follow our progress from the air as best you can. Until then, wait here. Make sure we aren't followed." Stanik saw Alaborap scan the southern island's shoreline, where they'd all come from.

"Aye, Cap'n," Murray grumbled. He clamored through the ovular hatch door, back inside the *Stingray*.

Eldadip and Vestonn continued hacking at vegetation, already three meters deep in the thicket. Alaborap took stock of the impossible jungle, watched them both work a beat longer, then turned to Glygorg. "Assist the others. Naughtadargh and I can handle the Cadets." Glygorg nodded, tested the zip ties around Hank's wrists, then drew a hatchet from a sheath on his back. He leapt up into the shortest palm tree, then used his momentum to spring up into the branches just over Eldadip. There, he made quick work of some tangled vines with a few hacks of his hatchet.

Stanik kept an eye on Alaborap. He peered out across the channel again. Stanik figured he was watching for the Candalonians. That's why Alaborap was sending his pilot away with the ship; he was hoping to draw them off.

To Alaborap's credit, Stanik knew the Stingray was rumored to be a veritable fortress, and its sour old pilot Murray would be locked safely in the cockpit if the warrior lizards chased the ship down. Interesting though that the atmosphere hadn't drained the Stingray's power, Stanik noted. Had the pirates realized firearms wouldn't hold a charge? Of course, Stanik reasoned. Otherwise, they wouldn't have marched into the *Blue Danube* so confidently.

After a good effort, the pirates grew weary of chopping their way through jungle. Stanik hoped for rest, but instead, Alaborap ordered the Cadets to take a turn beating back the tangled overgrowth. They were forced to labor through the night that way, under a veil of silver light cast by the white aurora snaking across the starry sky above.

38. THE RELIC

Onward they traipsed through a prism of colorful vegetation until the deep blue light of a new dawn bled into the sky. The Zirkulon sunrise made the sky dance with jewel tone purple and magenta. Clouds were cast as pastel orange, their wispy edges blending with the indigo daylight like swirls of cotton candy. Stanik figured the effect was a wild blue sun reacting with the planet's atmospheric gasses as he prepared his eyes for another day of ultraviolet light. While the light was still favorable, he kept his sights trained on Alaborap. The pirate had been quiet. He didn't conspire with his crew, nor did he offer instructions other than the occasional demand for Hank to send out a sonar pulse, checking their heading.

At one point, the thorn bushes grew so tangled that Hank got his tail stuck. His yellow skin was jabbed and torn at, but the pirates rolled their eyes and mocked his predicament before tugging him free with a rough heave-ho. They pressed on, but Hank struggled to slither forward with his fresh wounds. Alaborap stopped, peering back over his shoulder. "What's the hold-up?"

"Fish-boy can't keep up," Naughtadargh grumbled.

"You're the one who was playing too rough," Alaborap said. "You fix it."

The big furry brute huffed in annoyance and tied Hank's arms and tail to a length of rope, carrying the legless Hulgarian like a shoulder bag. Glygorg and Vestonn cackled together at the furry monster's ingenuity.

"No more stalling," the wolf-beast muttered.

Stanik scowled, but Vestonn caught him in the act. "Don't let it get to you," the pirate advised him quietly. "That's Naughtadargh's way of having fun. You best play along; you don't want to be on his bad side... they say he's one of the beasts of Doctor Gennaro."

Stanik had only come across one reference to the beasts of Dr. Gennaro. An ISF privateer claimed they'd discovered a Federalist scientist creating monsters in a lab out on the frontier. The privateer had been dishonorably discharged and the story discredited by the Piracy Prosecution Program. Stanik had never given such a wild story any credence. Plus, he reminded himself, pirates were all about theatrics. The taller the tale, the more it was told.

Vestonn, as if reading Stanik's thoughts, coerced his disbelief with details. "See, Naughty doesn't remember very much about his childhood. Just a big glass cage and a man in a white coat teaching him to read."

"Is that right," Stanik agreed just to make things easy.

"Yeah." Vestonn's tone was challenging. His solitary eye glared harshly at Stanik, the pupil small but demanding. "Hey Naughty," he called ahead, "hold up. Show Captain Crash-landing here your tattoo." Naughtadargh snarled, turned violently, and held out his left arm, where a bald patch of fur revealed puppy-pink flesh branded with black ink. It read 'NA2.DrG' in aggressive, digital block letters.

"Been there my whole life," the wolfman purred. "My very own laboratory birth mark." He flashed his fine maw of flesh-shredding teeth. "They say things about him, too," Naughtadargh said, nodding to Vestonn.

Vestonn shrugged. "They say I wear this bandana to hide the melted flesh of radiation burns… they say I was exposed to the atmosphere of Candalos Prime, and my right eye's gone sour, my face twisted and deformed. Have you heard that story?" As Vestonn said it, Stanik noticed the shiny, bubbly cracks of scar tissue puckering under the force of the brawny pirate's sickly grin. Vestonn waited a beat longer… which was long enough for Stanik to realize his question was not a rhetorical one.

Walt decided to take a dig at the pirate. "No, I haven't heard that one… but then, I haven't really heard of you." He enjoyed watching Vestonn's neck tense up, veins bulging as they worked to supply blood to his muscle-inflated chest and bulbous arms. Pirates liked to brag about their exploits; that was one of the first things he'd learned. A pirate's reputation was as precious to them as any share of plunder they were owed. Feigning ignorance was Stanik's best weapon: an insult to silence the man's ego.

"Don't feel too bad," Vestonn cooed in condescending wisdom. "Dirtwalkers[58] and purplebloods don't know much about the world beyond their Barrier. But the frontier worlds? They know us all. And they swear I wear this scarf for no other reason than to shroud my face." Stanik didn't understand what the pirate was getting at. Then, Vestonn reached up and pulled his paisley kerchief back, revealing a rippled, uneven mass of pink scar tissue. Some of it was discolored with dead white skin, and his opaque purple eye was a horror all its own. There was a milky frosted pus that seemed to seep from his socket into the eye itself, and the eyeball rocked slightly, unable to properly roam free in the socket. In the rising morning humidity, Stanik's stomach lurched, burning on empty. He couldn't even be sick, and so his revulsion cooked in his gut. "Watch yourself, mate. I'm radioactive," Vestonn said with a grin that wrinkled the wound in a truly evil way. The pirate chuckled to himself. He fixed his bandana over his scars again and marched on.

The pirates shoved the Cadets forward until

---

[58] **dirtwalker** – slang for a being who prefers to be 'grounded' on a planet or lacks experience traveling long distances through space. Comparable to the Terran nautical slur 'landlubber.'

everyone stumbled through a tangle of twisted brown vines. A half step down sent them all splashing into an ankle-deep pool in an acre-wide clearing. The Zirkulon sun broke the horizon, forcing its ultraviolet light through the jungle much faster than their party had managed. The colors of sunrise still made things easier to process, dousing the world in a poisonous but familiar yellow tint.

The water soaked into Stanik's boots as he surveyed the jungle billabong. It was perfectly round, defined in the forest floor with large pink stones, and at its very center, a pristine temple shimmered like a crystal palace. Clear water flowed into the site from four rushing streams.

"It's here," Alaborap noted confidently. He held his hands out, palms facing the ground as if he were absorbing energy from it.

"Weird," Eldadip whispered to Glygorg. Stanik stole a glance to see what she was talking about. In a tree across the clearing, there was an old spaceship tangled in the mighty branches of the largest tree. It was designed to reflect the style of an old Spanish War Galleon, one of the grand ships from Earth's distant maritime past. Stanik noted the name *Red Whydah* stenciled in scuffed paint along the bow.

"They're everywhere," Glygorg exclaimed.

Stanik scanned the treetops. They were littered with the carcasses of rotting spaceships. At least three familiar ship models caught his eye. Several others were so foreign, he couldn't say they'd been designed by one of the Federation worlds. The improbability numbed Stanik's mind. They were in a forest full of shipwrecks.

X   X   X

June 25, A.D. 2352
04:07 IST

A reverence settled over the group as Captain Alaborap led them across the shallow pool of water. He stopped at the mouth of the temple, then raised a hand, which brought his crew to a halt. "Naughtadargh, give me Argyle's chains," Alaborap ordered.

Naughtadargh obliged, unlinking the chain he wore around his waist like a belt. "Since you're so eager to solve this," Alaborap said to Argyle, "I'll let you go first."

Argyle said nothing, just sulked dutifully into the entrance. He was too weak to make a noise, and he doubted it would have done any good. He knew what Alaborap was doing; Argyle would trigger any booby traps the temple might have. On Candalos Prime, that dirty work had been left to the kid Pockam, but Vestonn had jumped in and saved him. It somehow felt fitting, that he would be that person now... at the foot of the alter he'd coveted so long. Argyle couldn't help but appreciate the irony. He was reaping what he'd sown.

The water behind Argyle sloshed as Alaborap followed him trepidatiously into the temple. With a deep breath, Argylesox took a careful but certain first step into the main chamber. The domed structure was wide, the ceiling tall, and the stones glowed hot pink with their energy. Intricate Candalonian hieroglyphs were inked in the stone from floor to ceiling, all leading the eye up to a circular opening in the middle of the dome.

In the center of the room, a pedestal cradled a strange device in architectural veneration. Argyle's heart skipped a beat; he was looking at the relic. His breath snagged in his chest, and he felt tears gather in his eyes.

"It's here," he exclaimed in a burst of emotions. "It's really here!" Goosebumps flooded his body as a strange nirvana overtook him as he realized his life's purpose; he was destined to discover the Goliathon. He gasped, completely overwhelmed by the moment.

The relic resembled a half meter tall bonsai tree, its trunk a mass of tightly wound bronze wires. Each metal branch was tipped with a ruby-like stone, which shot off tendrils of pink lightning sporadically at the crystal walls. Around him, the structure pulsated with light, glowing brighter as the electricity jumped from stone to stone. Argyle took a step, getting comfortable with the idea that perhaps there were no booby traps. A bolt of the pink lightning leapt out, singeing the air above Argyle's head.

"Watch," Argyle relayed back to Alaborap, pointing overhead. "The only trap here is the charge in the structure itself." Alaborap ducked into the chamber with Argyle. He gasped as he beheld the Goliathon.

"It's beautiful," Alaborap said quietly. For a moment they were equals again, standing in awe before their great discovery. Then, seizing the distraction, Argyle torqued his whole body and his chains yanked Alaborap down into the sloshing pond at their feet.

39. NAUGHTADARGH

Outside in the temple clearing, Eldadip heard the snapping of twigs and rustling of palms. At first, she thought it was a breeze cutting through the forest. It took her a moment to realize there was no breeze. The tropical air was humid and stagnant, and Eldadip's sweat was starting to feel like an extra layer of skin. It was probably more like a Hulgarian's stress coat, she corrected herself.

The forest around them creaked and rattled louder. In a cacophony of matted hair and rabid growls, a horde of Beniti clones spilled out of the ferns and fronds. They barked and snarled like dogs, backing the pirates and Cadets up to the walls of the temple.

Startled, the pirates mustered the Cadets in their midst. Eldadip had to suck her breath in through her mouth because Beniti's beasts seemed to travel in a cloud of putrid human body odor and feces.

Beniti emerged from the jungle in the wake of the clones' charge, stopping at the edge of the tidepool where he closed his eyes. Eldadip scowled. She thought they had rid themselves of the old fart and his never-ending supply of duplicates.

"In the name of the Sacred Order," the strange old man recanted in a trance, "they shall not sully this holy place. The Goliathon is not for them. It is for the Candalonians! God wills it!" He growled the last statement like a man possessed, and Eldadip could see his lips curling around his teeth as Beniti ended his prayer. The old man's eyes darted from pirate to Cadet to pirate as he marched towards them, his clones running in circles around them like bloodhounds around a Fallamon den.

The clones closed in. Their whooping barks sent chills up Eldadip's spine as the savage men chided like a cackle of hyenas. Naughtadargh ushered the pirates behind him. He swatted at their captives, too, forcing the Cadets into the temple's entryway.

"Get inside, all of you," the wolfman barked, cutting Hank free of his ties before urging him to safety. Eldadip cut one of the Cadets loose, too, then shoved him in the temple.

Outside, Naughtadargh planted his feet wide in a defensive stance. He squared his shoulders, blocking the arched entry. Unable to curb her curiosity, Eldadip stayed close. She could still see Naughtadargh's furry white flank barricading the entry.

At first, all she could make out was the wolfman's backside, his white tail sticking out through a hole in his navy breeches. His big, pawed feet seemed scraggily and thin, soaking wet in the shallow pool. Naughtadargh roared, and in a flash of daylight Eldadip saw a clone splash down at the monster's feet. The water ran red with its blood. Two more clones lunged at Naughtadargh. He flailed his massive arms, a flurry of razor-sharp claws that swatted away pouncing clone after pouncing clone. As he turned to bat down another clone, Naughtadargh moved out of view.

Eldadip ducked her head outside for a better view. Just then, Naughtadargh's awkwardly muscular right arm slammed down on a clone pouncing from the right. The Beniti copy's head ricocheted off a temple stone, and lightning jolted from the chipped piece, nearly hitting Naughtadargh. The wolfman paused, peering at the sparking stone, then wrapped his paws around the loose pink crystal. He hefted it over his head, threatening the clones. A trio of stray clones burst from the jungle behind Naughtadargh and leapt onto his back. The wolfman howled, bucking around and swinging the stone to shake them off. The beasts clung to him, tearing clumps of his fur, ripping flesh as they went. Blooms of deep crimson soaked Naughtadargh's fine fur in patches.

Their mutant ally shook violently, throwing two of the thrashing clones off his back. The stone crackled in Naughtadargh's hands, shooting jagged stems of electricity in all directions. Eldadip only heard the yelps of injured clones, cut short by a sickening popping sound, but she could not see what was happening to them. Lightning sizzled again, striking the one clone still clinging to Naughtadargh's bloody back. The energy zapped the savage clone, who disintegrated with a dull, wet pop. The jagged stems of light pushed further, electrocuting Naughtadargh where he stood. Strangely, Eldadip noticed the electrical phenomenon did not seem drawn to the pool of water all around them. Naughtadargh struggled with the pink stone, but he did not pop into dust like the clone. A pink jolt of power illuminated the wolfman's flesh and muscle and he yelped, his hair singed and frizzed. The sour smell of burnt hair was everywhere as Naughtadargh staggered forward a half step, then collapsed with a pitiful whimper in the shallow waters outside.

"No," Eldadip cried out. Her heart sank as she watched Naughtadargh's body floated helplessly in the pond. After years of close calls and lucky breaks, Eldadip thought, the Stingrays had finally lost an invaluable crewmember to the captain's Goliathon quest.

40. THE ZEALOT

The clones pushed into the temple like an angry mob, but the pirates and Cadets were ready for them. Alaborap and Argylesox were both soaking wet, however they were no longer grappling with each other on the floor as they had been when Stanik first ducked inside. Eldadip handed Jablon an extra sword. Hank and Stanik were unarmed, but at least their hands were no longer tied.

Stanik was not expecting to fight alongside the Stingrays, but there they were. He cracked his knuckles as the cavemen pushed and shoved. By now, he had noticed that all the clones shared a face and body with the zealous, bespectacled man leading them. On the journey to Laciport, Hank had mentioned a stout older man was with Alaborap in the caves on Zebulon 5.

Behind Stanik, Alaborap lunged forward, slicing

down two clones at once. The other pirates defended with equal efficacy, felling at least half a dozen clones right off the bat. Stanik cracked one in the face. The creature backed away, targeting the Fallamon instead. Stanik tackled the clone before it could leap at Alaborap's first mate. Glygorg nodded in thanks, then sank the blade of his sword into the clone's neck.

Stanik turned around in time to see Beniti marching in through the chaos of the fight. Alaborap skewered a clone very near Beniti, then got in the short man's face. "You are a strange, angry little man. You know that?"

Beniti spat in Alaborap's face. The pirate wiped his cheek, chuckling wickedly. Beniti drew his sword and slashed at Alaborap with such force, Stanik swore he could hear the blade ripping the very air, even over the echoes of battle. Surprised, Alaborap recoiled, backpedaling as he defended himself skillfully. Stanik tried to observe the pirate's footwork, but the pool of water sloshing around their ankles made that difficult. Beniti raged on, hefting his sword mightily. His face reddened and he knocked his glasses crooked, but even that did not deter him.

He seemed to be pushing Alaborap back, trying to get to the Goliathon, Stanik assumed. Considering what he had just witnessed a temple stone do, Stanik had no desire to see what might happen if Beniti was able to wield the relic itself.

Without thinking, Stanik rushed the pedestal, shoved past Argylesox, and yanked the Goliathon from its pedestalled perch. He turned to face Beniti.

"You want this," he mocked, "Come get it!" Beniti locked swords with Alaborap, shoved the pirate away, then froze, pointing the tip of his sword up at Stanik.

"You insolent little worm," Beniti growled. He raised his sword, ready to cut Stanik down. Brilliant rays of pink lightning burst forth in all directions from the Goliathon's branches. Stanik went numb as the lighting reached down in jagged lengths, wrapping around Stanik's body.

The lightning consumed Stanik, and he felt the relic burn hot in his hand. He hadn't felt that much in his arm in years! Instinctually, he tried to drop the relic, but he couldn't loosen his grip. Rivulets of pink voltage coursed through his hagron prosthetics. Then, it stopped.

Stanik grinned, lifting the Goliathon over his head as if in a game of keep away, taunting Beniti with it. He didn't drop dead like Naughtadargh, he realized, nor had he burst into dust. He held the relic as high as possible, and a column of rosy-white light erupted from the Goliathon's ruby-tipped branches. The burst of light shot through the hole in the ceiling, shattering pink stones as it went.

Shocked, Stanik jumped back. This time, he was able to release the relic. Beniti dived, catching the Goliathon centimeters from the water and soaking himself in the process. The older man was limber, and he rocked up onto his feet quickly, holding the Goliathon in reverence. He swung it at them all, pointing it like a sword, and began chanting. "Mahhk Ah-Tay. Kahl Guhr-ah. Shauck-ah-tuhr," he chanted with the cadence of prayer.

Stanik assumed this was Candalonia Mammalia[59].

The lightning intensified, then spread thin, popping in static bursts that curved back for Beniti. He gasped, growling in pain, unable to release the Goliathon. The relic fired electricity at Beniti clones picking them off one by one with crackling fury. The defenseless grunts disintegrated with a dull, sickening pop. Their ashes drifted lazily in the air; the reek of burnt hair lingered.

Stanik watched Beniti glimpse feebly up at the Goliathon, watching helplessly as its surging hot force reached down, constricting his muscles as the lightning traumatized his body. Then, with a blood-curdling screech, Beniti Juan Velirno burst into dust. A white plume of energy rocketed up through the center of the dome, and the temple stones absorbed the remainder of the charge, belching out a shockwave that knocked everyone to the ground. Stanik sprung up in time to see the Goliathon snap back into position atop its pedestal, as if magnetized there. The temple stones glowed white at their core, the structure humming like a power plant.

Stanik felt the stones under them shift. The pool bubbled and churned at their ankles as he retrieved Beniti's sword from the pool. "Argyle? What's happening," he blurted out.

"Your guess is as good as mine," Argyle said.

"Everybody out," Vestonn barked.

---

[59] **Candalonia** /ˈkændəˌloʊniə/ **Mammalia** – an approximate translation of the Candalonian language for the tongues of apes.

41. THE STORM

June 25, A.D. 2352
04:26 IST

The *Halogien Stingray* prowled low over the jungle just south of an intense electrical storm. From the cockpit, Murray was tracking a large group of Candalonians. He had discovered that the lizards swung from tree to tree to traverse the dense jungle. The storm winds were blowing southward, making it easy for Murray to see the trees that dipped north with the weight of the reptile brigade. Captain Alaborap had been heading north, and Murray had no way of signaling him.

Murray followed the path of swinging trees. "Grimtash," he cussed as he realized the Candalonians were headed into the dark clouds at the heart of the storm. The clouds catapulted bolts of pink lightning at the island below.

Murray noticed a large domed structure glowing pink in the jungle beneath him. The structure's bright glow sparkled off the pool of water encircling it, and Murray could see the tree branches surrounding it as they rocked and rattled with agitated Candalonians. Many of them crouched in the branches, their tails sticking straight out behind them to balance their weight. The trees trembled violently as the fierce reptiles hopped and hooted.

Murray activated an audio channel so he could hear what was going on outside. Over the whine of the Stingray's engines, the Candalonians croaked their chant: "Go-li-a-thon! Go-li-a-thon! Go-li-a-thon! Go-li-a-thon!" The call was eerie and inhuman, each syllable croaked out like a frog imitating speech. A hurricane wind pushed in from the south. Murray held the *Stingray*'s wheel steady as subsequent gales ripped hardy fronds and fragile ferns from their home in the soil.

Murray scratched his jaw, working his fingertips through his mutton chops as he considered his next move. He had to keep the *Stingray* circling. The solar sails had done their job, recharging in the sun despite the constant energy drain on Laciport.

Murray backed the *Stingray* off to give the storm more room for its tantrum. A volcanic burst of hot white light shot up out of the dome's center, and Murray could see pieces of stone crumbling away. Surely that was a sign his comrades had found the powerful relic. He tried his DashCom but still couldn't signal the captain. He cursed to himself, stopping mid-grumble as he noticed a shift… the Candalonian chants had ceased. The lizardmen were in full retreat.

Pink lightning sizzled up into angry storm clouds from the dome below, the bolts firing off in all directions. One tendril rocked the Stingray's mizzenmast, setting alarms off in a tizzy around the cockpit.

"Grimtash," Murray growled, regurgitating a string of obscenities as the ship wobbled like a toy top. He slapped at his console to cancel the security warnings, and the DashCom chimed. "Power cells at maximum capacity," his console reported calmly.

"Ooh," Murray sang with delight, "well, I'll be." The lightning hadn't damaged the *Stingray*… it had supercharged the vessel's power cells. That was an unexpected perk. No longer concerned with the lightning, the old pilot flew straight into the fearsome storm, lowering the ship over the temple.

Murray saw his captain splash out of the dome as waves of water crashed through the trees. Bloody hell, he thought as he watched the beaches disappear beneath the stormy sea, the whole island's sinking! Immediately, he dropped the *Stingray*'s lifelines from the cargo bay and eased the ship down among the trees, keeping track of how close he got to their towering branches. He activated the cameras in the keel and waited for his crewmates to grab a lifeline.

42. RAGING RAPIDS

Stanik was the last one out of the temple, trailing behind Alaborap as the pirates and Cadets swam furiously away from the surging waters. Geysers ripped open along the perimeter of the clearing as everyone scrambled for the overhanging tree branches that had dared to grow close to the Goliathon's energy. There were not many, and several were ripped away in the sound and fury of the belching geysers.

The *Halogien Stingray* roared in overhead, dropping six thick chains from its belly, each outfitted with a leather handle. Eldadip and Alaborap were the first to reach the lines. As Vestonn grabbed hold of one, Stanik realized the pirates had no intention of taking the Cadets with them. Stanik was not about to be marooned. He lunged at Eldadip's legs as the *Stingray* dipped, turning itself around. Stanik used his momentum to swing Eldadip right at Alaborap. He wrapped his left arm around Eldadip's legs as she tried to kick him off, then drew his sword with his right hand. Glygorg snarled, swinging in on his line. The nasty Fallamon kicked his clawed feet at Stanik, barely missing his mark.

His blade outstretched, Stanik took one good swipe at Alaborap's hands, which clenched at the leather handle on the pirate's lifeline. The strike nearly clipped Alaborap's knuckles, but Stanik felt it fall short, slicing air. Then, Eldadip writhed again, and her powerful legs loosened his grip. Stanik slid, grasping at her ankles, but toppled back into the rising waters below. Fortunately, he managed to fling his sword away so as not to risk injuring himself in the fall.

"It's been fun, Captain," Alaborap called down to him, tipping his tricorn hat before the Stingray hauled him safely into its hold, along with the other pirates. The ship's white belly turned its stern to the Cadets. Stanik could see its telescoping masts retracting as the vessel adjusted on a launch trajectory and roared away up into the clouds.

Stanik's heart sank. How had the Stingray managed to store enough energy to take off again? He wondered if the *Explorer* would have been able to–

"We have to get out of here," Hank shouted.

"Over here," Jablon hollered to them, pointing at a derelict spacecraft tangled in the branches of the tree he'd climbed.

"Follow Jablon," Stanik ordered, and Argyle and

Hank complied as quickly as possible. Hank made it first, by far the fastest swimmer among them. He hoisted himself up into the branches, then wrapped his tail around the thickest, lowest branch. He released his grip and hung upside down, reaching down to pull up Stanik, then Argyle. The water kept churning, racing them as Stanik lost the top of the temple amidst the raging water.

He focused on the climb, scrambling up through branches overgrown with twisted vines until he found Jablon's hand reaching for him, guiding him up the ladder on the stern-starboard end of the old craft. Stanik heaved himself up over the *Red Whydah*'s tired metal hide and onto its moss-covered deck.

Stanik rolled onto his belly, reaching over the side to hoist Hank up. Argyle clamored over the gunwale without assistance, huffing and puffing as he did.

Jablon started jumping up and down, rocking the vessel. The branches that held them snapped free, and the Cadets' shipwreck bobbed into the waves. Jablon rushed aft to the helm and threw a hefty lever. Metal clanked in protest, but the pilot steered them skillfully through the treetops that disturbed the water's surface.

"Where should I take this old wreck," Jablon asked.

"Let's see if it'll get us back to the *Explorer* crash site," Stanik reasoned. "We need to see what can be salvaged." He turned to Hank and Argyle. "Let's get below decks and check for leaks so this thing doesn't rip open."

43. CASTAWAY

Laciport – Day 39

"We've been scouring the sunken island on Laciport for some time now," Argyle reported softly into his DataCom. It was his first entry in a long time, as the Space Cadets and he had been focused on salvage and reconnaissance. Survival was key; Argyle's academia couldn't be his priority. Finally, he'd been able to rig a charging station out of some replacement solar panels Jablon pulled from the *Explorer*'s supply crates.

"It feels good to have my research files back, even if I'm not able to date my new entries. Laciport's power anomalies seem to have reset the DataCom's system clock. It also corrupted a few files, but fortunately my important Goliathon research is intact. Now that we've established camp, I intend to pick up my record-keeping." The Cadets had helped, each recounting their side of things. With all that logged, he was officially moving on to Laciport research.

"Despite several deep dives, Hank has not been able to locate the Goliathon temple," he told his DataCom. "During yesterday's expedition, he had a run-in with a cephalopod. Hank suspects the tentacled creature has nested, blocking access to the temple site."

"Admittedly, Hank and I have been met with obstacle after obstacle in our attempts to access the sunken island. I'm beginning to lose hope," he said aloud into his little device. Saying it out loud sank a barb in his heart. "It's become quite clear that Laciport seems to be… protecting the Goliathon site from our prying eyes… It's time to focus my efforts elsewhere." Argyle paused, thinking again. He'd made a rule long ago never to end his entries on a negative note. What else was there?

Argyle lowered the DataCom, mulling over the past few days. "I realize I keep referring to our time awake as 'day' but I should note for the record that we have become nocturnal to survive here. The harsh blue hue cast over everything creates quite the psychedelic experience, particularly with the vibrant floral selection indigenous to Laciport. It's fascinating, almost dream-like, but it didn't take long for us to realize it was causing long-term damage to our vision. The nighttime aurora offers the same spectrum of white light as a full moon on Earth. It's much easier on the eyes. The

Candalonians seem to have also made that adjustment, which does mean we're extra careful when we're out hunting, because they all are, too. It's fascinating to think that Candalonians had the tech to travel this far through space over two hundred years ago. In fact, it boggles the mind! Walt offered me that observation. The captain has been an active participant in my academic quandaries. Every dawn, after dinner, he's sat at the fire with me sit to discuss my theories and our daily observations. I find it quite helpful!"

Argyle paused, trying to remember what else there was to report. "Ah, yes!," he continued as the thought struck him, "I noticed a distinct odor, reminiscent of pine tar, the last few nights at our campsite and, just this morning, I found Candalonian tracks in the sand around the perimeter of our seaside camp. Seeing as there was only one set of tracks, I suspect it was the Cadets' former tour guide, the one who loaned them the *Danube*." Argyle waited a beat before adding, "I intend to make contact and study him. After all, it's not every day someone encounters a Lazarus taxon." He grinned and clicked the DataCom off.

Laciport – Day 172

Argyle's undated DataCom entries on Laciport quadrupled over the course of their stay. He'd confirmed his suspicions that the Cadets were being watched by the friendly Candalonian Jablon insisted on calling 'Chirpy.'

"I pinpointed the reptile's favorite hiding spots and cornered him there about ten days ago. Since then, we've spent each day going through the Candalonian's camp, examining each of his treasures. I'm keen on getting Hank's legs back.

"I've finally scratched the surface of translating this new variant of the Candalonian dialect. Today, I think I've translated our friend's name into English, meaning we can abandon Jablon's demeaning misnomer. If I'm not mistaken, our friend's real name is pronounced Nemega'an.

"We also established that he 'does not run with the pack.' This is his way of expressing that he's been cast out of the Candalonian social structures elsewhere on the planet. He attributes this to his trinkets and experiments. It would seem his scientific curiosity is what got him banished."

X   X   X

Laciport – Day 292

"Time keeps trudging on. I've spent recent days getting to know more about Nemega'an, who seems to be a bit of a gearhead. He has readily offered spare parts from his collection to aid in restoring the *Red Whydah*. Jablon and Stanik are hopeful that, with the surviving tech and emergency repair crates from the *Explorer*, we have a chance to get the old *Whydah* space-worthy again. I'm not entirely sure any of it will work, but then, I'm fine to die in paradise if that's our fate."

Argyle smiled to himself as he watched the sun set over the jungle river from a table at Nemega'an's camp.

Laciport – Day 392

"We've been here for three hundred and ninety-two of the planet's days," Argyle reported to his DataCom. He was waiting for their dinner fire to die out, for the blue Zirkulon sun was ready to break a new day. The others had already gone to bed. "I'm still unsure how long that is in Federation time, and calculating such things has never been my strong suit. But the planet is significantly smaller than Earth or Cliptorgia, so I guesstimate it's been about ten standard months. That means back home it's 2353 now."

Argyle glanced down at his notes, bulleted in pen on a stationary pad branded with the ISF logo. Stanik had pulled it from the *Explorer* crash for him. "Captain Stanik's right arm seems to be healing. Not only is there new skin growth, but it appears as if a few of the minor mechanics are in the process of being rejected by his organic material. I cannot say whether this is due to Goliathon exposure or not, but my suspicions are aroused.

"Also, our weapons hold a charge again, which has made hunting easier. I'm convinced the Goliathon was the cause of the planet's energy drain. But why has that power gone dormant? Perhaps submersion neutralized it? The Goliathon's electrical event wasn't conducted through the pool of water at the site. It was, however, easily conducted by the temple stones. The stones are crystalline; carved from large deposits of pink agate. I've no idea what to make of that yet. The electrical phenomenon suggests to me that I'm dealing with a yet-unknown form of energy.

"The most exciting development for our crew is Hank's new method for welding up the hull of our shipwrecked *Whydah*. Nemega'an showed us the technique he uses, and Hank was able to improve upon it considerably with the surviving tools from the *Explorer*. I suspect I won't be updating the DataCom as much while we focus on a potential escape."

X   X   X

Laciport – Day 549

The *Red Whydah* rocked in the surf off the eastern coast of Candalos South. Nemega'an had reassured them that his former pack was off to the west on their monthly hunt. The Cadets only had five more days before the Candalonian pack returned to that region. If they couldn't get their test flights done in that time, they'd have to relocate their whole operation before trying again.

"My doing, I'm afraid," Argyle confessed to his DataCom as he made another entry. "I had made the request a while ago that we try to keep our technology discreet. I don't want to influence whatever evolutionary growth these primitive Candalonians are going through. Fortunately, Captain Stanik agreed and made it a direct order.

"We've conducted two days of test flights in atmosphere, and Jablon and Stanik finally feel safe enough to attempt a wet launch. The ship's air seals are holding, the hull's been reinforced in weak spots and tested for strength, and Hank even managed to refurbish and install the *Explorer*'s gravity simulator."

Argyle leaned against the mizzenmast aboard the classic galleon-shaped vessel, finishing his DataCom entry. Behind him, Stanik was feeding cable down into the gunner ports. They'd need auto-turrets if they were lucky enough to make it back to the Outer Rim. There had been two spare turrets packed safely in cargo bins aboard the *Explorer*. Apart from a few dents and scuffs, they were the most pristine parts of the born-again *Red Whydah*.

Argyle placed his hands on his hips and surveyed the *Whydah*'s deck with Stanik. Jablon and Hank were fortifying a worn patch of the bow with a piece of the *Explorer*'s purple bullfrog nose.

"A banged-up ship for a bedraggled crew," Argyle said with a smile to his disheveled friends. For such clean-cut Terrans, Stanik and Jablon were now the spitting image of swarthy castaways. Just like the romanticized image of Terran maritime stories, their complexions had darkened, and their skin appeared leathery. Their hair had grown wild and their beards long. There was only so much a sword could do to keep hair in-check, after all.

Stanik patted Argyle on the shoulder. "You ready to get out of here," he asked.

"Not really," Argyle admitted. "I still have so many questions." It was true. Argyle had been holding back, but he was reluctant to go. It had been five-hundred-and-forty-nine days since they'd been stranded on Laciport; nearly two years in the planet's orbital phases by Argyle's estimation. He'd spent a great deal of that time cataloging flora and fauna, translating Nemega'an's dialect, and dusting off his foraging skills. He was disappointed that he had grossly overestimated how much time was needed to repair the *Whydah*, as he still had plenty of island to discover.

"Doesn't seem fair, pulling you away from all this," Stanik nodded at the island with a frown. "Getting here only has us all asking more questions."

"Well, I don't view the new questions as a failure," Argyle said. He meant it; he'd been thinking on it all through the night as he searched for solace in their departure.

"No?"

Argyle shook his head. "Certainly not. Think about those questions; how did the Goliathon get here? How did the Candalonians get here? Why did the whole island sink only *after* we interacted with the relic? Then there's the Goliathon itself; what elements comprise its metal coils or those ruby-like gems at the end of its branches? How do those create the energy phenomena we keep seeing?" Argyle laughed. "The list goes on. But the only reason I have all these questions is because we answered one very big one: is the Goliathon real? Yes. It's here. We saw it for ourselves. All the other questions stem from that one simple fact. So, I have my work cut out for me, but I'll take the new questions because it means I finally succeeded."

"I wish Cliptok were here," Stanik said. The thought seemed to stumble out of him. It certainly caught Argyle off-guard.

"I *am* sorry we lost her," Argyle nodded, being sure to make eye contact with his friend. The captain and he had formed quite an intellectual bond, particularly during their fireside chats. They'd maintained that tradition for the duration of their stay.

"I'm glad you don't think you failed," Stanik said. "It means she didn't die in vain."

"She certainly did not," Argyle encouraged. "The Goliathon is lost to the sea, which should keep it hidden away, and Alaborap has nothing but a tall tale and a reduced crew to show for all his efforts. Keeping the relic away from him was, in itself, a success."

"I agree," Stanik said. "I just hope Cliptok would."

Argyle shrugged. The captain had confided over many a campfire that he felt responsible for the loss of his gunner. They'd had so many conversations trying to rid Stanik of his survivor's guilt. There was nothing left to say, and it felt hypocritical to try, because Argyle also felt he was partly responsible for the loss. It would take some time to shake that.

At stern, Jablon checked the clamps on one of the

auto-turrets. Satisfied, he turned and lumbered past them both, his face streaked with grease.

"Outer Deck secured," Jablon said cracking his knuckles.

Hank jumped out of the water, hoisting himself up the ladder, his powerful biceps bobbing as he climbed. "Engine valves clear and those loose cables have been secured," Hank reported. Argyle could hear the Hulgarian's satisfaction ring in his voice.

"Excellent," Stanik said. "Let's get inside and fire this thing up."

Hank slithered down the ladder first, headed to the cockpit. Argyle paused on deck outside the hatch door, taking in the sorbet sunrise that streaked the sky before them. He sighed in admiration as a flock of furry mammals swooped low, flapping leathery wings as they tried snatching fish from the water.

Jablon stretched, stepping up next to them. "I'm really gonna miss this place," he said with a sigh.

"We've got other places to see," Stanik encouraged, "...*if* they reboot the mission," he added with a mischievous grin.

"Give it up," Jablon said, shaking his head. "They're gonna blacklist us and tuck us away somewhere."

"What're you thinking," Stanik mused, "soft retirement patrolling the mines over Jupiter?

Jablon grinned. "Not quite. I was thinking about… hunting pirates."

"What," said Stanik, his voice cracking. "You? In

the Outer Rim?"

"Yeah," Jablon said candidly, squaring his shoulders. "Yeah, I think so. I think if we get the chance, Alaborap's earned himself a real ass-whoopin'."

Hank crossed his arms. "You can say that again," he said gravely. "Outer Rim will be the closest settled system we can get to from here. I wouldn't say 'no' to a pirate hunt."

Argyle chuckled, enjoying one final moment in an atmosphere with fresh, breathable air. He ducked down into the cockpit and strapped himself in as Jablon locked the hatch shut behind them.

In the cockpit, they powered on all systems just like they'd rehearsed, and in no time, the *Red Whydah* roared to life, a far noisier ship than the *Explorer*. It was still not nearly as bad as some of the clunkers Argyle had hitchhiked in.

Argyle manned the first mate's console, where he pulled the lever to activate the ship's wings, which shrieked at the joints as they extended. Argyle winced for a moment, but his console light went green, and the wings locked in place as the Cadets demanded their ship out of retirement.

Jablon opened the throttle, letting the *Whydah* chug forward. If they'd managed to get the security cameras working, the Cadets might have noticed a slender green tail slip into a storage locker down in the cargo bay as the ship lurched forward. But they hadn't, and so they were none the wiser.

The locker clamped shut and the *Red Whydah* skipped shakily out of the water, speeding past the squawking airborne mammals, up towards the rising sun.

The launch computer traced a green grid up into the night sky over Laciport, and Jablon held course along that trajectory until finally, with one more uncertain sputter, the *Red Whydah* arched across the sky, ferrying the Space Cadets back to familiar stars.

The adventure will continue in
Space Cadets and the Pirates of the Outer Rim,
coming soon from Space Cadets Studios!

ORIGIN OF THE STORY

On June 25, 2005, a group of theater-kids set out to make a ten-minute short sci-fi spoof video. Enter Joe (Jablon), Dale (Cliptok) and Captain Stubing (Winzek). Upon seeing the footage, an eager Dale suggested, "we should try to make a series of these this summer. Like, ten episodes?" Winzek just wanted to be behind the camera. He had invested in a Canon ZR-200 MiniDV handicam, making this first cinematic experiment possible. So, the Space Cadets were born that fateful Saturday after a stage crew workday to sort high school theater equipment for the next season of shows.

Over the course of that summer and fall, they introduced Argylesox and Alaborap, Glygorg and the Goliathon, and accomplished their ten-episode goal (plus bonus features). Winzek spent the fall saving money to build a computer for editing the three hours of footage into a story. That goal was realized on December 16th, 2005, a day which also marked the beginning of Season 2 filming. That Season 2 story would evolve into the one laid out here. While much of it is the author's own, there are many creative gems that can only be attributed to the beauty of collaboration. Characters, circumstances, and even names from the Space Cadets universe would not be what they are without the collective subconscious of a group of bored theater teens living in the dreary Rust Belt at the dawn of the twenty-first century.

Season 1 of the series premiered at Norwin High School's (sci-fi themed) *Sadie Hawkins Dance* on Saturday, March 11, 2006 (in the very theater the group called home). It caused enough of a stir to keep the project going for three seasons over just as many years (June 2005 through January 2009), including a premiere of each season, a live performance with a limited run, homemade merchandise, and thirty tapes worth of 'Space Cadets' project footage.

From there, the Space Cadets story went to college, where it continued to evolve through the author's study of storytelling & performance. The ideas were refined into a 120-page screenplay version of *Space Cadets* Season 1 and 2, renamed *Space Cadets and the Legend of the Goliathon*. While at university, the story caught the imagination of test-reader & *Space Cadets Radio* co-writer Jordan Stine. Stine and Winzek galvanized their fast-forming friendship over countless rewrites of *Legend*. After several years of lurking in Ohio coffee shops, the two friends set sights on New York City, where the project would evolve once again.

In late May of 2013, Winzek hosted a private reading of the script with a full team of actors, for he and Stine were still eagerly perfecting it for submissions. In attendance were original Space Cadet

Chris Shendge and his roommate Sacco, both professionals in the world of sound design. While the challenges of filming even one scene in the script would cost far more than the team could afford, Shendge and Sacco were enthusiastic about adapting the *Legend* into an aural format. So, the *Legend* continued, this time as *Space Cadets Radio* (seasons 1 & 2 are still available on Spotify). The audio drama podcast managed to produce two full seasons, continuing to grow the Space Cadets universe through a sequel script, *Space Cadets and the Pirates of the Outer Rim*. Both seasons of the project were funded independently by the group, and the efforts to record, edit, and release that content took over four years.

Around that time, the world shut down due to coronavirus, and Winzek was coaxed back to his very first attempt to tell the *Legend*'s story... for he still had seventy-some pages of an abandoned novelization. All credit is due to his wife Monica, who has served as illustrator of the Space Cadets universe since 2016. Without her wish to 'read Space Cadets with all the details of a novel,' this manuscript would not exist.

Times have changed, the people who made it have changed, and the town feels like a whole different place. The story, too, has grown in many ways, evolving with the help of countless brilliant artists. Winzek hopes that, in this most complete version of itself, the *Legend* will live on, freeing him to tell other stories in the *Space Cadets* universe.

ABOUT THE AUTHOR

Award-winning author & entertainer Brent Winzek was born and raised in the hills of Pittsburgh, Pennsylvania, where, at age 17, he created the *Space Cadets* universe with the help of his quirkiest, most intelligent theater friends. He attained a Bachelor of Arts in Film Production and a Master of Arts in Theater from Bowling Green State University in Ohio, where he further developed the *Space Cadets* with collaborator Jordan Stine. The project continued evolving in New York City while Brent was working in various circles of the entertainment industry. He continues to write & produce strange original work from deep within the hills of Appalachia. There, in a forested hovel, he spins his yarns with the help of his wife and critters.

To explore other projects, visit
spacecadetsstudios.com

www.ingramcontent.com/pod-product-compliance
Lightning Source LLC
Chambersburg PA
CBHW030350030726
47497CB00002B/272